BEST LAID PLANS

A SAMANTHA TRUE MYSTERY

KRISTI ROSE

BOOKS BY KRISTI ROSE

Samantha True Mysteries

One Hit Wonder

All Bets Are Off

Best Laid Plans

The Wyoming Matchmaker Series

The Cowboy Takes A Bride

The Cowboy's Make Believe Bride

The Cowboy's Runaway Bride

The No Strings Attached Series

The Girl He Knows

The Girl He Needs

The Girl He Wants

The Meryton Brides Series

To Have and To Hold (Book 1)

With This Ring (Book 2)

I Do (Book 3)

Promise Me This (Book 4)

Marry Me, Matchmaker (Book 5)

Honeymoon Postponed (Book 6)

Matchmaker's Guidebook - FREE

The Second Chance Short Stories can be read alone and go as follows:

Second Chances

Once Again

Reason to Stay

He's the One

Kiss Me Again

or purchased in a bundle for a better discount.

The Coming Home Series: A Collection of 5 Second Chance Short Stories (Can be purchased individually).

Love Comes Home

BEST LAID PLANS

No "learn to be a PI" video prepared her for this

When Samantha True witnesses Wind River's most popular principal keel over dead she knows three things

1. He's been murdered
    2. Proving it will be impossible
    3. They're gonna think she did it

As she works to clear her name, Samantha learns "Principal Josh" is the king of slime balls. Eliminating suspects proves tricky when half the town has a motive for murder. It'll take the right private investigator to crack this killer's best laid plan.

Warning: May cause spontaneous laughter. This mystery offers witty banter, characters you'll want to be friends with, and is a perfect escape to the Pacific Northwest. Laughing out loud in public may cause curious glances from strangers.

BEST LAID
A Samantha True Mystery
PLANS

KRISTI ROSE

1

"I'M COUNTING ON YOU, Sam. You must be my eyes and ears. I'll need you to attend the Parent-teacher collaboration meetings and school events," Rachel said, taking the seat next to me. She handed me a piece of paper with the meeting's agenda. "Mom and Dad are super busy. They can't do everything."

"They can't come to a PTA meeting once a month? They managed it when we were kids," I said.

Rachel's deployment was set for the end of September. She'd brought Cora out over the summer to live with our folks hoping to make the transition easier. Rachel's ship was constantly going out to sea in practice runs they called workups. For every five-day break she got, Rachel flew out to spend them with Cora and us.

"It's PTC. Parent Teacher Collaboration, and you know what I mean." She sighed with exasperation.

I rolled my eyes.

Rachel was a tightly wound ball of anxiety and motherly hysteria, primed to blow at any second. Until this deployment, she'd never left Cora for a period longer than twenty-four hours and the separation was wearing on her. Her ship's deployment was scheduled for a minimum of four months, a maximum of six. That was a long time in kid years.

Rachel had decided Wind River Elementary, the elementary school we'd attended, wasn't good enough for Cora. Instead, my niece, who still picked her nose when watching TV, was going to the new ubercool STEM-based charter school called Village Garden School.

A ruse of a name if you ask me.

Mom said they picked the name to sound friendly and unthreatening. No aggressive or politically incorrect mascot either. Nope. The fighting carrot, Captain Carrot, with his wild sprig of hair, the leafy green part, and a bowler hat, was as menacing as the school got.

Personally, I thought it was a huge joke on the town. A dig at the hipster parents and their crunchy lifestyle. Because Wind River wasn't some quaint village. In fact, a meth house had been discovered on the outskirts of town. And as for the school's garden? It was currently a churned-up piece of land waiting for seed. Soon the Pacific Northwest rains would start and wash away anything planted if the school didn't hurry up about it.

My best friend, Precious, real name Erika, plopped onto the seat beside me and held out a napkin with three tiny blueberry scones on it. "Compliments of the PTC and How Ya Bean Coffee House," she said.

I took one. "That's a dumb name," I said. "PTC. Putting collaboration in the title doesn't make me want to work as a team any more than using association or organization."

Rachel took a scone. "I'll miss these. June knows what she's doing."

June was the owner of How Ya Bean and one awesome baker and barista. Her concoctions could make angels weep with joy.

"I might attend these lame-ass meetings if scones are served," I said under my breath.

My role as younger sister was to get Rachel to explode. She needed a good cry and to vent her steam. I was prepared to take the brunt of it, too. And if I wasn't? She'd twist my arm behind my back and remind me of all the times I'd ruined her—insert favorite anything. That list was long. That's why I continued to push at her buttons and nitpick at random, insignificant things.

"Just help me out here, Sam," she said with a groan.

"Okay, let me get this straight. You don't want me to be in charge of caring for Cora—dressing, feeding, offering life lessons, those sorts of things—but you want me to do things like attend PTC meetings, volunteer, and report back little tidbits about her school and teacher to you? You know how I feel about school."

Being dyslexic had not made school a fun experience. Even more so when a portion of the staff thought my inability to decipher language and symbols was me being stubborn and refusing to learn. Who purposely did that? Refused to learn?

Rachel said, "All the more reason for you to be here. You can pick up on struggles Cora might have."

Okay, I'd give her that.

Rachel blew out a frustrated sigh. "Besides, I'm not asking you to be her guardian because you've never cared for a kid before. It's not easy. You can't make them tater tots and sprinkle dried kale over it and call that nutrition. You have to keep track of when they poo and how they sleep."

I grimaced. I wasn't interested in anyone's poo.

She continued, "They need seat belts. They lack common sense, and they don't need a role model who throws caution to the wind." She gave me a pointed look.

I looked over my shoulder to see if she was talking about anyone else. Then I stuck my tongue out at her.

"You can help me *here*. Show her she's not alone. *Be here*. It'll make her feel good to know someone she knows and loves is on campus. *And* you can tell me if she's making friends. I need to know she's happy and adjusting well. I need to know her teachers are warm and loving. That this is a good environment for her. You can easily do this for me."

"Thanks, I think," I said. I was about to poke at her more but a tall woman with mousy brown hair pulled back into a topknot with expertly curled tendrils around her face stood and rang a bell.

I glanced at my watch. The kindergarten families had fifteen minutes to get all the pertinent information before we'd be shuffled out and the first-grade parents would be shuffled in. VGS was hosting us in their cafetorium, used both for lunch and assemblies. The room had been redone so that one wall was a row of three single-car garage door-sized folding windows that opened to the dry dirt yard called the garden. They were open tonight. Not the best choice in hindsight considering the wind would occasionally bring in puffs of dust.

"Take your seats please," Mousy Brown Hair lady boomed across the room. "Principal Josh Chapman would like to speak. I'm Mindy Cunningham, President of the PTC, and I'll be here to answer questions you might have about the PTC and how you can help. Our volunteers can do so much from home, so please come see me when he's done. We depend on you all to make this school great." She turned to the side and gestured to a tall, lithe man with a full head of light blond hair in tight curls. He was probably Rachel's age, but he hadn't grown up in Wind River because neither of us knew him.

I whispered to Rachel, "I wonder which one is the village idiot?" I elbowed her to show I was joking. She pinched my knee in response.

"He resembles Justin Timberlake," Rachel whispered. "Kinda cute."

Yeah, I suppose, if it was two a.m. and a person was inebriated, tired, and wore foggy contacts. But I sorta saw the resemblance. Maybe it was the coloring or the hair. He wasn't unattractive by any measure. Just not my type.

I said, "I think it's because he's not in uniform. You're not used to seeing men in regular clothes."

Rachel snorted.

Precious said, "There's better out there. And he's wearing pleated pants. I mean, who does that anymore?"

The man in question cleared his throat and beamed at the crowd. He would need to do more than smile to gain my trust.

Principal Josh—he told us to call him that—talked about bullying, behavior, and parent pickup. No buses, only mommy mode of transportation for the special snowflakes. He shared all this with a constant smile. Like the Joker who even when being evil smiled. I was underwhelmed by him and skeeved out by how he constantly touched people when he talked to them. Like Mindy Cunningham from the PTC kept getting her shoulder squeezed every time he referred to the *collaboration*. Or a parent in the first row when he called attention to their volunteer work.

Or maybe my annoyance was because men were on my crap list. Thanks to my probably decreased-kept-two-wives liar of a husband, I didn't have warm fuzzies about men in general, or Principal Josh.

I forced my thoughts away from Carson and the mess he left me when he was murdered and focused on Principal Josh's yammering. He was making extended length-eye contact and repeating the phrase "caring is sharing" to guilt people into volunteering for the upcoming Fall Festival, which was happening in a few weeks. Like me, many were looking at their fingernails or the ceiling.

Following a heavy sigh, Principal Josh introduced the school counselor, Danika Post, a petite woman with chestnut curly hair and an eye for fashion as told by her fancy high heels.

As Principal Josh spoke about her role, he placed his hand on her back and gestured to her like Vanna White did the electronic letters. She cast him a brief and furtive look of such loathing I sat up straighter.

"Did you see that?" I asked Rachel, who was nodding and smiling to whatever Principal Josh was saying.

"See what?" she asked out of the corner of her mouth. Rachel had always been a teacher pleaser. No chance she was going to give her attention to anyone other than Principal Josh when he was talking. Heaven forbid.

"Incredible that you missed the look the counselor gave Principal Josh, like she thought a dog turd was better than him."

Rachel elbowed me. "I doubt that."

I leaned toward Precious. "Did you see it?"

She nodded. "He disgusts her. Probably the pleats."

Principal Josh gestured to his staff then clapped his hands, cueing the audience to applaud the hard-working women, all the while his smile never wavered. Then, with a grand wave of his hand, he dismissed us. Rachel sprang from her seat, her grip strong on my elbow as she dragged me toward the principal and the open doors. I dragged Precious.

"Hi, Principal Josh, Counselor Post," Rachel said as she planted us in front of them. "I'm Rachel True. We've spoken on the phone before. And this is my sister, Samantha."

I laughed. I was sure they'd spoken on the phone

before a lot. A lot. Multiple times a week would be my guess, knowing Rachel.

"You don't have to call me Counselor Post. Danika is fine. I remember speaking with you." She held out her hand and shook Rachel's.

I watched her like a hawk hoping to see another glare. Maybe I'd imagined it.

"Cora has a great support system with my parents and sister. We've done what we can to ease her into this transition with me shipping out." She elbowed me. "But I want to know if she's struggling or acting out." Rachel pointed to me. "She'll try to keep things from me because she's afraid I'll worry."

I shrugged and smiled at Danika. "I'm not afraid she'll worry. I know she will." I glanced at Josh. His smile was still going strong. His pearly whites, probably veneers, glistened under the fluorescent lights. His tie had little stick families all over it. Yoga mom, karate son, business dad, and baby sister. Except each family on his tie was different. It was kinda cool. His overall appearance screamed "educator." Which was good considering he was in charge of a bunch of them. And up close he wasn't hideous or anything. I could see a certain appeal.

Danika put her hand out to shake mine. "You can reach out to me anytime."

I liked this counselor. She seemed straightforward.

Next, I shook hands with Josh. If that's what it could be called. We clasped hands, but instead of shaking, he tucked my hand between both of his and squeezed. Weird.

"And who is this with you?" Principal Josh asked, his

eyes on Precious. Precious awed everyone. She was super-model pretty.

She stuck out her hand. "Erika Shurmann, I'm a business and life coach." She shook Danika's hand first.

Principal Josh's brows shot up. "What exactly does a business and life coach do?"

"I help people level up."

Josh's focus on Precious intensified as he took her hand. He stood taller, shoulders broadening as he leaned toward her. When his button-down shirt stretched tight across his chest and side, I glimpsed two large overlapping squares under the arm extended to her. Like a patch or something a smoker might wear.

I did a sweeping inspection of Principal Josh. He had the telltale pucker lines of a smoker around his mouth, but his teeth weren't yellow thanks to the veneers. I glanced at his hands as he clasped them over Precious's outstretched one. Sure enough, right above the middle knuckle of Principal Josh's middle finger was a tinge of yellow. I'd put money on Josh being a smoker trying to quit.

"Do you have a card, Ms. Shurmann? I'm thinking of leveling up my personal life."

Barf. The nerve of this guy to flirt with parents around. Though, to be fair, Precious had this effect on men everywhere.

"Hard pass, Principal Josh, but if you're searching, I can give you the name of other companies." She pulled her hand free.

I choked back a laugh.

Danika cleared her throat and said to me, "Didn't you used to work at Toomey Studios?"

I had to think about the question. Working as a photographer for Toomey seemed like a lifetime ago. No sooner had I quit that job when my life went sideways. I'd been widowed, found out my marriage wasn't legal since Carson already had a wife, inherited a PI business I knew nothing about, was chased by bad guys, and then brought down said bad guys. Hard to believe that was six months ago.

Principal Josh turned his wide-eyed gaze to me and did the impossible. His smile broadened. "You're a photographer?"

I smelled a trap.

"Yes," Rachel said. "A high-quality one."

"My camera's broken," I said.

Rachel gave me an odd look. "No, it's not. You were just taking pictures of Cora at the beach today."

"Well, the film was giving me trouble," I mumbled.

"Aren't most cameras digital now" Danika asked. I dropped her down a level on the Like-meter.

"Did I say film? I meant screen," I said.

Principal Josh squeezed my shoulder, his fingers massaging. "We need a photographer for the Fall Festival to take pictures of the families from ten to one. We—" He chuckled. "By we I mean *the PTC* will have everything set to go. All you need is to show up with your camera and smile." His hand slid off my shoulder and rubbed my upper arm. "You could also help us get candids of the staff, PTC, and our environs for the yearbook. You seem like the best person for that."

I showed teeth and hoped it looked like a smile. The thought of taking family pictures that weren't of my family was a special kind of hell.

Rachel faced me, pleading with her eyes, "The festival is right before I ship out. Cora can see you supporting her school. You'd be doing a good thing."

Not knowing how to respond, I said nothing.

A rogue bird flew in from one of the open ginormous windows and buzzed us. Danika swat at it and squealed in fear.

The PTC president ducked and covered her hair.

Likely just as afraid as the humans and discombobulated, the bird circled and zigzagged over us erratically before colliding into the top pane of the lifted window and crashing to the floor. The little bird shuddered once. Then Died.

At my sister's feet.

Or mine too because we were standing side by side.

Rachel gasped.

I grabbed her arm. "Do not read into this."

"What am I missing?" Principal Josh said.

I stared at the little bird. A magpie.

Precious said, "It's believed if a bird dies at your feet something bad is going to happen."

2

I WOKE to my sister misting me with a squirt bottle.

"Pleeg," I said, blowing hair from my mouth while wiping the dew from my face. I rolled over and buried my face in the pillow.

"Get up." She pushed my head into the bed. "You have seven minutes before you're expected to take pictures at Fall Festival."

I'd heard through the grapevine, aka Precious, that the Village Garden School had committed to hosting the photography booth as part of a clever strategy to beholden the school to the community, to win over those holdouts that begrudged a different school outshining the regular old schools. Anytime a person looked at their picture, they'd think of the charter school.

"Go away," I mumbled. I'd stayed up way too late watching YouTube videos on how to be a PI.

I was living off the dregs of a small windfall left

behind by my lying bigamist husband. I'd used a portion to fix the air conditioner in LC, my classic Jeep Wagoneer. Working the case of my not-husband's unexpected death left me battered and bruised, so I'd taken a budget trip to Hawaii to reset. What was left was earmarked for rent and food. I needed to step up my game or else I would be dirt poor. I had my job at Ralph's doing the online grocery shopping gig but wasn't getting more than fifteen hours a week. LC, named after the explorers Lewis and Clark, drank those wages weekly in gas and oil.

"Sam, come on. People are lined up. Mom is there, and she said you better not make her look bad."

Oh, snap. Rachel had pulled out the big guns.

I flipped onto my back and squinted at my sister. "You're so mean."

She shrugged. "Mean would be to let you sleep past ten and have Mom come and get you."

True.

I rolled from the bed, groaning. "I hate taking pictures of smiling, happy people."

"You take pictures of us all the time." She pushed me toward the bathroom.

I stopped at the doorway. "I like you all. It's everyone else. All fake smiles while the dad is thinking he can't wait to go back to gambling away their mortgage money, or the mom is having an affair. Maybe he is, too." I snorted with disgust. From the floor I picked up yoga pants and changed into those.

Rachel raised her brows as she studied me "You've gotten cynical. One bad experience, and its changed you."

"Says the woman who hasn't dated since her fiancé died." I stepped into the bathroom to roll on underarm stink repellant, don a bra and a tunic style T-shirt.

In my bedroom, Rachel was lying across my bed. "I'm hoping time with Dad will do wonders for Cora. She isn't around men a lot."

"When Dad's done with her, she'll be a boss at picking her own fantasy league," I said. "She's an amazing kid, and that's all because of you."

"But maybe I should date," Rachel mused.

"Maybe think about that when you get back. You've got a lot on your plate." On Monday we would fly to Virginia with Rachel to see her ship out. Pretending that her deployment wasn't a big deal while focusing on everything else, regardless of how insignificant, kept us from impromptu crying episodes.

My phone rang, and we looked at each other.

"Ten o'clock," Rachel said. "You're officially late."

"Crap." I stuffed my feet in UGGs. I pushed my hair back with a fabric headband and ran to the bathroom to brush my teeth. "This is the bad omen from that bird," I called to Rachel.

She groaned. "I hope so. I know it's a silly superstition, but I don't need one more thing to worry about."

The ringing continued.

"Grab that," I yelled before sticking the toothbrush in my mouth.

"Not on your life," she said.

My mom and I might not agree with how my life was playing out, but I wasn't interested in making her look bad or upsetting her any more than I already did. She was the town mayor and one day aspired to run the world. Or the school board. Whichever came first.

At the door I grabbed my camera case. Then Rachel and I dashed out. I lived in a simple four-room apartment over my dad's newspaper. Living room-kitchen combo, bathroom, and bedroom. The place used to be an Airbnb and extra cash for my parents, so the decor was nice and inviting.

The newspaper office, and apartment, were half a block from the downtown park where the Fall Festival was happening. We didn't have far to hustle. But as we drew closer, I slowed. I wasn't about to rush up looking flustered.

The park butted up against the Windy River and was swarming with families. Countless booths ran the perimeter of the park and offered food, information for community programs, face painting, and so much more. The photography booth was near the entrance and set up to look like a library. Two tall shelves stacked with books were the backdrop surrounding a small stage. A line of people waited.

"Crap," I mumbled.

My mom stood at the head of the line with one hand on her hip and one arm around Cora. She raised a brow. "Is there a problem?" she asked.

Besides not wanting to do this, the hour too early for me, and I hadn't had coffee? Nope.

I was setting up my camera when Precious stepped

into the space. She held out a large paper cup that was filled with nectar from the gods.

"Is that coffee?" I took the cup and inhaled the steam coming from the tiny hole in the lid.

She nodded. "I figured it was for the good of the entire event and, particularly, the families that requested photos." She wore wild, flower-patterned black leggings under a formfitting black tunic and knee-high black boots. Precious was the descendant of Germans. She stood six feet with naturally platinum blond hair. Her personality was big, her breasts even more so. But her heart was ginormous. She'd pulled her hair into a pony-tail using a black Ponytail Beanie and looked the picture of a successful adult. Put together.

She continued, "And if you find that to not be enough,"—she pointed behind the bookcase — "June's right behind you."

I glanced behind the shelves. June and one other teenager staff were serving up drip coffee and scones.

I said to June, "Best part of this whole thing is knowing scones are right behind me."

She smiled and handed me a mini scone on a napkin. "On the house."

"You're a savior," I told her before shoving the entire treat in my mouth.

My mother cleared her throat, but it didn't keep the irritation out of her voice. "Samantha?"

"I got this, Mrs. True," Precious told my mom.

She turned to the crowd and explained the procedure for getting their picture taken. They were to put their names on the provided list in numeric order and include their phone numbers and email. I would catalog their names with the coordinating picture frame number. Precious also told them that mistakes were bound to happen so be patient and kind. Precious was a natural leader and organizer.

"Weren't you wearing this yesterday?" my mother asked. She gave me a pointed look after scanning me up and down.

"At least I'm here," I pointed out. I gave Cora a tickly hug that made her laugh then turned to the crowd.

"Okay, let's do this," I said, then groaned from annoyance. I'd rather be anywhere but here. Based on the surprised look on the faces of my mom and the families in line, I must have groaned out loud.

Forty minutes into snapping images of several families with plastered-on smiles, I was looking for an excuse to take a break when Principal Josh popped up. Hands in pockets and a toothy smile on his face, he said, "I suppose right on time is still considered on time. I'm a five minutes early guy." He rubbed my back. "This is a flattering look for you."

His mannerisms were so weird. Was he reprimanding me? Or flirting?

An appropriate response eluded me.

Principal Josh continued, "It takes a village to raise productive adults, Samantha. We appreciate you doing your part. But remember, you're a role model and be mindful of the message you're sending." He massaged my shoulders.

Reprimanding, I decided. See, here's the thing. Guilt didn't work on me unless it was from my parents. I wasn't wired like most people. Having dyslexia and struggling through school taught me that sometimes other's expectations were unattainable and that those requirements were on them, not me. Besides, it didn't hurt to teach kids that, even as an adult, we get flustered or have bad days.

I was about to tell Principal Josh with his Calvin and Hobbes tie, which was super cool, to kiss my heinie I opened my mouth to say something unkind but Principal Josh interrupted.

"Oh, the PTC ladies and I are meeting Tuesday after next at How Ya Bean Coffee shop. Come by and get pictures."

The only good thing about being the "school photographer" was the fact that the PTC met at a coffee shop. "I got a fair number of pics from the last meeting." I signaled for the next family to take their place on the stage.

"More is always a good thing. Besides, it's important to me you become a part of Team VGS." He squeezed my shoulder. VGS was Village Garden School, and I'd rather be on a team doing an excursion into hell than to go to another PTC meeting with the snooty moms with their Range Rovers and Hunter boots.

A tall woman with long straight brown hair and blue eyes came up to Principal Josh and cupped his elbow. She was dressed like everyone in the PNW: leggings, a T-shirt, and a long sweater-like jacket over it. She looked familiar, but I couldn't place her.

"Hey," she said to me then focused on Principal Josh.

He faced her, his smile wide and open. "Hey, babe, you all set to ease parent's minds?"

She stepped closer to him and lowered her voice. "Where did you get that water you brought for the run?"

As part of the festival a small 2.5 K kick off at eleven.

He shrugged. "I didn't have time to run to the store, so I grabbed your stock from the garage."

She groaned. "That's part of my"—she lowered her voice — "cache."

Principal Josh's smile wavered. "I'll replace it. Don't freak out. It's not like you need it today."

Babe's eyes went wide. Freak out might not have been impending, but it was now. Telling someone to not freak out is a stupid thing to do. He was being dismissive, and she was about to let him have it.

I snapped a few pictures, dismissed a family with a wave of my hand and told the next family to take their place. Hoping Babe and Principal Josh would continue their conversation without taking it elsewhere. I was nothing if not curious.

"I'll decide when to freak out or not. You helping your-self to my stuff without asking feels like I should freak out," she said vehemently.

"It's just water. It's not like you can't get more, and I said I would replace it." Principal Josh did not sound like he was smiling.

"Kids in front," I said like I was paying attention to my job and not the drama behind me.

Babe scoffed. "See that you do," she said. "And anything else you might have helped yourself to."

I bent to dig out a lens from my camera bag and watched her stalk off. She went across the park and behind a booth with a Danner Pesticide banner across the top. An older, tall, stocky man about the same age as my father was waiting there. He said something to her, and she gave him a dismissive wave. He looked slightly familiar as well.

I turned, curious to see Principal Josh's face. A tall teen with brown hair and side-swept bangs was inches from the principal.

"What do you want?" Principal Josh asked.

Nope, his Joker smile gone, replaced by a thin press of his lips.

"Wait till she finds out about the other stuff you took," the teen said with a snarl.

Principal Josh scoffed.

The teen leaned closer to Josh, fist clenched, his voice low and menacing. "You better replace everything, including the batteries and gas." The teen snorted, his nostrils flared. "Yeah, I know about that." The teen's anger was radiating off him.

I stepped off the stage, prepared to break up a fight.

"And what if I don't?" Josh hissed. "What are you going to do?"

"I have options. For starters, I can tell everyone about you and that lady getting it on in your car. And about your smoking habit. For starters."

Beside me, June gasped.

I was less shocked by the exchange, but more by the

teen's aggressive mannerisms. Like the kid had a chance taking on an adult. And to do so in such a public venue.

I shook my head with disbelief.

Principal Josh tossed back his head and laughed. The Joker smile had returned. He said, "Careful. If we're telling secrets, I think you might have a few you wouldn't want uncovered." He slapped the kid on the back and strolled off as if nothing untoward had happened.

I looked at June, confused. Anger etched her face. She rolled her eyes and returned to serving her long line of patrons.

I turned my attention back to the families in line. No one but me and June seemed to have seen and heard the interaction. I caught my mom as she, Rachel, and Cora were walking by.

"Hey," I asked. "Is it weird that Danner pesticide is here? Pesticide doesn't feel festive."

My mom picked imaginary lint off my tunic. "The school has a policy that when the property's sprayed with pesticides, parents can opt in or out on notification. Danner does the spraying. They're here to field questions."

I nodded to the booth. "That's the owners?" Father and daughter maybe?

Mom glanced at the booth. "Yes, sorta. You don't remember Laura Danner? Oh, I can't recall her maiden name. But she was a grade or two ahead of Rachel. She married Carl Danner. That's his father, Lyle, with Laura."

Realization dawned. "Carl was killed a few years ago,

right? Changing a tire on the side of the road and someone hit him?" The story was tragic.

Mom nodded, looking sad. "Yes, and it wasn't even his tire. He'd stopped to help a stranger. Left two kids behind. Levi and Lanie."

"She's dating Principal Josh?" I remembered Carl as a big, scrappy guy who looked like he could survive any situation. Not exactly in the same class of man as the principal. I wanted to slap myself upside that head. That was who the teen was. Levi Danner.

Mom smiled. "They've been dating for a few months. Good for her, she deserves to be happy. More importantly, it's probably good for Levi, too. He's struggled and having a good male role model in his life might be a positive thing." She licked her finger then wiped something off my face.

"Gross, mom," I said, jerking back.

"You're so pretty, Sam. You should take more time with yourself."

"I should take these folk's picture," I said and pointed my camera at the impatiently waiting family.

"You're so good at this, honey. Don't you miss taking pictures?" She draped an arm around Cora's shoulders, who was face deep into a shaved ice, and steered her away.

I looked at the irritated expression of the dad. Yep, I was so good at this. Not!

"Smile," I said with a fake cheery voice and bit back a laugh at the dad's scowl.

3

TUESDAY - SECOND WEEK IN OCTOBER

TWO WEEKS AGO, my parents and I had flown to Virginia to wave good-bye to my sister Rachel as she deployed on the Naval aircraft carrier Enterprise. We then spent the subsequent days coddling her six-year Cora who we now were responsible for.

Well, not me exactly. Rachel didn't believe I had it in me to be solely responsible for Cora. Instead, volunteering at Cora's school was my assignment. Spying on my niece, her friends, and teachers to make sure every day was butterflies and rainbows. Not a useful way to use my newly gained private investigator license and blooming skills, if you asked me. Not that anyone had.

Yet, here I was. Dressed in faded jeans with holes in my knees, a kelly-green long sleeve T-shirt, and my favorite canvas Jack Purcell low top white Converses. My destination was the local coffee shop. My task was to get candids of Cora's school's parent-teacher collaboration. A volunteer job I was told to do. Would I rather ride a horse buck naked through town before spending time with the Uber bossy hipster moms of Village Garden School? Yes, I would. A horse can speed through town. Time with the moms was gonna crawl.

On a whim, I printed up a flyer and cheap business cards for my PI business with hopes to leave them at the coffee shop. The worry of diminished finances weighing on me. My private investigator business wasn't bringing in any money. Because I had no clients. I had no clients because I felt like a poser, a pretend PI. That would only change when I changed how I saw myself.

"Morning, June," I called as the front door swung closed behind me. I'd wanted to arrive before the Barbie Brigade—Rachel's term, not mine—but they were already there.

"How ya bean?" June said with a smile. Petite, a natural blond with pink cheeks and cornflower blue eyes, she was the cutest and softest person I knew. She never raised her voice, always wore pastels, and looked sunny even on the grayest of days. She was a whiz with coffee. Starting from roasting the beans to adding any kind of sweet extra. Often, I depended on her creations to get through the day. As I was sure most of us did.

One day June would be a perfect addition to the Barbie Brigade; only she'd have to give up her pastels and her sunny disposition. For me, stay-at-home moms fell into one of two categories. The harried, haven't-brushed-their-teeth-or-hair-in-a-week moms. Or this group. The Hunter boots, yoga pants, tight T-shirts with the puffy vest over them. None matching but all coordinating. Their lipstick was precise. Their hair not mussed. It baffled the mind on how they achieved it.

My guess was they took their kid's attention deficit meds. But that was me being judgy.

"I have Unicorn Brew today. You want one?" June asked.

"Yes, please." Unicorn Brew was a shot of espresso and white-hot chocolate mixed with flavored syrup. Only, no one could guess the syrup's flavor. The drink made me a happy person, and June only offered it occasionally and without warning. It was the elusive drink we all wanted. There had been a time when she had it more frequently, but I think that was a ruse to get us addicted and to keep us coming back in hopes we'd get it again.

"Do you mind if I tack this flyer to your bulletin board?" I pointed toward the restrooms where a community board hung.

"Go ahead," she said and turned to the teen helping behind the counter.

That's the other thing about June. In collaboration with the school district, she sponsored teens and helped them build their work skills. Just helping my folks out with Cora was exhausting. I couldn't imagine running a business and working with teens who, biologically, were nitwits because of hormones.

I pinned my flyer and returned to the mommies, giving them my attention. All five of them.

"Everyone ready for pictures? Just act normal." Or their version of normal, I wanted to add. I plunked my camera bag on an empty table and took out my camera, setting my lens cover on the table.

"We are," Mindy, the PTC president, said. She wore a mustard yellow puffy vest and matching headband. She pointed to each person and said their name. Carlie, Dana, Annber, and Heidi. Each of them had been with the school since its inception two years ago.

I would never remember their names outside of today. That was how my brain worked. Their mommy uniforms didn't help. Only one of them, Annber I thought, was dressed in exercise clothes, of the Lululemon variety. Cropped shimmery silver yoga pants, matching sports bra with a thin dark pink hoody zipped only midway. Her makeup was flawless, her high ponytail tight and slick.

I pointed my camera in her direction. "You're okay with me getting you in your workout clothes? Some people aren't." Studio photography taught me people were particular.

She gave me a dismissive wave. "Of course I am."

"At least I caught you before you worked out." I shifted my attention to the camera screen.

Annber chuckled. "Um, no. This is me after a workout, but I believe in keeping it real."

I glanced up. "What do you do? Transcendental Meditation?" The only time I ever looked as picture-perfect as her was when I went to the hairdresser.

She smiled and wrinkled her nose. "No, I don't even know what that is. I do core yoga for muscle building."

I'd done that class. It was hard. And sweat-inducing.

Clearly, she showered afterward. No way she'd just come from muscle-building yoga. Why Annber pretended otherwise was anyone's guess. I let it go. Because who really cared?

"I'll be here in the background getting shots. Try not to look at the camera."

They blinked at me doe-eyed.

I glanced around the coffee shop. "Maybe switch tables so I can get June's cute menu boards in the background." I pointed to a section of tables along the wall away from where they were sitting by the window.

"We like these tables," Mindy said.

I looked through the camera viewfinder. "Okay, but the light from the window makes you look like you have a beard," I said. "Shadows do cruel things."

They moved.

I snapped a few pictures with June's artisanal chalkboards in the background. I loved how she changed the menu and also listed events that How Ya Bean hosted. Briefly, I wondered if *Ask the PI Anything* might be a good presentation and would help with business, but I didn't know a lot about being a PI so...

Principal Josh came rushing in. "Sorry I'm late, ladies. Education is never a nine-to-five job or confined to the school campus." He went from woman to woman and touched them somehow. A hug, a shoulder squeeze, a clasping of the hands.

He faced me and looked overly please. "Samantha, excellent. I hope you're getting good pictures."

"I am."

He looked at June over my shoulder. "Any chance we have Unicorn Brew today?" He gave her a wink.

"Yes, we do," she said with a smile.

Something seemed to pass between them. I think the mommies noticed it, too, because one bristled.

"Are we going to do this today or what?" Mindy asked. "I have groceries being delivered." Her ponytail was an arrangement of expertly made curls.

"Hey, there's enough of Principal Josh to go around," he said with a chuckle.

Behind the counter, a plate fell. I glanced at June who had a disgusted expression on her face.

"You okay, June?" I asked.

"What a mess," she said. Then gestured to the floor.

"June? My coffee?" Principal Josh asked.

"It's coming. Give me a second," she bit out before disappearing behind the counter to, I assume, clean up whatever spilled.

"Ladies, get out your calendars," Principal Josh said.

In unison, all five-women whipped out planners of various sorts. Some electronic, some paper and decorated with Washi tape and stickers.

"We have much to talk about. Don't forget, Samantha is our in-house photographer. You can call her anytime if you need or want pictures. Her goals are to capture the greatness of Village Garden School and the work you women do."

"Um, I am? My goal is what again?" Because I was pretty sure my goals were about making money and this gig paid nothing.

Josh turned to me. "Samantha," he said, hands extended, "give me your hands."

I set my camera down to do as he asked. He closed his hands over mine, like one of those double-fisted hand-shakes that was supposed to make a person feel like the handshaker was really, truly interested in them.

"Samantha." He held tight to my hands but said over his shoulder, "Help me out here, ladies." His attention back to me, he continued, "I'm a firm believer that educa-tion is..."

"A three-hundred-and-sixty-degree process," the ladies said in unison. Even June. They all did this hand thing where they made a circle in the air. I'm guessing Principal Josh would have done the same had he not been holding my hands.

"Yes, three-hundred-and-sixty degrees. You know what that means?" He smiled and leaned in closer to me.

"That you end up where you started?" I felt like I stepped into some bizarro-world TV show where everyone was a Stepford something or other.

"It means, Samantha, all of us have to raise these chil-dren. All of us have to do our part. Because if we don't, who suffers?"

"The children do," the robot ladies said.

The creep factor rose significantly.

Principal Josh put one hand on his heart and the other hand over my heart. Warmth radiated from his splayed fingers as he touched me in places I wasn't comfortable with. The urge to brain him with my camera was strong. Like a force compelling me to do it. Someone in the group gasped. My distaste was likely expressed on my face.

"Feel that, Samantha? That's the heartbeat of our children. That's how we make and raise successful adults. Through our love and desires." His hand lingered, my skin prickled from his touch and the uncomfortable nature. He winked. "Sharing is caring, Samantha."

"I'm not making the connection." I pulled away.

June called Josh's name, and he went to collect his coffee. I wiped my hands down my pants. He came back and faced me with a wink and a smile. Then a buzzing sound came from his pant pocket.

Principal Josh pulled out his phone and did some finger pressing and swiping. "I have a spot on my calendar with your name on it. Thursday at four. I'll go into more details then." He flashed me a dazzling smile.

"Um," I said, confused. Were we talking about kids or was he flirting with me?

Principal Josh stared at his screen then frowned. "Oh dear," he said and faced the mommies. "I have to cut this meeting short. Looks like the superintendent is bringing the school board by for a surprise visit. You all forgive me, right?"

They murmured various things, each looking at each other with questions on their faces. Carlie stood and crossed her arms. I knew that was her name because she was wearing a coral puffy vest and I'd matched the sounds. Coral. Carlie. Her Hunter boots were a glossy silver that highlighted the glitter in her tights.

She said, "Principal Josh, are you sure you're free

Thursday?" Her gaze flicked to me. "I thought you had an appointment?"

"I'll be shifting things around. Everything will be fine, Carlie. Samantha has potential, and I'd like to help her discover it." He gave me a wink over his shoulder.

Did he think winking was his superpower? He must because he did it *all the time*. Perhaps he thought the act was endearing enough to override his creep factor? Never had I ever wanted to poke someone in the eye as much as I did this guy and his winking eye.

Frankly, I was okay leaving any potential of mine undiscovered, especially by him. After all, he'd done enough discovering of my potential when his hand had been all over my chest. Flustered, I shoved my camera in its bag, ready to vault from this place.

Carlie put her hands on her hips and glared at me. "Well, what about the issue with her niece? Annber was telling us about it earlier."

I paused my packing. "Wait? What issue?"

Principal Josh gave me a dismissive wave. "I'll handle it." He glanced at Annber. "I thought that was between us."

Annber turned pink and gave an embarrassed shrug.

Carlie wasn't going to let it go. "Her niece sexually harassing another student is a big deal, Principal Josh. I hope *you are* handling it."

A piercing buzz sounded in my ears. "Come again? Sexual harassment?" What in the flim-flam was going on?

Principal Josh faced me and said, "We can discuss it Thursday." He turned back to the others. "Now, let's focus on the school real quick. When Mindy and I last met we went over fundraising ideas so she'll share with you. Our meetings are *very* productive, aren't they Mindy?"

She beamed. "Yes."

Principal Josh said, "I'll see you ladies at our appointments. Thanks for being a part of this with me. Without you smart, amazing, and strong woman, where would I be?"

Carlie grunted and crossed her arms.

He said, "You too, Carlie. You're special, and what you do is like no other." Instantly her ruffled feathers relaxed, and she blushed.

"Enjoy your Unicorn Brew, Josh," June called.

Principal Josh picked up his thirty-two-ounce coffee and gave June a salute. "Where would I be without you?" he asked her. He gave everyone a toothy smile and breezed out the door.

I was still a few seconds behind with the whole Cora and sexual harassment thing. I said to Annber, "Care to explain?"

"Only that your niece touched my daughter in places she shouldn't."

Carlie's upper lip curled. She sneered, "She rubbed her hands up and down Annber's daughter's torso, like that's allowed."

Somehow the pieces weren't connecting. I looked around the coffee shop confused.

June threw me a bone. "It's those sequin shirts. The ones that change images if you rub up or down."

Click. I said to Carlie and Annber, "Are you saying

you're accusing my niece of sexual harassment because she rubbed up and down on Annber's kid's shirt?"

Annber nodded "Yes. Made my Kali uncomfortable. Touching another body is *not okay* unless you have expressed permission."

"They're six," I said. "They eat their boogers."

The mommies sat back in horror as if such a concept never existed in their world.

Carlie snarled, "You can handle it on *Thursday*. Hopefully, you'll have a better defense than your niece is too stupid to not know better. And to think your mother is the mayor."

I wanted to beat her with her Hunter boots. Instead, I channeled my anger toward Principal Josh and his inability to defuse this situation. And for letting me learn about this the way I had.

"Oh, hell no," I said and jerked up my bag, "we're gonna solve this today."

4

TUESDAY

I BROKE several laws driving the three blocks to Cora's school. I hoped to catch Principal Josh before he went into the building. This conversation would not go well. The chance of me not yelling was slim. But that's not why I wanted to catch him outside. Imagining myself confined to a space behind a closed door with the man made my protective radar vibrate like a struck tuning fork.

LC listed to the side when I took the turn into the school parking lot at a high speed. Principal Josh was walking toward the front door and I pulled across a parking spot. He paused, tipped his head back as he finished the last of his Unicorn's Brew, then tossed it in the trash. The cardboard cup bounced off the can and fell to the ground.

Josh paused and stared at the front of the school while surreptitiously kicking the cup behind the trash can. He then took a small object from his pocket and held it to his mouth.

Shut the front door! Principal Josh was vaping.

On reflex alone, I snatched up my camera and went to remove the lens cap. Only it was gone. Left behind at the coffee shop. Having done so shaved seconds off my sighting Josh in the viewfinder. I held down the shutter as I brought him into focus.

Proof, evidence, or blackmail. My gut told me these images were gonna come in handy.

Josh Chapman was amazing, and I didn't mean that in the most complimentary way. Currently, an epidemic called vaping lung disease was sweeping the country. Little was known as the first incident occurred a short time ago, but from what Dad had said, something was in the vape juice that was making people sick. Two people had even died.

And here was Mr. Marvelous-school-principal puffing away as if the juice in his vape pen couldn't possibly contain deadly consequences. What made a person do that? Hubris?

Faster than he'd whipped out the vape pen from his pocket, he tossed it in the trash can and stepped away.

Danika Post pushed through the front doors of the school. The schoolcounselor took one look at Josh and turned around, apparently to go back inside to avoid him.

I kept my camera focused on them, wishing I could read lips.

Before she could go inside, Principal Josh caught her by the elbow, but she pulled away and attempted to skirt him, keeping her oversized purse between them. They had a brief exchange that looked unpleasant. He made a lazy lurch toward her, but she was quick to put distance between them and scurried off, never looking back. Josh leaned one hand against the building and watched her go.

When he turned to go into the entrance, I slipped my camera onto the floorboard then sprung from LC and called his name. Either he didn't hear me or ignored me, I don't know. He went inside.

The school, housed in the old community center building, was downtown, tucked between a bank and a building waiting for a purpose. The recent remodel of the VGS had done an excellent job of making the building look like a school, except for the double glass front doors. A clear security issue if you asked me.

I flung one side open and stormed the lobby while counting to ten to compose myself. A large crescent-shaped desk created a barrier between the front door and what lay after. Willa Rivers, June's mother, sat at the desk. She gave me a happy smile. A second lady, her desk plate reading *Jami Walters, Fiscal*, sat next to Mrs. Rivers.

"Hello, Samantha, how are you today?" Mrs. Rivers rose to greet me.

"I'm great, Mrs. Rivers, how are you?" Mr. Rivers, a farmer, had died when June was a toddler. Mrs. Rivers turned their farmland into endless flower beds that were stunning in spring and autumn.

"Doing fine. What can I help you with?"

To my left were two offices. The door farthest from me

was closed with a placard hanging on the wall that read *Principal Josh Chambers*.

Man, he was quick. I'd been seconds behind him, and yet he was already safely behind the door.

"I need to speak with Principal Josh. Apparently there's an issue with my niece?" I played with the pen on the desk, stretching the chain that kept it from being stolen.

"Are you on his schedule? I'll have to check, but I believe I cleared his schedule because we're getting a surprise visit from the superintendent and school board any minute now so..."

"I only need a second." My impatience pushed back against her resistance. "He may have added me. We talked at How Ya Bean and made an appointment."

She huffed. "That man! It would be just like him to add a mom into his day when I tell him to leave it free." She wiggled her computer mouse, and the unit began to hum.

I had to strike while the iron was hot, as they say.

"Sorry, Mrs. Rivers." I scurried around the barrier toward his door. "Only need a minute to give him a piece of my mind."

I'd made my move as she was lowering herself into her chair, causing her to hover as if she debated chasing after me. "You can't go in there," she said halfheartedly before she plopped into her chair. "Why do I bother? Women come and go all the time."

I flung the door open and spotted Principal Josh slumped with his side against his desk, one hand pressed against the desktop and the other on his chest. His head down.

My temper got the best of me. "You can't let that Stepford mom drop a serious bomb like that and expect me to wait a few days to resolve it. Because that would really make you the village idiot. Which you might be considering you've likely broken some confidentiality law." My raised tone echoed off the walls. Fury clear in the sharp and biting crispness of my words.

"Samantha, please," he said in his soft be-kind voice. He continued to rub his chest.

As I kicked the door closed I said, "You're lucky I didn't brain someone with my camera back there. I'm half tempted to clobber you. How is it that a group of women know my family's business before I do?" The door slammed with a resounding bang.

"Samantha, please," he said again, only the words were slurred. He looked up at me. His face was a stark white, ghostly, and glistened from sweat. He picked up a half-empty twelve-ounce water bottle. Inside, the fluid was light pink, and on the bottom, an effervescent tablet was breaking down.

His hand trembled as he lifted it and took several gulps, looking overly exerted from the task. Water ran out the sides of his mouth and onto his shirt.

I took in his surroundings but nothing else seemed off. Laptop open, three pens splayed out next to a notepad, a cell phone, the lid to the water bottle, and an inhaler.

My brain tried to compute. He'd been fine a few minutes ago chugging his coffee and even hanging with the organics only Hunter Boots Moms. His hands had been everywhere, touching and squeezing everyone. Ironic that he was accusing six-year-olds of sexual harassment when he couldn't keep his hands to himself. But as much as I wanted to resolve this issue with Cora, his appearance was more pressing.

"Josh?" I stepped toward him.

He slouched, his shoulders rolling inward, and sucked in a ragged breath.

"You don't look so good. Here, let me help you sit." A couch was up against the wall to my left. I reached out, but he brushed my hand away with more strength than I expected considering he looked like death. Not the warmed-over version either, but the one that was already in a pine box.

"Water," he rasped and held out the bottle.

"There's water in there, Josh."

The bottle slipped from his hand. "Water," he said, only it sounded like "wa-er."

"Have a seat, and I'll get you water." I tried to take his arm and steer him to the couch. He slapped at me but missed, swatting at air instead.

He gasped. "Hands. Off," he boomed.

I jumped, surprised by the force behind his words.

Confused and frustrated, I dashed for the door and help. As I reached for the knob, Josh made this gross gurgling sound. Dread filled me. When I turned back, Josh was listing away from the desk. He swayed once, then fell forward like a downed tree. His head struck the front corner of his desk in a *thunk* that sounded like a water-

melon smashing against concrete. Bile rose in my throat
and out came a scream I hoped would bring the walls
down.

I rushed to him. The impact of colliding with his desk
had broken his fall and forced him onto his right side.
Blood gathered at the laceration on the left side of his
head. His eyes were open and vacant. They stared at
nothing.

"Josh," I yelled and nudged his shoulders. I didn't want
to shake him because of the wound to his head.

His office door flung open. Mrs. Rivers gasped.

"I didn't—I couldn't—he—," I didn't know what to say.
I'd just witnessed a man dying and had done nothing to
save him. I wasn't sure I could've done anything, but that
was irrelevant. I should've made him sit down. All the
"should haves" were rushing through my mind.

"What have you done?" Mrs. Rivers said, horror on her
face.

"He fell," I said. "Get help." I'd taken an emergency
response class and recalled that in times of shock, and I
was guessing this was one of those times, people needed
specific instructions.

"Call 911, Mrs. Rivers," I commanded with authority. I
searched Josh's wrist for a pulse. Finding nothing, I
scooted away from the principal, my eyes on his Calvin
and Hobbes tie. I loved that comic strip.

Outside in the main room Mrs. Rivers was on the
phone. Moments later, she came to stand in the doorway.

"Is he dead?" she whispered. Behind her, someone
gasped. Jami, I assumed.

when I turned he was falling over. He hit his head on the desk."

Oliver Gee, another cop came in. "Cleared the area. Saw nothing suspicious. No one out on the property." He told Leo. "I have Smith monitoring the premises."

Officers Smith and Gee were the least experienced cops on our small-town force.

Leo nodded to the office ladies. "Go take their statements." He said to me, "Chief Louney is on his way."

I groaned. DB Louney, our police chief, was a tool. He'd only gotten the job because he was good looking and his dad had the position before him. But he lacked an ability to think of anything other than himself or to connect two rational dots. He liked to take the easiest path possible. I would know. I'd been his chemistry partner, and he'd cheated off *me* to pass.

I was the sole witness to a man dying. And it had been an awful experience. And now I would have to retell it to Dweebie.

As if thinking his name evoked his presence, the front door opened and DB strolled in. He wore his uniform shirt tight to show off his physique.

Mrs. Rivers jumped to her feet. "Thank God you're here, Chief." She pointed a finger at me. "She killed Principal Josh."

5

TUESDAY

I GASPED. "I did no such thing," I said.

"Just relax, Sam," Leo whispered. "Let me handle this."

DB came to me, walking like there wasn't any rush, as if a dead man wasn't in the room behind me and we had all the time in the world.

His thumbs were hooked into his utility belt, his arms flexed, his preferred posture to show off his big guns, as he liked to call his biceps.

He paused at the doorway and looked into Principal Josh's office. "He a goner?" he asked the EMT inside. His eyes flicked to me when the EMT confirmed it.

Leo stuck his hands on his hips and said, "I know what you're gonna say DB, and you're right. We need to evacuate the school. Officer Gee's secured the premises. He didn't see anyone, and Officer Smith is still out there monitoring things. Here's what we know." He reviewed the events.

"Yep, we need to evacuate the school. Any thoughts on the best way to do that?" He asked Leo.

I stuck my hands under my legs and bent forward. I'd experienced shock before and could tell it was settling in. My hands were shaking, and soon my body would follow. Sometimes, I liked to upchuck, too. I swallowed convulsively.

Leo asked Mrs. Rivers, "How would you notify parents if there was an issue?"

"We'd send a text alert and an email. We also have a system where we can set up a voice message and call everyone." She was standing with her arms crossed, sending occasional glares my way. June looked so much like her. Both petite and blond. Her anger and accusation were upsetting. How could she believe I'd do such a thing?

"Are you up to sending out an alert?" Leo asked.

Her gaze flicked to me. "Not with *her* right there."

DB faced me, a wry smile on his face. He surveyed me, I presumed an attempt to make me squirm. But I stared back. His droopy-eye stare had nothing on the vacant soul-has-left-the-body one Principal Josh had. That look was forever burned in my mind.

"Let's take her to the cruiser and let her sit in the back," DB said.

"What?" I cried.

Before we could say anything further, the front door opened, the superintendent and the five-member school board came into the lobby, my mother behind them.

Alice Andrews, the school Superintendent, surveyed the room, her smile fell, and she said, "Has something happened? We're here to talk with Josh Chapman and tour the school."

"Samantha?" My mother stepped up to the barrier desk.

I tried to smile but my teeth were chattering.

Mrs. Rivers pointed to me. "Josh is dead, and she killed him!"

Leo groaned. Mom gasped. Alice Andrews laughed nervously. My teeth clanked together.

"I *did. Not. Kill. Him,*" I said.

Mrs. Rivers wagged her finger. "Whatever. My guess is you were angry because of the sexual harassment accusations made about your niece. Annber Greene was just here this morning complaining."

My mother straightened, her features hardening. Dad, Rachel, and I called this her pit-bull lawyer look.

Mrs. Rivers continued, "You even told Josh he was lucky you didn't brain him with your camera."

Alice Andrews covered her mouth but continued to laugh. The sound was so out of place it came off as abrasive, causing me to wince.

Alice leaned against the wall, waved her hands in the air as she sucked in a deep breath. "I'm sorry, I do this when I'm nervous." She covered her face as her shoulders shook from restrained chuckles.

Whoa. Weird.

Lydia Delahooke, a school board member, said to Alice, "Maybe you're laughing because you're happy, now your niece can take the position." She held up her index finger. "But only in the interim."

"Folks," DB said to the group. "We have to ask you to leave."

"If you have a student here, please step outside and wait. We'll be dismissing the students shortly," Leo added.

I grabbed at Leo's arm. "Did you hear what Mrs. Delahooke just said?"

He squeezed my hand. "We'll talk to both her and Mrs Andrews."

DB ushered everyone out but my mother, who'd skirted his efforts. When he went to take her elbow, she jerked back and said, "Tread cautiously, Chief. I'm a lawyer, and that's my daughter." She stared DB down.

"Mrs. True, please. This has all just happened. What we know is Josh is dead. From what the EMT thinks is a head injury, and Samantha was the only person in the room when it happened."

"He hit his head when he fell over," I said. The memory of his blank-staring eyes as he went down will forever be burned on my brain.

"She pushed him," Mrs. Rivers said.

"How would you know? You weren't in there," I shouted then shivered.

Leo took a package from the EMT, broke it open, and shook out a thick wool blanket. He wrapped it around my shoulders then pulled it in tightly.

"Shut up," he mumbled. "Don't give him anything." He jerked the edges of the blanket together, which made me look at him.

"Do you understand?" he whispered.

I did. I gave a slight nod and considered the situation I

was in. Whether or not I liked it, whether or not I wanted to believe it, I was the prime suspect should Josh's death be ruled a homicide. In the true crime world, there were endless stories of innocent people going to jail for life or taking a plea deal because to maintain their innocence meant a harsher sentence, but to plea meant a chance at life outside of prison. The justice system was a twisted entity where reality was frightening. Guilt, after all, was determined by how one *perceived* facts.

Leo did not want me to give DB, or anyone in this room anything that could be used against me in court. I blew out a breath and tried to calm myself, tried to get a grip. What I needed was a good cry or sugar. Either would suffice. Both would be awesome.

DB came over to Leo. "We need to divide and conquer." He glanced at me. "She needs to be questioned."

"I already have her statement," Leo said.

"Maybe, but what Mrs. Rivers said sounds like motive. We need to do more at the station."

Leo blew out a sigh. "I'm happy to do the crime scene if you want to take the questioning," Leo offered.

Initially, I wanted to protest. I wanted Leo to question me. I trusted him. I opened my mouth to say something, but he shifted and stepped on my toe, a warning to keep my trap shut.

I listened to them work out the logistics of releasing the students. Leo was methodical and organized, and I knew then that I'd want Leo to process the crime scene. There would be no question about the chain of evidence.

There would be no stone unturned. DB was a selfish, lazy, and careless individual. I knew this. Leo knew this. Anyone with a brain and observation skills knew this. DB was not the sort to collect evidence from a scene unbiasedly. Leo had been right telling me to hush. My toe ached as a reminder of my near miss of stupidity.

"Officer Gee," DB called across the lobby. He waved the young officer over. "Take Miss True to the station for questioning." He smiled at me. Not a kind smile either. A smug one. "Guess who's taking a field trip to the police station."

My mother darted around the desk barrier to where we were. "Excuse me," she said to DB. "I'll be going to the station with her and, as her lawyer, I can tell you she won't be saying anything."

DB sighed and hung his thumbs from his utility belt. "Mrs. True, are you even licensed anymore? Go on home, and Samantha will call you when we're done."

My mom straightened, and I wanted to warn DB. He'd unknowingly dismissed her and the law in one statement. Something only stupid people did in her presence.

"I beg your pardon?" she said with a steady tone that edged on lethal. "Did you just dismiss representation for this woman when counsel was evoked? And do not forget Dwayne Butler Louney, that I'm also the mayor of this town. I'm in charge of appointing the proper person for your position. I may not have been the mayor when you were initially appointed, but I'm the mayor now. Watch your step. Now would not be the time to have me think you're inept at your job, would it?"

I sucked in a breath. For all her good intentions, she'd just made everything worse.

DB's eyes narrowed. "Excuse me, Mayor. All I wanted to do was question Samantha. She's not being charged. I'm assuming, as a lawyer, you remember how the process goes."

My mother's right brow cocked. "And you can do so in the presence of her attorney."

Chances were strong we'd go around and around here. I said, "Mom, why don't you grab Cora and take her to Dad. I'll go over to the station and wait for you there." I raised a hand. "I promise not to say another word until you get there. Though I've already given my statement to Officer Stillman."

My mother crossed her arms and smiled up at DB. "She's already given her statement. Perhaps you should read that and invite her back should you have more questions. Unless you're charging her?"

DB looked from mom to Leo then me. Leo stepped up to DB's side and said in a quiet voice that both mom and I could hear. "There's no weapon. There's no motive. Worst case she shoved him, and he fell and hit his head."

DB glared at me, glanced at Josh's office, then refocused on my mother. "Madame Mayor, Josh Chapman was a member of your community. He has rights as well. I know it's inconvenient for Samantha to keep telling her story, but if there's more to this scene than what we see, Samantha might hold our strongest chance of resolving this. Is there any harm with her retelling the sequence of events?"

Mom bristled. "No, so long as she has a lawyer present."

My spidey-senses told me there was something more to this picture. Maybe it was from the forensic classes I took in college or all my true crime TV watching, but something was off. Like Alice Andrew's reaction. Maybe whatever was eating at me wasn't as nefarious as murder, but maybe it was. My guess was there were several layers to Josh Chapman, and the good people of Wind River were about to peel them back.

DB's voice boomed across the lobby, "Gee, take Miss True to the station." He studied me. "I want to hear it directly from you what happened in there. Why Mrs. Rivers thinks you killed her boss."

My mom slapped her leg in frustration.

I went to stand, but the shock of the events left me lightheaded. Leo offered me a hand and pulled me up. I held onto his arm for strength as I steadied myself. My legs were weak and trembling. My nerves were frayed. I wasn't sure I could make it out the door much less to the station, but I wasn't sharing that with anyone.

"What about Josh?" I asked quietly.

"What about him?" DB said. "He's dead."

Leo said, "He'll go to the medical examiner in Vancouver. We'll know more after they do an autopsy."

I nodded, mostly because I didn't know what else to do.

Leo stepped closer, his voice low. "Don't do anything stupid, Sam."

We made eye contact. "Gosh, how do you mean? I

watch a guy die and immediately requested the police. That's turning out to be stupid." I cut my eyes to DB.

Officer Gee came to stand next to me.

DB said to him, "Make sure she has a comfy chair. We might be here a while." He gave me a pointed look, one that said he was going to be a butthead and he intended to make me wait as long as possible.

My mother huffed. I calmed her by putting one hand on her arm. "Get Cora home. I'm okay. I'll call you when I get home."

She shook her head in disagreement. "You need a lawyer."

"I'll take care of it." I met her gaze with a steady one of my own to reassure her. She nodded slightly, and I turned to DB.

I said, "Take your time. My lawyer is in Seattle, and it'll take him a while to get here. I won't be talking without him present."

DB narrowed his eyes, then with a sharp nod of his head, gestured for Officer Gee to get me out of there.

"If you aren't home in a few hours, I'll be going down there," she said sharply, more for DB than me.

I tried to give Leo back the blanket, but he told me to keep it. My mother pulled me into a hug. She whispered, "Try to document every little detail you can recall. With no one knowing. Deep breath, Samantha. It's game on."

I nodded in understanding. "Game on" in our house meant we needed to suck up everything we were feeling and focus on the issue at hand. In this case, it was Josh being dead, and me being questioned. I could fall apart later. Game on meant there were also no do-overs.

Outside, I handed Oliver Gee the blanket then pulled my phone from my back pocket. The number went to his direct line.

"Tyson Lockett," he said upon answering.

I could picture him behind a desk in a thousand-dollar suit, tugging at the neckline because Tyson would rather hang ten. He probably had his shoes off under his desk. He was a barefoot instead of dress shoes kinda guy.

"Hey," I said to Tyson with false cheeriness.

Next to me, Oliver Gee startled. He looked shocked, probably because I had the nerve to use my phone in his presence, Oliver gestured to the phone. I pushed him away.

To Tyson I said, "How would you feel about coming down to Wind River for a visit?"

Lockett hesitated. "Why?"

"Oh, nothing major. Just a possible murder and the moderate probability I'll need a crack-shot defense attorney such as yourself."

6

I EXPLAINED to Lockett that I was standing in the presence of Officer Gee and on my way to the station. He gave me strict orders to say nothing. Not even "mm hm" or "uh-uh." I figured those were easy enough instructions.

After I hung up, Office Gee gave me a dirty look. Oliver was my height, dirty blond hair, and an average watt bulb, if you know what I mean. We'd been on the yearbook staff in high school together.

"What? If I were under arrest, I'd be entitled to one call, and I'm not under arrest. I'm cooperating with the police to answer some questions. I believe I can say no, and you all would have to 'bring me in.'" I did air quotes.

He looked caught between a rock and a hard place, his expression pained. Either that or he had bad gas.

I held up a hand to stop him from saying anything. "Don't worry. I'll be compliant from here on out." I pointed to the station four buildings away. "We walking, or do you need to drive?"

"Why would we drive?" he asked, puzzled.

I shrugged as he fell into step with me. "I dunno. Maybe you drove here and don't want to leave your car at the school." I tucked my phone in my back pocket.

He took off his hat and brushed back his hair, then grimaced. "I, uh, just ran out the door when the call came in. Didn't even think about driving." He said the last part as if self-reprimanding.

"First dead body?" I asked, cavalier.

He nodded.

"Mine, too." I shivered and ran my hands up and down my arms. I remembered Lockett's words and shut my trap. Because what I wanted to do, needed to do, was talk about it. I fiercely needed to process what I'd seen. Everything was surreal. A part of me was waiting for someone to come clean and say it was a joke. This was my default when given situations out of the norm. When Lockett told me my not-husband Carson was dead and still legally married to someone else, I'd had this same sense of being out of body. Of the events happening around me and not to me. I'd also had a terrible feeling then, and I had one now.

Not to say the death of someone was a cut-and-dried situation, but I couldn't shake the feeling that things were going to go sideways real fast.

And then there was Rachel. How would I drop the bomb that her kid's principal was dead, and I'd witnessed that death? Or worse—that the Police might accuse me of killing him? Never mind that some mom accused Cora of sexual harassment. Holy crap, she would flip out.

Oliver held open the station door for me and escorted me into the lobby. Many a tree lost their lives in the decorating of the lobby. Wood front desk, wood bench, wood chairs, and wood floors. He gestured toward the door behind the front desk clerk, Pamela Hopkins. She was reclined back in her office chair, reading a book. She was a tall, lithe woman who liked to run marathons and write erotic poetry. She had a pixie style haircut and wore flannel and plaid. She'd been three years ahead of me in school.

"Is it true?" she asked, jerking upright in her chair. She glanced from Gee to me. "By the look on your face and lack of color in your complexion, I'm going with yeah, it's true." She shook her head.

"I'm taking Miss True to the interrogation room." He gestured for her to open the door separating the lobby from the offices.

Pamela raised one perfectly tweezed brow.

"I witnessed it." I mentally slapped my head. Lockett had said to shut up. I was doing a terrible job of it.

"Chief Louney will be along shortly," Oliver said.

"Can I get you anything while you wait, Sam?" Pamela asked. She pressed something under the desk, and the sound of a latch releasing and a steady buzz came from the door.

Oliver pulled the door open.

"I'd love a water," I said, then touched my stomach.

"And an antacid. I'm not sure if it's the Unicorn Brew or Josh dying, but my stomach isn't right."

"June has Unicorn Brew today?" Pamela asked.

I nodded.

She slapped at the table. "The one day I skip the coffee shop, and she has Unicorn Brew. As soon as I get you water and an antacid, I'll get one. Oliver, you want one?"

He nodded vigorously then gestured for me to precede him. Which I did. I was certain DB wouldn't like me having a drink. I imagined he'd want me to be as uncomfortable as possible.

Oliver showed me to a small room with a simple table and three chairs. All wood, of course. I dropped in one by the wall and kicked my feet up on another. "I'll be here."

Oliver gave me the thumbs up and closed the door behind him when he left. A few minutes later, Pamela came in with a large water bottle and two antacids.

When I'd been in the room uninterrupted for five minutes, I took out my phone and texted Precious.

Holy Crap. Have you heard about Principal Josh?

She said:?

DEAD. And I was there when it happened.

OMG. How awful. What happened? She sent a GIF of a person looking stunned.

I don't know. He just collapsed in front of me.

I'm leaving work now, coming to you

Don't bother. I'm at the station. Dweebie wants to question me. Can you come over later?

Text when you're sprung

I sent the thumbs up.

Using my phone's note app, I got down to doing what my mother told me to do. I put as much as I could remember in writing. Or in my case, drawings. Being dyslexic sucked, but the tradeoff of stellar memory was coming in handy today.

My drawing was rudimentary. Josh's basic furniture the landmarks in the square I'd labeled his office. Details were what I was after. A case of water was in the corner to the right and behind his desk. A packet of pink homeopathic antacids was open and spilling out on his desk.

The fizzy water he'd been drinking.

A laptop, closed. His phone, the screen dark. No pictures of family on the desk or shelves. I closed my eyes and saw the room in my mind's eye. The yellow and light blue made the office cheerful, but there was nothing personal in the space. Not a plant, a picture, or even a doodle on a notepad. Because there was no notepad.

I eased back in the chair and stared at the ceiling, thinking of what that meant about Josh. After finishing the water, I let myself out to go to the restroom, took a second water bottle from the break room by the bathroom, and was back in the interrogation room reading a magazine I'd also collected on my journey out when DB showed up.

He reversed the chair so he could straddle it and rested his arms along the backside. He stared down at me before his gaze flicked to the water bottle and his lips tightened briefly.

"You run a tight ship," I said with a straight face. "It's been awful sitting in here, alone, waiting for you."

"I wouldn't have even given you water," he said. He glanced at the window over my head. I assumed someone, likely Leo, was behind the glass. However, chances were also high no one was behind the mirrored glass and he was trying to catch a glimpse of his reflection.

I pointed to the bottle. "That's not mine. It was in here when I got here." I didn't want anyone to get in trouble.

He gave me a dead-eye stare. "Tell me what happened?"

"I already gave my statement." I figured Lockett would allow me to say that.

"Yeah, but Stillman hasn't typed it up yet so I don't know it."

I pursed my lips. "I'm not sure my lawyer would think that's a good idea. He told me to keep my mouth shut."

"He? Not your mom? I thought you were bluffing." DB straightened in the chair.

"My mother has enough on her plate."

He nodded as he mulled over what I'd said. It was anyone's guess how he was interpreting it. Did I do something wrong? Why had I called a different lawyer? Was I hiding something from my mother? No telling where his prepubescent-stunted devious mind was going.

"What was your beef with Josh Chapman?" DB asked.

I smiled.

"How did you know Josh Chapman?" he asked.

I continued to smile.

"Why did you kill Josh Chapman?" He leaned onto the back of his chair and narrowed his eyes.

I knew he'd asked this to get me to protest. To get a reaction. This time, I showed teeth with my smile.

"Dang it, Samantha,"—he pounded a fist on the table — "you better start talking. You look awfully suspicious here."

"I told you my lawyer said to not say anything. When he gets here, we can talk."

DB put his hands in the air. "And when will that be?"

I glanced at my watch. "If he left right after I called him, then in an hour, I suppose."

DB sighed wearily and closed his eyes.

"It's not yet noon. We got time. I'm not going anywhere," I said. DB wanted to make me uncomfortable. If I showed him how nervous I was, he'd get a buzz from it and keep me here forever. Power over people was his crack.

"This isn't a game, Sam." His upper lip curled. "A man is dead."

"I know," I said, my voice low. "More than anyone." I'd been present when life left Principal Josh's body. I'd looked into his eyes as he fell over, and there was nothing. Not fear, not relief. No light. Nothing. Because he was already gone. And experiencing the passing of someone was unlike anything I'd gone through before. Fear, uncertainty, and guilt were emotions waiting to erupt. Jerking DB around was the only way I could keep that underlying current in check.

He narrowed his eyes. "What does that mean?"

Uncertain what to say next, I shrugged.

He pounded his fist into his hand. "Dang it, say something."

"Is it true you went to the Taylor Swift concert in Tacoma?"

"What?"

My question caught him off guard. "I heard you did, and you went by yourself?" I held up a hand. "I'm not judging. I like Taylor."

He reared back. "I wasn't alone."

The lack of further explanation made me think we'd entered a semantics game. Rachel and I used to do this as kids. The trick was perspective.

"Okay, let me rephrase the question. Not counting all the other people in attendance, did you go alone? Meaning...did anyone ride with you or meet you there?" By the shocked expression of his face, I was on to something. I smirked.

He leapt up, his sudden movement knocking his chair onto the floor with a loud *bang*. "We aren't talking about me!"

I kept my tone matter-of-fact with no intention to make this situation more difficult. "And I'm not talking until my lawyer gets here. If you want to have a chat, we can talk football, or the weather, or you can tell me how awesome the Taylor Swift concert was, but I'm not saying anything until my lawyer gets here."

A knock on the door stopped our conversation.

"Come in," DB boomed.

Oliver handed him a piece of paper. DB read whatever was on it then balled it up. He pointed a finger at me, the paper a wad in his fist. "You can just cool your jets in here by yourself until your lawyer gets here."

"This means we aren't going to talk Taylor music? Because I really like her. All that angsty break-up music." I stretched my legs out, resting them on the overturned chair. "Bummer."

DB shook his head at me, glaring. Then stalked out. Oliver gave me a look of part wonder and part fear.

I smiled.

The door slammed behind them.

I slouched in the chair, resisting the urge to text anyone in case DB was watching through the two-way mirror.

The door opened partway, and Leo leaned in.

I gave him a finger wave.

He looked tired. His dark, closely cut hair was mussed as if he'd run his hand through it a thousand times. A five o'clock shadow darkened his jawline, and it wasn't even noon yet. He narrowed his gray eyes, not in anger, but in pleasure. "Taylor Swift? Really?"

"Curious if it was true, and now I know. Do I have you to thank for the note and the peace and quiet?"

"Nope, your mother. The school board and your mother requested an immediate meeting. Word is getting out. Media has caught wind."

Slammed with the full magnitude of how this would rock our community, I said, "Did all the kids get picked up okay?"

He nodded. "You doing okay?"

"It was awful, Leo. The look in his eyes, or the lack of it..." I inadvertently shivered. "Awful."

He looked lost in his own memory when he said, "Yeah, that's a hard thing to see."

"I won't ever un-see it, will I?" The question was rhetorical as my mind's eye replayed the last minutes of Josh's life.

"Hey," Leo said softly. "Can I get you anything?"

I shook my head. "I'm glad you were first to get there."

"Me, too," he said and backed out of the room, closing the door quietly behind him.

7

TUESDAY

LOCKETT SHOWED UP AN HOUR LATER. I told him the whole story, and he had me repeat the key parts to DB, who then made us wait in the room an additional hour before letting us go. By the time we got to my place, it was dinnertime. I called home and touched base with my parents, then texted Precious. Though I wasn't hungry, Lockett convinced me to eat. While I took a shower, he ordered delivery.

When looking for a silver lining following the death of my fake husband Tyson Lockett would be it. I hadn't liked him at first, after all, he'd been tasked with delivering the bad news about Carson. But I'd call him friend now.

Precious arrived with my dad in tow. Worry drove his need to see in person that I was indeed okay.

I was on the couch, my feet tucked under me, my hair wet from the shower. Dad surveyed me. He tapped a packet of papers, folded lengthwise, against his palm.

"I'll report to your mother that you appear to be holding up okay." Dad's furrowed brow showcased his worry.

"I *am* okay." My voice was calm, strong. My best attempt at reassurance.

"No one is okay after witnessing someone die." He rubbed my arm to comfort me.

I smiled slightly. "Well, that part wasn't what I was referring to."

He kissed my forehead. "It's been a helluva news night," he mumbled.

I nodded to the papers. "What do you have there?"

Dad's reading glasses hung from the neckline of his plaid button-down shirt. He put them on while cracking open the sheets. He looked every bit the investigative reporter. His gray hair was a tad too long because he was too busy following a story. His blue eyes bright with excitement. Dad had something he wanted to share.

"I researched Josh Chapman." He cleared his throat and glanced at me over his glasses. "Toby did a little as well, visited the dark web I'm guessing. I said I'd pay him, but I don't know his rate."

Toby was another silver lining from the husband fiasco. Hired to do Carson's IT work, I'd inherited him when I took over Carson's PI business. Tall, pale, insanely thin, stoned half of the day, Toby Wagenknecht was Shaggy to my Velma. Obviously, Precious was Daphne.

I waved off the comment. "I'll take care of it. What did you two find out?"

"Josh was from Port Angeles, but he bounced around a

lot before he landed here six years ago. Taught in special education at the high school, kids with behavior issues. He piloted a program for troubled teens identified as high risk for dropping out. It was his experience with both general and special education students that made him a candidate for VGS. Your mom says he was a lock for the job, only Alice Andrews was a holdout. She wanted a different candidate."

The special ed part bothered me. It takes a special person with a teacher's heart to work with struggling kids. Josh didn't strike me as having the skills or desire. He was an all talk kinda guy. Kids in special education, myself included, needed teachers who walked the walk. "What kind of program was it he piloted?"

Dad glanced at his paper. "Teaching them computers and coding. Skills for the modern age."

"How did he become an administrator?" The leap from special education to the big office sounded too large.

Dad said, "He had the degree. And his programs showed good success rate. He'd held several education positions in Port Angeles, coming down through the Kitsap Peninsula, and then Chehalis. I asked your mom, and she said reducing the dropout rate has been a struggle for Wind River. This was the selling factor in hiring Josh."

Dad held up his index finger. "But get this. Toby found Kitsap School District flagged his human resource file, but he couldn't tell what for. I called up and spoke with the head of HR there. She was definitely squirrelly about Josh. Wouldn't say a thing."

My natural curiosity came from this man. Investigative reporter. Private Investigator. Not much difference in my opinion. He handed me the papers.

Looking through them, I said, "He was never married. No family."

"Go to the last page," Dad instructed.

I flipped to the end. I gave a low whistle and looked at Lockett. "Josh has serious money in his bank account."

"How serious?" Lockett asked, coming to stand next to Dad.

"Almost two million dollars." I held out the financials for Lockett to peruse.

Dad crossed his arms. "Lots of things can explain this. Maybe he inherited his parents' life insurance. Maybe it's part of a settlement."

I shrugged. "Sure. Or maybe there's more to it."

Precious collapsed on the couch next to me and kicked off her stupidly high heels. Her hair was knotted into a French twist. Her makeup was immaculate even though the day was nearly over. She wore a silk navy shirt with tiny flowers on it and a bright yellow skirt. Her coach's whistle hung from a navy lanyard around her neck.

"And we'll find out what that is." She pumped a fist.

Lockett warned, "Cautiously. We'll do everything cautiously to not give the police more to hold against Sam." He held my gaze. "I'd prefer you do nothing until we get the full picture of what Josh died from. He might have had a heart attack for all we know."

My dad sat on the coffee table in front of me. "I want you to walk me through everything."

I blew out a sigh. What was everything? Where did this story start? With Rachel at the open house? The moment I stepped into his office today, angry?

"Did you know a mom complained that Cora sexually harassed her daughter because she was swiping up and down on one of those sequin shirts?"

Dad reared back and looked at me as if I'd just told him his fantasy league would bomb. An inconceivable notion.

I nodded. "Yeah, Josh told me to meet with him Thursday to discuss it, but fat chance I was going to wait two days to sort this out."

"And?"

"And he died a few minutes after I stormed into his office to confront him." I grimaced. "It was awful, Dad. There wasn't anything I could do. At first, I thought he was choking, but he could talk. He was sweaty and pale and asking for water. Though his words were slurred. And there was nothing I could do. Or at least I hope there wasn't because my reaction..." I shook my head, trying to forget the image of his last expression.

We sat in silence.

Lockett broke the quiet. "Do you think his death was... ah... more than it seems?"

We locked eyes. "Do I think Josh was killed?" I shrugged one shoulder. "I dunno. I know I didn't kill him, and I also know his last few minutes weren't easy or peaceful."

A rap on my door made my pulse quicken.

I expected DB to show up at any moment and arrest me. Logically, I knew he wouldn't, but back in high school when we'd been partners in chemistry, he'd sucked at doing experiments. His solution was to make a conclusion, then write the findings and hypothesis to fit. Was I going to be treated like a conclusion? My gut said yes. Because that was the easiest path to a solution.

Everyone's attention bounced between me and the door.

"It's probably the food delivery guy," I said, more casually than I felt.

I whipped the door open and braced myself for whatever was on the other side.

Toby stood on the other side with bags of food in both hands. "Someone order delivery?"

"We did." Lockett came forward and took the bags from Toby. "It's good to see you, man. Can you come in and eat with us?"

Toby glanced at his watch. I glanced at the clock on the wall. We were getting close to his high time. The hours where he liked to get stoned and watch Scooby Doo or Northern Exposure reruns.

"Yeah, I got time. Besides, the PoPo is down there sitting in their car. I figure they're headed up and sticking around might prove interesting."

I glanced at my dad and Lockett then stepped out to the landing and leaned over the rail. Below, parked along the curb, a police cruiser idled. The cop inside appeared to be sitting in silence. His profile was one I knew well. I stuck my ring and index finger in my mouth and let a shrill whistle loose.

The dude in the car, Leo, dropped his head into his hands. Figuring he was struggling between doing the right thing and doing something stupid, I decided to make things easier for him. I was going to him. Because there was no telling if being here was right or stupid. I moved to the top step when he opened his door and climbed out. I waited.

He stood at the bottom of the stairs and looked up at me. "I shouldn't be here."

"Then go."

We continued to survey each other.

I broke first. "Or you could come in and have some food that Toby just delivered and tell us what's on your mind. Because why else would you be here if something wasn't eating at you?"

He blew out a heavy sigh then climbed the stairs. Once inside, I closed the door behind us.

"Leo, you know Tyson Lockett."

The men nodded at each other. If Leo found it odd that my lawyer was the best friend of my dead fake-husband, he kept his trap shut about it.

Precious set out the food and walked around handing out plates to everyone. "Dig in," she said. "We can all pretend today hasn't been a terrible-no-good day."

A bright yellow sack the size of a softball, made from felt and shaped like a curling bunch of bananas, hung from around Toby's neck.

I pointed to it. "What in the world is that?"

Everyone looked at Toby. He followed the trajectory of my finger and glanced down at his chest. He caressed the felt sack. "This is Lady Marmalade's travel carrier."

Leo's lips twitched as he cut his eyes to me.

I said. "And Lady Marmalade is...?"

Toby set down his plate and gently stuck his hand in the belly of the banana. He pulled out a brown ball of... well... I don't know what it was. I stepped closer.

"Is that a squirrel?" Dad asked.

Toby grinned. "A sugar glider. She's my emotional support animal. Remember when I got shot?" He gave me a pointed look as if I were the one who pulled the trigger when, in fact, I had been the one who offered him several outs to the situation prior to the event.

"You have got to be kidding me," Precious said. "The bullet grazed you."

Toby gasped and cuddled Lady Marmalade to him. "And that's supposed to be less traumatic? I suppose when you all were held up at Junkie's, you were only sorta robbed because they didn't take anything from you personally."

"He's got you there," I told Precious. "I think you might be jealous you didn't think of getting an emotional support animal."

She huffed and plopped on the couch. "Maybe."

"Can I hold her?" I asked Toby.

He shook his head. "We're still getting to know each other. Watch this." He set Lady M on my kitchen counter and gave her a small pellet of food he took from his pocket. Then he stepped away. We stood quietly as she worked over the tiny bit of food. We watched her. She watched us.

"Okay," Toby said. "Ready?"

Was he asking the sugar glider or us?

Then he gave a sharp, short whistle and held out his hands. Lady M leapt into them. He cooed, rubbed her against his face, and then slid her back into the pouch.

"Cool," Dad said. "I might want to do an article on you and Lady Marmalade."

Toby nodded and grinned. "Yeah, we can do that." He reached under his T-shirt and lifted out the lanyard with his vaping pen dangling from the end. He was seconds from putting it to his lips when Dad knocked it out of his hands.

The force of my dad's swat broke the vape pen from the lanyard. It fell to the floor, bounced, then skid its way under my couch.

"What the frack, Mr. T?" Toby cried.

Lady Marmalade hissed.

Toby immediately went to sooth Lady M while glaring at my dad.

Dad took a small notepad from his pocket. "Story breaking tonight. In fact, I have to head downstairs to get the story to press. Over twenty people have been hospitalized with this vaping lung disease. And the best guess is the juice has been tampered with. Three people have died."

Toby gestured to my couch, where his vape pen had

gone. "We all know this. I use non-nicotine flavored juice and I heard it was only the nicotine based ones. I have nothing to worry about."

Dad shook his pen at Toby. "Ah, but that's where you're wrong. They haven't ruled out the non-nicotine vials. The person hospitalized today apparently was using non-nicotine vape juice. No specific flavors have been identified. They're looking into non-nicotine based juice."

Toby paled. He lifted the hem of his shirt around Lady M and began wiping his tongue off with the end.

I glanced at Leo. Then Lockett. Then I lunged for my camera and whipped it out of the bag. My fingers fumbled to bring the screen to life.

In my head, I saw today's events play out. Josh by the garbage right before Danika came out. "Josh was vaping today."

Dad shook his head. "I don't think he was a smoker."

Leo said. "There were two vials of vape juice in his desk drawer."

I showed the image to the group.

Leo again, "But we didn't find a vape pen on his body."

I slowed the playback in my head. "He threw it away. Only he missed and kicked it behind the trash can outside the school." I squinted. "Wait, that might have been his coffee cup. Either way, it's the can on the right if you're facing the building."

Dad's phone pinged. He glanced at the screen. Then at us. "Another vaping lung death."

"How many in our area?" Precious asked.

Dad said, "The first three were on the east coast." He tapped his phone. "This latest one is in Portland."

Toby slumped against the counter and stroked Lady M's head, which was poking out of the banana. "Jeez, Mr. T, you probably saved my life."

I wagged my finger at him. "No vaping until the police get to the bottom of this. There's no emotional support animal good enough to make you feel better about being dead."

Toby nodded solemnly. "I can do that. But as soon as they rule out the flavor I'm—" He looked hopeful, desperate. Addicted.

"Nope," Leo said. "Only when they know for sure the cause and not before then." He pointed to me. "What if this killed Josh Chapman?"

Toby, already a pasty white, turned gray. "You guys are killing me."

"We're keeping you alive," Precious said.

Leo moved to stand in front of the door. "I have to go. Samantha, I want you to take that picture to the cops first thing."

Lockett said, "I'll take a copy tonight."

Leo nodded. He pinched the bridge of his nose before speaking. "There's something that needs to be said, but I need to know it'll be held in the strictest of confidence."

Toby, over his shock of not being able to vape, dumped a half carton of white rice on his plate. "Everyone thinks my brain's fried, anyway. I could spill state secrets, and everyone would think I'd made it up." He poured Moo Goo Gai Pan onto his rice.

Leo met my gaze and held it. "You said something to me that's not sitting right. Josh's eyes?" He arched a brow, indicating I should talk now.

"They were blank before he hit his head. I'm no expert, but he was dead before he fell over. Or I suppose he fell over because he was dead."

Leo nodded and appeared to be contemplating my words. "Maybe he was a victim of this vape juice tampering. Maybe not." He faced my dad. "Any of these people die quickly?"

Dad shook his head. "Within twenty-four hours, but they were hospitalized first. None as suddenly as Josh."

Leo faced me. "With your picture, we can make sure the vaping is fully investigated. But if that fails to produce anything... Listen. Right now, DB is going with the cause of death being a blow to the head. And if the medical examiner verifies, if it's not the vaping lung, then DB will look right at you." Leo nodded to Dad's papers. "You need to get in front of this. Dig into Josh's life."

"I didn't kill him," I said. Because I couldn't say it enough. "Maybe he died from natural causes?"

Leo arched a brow. "Not with your luck. Let's hope Josh was a victim of this vaping lung disease."

There were no truer words.

Lockett said, "Leo's right. If Louney has enough circumstantial evidence and the district attorney likes it, they can charge you with manslaughter in the second degree. That's a class B felony."

Leo said, "Up to ten years in prison with a fat fine, too. Twenty K."

Precious whistled. Lady M popped out her head.

I thought of that bird that had died at both Rachel and my feet. Bad omen came to fruition today. "I would not do well in prison," I said.

"Fo shizzle," Toby said.

8

NOTHING BOOSTS one's self-esteem like needing a job and having to take a position with their successful and savvy, entrepreneurial best friend. Said no one ever.

Oh, that and being suspected of murder.

I'd tossed and turned all night with one nagging thought. If the medical examiner determined Josh's death to be a homicide, then DB's shortsightedness would put me right in the crosshairs of his scope. I was sure in the history of time there'd been flimsier motives than defending one's niece against accusations of sexual harassment. Particularly when said niece was only a few years out of diapers.

Man, I hoped Leo found that vape pen, and they discovered Josh was the victim of whoever was spiking liquid nicotine vials.

Or, better yet, maybe he had a family history of heart

disease, and he was the victim of bad genetics and too many carbs and saturated fats.

Either way, I was knee-deep in this and sinking fast.

I needed a plan. A safety net. I needed to CMB. Cover my butt. In school, there should have been teachers to guide me, but a fair amount let me down. I couldn't trust the judicial system to be any different.

Only, I wasn't sure where to start. And Russell True, my brilliant father, once told me if a person sat on a problem long enough, a solution would present itself. Doing so created distance, and maybe then I'd see everything through a different lens. Though "long enough" seemed like an ambivalently unsafe amount of time. Easily confused with being passive. So, I gave myself forty-eight hours to get my act together, and if I didn't have a plan by then, willy-nilly it would be.

In the meantime, I needed money and Precious needed help.

Dressed in navy capri leggings, a navy cotton skirt, a white T-shirt and Klogs, I drove to Camas to be a personal assistant to one of Precious's clients.

A quaint town on the Columbia River, Camas was beautiful, charming, and home to a paper mill and, some days, a ripe smell. My phone GPS was winding me up the mountain away from the river.

Precious's call interrupted the nasally GPS voice.

"What?" I said into my phone's speaker. "I'm trying to find the place now."

"Okay. There's something I should have told you before you took the job," she said.

I pulled to the side of the road and turned on my hazards. "How bad is it? Because I don't think I can take anymore."

She cleared her throat. "It's not bad."

I scoffed. If it wasn't bad, then why didn't she tell me this at her office this morning? Riddle me that.

"It's not even a thing, really," she hemmed.

"Precious, just say it. Because I'm sitting on the side of the road, and I'm going to be late." A true crime in her opinion.

"Okay, so AJ is great."

"You already said this. He's also sexy and off-limits because it's against company policy to date clients. But you're good with me going because you figure Carson jacked me up for a good long while. We've gone through this today, too. What aren't you saying?"

She blew out a frustrated breath. "I think he's hiding something. I think he might fire me, and I need you to feel him out to see if that's true."

I shook my head in confusion. "What are you talking about?"

"There's another company out of Seattle that's been trying to poach my clients. They've copied my ads, they've cold-called some of my clients, and they even have a representative who resembles me. I think they're going to take AJ away from me. Think about it. He's the client that can keep on giving. He can tell his teammates about me. If he gets traded to another team, he can tell those teammates about me. Endless customers."

Currently, AJ was the backup quarterback for the Portland Pioneers NFL team. "If he gets traded to a team in Florida, those teammates will have no use for you," I said.

"What if I want to expand?"

Precious takes over the world, one unorganized and mentally frazzled person at a time. I could see it happening.

"What you want me to do is to be a double agent. You want me to be AJ's personal assistant, but also find out if he's considering jumping ship for this other company. What's their name?"

"Sky's The Limit." She blew out a snort. "Dumb name, right?"

"Visualize the results you want," I said. "Then make a plan on how to get there." She'd said this to me a thousand times.

"Oh, shut up. I've spent so much time with AJ, but this company could easily pick up his trigger point and promise him the moon."

"Trigger point? What would that be?"

A long pause. "I can't tell you that. Client confidentiality."

"Let me get this straight. I'm to do this guy's laundry, grocery shopping, and walk his dog. I'm also supposed to snoop around to find out if Sky's The Limit is trying to get him to reach for the stars?"

"Yes, sounds perfect."

"For you, it does. How would I know if they're trying to poach him? You want me to eavesdrop? Are you that kind of company?"

Precious grunted her frustration as she processed my question.

I continued, "Do you really want him to stay if he wants to go?"

She snapped back a reply, "If AJ wants to go because he's not getting what he needs from me, then that's fine. I've achieved my goal. But if AJ left because someone else has sold him a line of BS using prosperity-thinking techniques, then I'm *not* okay with that."

Prosperity thinking was Precious's soapbox. Just because a person imagined wealth and success didn't mean it would happen. Her rant went on about adding the hard work and common sense component to it. She'd based her company on the premise. How to map out the steps needed for success. And reminding her she used to be all-in on prosperity thinking would be pointless.

"So, AJ wants to be rich and famous," I said. He was, after all, in the NFL. He probably had certain expectations.

"No, AJ wants to see his dreams come true, and he's getting impatient waiting for that to happen," she huffed.

Fair enough.

I promised Precious I'd do what I could.

AJ's house was in a gated community that overlooked the Columbia River. He didn't appear to be hurting for money. I used the access code Precious gave me and arrived at his door with one minute to spare.

AJ Gunn was of mixed raced and hotter than a romance novel cover model. He was beautiful. So pretty, looking away was hard. He wore his dark hair shaved so close to his head; it looked like his head had a five o'clock shadow. Lashes unfairly bestowed on a dude framed his green eyes. His physique was that of a Greek god's and with the trend of talented able-to-scramble-and-make-big-plays quarterbacks, AJ was old school and liked the comfort of the pocket. When forced out of the pocket, AJ spent too long looking for an open receiver. And boom. Sacked like a bag of potatoes. My dad said he'd never pick him for his fantasy league should he get more field time. But these were things I wouldn't tell AJ.

"I'm Samantha True." I stuck out my hand and pretended his green eyes weren't making me want to giggle like a teenage girl meeting her celebrity crush.

"AJ Gunn. Erika speaks highly of you." He stepped back and gestured for me to enter.

"She kinda has to. We've been friends forever."

The smile on his face wavered.

I rushed on, "Oh, that doesn't mean I'm going to share your secrets and sell scraps of your hair or anything. I'm trustworthy." I grimaced. "Of course, telling you that probably makes me appear even more sketchy. Let's start over. Why don't you introduce me to your dog?"

His smile broadened. "Good idea. Follow me. He's outside enjoying the sun. He loves it there."

He led me through a one-story house with lots of glass on the backside and wood on the front. From my guess, the bedrooms were to the left, the kitchen and garage to the right, and the central space was the living and dining. The house wasn't insanely large but spacious. The minimalistic style decor done in shades of white, black, and gray made it appear larger. Playing on the enormous flat-screen TV mounted over an equally large fireplace was last week's Pioneer game. AJ had come in at the last quarter because Keith McVay, MVP quarterback of the year every year, had taken a hard sack, landing on his head.

AJ pointed through the window where an Airedale lay stretched out in the sun. "That's Simon."

"He's gorgeous," I said. "How old is he?"

"Three. Lots of energy. The neighborhood has a dog park, and if you could get him down there when you come, that would be great."

I was scheduled to help AJ twice a week.

"I'd love to." This gig Precious hired me for was the bomb.

AJ opened a glass slider and whistled. Simon leapt to his feet and dashed for AJ. When he bounded through the door, he passed by AJ and lunged for me, tail wagging fiercely.

"Hey," I said, bending down. "Hey, Simon." No hold-out-your-hand for this guy. He was one of those dogs that never knew a stranger. "Fierce guard dog you got here."

"Yeah, he's worthless. He'd sell me in a second for a dog treat," AJ chuckled.

Simon's feet were up on my thighs as I gave him a good rub to the sides. "We're going to be the best of friends," I said. "You know why? Because I can tell you're a good listener." When I scratched his ears, his tongue lolled out of his mouth.

"He's crap for giving his opinion, though," AJ said. "In case you need feedback."

I shrugged. "That's what Precious is for. Perks of being the BFF to a life coach."

"Precious?" A smile teased at his lips. "Are Erika and Precious the same person?"

I glanced at his face and grimaced. "Um... you can't tell her you know."

He broke out into a full smile. "Oh, I'm gonna tell her. Sorry. I now see her in a completely different way."

I groaned.

A door slammed near the kitchen, and a tall teen came into the room. He was clearly a relative as the resemblance was remarkable.

The teen said, "Hey bro, whose POS is that in the driveway?" He wore his jeans low on his waist and a long Tupac T-shirt. Earbuds dangled from his ears.

I raised my hand, ready to claim the so-called piece of shit. "That's my POS, and I'll thank you to keep your voice down. If LC, the POS in question, hears, he'll become temperamental."

"LC?" AJ asked.

"Lewis and Clark. That POS and I have been on many adventures."

The teen shuffled. "It's a cool ride," he mumbled. "Old school. Sorry for calling it junk."

"Apology accepted." I wasn't going to split hairs that he called LC more than junk. While some people defended their dogs or children, I defended my ride.

"Samantha, this is my kid brother, Troy. Tee-Roy, this is Samantha. She works for Erika. She'll be here twice a week, but she's not your errand girl."

"She's your errand girl," Troy snickered.

"Yeah, when you finish high school, go to college, graduate, and get a job, you can hire someone to do the things you dislike doing, too." AJ planted his hands on his hips.

This sounded like a common refrain.

"Jeez, this again? Are you ever going to get off my back?" Troy rolled his eyes and skirted around the large kitchen island away from AJ. "I'll be in my room if you need me." He did a fast shuffle toward the other side of the house. But not fast enough, apparently, because AJ did a quick juking sidestep and came up beside him. AJ inhaled loudly.

"Aw, man. Stop sniffing me. I'm not stoned. I wish I was, though, and who cares if I was? It's legal." Troy batted his brother away.

"It's legal for people over twenty-one. That's not you. You want to live here? You live by my rules," AJ said.

Troy's upper lip curled. "You sound like Mom."

"She had a point," AJ said.

Troy pushed his brother away and bolted for what I assumed was his room.

AJ turned to me and shrugged. "Kids."

"I hear ya. I got a six-year-old niece accused of sexually harassing a kid in her class." I made light of it, but it wasn't a joke. Because I'd followed that thread of a story, it led me to Principal Josh's office and his death.

"What?" AJ said. "That's not a thing."

"One would think it's not a thing," I said. "One would be wrong."

AJ shook his head in disbelief. "Count your blessings. As they get bigger, the problems get harder. My mom's sick and in Arizona undergoing treatment. I've been picking up the slack. Every week it's something new with him. He was arrested a month ago and was given one chance." AJ held up one finger. "One chance to get his act together, or else he goes to juvie. You think that would motivate him."

I didn't have any advice. "Some people like to learn things the hard way."

AJ glanced over his shoulder toward the bedrooms. "Something squirrelly is going on. I've got charges on my credit card that don't make sense, and Troy is locked down tight. I'd be more successful getting info from an opposing team's play caller than my brother. I tell you this because when the team is on the road, you'll be here alone with him. I know it's not part of what Erika asked you to do, but if you could keep an eye on things... Maybe even solve the mystery of my brother." He laughed as if he were joking. "I could use a miracle. I got enough of my own issues." He glanced at the TV where the game was playing.

I cleared my throat. "I can help you with the first one. My other job is a PI. I can look into some things for you." One day I wanted not to feel like an imposter when I told people I was PI.

His brows shot up. "Seriously?"

"No joke." No need to point out that if I were a sought-after PI, I wouldn't be working for Precious.

"You're on," he said in awe. "You're a Jill of all trades."

I laughed at his positive spin. "Sure. That sounds good.

Once I have everything here squared away, I'll help you with your other problem, too." I pointed to the TV.

AJ tossed back his head and laugh.

"Okay," I said and clapped my hands together to bring us back to the job at hand. "How about you show me what's what, and let's get started."

AJ's grin was wide, his green eyes twinkling. "Best thing I ever did was hire Erika Shurmann."

9

WEDNESDAY

WORKING for AJ would be a snap. Finding out what his brother was up to was going to be harder. AJ gave me the rundown of the situation. Troy had been arrested for shoplifting. Twice. The second time, the judge wasn't as forgiving just because Troy was the kid brother of an NFL second-string quarterback. He gave Troy one last chance. He mandated Troy do both community service time and a teen-scared-straight program at the Vancouver Community Center. Mess up again and Troy went straight to juvie, didn't pass go, and didn't collect two hundred dollars.

AJ said a court order restricted Troy to the house unless he was out doing one of two tasks, cleaning up the side of the road per his community service or attending the program. The program confused A.J. Frequent charges on his credit card from the program were popping up, but there was nothing to show for it. And Troy had no answers. Or did but wasn't sharing them.

Where to start? That seemed to be the million-dollar question. Where did I start with Troy and my own situation? What I needed was a mentor, one who wasn't my dad. And the YouTube videos only went so far, and there was no way I was going to ask Leo.

That's when inspiration struck.

Mrs. Wright! She had an entire closet dedicated to nosing into other people's business. I'd discovered this when I did a job for her. She'd been in a battle with the lady down the street over a promiscuous cat.

On the drive to Mrs. Wright's, I called Toby and asked him to do some digging into the charges and the school. And while he was at it, dig more into Josh. A plan was taking shape. At least in my mind.

Mrs. Wright was sporting dyed magenta hair and a Def Leppard shirt with *Love Bites* in large letters across the top.

"Hun, what brings you here?" she asked in a thick Jersey accent.

Behind her, the TV boomed at a volume that made the windows rattle. I winced. "I need some help. I was wondering if maybe you could give me some guidance."

She held up her hands and yelled, "I don't do fake IDs. I can get you connected to a guy on the east coast, but after that I wipe my hands of it. I don't wanna know anything about your plans to go on the lam."

I tilted my head in confusion. Maybe with the TV noise, I was getting mixed information? "What are you talking about?"

"That you offed that hunky principal."

To Mrs. Wright's credit, she wasn't fazed after calling me a murderer. And she offered to help me get a fake ID. Good to know.

"Who said I killed him? And would I be standing here if I had?"

"Bail, sweetheart. And you're gonna beat feet before that buffed-out buffoon of a police chief locks you up and throws away the key. You were all the girls could talk about at the community center's Bunco game last night."

"Had I known, I would've shown up. Maybe answered some questions." I was joking, of course. "Any chance Mrs. Rivers goes to Bunco?"

Mrs. Wright aimed her index finger gun at me and pulled the trigger. "Bingo."

I huffed in frustration. "That lady. Not a lick of sense. I haven't been arrested, and Josh might be the victim of that vaping lung disease that's going around." I pointed both thumbs to my chest. "Guess who's not the killer. This girl."

She looked puzzled. "So why you here?"

"About my PI business."

"Ah," she said, then held up one finger. She turned and yelled, "Earl, turn down the TV. Samantha is here, and she can't even hear herself think. Put your hearing aids in, for the love of Mike."

"Quiet, devil woman," Earl yelled back, and the volume went up.

She shook her head in annoyance and signaled me to follow her. She led me through the house to the back room. She closed the door, shutting out the sound. I sucked in a deep breath, enjoying the silence.

"Ah," she said. "I don't know how much longer I can take it."

"I would have cracked by now," I admitted. "It's amazing how quiet it gets in here."

"Soundproofed the room. I also have quiet when I go to Mrs. Long's. I go a lot." She smiled. "The kittens are getting so big." She whipped out a phone and showed me pictures.

She caressed the screen once before shoving the phone into her back pocket. "Tell me about the dead principal."

Retelling the story was getting easier.

"Vaping lung? Hmm. Who'd have thought? I've heard lots about the virtues of the educator. No vices, and certainly not vaping."

"Saw it with my own eyes." I made like I was crossing my heart.

She nodded in acceptance. "You mentioned guidance? What exactly do you want from me?"

That was Mrs. Wright. Straight talk all the time.

"I need to find out what a teen is up to. If he's up to something at all. I have his schedule, I'm looking into his online behavior, but other than following him, how do I get into his business?" What worked for tracking Troy might work for getting to know Josh, too, theoretically. Posthumously.

She looked at me like I'd just asked the dumbest question in the world. Which I might have. "You follow him. You track his comings and goings. You see who he hangs out with and go talk to them when your guy isn't around."

Mrs. Wright wasn't a cop. Earl had been. He also ran a gun range, hence the hearing issues, and had been a PI at the end of his career. As a cop's wife, Mrs. Wright had picked up all the tricks of the trade.

I rolled my eyes. "I know *that*. But I can't be on him twenty-four seven. I like to sleep."

Mrs. Wright responded with an eye roll of her own. Hers was far more dramatic. "Such a delicate flower you are. A real snowflake."

I pointed to her closet that stored gadgets and spy goodness galore. "Oh, come on. You can't tell me there's not something in there that can help me."

She pointed her index finger at me and cackled. "Now, that's a different question and one you didn't ask."

Annoyance flashed over me.

She continued. "See what I did there? The first lesson about being a cop or a PI is knowing which questions to ask. You already knew you needed to follow him. You already knew you couldn't do it twenty-four seven. Your real question should have been what device can I use to help me track his movements." She slid open the closet door and paused before the shelves, her hand starting at the top then slowly worked down as she scanned the shelves.

"Here." She took a box from the second to last shelf. "This is a tracker. You can put it on his car, then track each of his stops from your computer. It only stores information for forty-eight hours."

I took the small box and smiled. "I knew you'd know."

"When you talk to people he comes in contact with,

think about what you want to know before you start the conversation. What's your end game. And remember, people can tell you what they don't like more than what they like, and what they did yesterday but not the day before unless something significant happened. You get what I'm saying?"

I nodded.

"Use these tricks to get what you need." She held out her hand. "That'll be twenty-five bucks for the tracker."

"Advice for free?" I asked as I dug money out of my pocket.

"This time," she said with a smile.

I left Mrs. Wright's and went to Ralph's Grocery store where I worked part-time. I needed to check the work schedule. And tell my boss Lason about my situation with the cops. I'd rather he heard it from me.

The conversation was awkward, and it didn't escape my notice that Lason took a step back when I gave him the story. As I feared, he kept me off the schedule for the following week, as a precautionary measure, with promises to put me back on as soon as I was no longer in the spotlight.

Back in my car, I got a text from Toby to call him when I was free, so I did.

"Dudette, guess what I found?" he said and followed it with a long inhale.

I gasped in horror. "Are you vaping?"

Toby scoffed. "I'm not a nitwit. I'm sucking on an old empty vial, pretending, if you must know. Now, you want to be my mom some more, or can I tell you what I found? Because it's goooood."

I chuckled. "I can only imagine."

He sighed. Lady Marmalade cooed in the background. "Troy attends the Recode and Reshape program, a rich kid version of the scared straight program. It's a joke. Nothing about the program scares me. I mean, they teach them to learn to code. If that's so scary, then I'm Captain America of coding because I'm wicked good and go to dark places on the web."

I laughed. "Yes, you are the superhero of the cyberworld."

"Anyway, Recode and Reshape is a private company that has a contract with the community center in Vancouver to run the program, and guess who's the instructor?" Toby snort-laughed. "I mean, *was* the instructor." His voice sobered instantly. "Sorry, Sam. I didn't mean to laugh at your dead guy."

I groaned. "He's not my dead guy, and Josh was the instructor? How come that didn't come up in Dad's research?"

In my mind's eye, I could see Toby shrug. Then he slowly inhaled. A pretend vape.

Some habits die hard.

He said, "Because he asked me to look into his background. We were focused on where Josh came from."

I pulled out of Ralph's parking lot and pointed LC toward Mrs. Wright's again. "Who owns the private company that employed Josh?"

"I'm still digging into that. It's an educational company

called Pay Forward for the Kids. It's got a lot of redirects. When I know, you'll know."

Redirects were used to cloak what the web owner didn't want people to see.

"Okay, Toby. Thanks. Anything you find, send to my dad. If I have more questions, I'll give you a ring."

"You know the drill. Not between the hours of—"

"Yes, I know when you get high." I laughed and hung up.

The drive back to Mrs. Wright's was quick, and she met me at the door.

She arched a brow. "What did you forget?"

I showed her a handful of twenties and said in a low voice, "A way to pick a lock?"

She shook her head in pity. "Oh, hon, you're gonna need more than a tool. Come in, let me show you what I know."

10

THURSDAY

PRECIOUS AND I HAD A PLAN. And it comprised of breaking and entering.

Leo had called when I was leaving Mrs. Wright's. The medical examiner was still working on Josh's autopsy, but there were no signs of an inhalation injury, seen in the lungs when they reacted to inhaling a caustic substance. Dad had said an inhalation injury tied the other vaping patients together.

This didn't completely rule out Josh being a victim of the current vaping crisis, but it reduced the odds greatly. And increased the odds that DB would look at me. Leo said they found the vaping pen and vial, and the lab was testing it. But it would be awhile before we knew more.

Hence the B and E plan. I needed more info on Josh. More than Toby could find. And I was starting with his work office.

Because the Village Garden School is housed in what

used to be the old community center, Precious and I knew a few things about how to get into the old building without using the front door.

We'd both spent time there in our teen years, and when your parents were upstanding members of society, finding ways to experiment and not be seen became a quest. With Precious the lookout, Hue and I had explored the off-limit areas every chance we got. Maybe that's why Leo hadn't liked me so much in high school. He thought I was a bad influence on Hue his kid brother. Which wasn't true at all. All three of us were equally bad influences.

Those old skills were going to get me into Principal Josh's office. Because I was part chicken, I didn't want to commit breaking and entering alone and convinced Precious to go with me. We waited until all threads of daylight disappeared, which in the Pacific Northwest during mid-fall comes a little after seven p.m. By winter, it would be pitch black around five.

Toby had given me a device to plug into Josh's computer that would link it to Toby's, and then my tech genius friend would scan it. Mrs. Wright gave me a lock-picking kit and a quick education on the various locks and how to break in. This was for Josh's office door, but a skill I could see coming in handy later on.

On the roof of Village Garden School was a trapdoor that lead into the attic. Back in my teen days, the lock had been broken, and I hoped that was the case today. Banking on the school districts desire to cut costs when the school was undergoing renovations.

Dressed in all black, Precious tucked her blond hair

into a black cap and ran black streaks down her face. I
wore a dark hoodie and before we set out on foot, pulled
up the hood. We tried to stick to the shadows of downtown, an incredibly hard task thanks to my mom who'd
carried out her restoration plan and had new streetlights
installed. Stupid lights lit up the town as if the sun were
shining twenty-four seven, or so it seemed when one was
trying to stick to the shadows.

With my back to the Village Garden School, I stared at
the steel ladder fixed to the side of the bank, an escape
route dictated by fire code. The ladder started six feet
from the ground, and ran up the side of the building to
the second floor. A quick hop from the ground and some
upper body strength—thank you, yoga—had me climbing
the rungs, Precious behind me. At the top, we pulled
ourselves up over the ledge and onto the roof.

Across a two-foot opening was VGS's roof. A leap of
faith separated me from my fact-finding mission. Precious
and I had done this several times as teenagers. As I looked
over the ledge and down the two stories to the concrete
below, the leap looked far scarier than it had as a teen.

"I can't do this," Precious said, looking at the ground.

"Visualize yourself making it across," I said.

"I only see myself falling," she grumbled. "And there's
no realistic strategy I can envision that will save me."

I cuffed her along the shoulder. "That's not being positive. But if you fall try to land on your legs and bend your
knees on impact. Better break those than your head."

"You're not funny."

"I wasn't being funny. I don't have a choice here. My

freedom is on the line. And you know how DB is. Once he starts down a path, he'll see it through until I'm sitting in the electric chair." Even in the dark I could see Precious roll her eyes.

"Washington doesn't have an electric chair or the death penalty."

"That's not the point," I said. I backed up to give myself enough of a running start.

"I'll meet you at the front doors," she said.

I wiped my sweaty hands down my jegging-clad thighs. "I don't think I can open the front doors without setting off the alarm."

"Then I'll meet you at Josh's window." She pointed to the ledge. "But I can't do that." She put her hands on her breasts. "These bad boys will get in the way."

She had a point.

"Okay, the window it is." I strapped on the mini backpack that held the tools we anticipated needing; Mrs. Wright's lock picking tool and a computer thingamajig from Toby.

"Hold on to your titties, kitty," Precious mumbled.

Without the crack of a start gun, I sprinted toward the ledge. When I reached the end, I pushed off like an Olympic hurdle jumper, my arms and legs wind-milling as I flew over nothingness. I landed on the other side with an "oomph," falling forward onto my hands.

"You okay?" Precious whispered loudly.

"Yep." When concocting this plan I'll admit I'd gotten a little excited. Who gets to do stuff like jump off or break into buildings for their job? Actors and criminals, that's who. And Samantha True. But the reality was a whole lot suckier than what I'd envisioned. My palms burned from scuffing the rooftop.

From the backpack, I took out my headlamp and put on the red light. The hatch into the attic of the Village Garden School was in the far corner of the building. If memory served, inside was a door to a stairway that would deliver me to the second floor.

I was right about the hatch lock, still the same old broken one from my teen years.

Scary how freakishly easy this had been. I opened the hatch and aimed my headlamp light, which I flipped to white, into the attic space. But this part wouldn't be easy. The attic was creepy as all get out. Creepier than that. To get in I had to descend four steps. Not a lot in daylight, but huge in this moment. The stairs, old wood, looked rickety and were covered in dirt and dust.

I swallowed, forcing back dread and ignoring my fears. I wished Precious was with me. I reminded myself that prison time for a crime I didn't commit was why I was staring into this black hole filled with cobwebs, and more than likely enormous vampire spiders were their occupants.

On a whimper, I stepped onto the middle stair. It bowed with a groan. Using my photographer's memory, I pictured the space way back when trying to locate the door that would take me out of the attic.

Boxes and furniture in various states of disrepair were clustered together in pockets of the attic. The fear part of my brain whispered that anything or anyone could be hiding behind them. Logic called me a moron. Regardless, this was a prime setting for a scary movie.

I recalled the location of the door. I had to pass bookshelves, towers of boxes, and a collection of desks, some lopsided from missing legs.

Fearing my headlamp light wasn't enough, I added a heavier flashlight from my pack because I could use it as a bug killer and cranium smasher. My light cast shadows on the attic junk that were weird in shape and made the scene scarier, if that were possible. Fear made goosebumps scurry across my skin.

With the roof hatch still open, I debated leaving it that way since the moon brought in some light. But there was no way I would exit from here. I was going out the window Precious was coming in. Or if spooked enough, I wasn't above going out the front door. I didn't care about the alarm, so long as I got what I came for.

On the count of three, I would close the hatch and dash for the exit.

One, two... I couldn't do this. I stared back up at the hatch and out at the dark sky.

One, two... I blew out a breath. I would suck in prison. If I couldn't even make it across a dark room, how would I survive in an environment scarier and tougher?

One, two... I stomped my foot in frustration, and something scurried across the floor away from me.

I choked back a scream.

Suck it up, buttercup.

One, two, three! I let the hatch slam closed and jumped off the stairs, then made the mad dash across the attic, sweeping my beam across the floor as I went. My heartbeat pounded madly in my chest and echoed in my ears.

Every time I passed a large group of items I hunched over, envisioning those items coming down on me, or worse, someone popping out from behind them.

I made it across the room in seconds, and with momentum and fear driving me forward, I didn't pause to try the door, just rammed it with my shoulder. It flew open on impact and sent me into the stairwell. I tripped over the threshold, launched into the air toward the stairs, and descended them ass over teakettle, knocking myself in the head with my cranium smasher flashlight.

Thump thump bump bump.

Thankfully, there were only five stairs before the landing where I came to a stop. My body screamed in protest, a late reaction to the impact. A long deep groan was pulled from me as I tried to sit. I'd made a huge cacophony of noise, so if anybody were in the building, I'd soon be discovered.

Needing another moment to recoup, I flopped back and stared at the ceiling and waited for the cops to show up. After what felt like an eternity, nobody came, so I used the stair rails to pull myself up.

I forced myself back to the attic door and eased it closed. A sign taped to the door read *Attic, Employees Only*. A second, hand-drawn sign was attached that read *Monsters Await*.

My headlamp had come off in the tumble and was resting on the second step down from the door. I picked it up on my way and slowly took the steps down. My flashlight waited at the bottom of the stairs, the beam extinguished. I snatched it up.

Using the headlamp's red light, I scanned the second floor. Even with the walls decorated with cute, joyful pictures of children, I was freaked out. I hurried along to the stairs and stuck to the side away from the windows as I made my way down to the first floor, taking care not to shine my headlamp out.

Time to see if I was an apt student.

In school, I'd been *meh* about some subjects, but this one had interested me, so fingers crossed. I knelt before Josh's office door and read the lock name. Awesome. I had a tool for that.

To make sure I was working smarter and not harder, I tried the handle. The door was locked.

Using the two tools Mrs. Wright had sold me, I did as she instructed and popped the lock in seconds.

That song, "Breaking The Law" popped into my head.

I turned the knob, gave the door a shove, and let momentum carry it open.

Creep factor to the max. A man had died here. Was his soul still here? What did they say about a soul at unrest? Was that Josh? Would he haunt us while here? I trembled with unease, my legs wobbly. I flashed the light around the office, then stopped where Josh had fallen.

A tapping sound came from inside the room. I rocked back on my haunches and weighed the merit of getting busted versus seeing a ghost. Neither were high on my must-do list.

"Sam," a voice whispered.

I whimpered and ran the light through the room again.

A face clouded in black with dark streaks under its dark eyes was pressed against the window, looking in. Its presence was so off-putting and startling, I screamed. The face screamed, too.

Oddly, the scream was something I was familiar with. Precious and not Josh's ghost.

I ran to the window and slid it open. "Jeepers, you scared me."

"I scared you? I thought you'd seen a ghost," she whispered.

"I thought you were the ghost," I said. "I'm so freaked out right now I want to leave."

Precious looked like she wanted to as well. She chewed her pinky nail. "Where did he die?"

I turned and pointed my light to the spot where Josh had fallen.

"I've got the willies," she said.

"Try being in here," I mumbled.

"Get the computer information and let's go," she said.

I took the computer scanner from the pack, then popped the screen from the window. I handed her the backpack. "I'm coming out this way. There's no way in all that's good and holy I'm going back through that attic."

"Good plan."

I flashed light over Josh's desk then gasped. "His computer's gone."

Precious groaned. I turned in time to see her slap her forehead. "I bet the cops took it."

All this for nothing.

"Okay, I'm coming out," I said.

In front of the window was a credenza. On it was one picture. I hadn't seen it on my initial visit. But this was of Josh at the opening of the school cutting the ribbon with Mrs. Rivers and the school board by his side.

"Mrs. Rivers," I said, just as I was about to put a foot on the credenza.

"What?"

"She had access to his calendar." I made eye contact with Precious. "It's better than nothing, right?" I needed encouragement to turn around when what I really wanted was to go out the window.

"We came for something. You don't want to do this for nothing."

"Poop," I said. I did the count-to-three thing again and ran across Josh's office, leaping over where his body had fallen, and into the main outer office.

Dropping into Mrs. Rivers's chair, I booted up her computer and plugged the device into the USB port. Like Toby had instructed, I clicked on all the right icons and let the device do its magic. Various windows popped up, allowing glimpses into Josh's calendar, a few photos, and Mrs. River's email program. The windows flashed across the screen in quick snapshots, occasional words or images flashing by.

A stock photo of two people standing on an island beach, water lapping at their toes caught my attention.

Someone had added graphics and text to the photo.
They'd drawn a dark heart around the couple, an arrow
pointing to them, and what looked like a handwriting
font that read, *me, you and Fiji*. But as fast as it had
flashed on the screen, another email or calendar page
replaced it.

Twelves minutes later, I was in the grass next to
Precious. One minute after that I was popping the screen
back on the window.

Precious and I parted ways at her car, her claiming a
need for a shot of something strong to calm her nerves
and a hot bath.

Though I felt the same need, especially the need to go
inside and turn on all the lights and check under my bed,
the unsettled feeling of having failed on my objective was
stronger.

What if Mrs. River's computer yielded nothing? What
if that image had been a spam email? I'd texted Toby to
keep his eyes open for the picture to see if it meant
anything.

Then I leaned against LC and questioned my feelings
of dissatisfaction while attempting to listen to my gut.

In response, I got the answer.

Josh's house. That's where I needed to go.

I parked LC two blocks from Josh's house and jogged
up a back street and then over, cutting through a neigh-
bor's yard.

Josh lived in an older neighborhood where the houses
were more spaced out and many of the homes smaller,
pre-war built. I approached from the back, there were no

lights on, but when I got within fifteen feet, I made out Leo sitting on the back stoop.

I stopped short by a tree and waited to see if he noticed me.

"You can come out," he said.

I stepped from the shadows. "What are you doing here?"

"Don't you think one breaking and entering a night is sufficient?"

"I have no idea what you're talking about." I stuck a hand on my hip.

"You have a cobweb with the spider still attached on your shoulder."

I screamed, whipped off the hoodie, and tossed it to the ground.

Guilty as charged. I gave him an apologetic smile.

He held up a hand. "I assumed you'd hit both places and I figured I'd let you in here. I'm collecting stuff from Josh's house for evidence. You might have enough time to scope out the place before I have to go in." He leaned back, pushing a hand against Josh's back door. It swung open.

I rushed to the door but stopped at Leo's feet. "How did you know I went to the school?"

Leo smiled. "Sweetness, know this. When it comes to being a cop, I'm like Jeopardy. And you? You're like Wheel of Fortune." He pointed to his chest. "Jeopardy." Then pointed to me. "Wheel of Fortune."

I gasped. "Wheel of Fortune can be hard. You have to have some sense to solve those puzzles."

One brow shot up. "Do you?" He glanced at his watch. "I have to be back at the station in an hour."

"Eep." I dashed into the house.

A laptop was sitting on the kitchen table, and I plugged my device into it. While it did its work, I walked through and took panoramic pics of his place. I was sure there was something here I was missing because of my hurried state.

On a whim, I opened a hall closet. A variety of coats for all weather hung there, but the size was off, like the closet was too shallow to be a real closet.

Having married, not legally mind you, a man who kept a secret room over his place of employment, my mind instantly went to that idea. I pushed the coats aside and searched the panel for any irregularity. A small indention was at the top left corner of the wall. It was big enough to put fingers in, which I did, and I slid the panel into the wall, like a pocket door, revealing the true depth of the closet and a butt ton of Chromebooks. All of them with asset labels from the school. Oddly, a roll of new asset tags sat on top of the laptops. I zoomed in and took pics of the label roll.

"Hey, Alex Tribec," I yell over my shoulder. "What do you make of this, Mr. Smart Guy?"

11

FRIDAY

DB WAS COMING out of the newspaper as I was heading in. The way he walked, his arms puffed out at the side, forced me to back up. He didn't even bother with a pleasantry or courtesy. I stuck my tongue out at his back as he walked past me.

"Oh, Sam," he said, as if I were an afterthought. He turned and stepped toward me. "I just came from seeing your father."

"I figured since you're coming from the newspaper that my father owns." I leaned toward him and said in a conspiratorial tone, "What were you doing? Putting an ad in the personals? Looking for a girl? You know they have online apps now. It's super easy. Even a chimp like you can do it. Just swipe left and right. But I hear swiping up to say you super like someone is super creepy." I waved my thumb like I was swiping in both directions.

"Ha ha." He stuck his chimp thumbs in the band of his

uniform's utility belt. "Actually, I popped in to give your father a press release about the murder of Principal Chapman. You'll be interested in this tidbit. The medical examiner did a forensic autopsy on Josh. You know why? Because his death was suspicious. And she's leaning toward homicide as his manner of death. Only waiting for a few more reports to come in. But I think it's safe to say preliminary reports indicate Josh Chapman was murdered."

Murdered. And I had witnessed the end game. I'd seen the "just desserts".

I pressed my hand to my churning stomach.

DB chuckled before he continued, "This is the fun part. You're our person of interest. I shared that with the newspaper. How you were there when it happened and how you and Josh were in an altercation. How Mrs. Rivers heard him tell you to get your hands off him."

Cripes. My dad had to run an article informing the community and beyond that his daughter was the possible murderess of Wind River's favorite principal. Leo had called it—I was screwed six ways to Sunday if I didn't get this thing worked out. Once the story broke, I'd become *persona non grata*, especially with the Hunter Boots Moms, and digging into Josh's life would become exponentially harder.

DB tweaked my nose and smiled. "What's the matter, Sam? Cat got your tongue? No cute retort? Right now, you're my number one suspect. You look pretty good, too. Who else wanted to kill Josh? He was Mr. Popular in this town. Except with you."

"Why would I want to kill Josh? I just met him. I didn't dislike him. Besides, I don't have a history of killing people, or I would have taken you out in chemistry class for cheating off me."

"Is that a threat?"

I scoffed.

DB continued. "You better mind your p's and q's, Samantha. I'm watching you." He put two fingers to his eyes and pointed from them to mine. "I'm watching you."

"Watch all you want because I'm innocent. And while you're watching me, a real killer is getting away."

DB blew a raspberry and looked skeptical. "They all say that."

"I'm telling you, DB. He was dead before he fell over."

"Is that a confession?"

Angry with his single-minded focus, I pointed my finger in his face, but before I could say anything, my mom shouted my name from across the street.

Both DB and I turned.

She was rushing toward us. To me she said, "Not another word."

Upon reaching me, she took me by the upper arm and said to DB, "You will do a good job on this, DB, because the leaders of this community are watching to see how this unfolds. Be mindful you have a review coming up, and to screw this up and wrongly accuse someone would not help you any."

Then, with her grip firm, she propelled me into the newspaper office. My dad and the paper's right-hand-woman Stella, were waiting for us in the lobby. Probably watching from the window.

My mother let go of my arm and reprimanded me, "Do not talk to him. Ever. Without your lawyer. You know better."

Frustration and irritation were the emotions I was working from. "I didn't do anything. I shouldn't have to worry about what I say."

Mom shook her head. "Any person who's considered a suspect has to worry about what they say. They can use anything against them. You're lucky your father saw him talking to you and called me."

"This is serious business." Dad gave me a pointed look, which I interpreted to mean I'd better get busy and solve this crime.

"Did you know Josh was teaching at the community center in Vancouver? He was working with kids at an alternative juvie program."

Dad's brow arched.

Mom nodded. "Josh came with an impressive resume."

"Okay, he had an impressive resume, but didn't he also have a history of leaving on bad terms?" I asked Mom.

She shrugged one shoulder. "Nothing that wasn't easily explained. Situations where either side could easily be argued. More a situation of 'he said, she said,' which are hard to substantiate."

Dad chimed in, "He moved around a lot."

Mom said, "And all his moves were for advancements. Logical."

I looked at my dad. "Did Toby get back to you with

anything?" Because even though Josh's moves were easily explained, there might be something else ready to be discovered. I hadn't found Josh as charming as everyone else. He'd put my spidey sense on alert. Not full pinging, but still. Josh wasn't who he seemed. I mean, he had a closet full of Chromebooks. What was that about?

Dad said, "Toby's been pulling things and sending them to me. Nothing major has shown up yet. Lots of invoices, though." He gestured for us to follow him back to his office.

"Please tell me you aren't doing your own investigation?" Mom asked.

Dad and I said nothing. She covered her eyes and groaned.

Once in Dad's office, he took a paper off his desk. "Toby said to show you this."

He handed me a printout of the image I'd seen. Attached was an email from drgnbait@techsavvy.com, making the request to get away.

It read, *The heat in WA State is not my type of heat. Let's blow this state and go somewhere with the right heat. Time to enjoy the payout from the hard work.*

Josh hadn't replied to the email, but Toby found a second email to drgnbait that included a confirmation email showing the purchase of two one-way tickets to Fiji for a Mr. And Mrs. J and J Chapman.

A third email chain with Fiji in the body or subject was from Mrs. Rivers to June and included a screenshot of Josh's calendar that showed the flight departure date for Mr. and Mrs. J and J Chapman to Fiji. In the email from

Mrs. Rivers, she said to her daughter, "Fiji. A dream destination. Travel Weekly rated it a top ten honeymoon
destination."

Last was an email to Josh from the airline less than
twenty-four hours later, stating that one ticket had been
fully refunded.

Dad said, "And look at this." He handed me more
papers.

I scanned the sheet. "This is an invoice from June's
coffee shop. It's for pastries and coffee to the sum of two
thousand dollars." I glanced between my parents. It took
me a second to connect the dots. "What does a person get
from a coffee shop for two thousand dollars?"

"It's probably for a function June catered," Mom said.

"How many people are you feeding for two grand?
We're talking coffee and pastries. How many people are
employed at Village Garden School?"

"Staff and teachers number forty-two total," she said.

That's it? I expected more for two grand. "Forty-two?
The math doesn't work. Let's say at twenty bucks a person,
that's not even eight-hundred and fifty dollars. What did
he spend the extra grand on?"

Mom looked irritated. "The startup of the school has
been expensive. Maybe this invoice is for cumulative
events?"

I showed her the paper. "It doesn't read like that." Just
one more thing that wasn't adding up. That was the story
of Josh. "Can I keep this?"

Dad nodded. "I have everything stored in a file."

Mom warned, "You should stay out of this, Sam. Nosing around in this business won't serve you well."

"Having DB investigate this is taking a far greater risk, as far as I'm concerned," I said. "I think I'll head over to June's. See what I can find out."

Dad put his hand on my shoulder. "You don't have much time. I have to get what DB told me up on the website soon or else he'll think I'm playing favorites. I can't leave your name out of it."

I gave him a hug. "I know, Dad. Just give me a few minutes to get to June's before you hit publish."

"It'll be in Monday's edition, too."

Dad did a print run on Thursday and Monday, but updated the paper online daily.

I said my goodbyes and ignored the worried look on my parents' faces. Because Josh had asked me to take pictures for the school's yearbook, I decided I wouldn't stop because he was dead. The probability that the killer was connected to the school was high.

I stopped at LC long enough to collect my camera then walked to How Ya Bean. The Real Housewives of Wind River were all in attendance, sitting around a table, iPads out, wearing UGG boots, with leggings and tunics. No one was dressed in exercise clothes.

June stood behind the counter, face drawn tight. Typically, she greeted customers when they walked in with, "How ya bean?" but not today.

The PTC mommies gave me the stink eye. I made my way to the counter to order. "Hey, June, how's it going?"

She looked at me, but I got the feeling she didn't see me. "What can I get you?"

I touched her arm. "You okay, June?"

She jumped liked I shocked her and stepped away. She appeared startled to see me. "What are you doing here, Sam?"

My guess was that her mother had fed her theories about me to June.

"I was hoping to get a cup of your amazing coffee and some pictures. Until I'm told otherwise, I'm still taking candids for the school per Josh's request." I added the last part for good measure.

"My mom said—"

"Your mom thinks I pushed Josh, and he hit his head and died. I know. But that's not true. The medical examiner hasn't determined the cause of death. At first the cops thought he might have been a victim of that vaping lung disease that's been in the news."

She blanched. "That's awful. How did they find out he vaped?"

My answer was to shrug and pretend I didn't know. The less I shared, the better off I'd be. If I could get her to doubt her mother's chatter, maybe I could keep the gossip to a minimum. "You've known me for a long time, June. My husband was married to another woman, and she's still alive. If I were a killer, wouldn't I target her?"

June looked skeptical, but she appeared to weigh my words.

"I watched him die, June." My voice cracked on the "d" word.

"Was it awful?" she said.

"Awful is an understatement."

She lowered her voice, her hand over her heart. "Did he suffer?"

She seemed pained to imagine it, and I wanted to soften the blow the best I could. From what I'd seen, Josh had been her friend.

"It was quick." Relatively speaking.

She shook her head and swiped a finger under her eyes. "He's really gone."

Timing was something I needed to work on, but not today. "Josh mentioned you'd catered a few school events. That must have been fun. Or stressful, considering what all you had to do."

She shrugged. "Catering is not the best word. I mean, I supplied a few boxes of coffee, cups, and pastries."

"If I wanted to have something catered by you, what would two grand get me?"

June reared back. "Two grand? How many people are you thinking of inviting? I've never done over seventy-five dollars. On average, I charge fifteen a person. So if you wanted something catered, then just add that by how many you want to invite."

Did I whip out the invoice? Yep.

"Look." I unfolded the paper. "I found this. Does it look right?" I didn't want to assume, right? Perhaps there was a logical explanation.

She shook her head, and her mouth pressed into a hard line. She slapped her hand on the counter and left me standing there.

She was a woman bent on a mission as she stomped to the back of the cafe. I followed, went to take off my lens cap, and then realized it was still missing as I walked behind June.

"Smile, ladies." I took a shot of the mommies.

Past the bathrooms were June's office and the stockroom. June was standing in her office at the computer, mumbling.

"June?" I stepped beyond the threshold and was surprised by the clutter. June was such an organized person, well put together. But this office had stacks of paper everywhere. On a cork board over her desk hung five sheets of paper. A quick glance showed two newspaper headlines declaring Josh's death. Two personal articles about Josh and his part in the community were from my dad's paper and a group email about coordinating some sort of ceremony for Josh. In the seat of her desk chair was a large box, overflowing with odd and ends of clothing, a purse, and store bags from local shops.

"What's all this?" I nodded to the wall.

She clapped her hands inches from my face. I jumped back.

"Focus, this is about that invoice you have." She pointed to the screen. "Look. My invoice doesn't match his. That invoice was for a small group of twelve people. I added a little for tax. My note says right here it was for the office staff. Not teachers."

I stepped around the desk and looked at her screen. "How did you give him this invoice?" Her notes were on her invoice, but they'd been removed from Josh's.

"PDF," she said.

Easy enough to change with the right software. "You know Toby Wagonknecht? He can set this up so your PDFs can't be altered." I was sure that was a possibility.

"That snake changed my invoice." Instantly, she clapped a hand over her mouth.

"Looks like it," I said. "I heard him arguing with Laura Danner at the fair. He helped himself to the family's cache of water, too."

Through her hands, she said, "I shouldn't say anything ill about the dead."

"But?"

She shook her head. Her eyes wide.

"Wasn't he dating Laura Danner?"

She nodded.

"So it's not such a big deal that he takes her water? I'm sure he was going to return it." I needed someone to fill in the blanks, and June might be able to do that. "It's not like doctoring invoices."

She dropped her hands from her mouth. "Only the Danners are real big on self-sufficiency. Taking their cache is a big no-no."

I leaned against her desk. "I don't get it. Isn't every one big on self-sufficiency?"

June's expression said she was questioning my IQ. "Self-sufficient. Like homesteading. One step removed from being a prepper."

The difference? I wasn't sure. Perhaps it was about philosophy. Regardless, June had said "prepper" like it was a dirty word. And if June was throwing shade on the prepper philosophy, I could see the rumor mill twisting Laura's practice to match just for the shock value aspect of the gossip.

"Is this common knowledge? About the Danners being self-sufficient?"

June sighed wearily. "I don't think Laura wants people to know. Josh let it slip once. Apparently, this lifestyle was something Laura and Carl embraced, and she kept it going after he died."

This gave Josh's actions new meaning. Laura's surplus meant more than being prepared. "No wonder Levi had been upset. I wonder what else Josh was up to."

June shook her head, and as if the action cleared away some fog, she jumped. "I need to get back to the front." She picked up the box of assorted items from her chair and hefted it to her hip.

"What's that?" I peered into the box.

"Lost and found. I try to clean it out every few weeks. You'd be amazed at what people leave behind."

"And never come back to get apparently," I said. The contents were numerous. "Come to think of it, I believe I left my lens cap here." I gestured to the box, asking for permission to dig through.

She nodded. Sure enough, I found the cap against the side of the box next to a bag from a local headshop.

I held up the bag. "Pot? You'd think someone would come back for that."

June shook her head. "Vape juice." Her eyes went wide. "Levi Danner's vape juice. He was here having coffee when his mom came in and made him leave. The bag was under his chair."

Levi vaped? Interesting, and clearly a secret if it were true. "He never came back for it?" I picked inside the bag. Just like a kid, he'd bought marshmallow flavor. Yuck.

June shook her head.

"Maybe it wasn't his." Because I imagine vape juice didn't come easy or cheap for a teen.

"Anything's possible." June's expression said she wasn't buying it.

With the box on one hip and her hand on my shoulder, she pushed me out the door as she said, "I really have to get back to the front."

Once outside her office, she slammed the door and stalked off.

12

BEFORE I COULD FOLLOW, a woman came out of the restroom. She stopped by the bulletin board and ripped my number off the ad I'd posted. I'd made one of those old-school ads with the proposition on the top of the page, *Need a PI?* and the bottom was a row of cut strips with my number on it. June turned the corner out of sight.

"Can I help you?" I put my finger on the ad pointing to my name. "I'm Samantha True." I held out my hand.

The woman, average size and my mom's age, wore her dark hair in a short bob. She was dressed in black slacks and a silky white blouse with black polka dots.

"Gillian Reid."

We shook hands. She glanced at the number she'd torn from my ad. "I'm not sure I want to hire a PI, but the police have blown me off, and I don't know what else to do."

"The Wind River Police?" I wouldn't be surprised if she said yes.

"My car was broken into earlier today and my brief-case stolen. And your cops took a report and wished me luck getting it back. But I need it back." She sounded desperate.

"Why don't you walk me through it, and I'll let you know if I can help." I was doubtful. Her briefcase could be in any trash can anywhere from here to Seattle for all we knew. I gestured for her to lead the way back to the coffee shop's main room.

We went around the corner, and I pointed to a table away from the mommies, closer to a row of four people banging away on their computers, looks of constipation or concentration on their faces. I caught a few glares from the mommies.

"Can I get you a coffee?"

Gillian shook her head. "I—"

June came from around the counter toward us. "You all ordering anything? Because if this is business, then you need to take it elsewhere."

Not gonna lie, I was caught off guard. "Is there some rule or something I don't know about?" I had no problem buying drinks and supporting June's business. I under-stood how frustrating it could be to have people loitering.

June cut her eyes to the mommies. She pointed to the line of people on computers. "I have those tables reserved." Then she pointed to the schedule that hung over the mommies on the wall. "Right now, they're reserved for the writers. See what the board says."

June had designated times listed on the board. Next to the time were symbols or emojis.

I glanced at my watch and pointed to the schedule. "It has a book by the time." I pointed to the computer people. "They aren't reading."

"They're writing books. This is their time. If you want to get on the schedule, submit a form. Until then, you need to take your business elsewhere."

I pointed to the mommies who were shooting me angry looks. "They're not on the schedule."

Again, June pointed to the schedule. "Yes, they are. That's them, the schoolhouse." She stepped closer and said in a voice so low I strained to hear, "You have to leave. They're reading the article about Josh on the paper's website." She slid her eyes to the side to show she meant the mommies.

Now June's behavior made sense.

I said to Gillian, "Why don't we take this outside, and you can walk me through everything."

Gillian was already moving toward the door. "My pleasure. Let's get this over with. I can't wait to get out of this town."

Gillian Reid was an independent forensic accountant who was hired to complete an audit. Gillian purposefully left names out of the conversation, but said she'd come to town for two meetings, one of which was canceled at the last minute. After her first meeting, Gillian tossed her briefcase in her trunk and went to the market to get a drink and some snacks for her return drive to Portland. While she was in the store, someone had stolen her briefcase. Hopefully, this was also when the CCTV cam that Chuck had installed outside his market picked up the entire burglary.

I explained this to her and that I'd need more information if the video turned out to show nothing. "If you hire me, I sign a confidentiality contract." I assured her. We completed the paperwork at the table outside June's.

Turns out, Gillian had been hired to audit Josh's spending. Her stolen briefcase carried all the documents she'd compiled against Josh. Documents she needed to produce to get paid.

"Who hired you?" The list was short because the person would have to be someone with access to school financial accounts.

"Alice Andrews," she said.

"And who was the canceled meeting with?" I had my notebook out on the table.

"Jenna Miller."

At my blank look, Gillian continued, "She worked with Chapman in his other districts and was arrested for money laundering while at Kitsap School District."

Gillian and I parted ways with my promise to call her with information within twenty-four hours. I sent Toby to Chuck's to try and get the footage and follow up with any leads, like car tags, if we were to be so lucky.

The district office for Wind River School District took up space on the third floor of the City Hall building. Alice Andrews had been superintendent of schools for over three years. My parents often went to dinner with Alice and her husband. And both were in my dad's fantasy football league.

An old, temperamental elevator with the retractable fence across the front deposited me on the top floor following a slow creak of its doors opening and a hard push from me to get the fence to retract.

The district secretary, Tammy McCoy, looked up from her desk that held court in the center of the small waiting room. I knew her from community events. Behind her desk were two office doors, each one off to the side.

She said, "You're better off taking the stairs."

"I feel lucky to be here." I glanced back at the elevator, wondering why I hadn't noticed it was sketchy before. Probably because I always took the one flight up to my mom's office.

"Don't think you aren't. How can I help you, Samantha?" Tammy was a well-put-together mom. Her clothes weren't the most fashionable, but classic. Her makeup was simple. Her hair full, eighties style with bangs. And considering it was making a comeback, the look worked.

"Any chance I can speak with Mrs. Andrews? I'm working on a case regarding a theft and just had a few questions." I showed her my PI badge.

She smiled. "Nice badge. Kinda cool."

"It's just the little certificate that comes with the license." A photo accompanied the certificate. Mine was a hot mess. I couldn't stop laughing the entire time I was trying to take it. Doing so made me feel like a poser, and that's what had cracked me up. On a whim, I'd gone with it.

I tapped the metal badge. "I bought this online."

She chuckled. Then did some clicking on her keyboard. "You're in luck. She has fifteen minutes before her next meeting. Let me give her a heads up."

She picked up the phone, pressed two buttons, then said, "Alice, Samantha True is here. In an official private investigator capacity. She has a few questions for you regarding..." She raised her eyes to me.

"Gillian Reid," I supplied.

She repeated the name, waited a breath, then hung up. "Right through that door." Tammy pointed to the door on the right.

"Thanks." As I made my way to the door, it swung open, and Alice Andrews beckoned me inside. She closed the door and gestured for me to take a seat on one of the two round club chairs in front of her desk. Her office was light and airy and done in pastels of blue and yellow and green. Pictures of all the Wind River schools hung along one wall.

I said, "Did Ms. Reid call you?" Hopefully Gillian had broken the news about the theft.

Mrs. Andrews nodded. "Yes, and I'm surprised, actually. Who would want to steal her work?" She snorted with disdain. "I mean, Josh Chapman would've absolutely stolen her work, but he's dead." She ended with a smile. A genuine expression of pleasure.

The hairs on my arms rose. "I take it you're pleased that Josh is dead."

Her smile wavered. "Oh, no. I wanted him alive. I wanted to take him down. Watch him burn into nothing but dull gray ashes. But I didn't get that, and this is the next best thing." She shrugged like we were talking about something as casual as the weather. Not a dead guy.

"Um, I'm sorry to ask, Mrs. Andrews, but did Josh do something to you personally? You seem..." I debated my words. "Angry?"

She slapped her hand on her desk. "I am angry. I never wanted that snake oil salesman to run VGS, and he knew it. A man that shifty can't have the best interest of the children at heart, and that just sticks in my craw. It's all about the children."

She looked away. From the YouTube videos I'd been watching about interrogation and reading body language, Alice Andrew's actions told me she had fed me a lie.

Drawing from what I knew about Josh, I said, "I'm guessing Mrs. Reid found padded invoices. Why don't you tell me about those."

Mrs. Andrews's cheeks went bright red and her eyes widened. She shook her head.

I pushed. "Mrs. Andrew's, padding invoices was Josh's MO."

She clasped her hands over her mouth, laughter eked out. She said through her fingers and chuckles "I'm sorry. I laugh when I'm nervous."

She'd done this at the school the day Josh died.

I said, "You aren't the only one he was taking advantage of."

After a long pause said through her fingers, "But I bet I'm the only one who appears to be in cahoots with him."

I blinked in surprise. "How so?"

She sighed heavily and leaned back in her chair, rubbing her hands up and down her arms. "Truthfully, I don't know. I can barely manage my smartphone, but according to Gillian, he forged my signature and had enough of my information to open a joint account. All the overages he was taking from the invoices were going into this account. And it looks like I was withdrawing them."

Her eyes filled with tears but she held them back.

"And you were using Gillian to prove that not only was he embezzling, but you weren't involved."

She nodded.

From my bag, I took out a small notebook and tapped the pen against the paper. Playing a hunch, I said, "Did you ever figure out what he was doing with the Chromebooks?"

Mrs. Andrews shook her head. "He reutilized them."

I shook my head. "What's that mean?"

"When assets are old, we have to move them off the balance sheet. Typically, when reutilizing items like furniture or equipment, we sell them on the state website, and the proceeds come back to the school. Josh said he sold the Chromebooks on a private site. He sent me an invoice for all new laptops, but I refused to sign it. The ones he had were only two years old."

I jotted this down in my notebook. So Josh said he sold the Chromebooks but really he'd stored them in his closet and was putting new asset tags on them, logging them as the newly purchased Chromebooks. "You might want to go over to the police station and tell them this. Mention you're looking for Chromebooks."

She gave me a skeptical look.

I continued, "They might have come across your equipment, and they need to know Josh was being investigated."

Mrs. Andrews squirmed in her seat. "I suppose since I've now told you, it would be in my best interest to inform the police before they hear it from anyone else." She slammed her fist on her desk. "Darn that man. He's been nothing but trouble. Even in death, he'll ruin me."

I didn't share with Mrs. Andrews that her outburst gave emphasis to the idea that she had the motive to kill Josh. I thumped my notepad against my thigh. "How so?"

"I thought I could handle this quietly, but that was a pipe dream. I'll have to tell the board the truth. I'll probably lose my job." Her mouth turned down, etching her face with deep creases of sadness.

When it came to offering comforting words, I sucked, so I skipped it. "Okay..." I tapped my notepad against my leg. "I'm sure Mrs. Reid will keep you up to date."

Mrs. Andrews stood, and we shook. Her hand trembled in mine.

I said, "Last question. Someone mentioned you wanted to hire your niece? Who's your niece?"

"Danika Post. Now there's a person invested in children." Alice shook her head.

Years of schooling my features came in handy as I masked my surprise. I let myself out and took the stairs out of the building. On the sidewalk, my phone buzzed.

Incoming call from Toby.

"Tell me you got something." Toby was my ace in the hole.

"With your trunk burglar? Not yet. Still waiting for Chuck's video. The man moves at the speed of a sloth," he said irritably.

Pot calling the kettle black, but I kept my thoughts to myself. A cooing sound filtered through the phone.

"How's Lady M?"

Toby said, "Great, very happy. Until I get in the car. She hates that. Anyway, I cross-referenced the numbers on that roll of asset tags you took pics off." Having seen the stack in Josh's closet and the new roll of asset tags, I'd acted on a hunch.

I said, "And let me guess. You found an invoice billing the school for new Chromebooks."

"Yep. The invoice is from an educational website called Pay Forward For The Kids. Supposedly a not-for-profit that gets products wholesale and passes along the savings to school districts. Or lets schools sell products via the site."

"How does this site make its money?"

Toby sighed. "Site says add five percent of the final sale bill."

"Why the sigh?" Toby was easy to read. Without his vape pen to calm him, he was quick to be irritated.

"The site's kinda lacking."

"Lacking?" Were his professional expectations coming out, or was his gut telling him something I needed to know?

He harrumphed. "The page looks professional

enough. A simpleton could have set it up though, maybe three pages total. No testimonies. No evidence they do what they say. It's like a dummy site we created in school when we were learning to code."

His words "a dummy website" struck a chord. How far would Josh go to run a con? A dummy website wasn't out of the realm of possibility. I switched gears. "How fast can you pull up any emails from Alice Andrews?"

Clicking sounds came through the line, and then Toby said, "They're up."

"Send them to me, please. I just had a chat with Mrs. Andrews, and she's carrying a boatload of anger toward Josh. My guess is he was blackmailing her." I told Toby about the joint account and how Josh made it seem like Alice Andrews was his partner in crime.

He hooted. Lady M echoed it. "Found them. I'd say she had anger. The last ten emails from her are threats. And I quote, 'burn you down until you're nothing but white-hot-ash.'"

"Whoa," I said and turned to stare up at the top-floor window that looked into Mrs. Andrews's office. "Maybe she killed Josh. With him dead, she could sweep every-thing under the carpet and give the job to Danika Post, her niece." I kicked the curb. "Trouble with this entire case was the person in the room when the victim died was me. So the actual crime happened elsewhere, and who knew when. Or how. I really hope she didn't do it. I hate when people I know are killers."

Leo pulled up to the curb in a police cruiser and idled. I held up one finger. The universal sign of wait a moment.

Toby laughed. "Don't forget to get evidence while you're trying to prove there's a killer among us. It's making me paranoid of my neighbors."

Yeah, evidence. That's the thing about this PI gig that differed from being a studio photographer. If I took a picture that just wasn't right, I could photoshop it. Sucking at being a PI wasn't an option. Not when lives were at stake. And I was determined to do this job to the best of my abilities. I just hoped my abilities didn't suck.

13

FROM THE DRIVER'S seat of his patrol cruiser, Leo propositioned me.

Well, he propositioned the private investigator me.

"I'm riding out to the Danners. Need to talk to Laura about Levi. How about you come along and see if you can get some questions answered about Josh."

My response was to climb into the passenger seat. The last few nights' sleep had been fleeting. Instead of lying there frustrated, I'd tried to build a picture of Principal Josh. I began by taping evidence of his scams to my wall. The invoice from June's. The invoice for water, billed to the school board for twenty cases and dated the day of the festival. The picture I took from inside his closet. The sketch I'd made of his office the day he'd died.

I liked this guy less every day, though I didn't see anything worth murdering over.

My main objective with Laura was to find out if Josh

replaced the things he took. He'd had plenty of time. And to ask what else he helped himself to besides water, batteries, and gasoline.

The Danners lived on five acres of land close to Wind River's city limits. What once looked like lots of open space and a simple house, I now saw as potential to be self-sufficient in a disaster. Specifically, an erupting volcano. Off from the road were three buildings. The house, a barn, and the business, a square concrete building. Cows and goats roamed the large fenced spaces between the house and the business.

At the entrance to their driveway, a dirt road, stood a large sign for Danner Pest Control with a picture of a stink bug toting a large arrow on its back that pointed to the driveway. The drive was a long road that split about a quarter of a mile down. To the left was the business and to the right was the house. We went left.

The business was a brown, square, one-story building. An area in front of the office had been graveled, and large wood parking stops shaped like logs marked six spots. One was taken.

The house, a simple well-maintained ranch was painted a rusty red with white trim. A large barn painted the same colors stood a football field's length behind it.

I was curious about Laura Danner and her children, specifically Levi. From my limited exposure, the kid hadn't been happy with Josh and his philandering, help-himself ways.

"June said Laura and Carl were big on being self-sufficient." I pointed out the window. "They're way better prepared than I am. I mean, I'm good with nature stuff, knowing what's safe to eat, making a fire, so I'd do okay in a zombie apocalypse. But should a volcano erupt and there were no grocery stores, I'd be up a creek."

Leo scratched his head, giving my statement thought. "That probably comes from Carl and Laura's background. Both are Cowlitz, and as a tribe, we pride ourselves on being prepared for all possibilities."

I needed to be prepared on so many levels in my life.

"Did you know Levi Danner got in Josh's face at the Fall Festival?"

Leo shook his head.

"What's Levi like?"

Leo shrugged. "Laura and Carl worked hard at their company, and now she does twice the work since Carl died. She's trying to get Levi involved, but he's going through his own stuff from losing his dad. It's hard being fifteen with no man around to guide a young boy. And I can't see Levi opening up to Josh and letting him in. He's known me his entire life, and I struggle to get through to him."

"He's not gonna warm up to a man helping himself to his family's cache."

Leo grunted. "True. Levi was arrested a month ago for shoplifting. Was running with a bad crowd. I wonder if there's a correlation between that and Josh coming into his mom's life?" He arched a brow at me.

I wrote the question in my pocket notepad. "Or at the very least it started when Levi noticed Josh was helping himself to their stash. How is Laura keeping Levi out of trouble?"

"He's been doing community service with me, helping at a soup kitchen, working on the reservation, helping with small construction projects, and he plays on my weekend flag football team."

I swiveled in my seat to face him, hurt that this was the first I was hearing about his weekend activities. "What? You have a team? How did I not know about this?" I loved playing football.

"Because it's for teens. Something for them to get involved in because they don't want to do it at the high school level." He gave a nonchalant shrug. "So I run a weekend game. I have enough teens to have two teams."

"You do this by yourself?"

"Oliver Gee from the station and Tupi Wildhorse help. When Hue's home, I get him involved." Hue was Leo's kid brother and one of my closest friends. Tupi was the high school mechanics teacher. He was Leo's age, and his first name was Herman, which he hated. He used his middle name instead. Tupi also belonged to the same find-Bigfoot-research team as Precious.

"Hue knows you have a flag football team and never told me? I'd love to help. I could even be a ref or something." I was kinda iffy on the rules of flag football, but I could study up. I'm sure there were videos about such a job. I preferred the competition of the game. And winning. I liked to win.

"Yeah, that'll be a hard no. You become a crazy person when your team isn't winning. Besides, when you go to prison, you can get your own team there." He gave me a large open mouth grin.

I wasn't sure which fight I should pick first.

"Look, we're here," he said, feigning mock surprise, and put the SUV in park.

Like I didn't know this was some dumb attempt to stop the discussion. The man was a chicken.

"I'm not done with you," I said.

"I'm not worried," he said while opening his car door.

"You should be," I mumbled then got out of the car.

I didn't know what to expect from Laura now that my dad's story was out. No telling how she'd react to me being the person of interest in the death of the guy she was dating.

Leo held the door open, and we went inside. The lobby was a standard square with a counter at the center and two offices on the right side. Each office had a door and a large window. The first office was dark, the door closed. The second was lit up.

Levi was at the counter, looking less than thrilled. His eyes lit up when he saw Leo.

"Hey, Coach, what up?" He gave him a chin nod. "I mean, Officer."

Leo extended his hand to shake. "Levi, nice to see you helping your mom. I hope your knee's feeling better. We have a big game this weekend."

Levi's eyes narrowed.

Leo continued. "Last time we played Tupi's team, they beat us."

"We're gonna take them this time, Coach." His words were heavy with determination.

Leo crossed his arms and rocked back on his heels. "I sure hope so. Because I bet Tupi that losers have to buy the burgers, and I'm counting on that coming from his wallet."

Levi pounded his hand into his fist. "You got it, Coach. We'll make them eat it." He laughed.

At first glance, his shaggy hair, slouchy jeans that looked like highwaters but were all the rage these days, and a Prince T-shirt gave Levi a casual, sloppy appearance.

But his mannerisms said otherwise. He surveyed the room under a slit gaze, as if expecting something to pop out. His hands, when not in use, were fisted, and his shoulders were hiked to his ears.

Anger. The kind a kid gets when they think the world is out to get them. I'd been familiar with that type of anger myself. Maybe that's why I could see it.

But all that aside, Levi Danner's one positive attribute was his desire to please his coach. He held on to every word Leo said and was quick to assure Leo he wouldn't let him down.

Leo cupped Levi on the shoulder. "I'd love to talk strategy with you, Levi, you've got a sharp mind for it, but I need to speak with your mom."

A slight pink erupted on Levi's cheeks, and he ducked his head to hide it. "She's in her office. Just knock." He pointed to the office with the lights on.

Leo led the way and did the knocking. Through the

window, Laura gestured for Leo to come in. When I walked in behind him, Laura looked surprised.

Leo started the conversation. "Laura, I have a few questions for you. Is this a bad time?"

She looked between Leo and me.

"A few questions about what?" She eased out of her chair and looked out the window toward Levi.

Leo rushed to say, "Oh, no. It's not about Levi. He's doing great."

She collapsed back in her chair with relief. "I thought maybe he was in trouble again."

Leo said, "This is about Josh Chapman."

Again, she looked between me and Leo before saying, "And she murdered him."

Leo shot me an apologetic look. But before I could say anything, Levi came into the office.

He said, "Mom, I gotta run." He glanced at me. "I got that thing."

She nodded. "Okay, but come right back when it's over. You're still grounded from using the car for anything but errands."

Levi's shoulders slumped. "Fine," he said. I envision the eye roll. He clomped out her office.

Laura said to Leo, "I'm not comfortable with her being here. You have questions? Fine. But why is she here?"

"Because I'm being accused, and I know I didn't do it," I said. "I'm trying to figure out who did."

"Said the woman who married a crook. Or pretended to be married to him," Laura said.

Not that I knew he was a crook when I married him. He had to die for me to find out the truth.

Laura continued, "Besides, lots of people in prison say they're innocent."

She had a point. There was an entire podcast series about such issues.

"I'll go wait outside." I gestured toward the door and his cruiser. Leo and I had discussed this in advance in case Laura wouldn't be welcoming. Our end game was to get answers.

Outside, Levi was skirting around the building. I followed the teen.

I found him on the backside, the aroma of tutti-fruity wafting in the air, and he was righting a large rusty tin bucket.

"Dude," I said. "Haven't you heard how bad those things are? Like, no joke. People are dying from something called vaping lung disease. It's been in the news." I remembered what June said about Levi leaving behind some vape juice vials.

Poor kid nearly choked on the pen from surprise. In his haste to block the bucket he ended up turning it over displaying his hidden stash of vape vials. He quickly reset it then swiped a vape pen from his mouth and tried to hide it in the folds of his hand.

He stood stock straight. "I don't watch the news."

"Well, when you have adult vices, maybe you should develop some adult habits to keep yourself informed. Just a thought."

"You gonna narc me out?" He toyed with the vape pen.

"I won't tell your mom." I leaned up against the wall.

"Yeah, like I believe that." He stared down at his hand. "You going to say something like, 'I won't have to because you'll tell her.'"

The kid was snotty, but there was an underlying tone of fear in his voice. Personally, I believed if a child still feared their parent, then there was hope for the child.

"No, I'm not going to say that." I didn't point out I hadn't said I wouldn't tell Leo. "You should at least google the stories. They're scary."

He nodded, perhaps his way of saying he would. Teens were hard to read. "You're the girl who killed Principal Josh, right?" He side-eyed me as he relaxed against the wall, tucking his vape pen away.

"I'm the girl who was in his office when he died, but I didn't kill him." I was getting used to saying this. "He was dating your mom, right?" Weird that Levi called him Principal Josh.

"Was. But she dumped his sorry ass—I mean butt. Sorry." He stared at his hand, likely jonesing for a puff of his pen.

"Was this before or after he took your mom's water, batteries, and gas?"

Levi straightened. "How'd you know about that?"

"I was there when you confronted him at the fair." I mimed like I was taking pictures. Levi nodded in understanding.

"Principal Josh was a dirtbag. He didn't deserve my mom."

Said like a kid who wanted the one thing he couldn't have, his father.

"She seemed mad about the water." I was hoping the kid would open up a bit.

Levi shrugged.

I pointed to the barn. "Is that where you all keep everything? You know, I keep seeing articles about how St. Helens could erupt again or Rainer, which means Tacoma would be G.O.N.E. Gone. Stockpiling is smart. I just don't know where to start."

There was a long pause before Levi said, "There are books out there. Good ones to get you started. There's no shame in being prepared."

"None," I agree.

"But Principal Josh used to tease us. Saw no point. Even broke the lock when he took the water."

"Did he fix it when he replaced the water?" I still didn't have my initial question answered.

Levi scoffed. "Mom kicked him to the curb right after. I guess that's why he never bothered to replace the water or the lock."

"And then he died," I said.

"Because you killed him."

"I didn't kill him," I said in protest. "Aren't you supposed to be somewhere?" This kid irritated me.

Levi snorted. "Juvie for rich kids, but I doubt it matters right now because my teacher died."

I gasped. "Your teacher died?"

"Yeah, because you killed him." Levi laughed.

The pieces came together.

"You're in the Recode and Reshape Community Program?"

Levi nodded but wouldn't meet my eyes. Ashamed maybe?

"Is there a kid named Troy Gunn in your class?"

Levi pushed off the wall and stepped away. "I dunno. I'm not allowed to talk to the other losers."

I let him go, watched him walk across the field to his house. I stared at the barn. What did it look like inside with the Danner family stockpile?

"Samantha?" Leo called from the front of the building.

I pushed off the wall and went back to the front.

First thing I did inside the cruiser was narc out Levi and the vaping.

14

FRIDAY

AFTER LEO DEPOSITED me off at my apartment, I opened the door to find Toby and Precious lounging in my living room. I tossed my backpack to the floor and went to the fridge for a green apple kombucha.

"We're going on a field trip," Precious squealed as she jumped to her feet.

"Field trip?" I glanced at Toby. A vape pen dangled from his lips. I assumed it was empty. Lady M was cocooned in her banana-shaped pouch that hung from around his neck. Toby might not vape with addictive juice, but obviously the act of vaping was a habit.

A quick glance at my watch told me we were just after high time. "Are we cutting into your private driver time?"

"Dudette, who cares about private driver when there's a field trip?" He puffed on his pen. The smell of biscuits and gravy filled the air.

I gasped. "Are you kidding me? People are dying from

vaping, and you can't even go,"—I counted on my fingers the days since we all met— "three days? Are you crazy? You say there's no nicotine in there, but clearly you're addicted."

Precious pointed a finger at Toby and laughed. "Told you she'd flip out."

Toby stroked Lady M. "Chill." He patted down the air in a way to emphasize I needed to simmer down.

I crossed my arms.

Toby tapped the vial. "It's an old vial. Found it rolling around in my car." He puffed in defiance.

"Oh, well, in that case, an old vial is fine. I mean, these toxic vials could have been around for a year and only started coming out on the market based on shipping and store stocking." I turned to Precious. "The news hasn't said for sure how old or new the vials are, right?"

She sat on the couch and tucked her feet under her. "Nope. Only that people were dying."

We both gave Toby a pointed look.

He sighed and whipped off the lanyard attached to the pen. "Fine." He handed me the vial.

"Thank you. Besides, the smell of biscuits and gravy is making me hungry. Okay, tell me about this field trip." I tucked the vial in a junk drawer in my kitchen.

"I got the video from Chuck's. Took forever. He sent it over during high time. I was eating Doritos and chilling and thought what the heck? It's not like I had to be overly observant. I needed to catch someone jack open a trunk. So I gave it a look-see. Boom. Right in living color. Chick gets out, pops open the car with an auto slim jim in, seriously, three seconds. She reaches in, pulls the trunk latch, then locks the car behind her," Toby said. "A pro."

I said to Precious. "Remind me to put a slim jim in my toolbox."

She kicked her legs onto my coffee table. "Already ordered one."

Toby snapped his fingers to get our attention. "Here's where the pro goes amateur stupid. She takes the briefcase and gets back in her car, a beat-up Rav-4. Then she does a U-ey right there in front of the market. Clear shot of her license plate front and back. Took me five minutes to track it on the DMV site."

Precious gushed, "It belongs to someone who knew Principal Josh back when he lived on the peninsula."

I said, "Any chance her name is Jenna Miller?"

Surprise showed on both Precious and Toby's faces.

Precious asked, "How did you know?"

I leaned against the bar. "She had an appointment with Gillian and was a no show."

Precious clasped her hands together in excitement. "She's our field trip destination."

I shook my head. "The last field trip we went on Toby was shot. This Jenna Miller was watching Gillian for an opportunity to take her briefcase. How far would she have gone to get that briefcase had Gillian not put it in her trunk and gone into the market? It would be stupid to assume she's not dangerous."

Bringing up Toby's gunshot wound made him massage his shoulder where the bullet had pierced.

Precious scoffed. "This time we'll just do a better job of

visualizing our goals and possible outcomes. We'll make contingencies."

Toby rolled his eyes. "I'm not visualizing anything. That didn't work last time."

I looked between my friends. "If we go, I'm not approaching the house by myself. I'll need backup."

Toby touched his nose with his index fingers and blurted, "Not it."

Lady M popped up from her cocoon. He touched her nose with his other finger. "She's not it, either."

Precious threw up her hands in exasperation.

Toby shrugged casually. "This time, I'm staying in the car."

"Then why are you going?" I asked.

He snort laughed. "Dudette, because why would I miss it?" He gave me a look that told me he thought I was crazy.

I said, "I hope you did some digging into Jenna Miller. Gillian Reid told me she'd been arrested."

Toby glared at me. "I might have been high. That doesn't make me stupid." Then he smiled smugly. "Jenna Miller was the one who got arrested when charges were pressed by Kitsap School District. She and Josh got busted selling reutilized equipment online."

The pieces were coming together, albeit at a snail's pace. I said to my friends, "Josh is being investigated by the Wind River School Board for fraud, embezzlement, and money laundering. Jenna was arrested for what sounds like the same thing in Kitsap County. Josh wasn't arrested. Why?" I raised a brow at Toby.

From beside the couch, he picked up a messenger bag then took out a laptop. "On it."

"Regardless, Josh ends up here where the games continue," I said as I fit the scenarios together.

"Then someone murdered Josh." Precious's tone ominous.

I nodded while thinking. "And yet, Jenna Miller comes to town and steals a briefcase with evidence regarding Josh's con here in Wind River."

Precious added. "Odd to steal a briefcase that has evidence of your past when that past is public record."

I wagged my brows. "Isn't it, though? Unless there was proof in that briefcase that Jenna Miller was still up to no good."

"Got it," Toby called. He pointed to the screen. "Josh paid a fee and did community service but no real jail time."

I picked up my backpack.

"She could be a killer," Precious said with glee as she jumped to her feet.

I pointed the finger at her. "Exactly why we shouldn't drive up there and get in her face."

Toby shook his head "No, she's harmless. Gillian knows who she is, and Jenna Miller didn't kill her. She just took the information."

Precious snorted. "Which is stupid because Gillian already knows the information and where to get it."

"Jenna's actions don't make sense," I said. "Jenna Miller is probably a crazy person." I slung my pack over my shoulder.

Precious picked up her purse. "All the more reason to take a field trip now. Let's get going. Toby?"

He shut his laptop with a click then bustled past Precious to reach the door first. "I call backseat."

Precious said, "That's not a thing. You're supposed to call shotgun."

Toby snorted. "Not on your life. And before you ask, I'm visualizing that this trip gives us answers, but I also want to keep my health and body in its current state."

Precious said, "I want to find out if she killed Josh."

I said, "I don't think it's going to be that easy."

"Stop being so negative," Precious said. "Start thinking in positive terms. Then you set an action, and we make that action a reality."

I said, "We're not going to make her a killer if she's not one."

Precious opened the door. "We'll never know anything if we continue to stand here talking about it either. Now move your butt." She pressed her key fob, and her SUV came to life one floor below us. "Hold on to your titties, kitties."

Jenna Miller lived on the second floor of a two-story walk-up apartment complex on the far outskirts of Seattle. So far out, the city skyline wasn't visible, the only view the brown buildings surrounding hers.

On the two-hour ride up, we'd made an exit strategy in case she gave off violent vibes. Toby waited in the car while Precious and I went to the door.

Jenna answered after the second knock. She was short, petite, with long bland brown hair, brown eyes, and a cute pixie nose. She wore cropped jeans with rips created the natural way, showing off their excessive wear, and a flannel shirt with a tank top underneath. Around her ankle she wore a large black state-assigned bracelet. From beneath the frayed hem of her jeans the upper body and head of a dragon tattoo twisted around her ankle and ran up her leg.

"Hi," Precious said. She held out the picture of Jenna doing the U-turn in front of the market. "Is this you?"

Jenna looked at the photo, blanched, and shook her head. "Nope. Wrong person." She went to close the door.

Denial was the state many of Precious's client came to her in. Jenna Miller was no different. Precious gave me a solid shove in the back, sending me forward into the door and Jenna.

We tumbled. Jenna, landing on the floor of her small living room, me on my knees in front of her.

Precious entered and slammed the door behind her.

Jenna said, "Come in."

I said, "Jeez, so much sarcasm." I looked at Precious. "Makes me think she doesn't mean it."

I pushed up from the floor, surveying the small space on my way up. A loveseat, an average-sized TV in a stand that looked wobbly, and a large computer desk with some serious equipment humming away on it.

I gave Precious's shoulder a light shove. "Way to go, Precious. What if she's a killer? Did you think of that?"

Precious offered Jenna a hand up. "If she is, she'll do it with a drink or food or something, so don't take anything she offers. But I don't think she is." She looked at Jenna. "Are you a murderer?"

Jenna batted Precious's hand away and got up on her own. "No, I'm not a murderer."

"But you're a thief," I said and pointed to a leather briefcase leaning against the desk. "I bet that's not yours."

Precious waved the photo in Jenna's face. "I bet you acquired that bag when this picture was taken."

Jenna pointed her finger at the door. "Get out before I call the police."

Precious made herself comfortable on Jenna's couch. "If you were going to call them, you would've already made the dash for your phone." Precious pointed to me. "She has some questions for you. Once you answer them, we'll leave. No biggie. Close your eyes and picture this. Sam asking you a few questions, then us leaving. That can happen, but it's up to you."

Jenna's gaze darted from Precious to me and back again. "Who are you people?"

Precious pointed to me. "She's the girl on the hook for killing Josh Chapman."

Jenna crossed her arms. "Good. You did the world a favor. I'd shake your hand, but I'm not feeling so friendly to either of you."

"And strong feelings of dislike for Principal Josh, I see," I said.

She snorted and plopped into her desk chair. "He ruined my life. And telling people to call him Principal Josh made me want to vomit in my mouth."

"He's ruining my life right now," I said.

She smirked. "Yeah, that's how Josh rolls. Or rolled."

"Any chance you killed him?" I asked. "That'll take the heat off me." My gut told me she didn't. My gut had also told me marrying my fake-husband Carson one weekend in Vegas was a good idea, and we know how that turned out. So, there's that. But I was going to be positive and go with Jenna not being a killer.

"Not that I didn't want to. Often, I would dream about him getting hit by a bus or getting poisoned by one of those fizzy water tablets he liked so much, but that's as far as it went. I've already lost my career and reputation because of Josh. I wasn't about to do more time because of him."

"Fizzy water tablets?" Precious asked.

She smiled wickedly. "Yeah, his taste buds were jacked up so he flavored everything. Tabasco on popcorn. Flavor tablets in water. Extra strong coffee. That sort of thing."

I leaned against the wall and gestured to the briefcase. "So why take the bag? Josh is dead. The school board can't charge a dead man. But you can be charged with burglary. You're willing to go to jail for that?"

Jenna dropped her head in her hands. "Taking the bag was a momentary lapse of judgment. Please don't tell my PO." Parole officer. When she looked back up, shame colored her cheeks.

I glanced at the ankle bracelet. "And how are you even allowed out of this pleasant abode you call home?" I gestured to her barren and sparsely decorated apartment.

Jenna curled her lip and looked at me like I was

stupid. "It's a tracking device. I'm allowed to leave. I just have to tell my PO where I'm going out of the county."

Precious said, "But omit things like breaking into cars and stealing stuff." Precious tsked. "Why don't you tell us about this 'lapse in judgment'?" She did air quotes.

Jenna tucked her legs up to her chest and wrapped her arms around them, dropping her chin to her knee. "Some auditor reached out to me and wanted to ask me a few questions. Brought up the whole incident with the school board. So I drove to some small town—"

"Wind River," I supplied.

She nodded. "Yeah, I'd found a picture of her online, and when I went to our appointment, I watched her put her briefcase in her trunk and go into the market. That's when the idea struck and I couldn't get it out of my head. I thought, maybe, if she lost all her paperwork, then she'd go away or give up."

"Did she tell you that you weren't who she was after? That she was trying to get an understanding for Josh?" This was what Gillian had told me.

Jenna shrugged. "Yeah, but I didn't believe her. Every-thing connected with Josh is one giant, hot, steaming pile of sh—"

"You're telling me," I said. "I know this isn't your favorite subject, but could you tell me what happened between you and Josh and why you lost your job?"

She looked ready to dash out the door. Her eyes darted from us to the exit as she gripped her legs, knuckles going white. So I gave her a little nugget.

"I ask because I found a closet full of Chromebooks in his house."

Jenna gasped. "I don't know why I'm surprised. That's Josh's MO. I worked in the IT department for our district. Josh and I started dating." She rolled her eyes. "I was such a sucker. Anyway, he asked me to show him how to build a website. So I did. It's so easy. He asked me to show him how to monetize one and add e-commerce. I did that, too. And like a dumb-dumb, I used my own name on all the forms as the examples. My digital fingerprints were all over it."

"What was he pretending to sell?" Precious asked.

"He had memorabilia he wanted to get rid of. I assumed it was for that. He hinted he was often strapped for cash, which was why we ate at my place a lot and never went out to dinner, or any place really." She looked between Precious and I. "You getting the drift on how much a sucker I am?"

"Was," Precious said. "You were. You aren't anymore."

Jenna scoffed. "I took a woman's briefcase."

I said, "So you built a website, and he took it over."

She nodded. "I figured he was selling his own stuff for money. I mean, I was partially right. But he was selling stolen stuff."

I thought of the invoices. "Then he'd turn in invoices from that company for products he never bought or services he never used and pocket the cash."

Jenna pointed a finger at me, telling me I'd nailed it. "Josh took it a step further. He'd reutilize equipment before it was due to be replaced and sell it from his website. Most of that stuff goes to a storage facility that no one can keep track of anyway. Inventory sheets are notoriously inaccurate. Josh capitalized on that, sold the stuff and pocketed the cash."

I slumped against the wall. Josh had been savvy. And greedy.

I picked up the briefcase. "I'm taking this with me."

Jenna nodded. "Good. It's been staring at me since I took it, accusing me with its silence."

"Is everything in here? I'm sure the woman who owns this might overlook this entire thing so long as she can move on."

Jenna said, "Tell her I'm sorry. I freaked out and made a bad choice." She nodded to the bag. "She did a fabulous job, pointing all the fingers at Josh. I wish I could use her stuff in my case."

"Are you still battling the school district?" Precious asked.

"I'm thinking about it. I can't get any IT job because of my record, so I'm stuck working from home."

Something flickered over Precious. She straightened and smoothed down her shirt. She was going into life coach mode.

"Many people would kill to work from home." She snickered. "Maybe kill isn't the right word. But instead of looking negatively at your situation, find the positive. What is it you do?"

Jenna studied Precious before answering. "I make book covers and graphics for authors. I build websites, too."

"Are you any good?" Precious asked

Jenna shrugged and looked away. "Yeah, I think so. All my clients are repeats, and they tell their friends."

Precious crossed her legs and leaned toward Jenna. She touched her on the knee, drawing Jenna's attention to her. "Have you ever considered that maybe doing this is right where you're supposed to be? Yes, you got here in a way that was less than pleasurable, but look what you created out of that bad situation. And you bring happiness to people. Readers see your covers, and like a piece of art, they marvel at it and are called to respond. Powerful."

Jenna was enraptured. "I never saw it that way. I've been so angry."

Precious shook her head. "All that anger is holding you back. Time to let it go."

Jenna nodded, one slow head bob after another. "Yeah, time to let it go."

Watching someone transform before your eyes is an amazing experience. Jenna's shoulders straightened. Her chin came up from her legs, which then unfolded. She crossed them and sat back in the chair with a smile.

Precious pointed to the bland white wall of empty space over Jenna's desk. "Change that. Put something there that inspires you. Something that creates happiness."

Jenna stared at the wall in wonder.

Precious stood. "We have to go. Give me your email, and I'll send you some good reads to get you started."

Jenna scratched out the information on a notecard and handed it to Precious.

I slung the briefcase over my shoulder. "All right, we're out. Thanks again." We exchanged a few awkward smiles and let ourselves out, leaving Jenna to stare at the white space over her desk.

"I'm surprised you didn't recruit her as a client," I said as we approached Precious's SUV.

"Nah, she's looney tunes."

I stopped short. "What? What makes you say that?"

Precious stopped and faced me. "Okay, maybe she's not full-on crazy, but there's only so much I can do with people who like to be victims."

"But she seemed sincerely interested in what you said about changing."

Precious nodded. "Sure, and she'll go out and buy something, and for a while, it will work until something bad happens, then she'll go into a tailspin. She needs a good shrink. I'll send her a list of books and a few names. Maybe it'll get her on the right track."

"Well, that was nice of you," I said.

She nudged my shoulder with hers. "All I could think about was that scene from Billy Madison where the killer marks an X across someone's picture because they've struck them from the list. I didn't want to get us on her list in the first place. Not after we kinda stormed the place and all."

I laughed. "Good idea. You think she was telling the truth back there? I don't think she killed him, but this was too easy."

Precious side-eyed me and smirked. "Make no

mistake. That girl was straight-up lying about something. I haven't put my finger on what yet."

Yeah, my spidey-senses were saying the same thing, but when Toby was able to access Jenna's parole records, nothing eventful stood out.

Something was off. I just didn't know what.

Autumn in Western Washington was my favorite time of the year. The temperature called for hoodies and fashion scarves, yet the days were sunnier than gray. Soon, the sun would be stuck behind clouds and as elusive as Bigfoot.

Today was one of those perfect days that reminded locals why they put up with the gray days of winter. Mount St. Helen and Mt. Adams stood like majestic sentinels below a baby blue sky. I decided to go for a run. Exercise helped me clear my head and look past the forest for the trees. I wasn't anywhere near understanding what had caused Josh to keel over and who might be behind it.

Gillian was happy to have her briefcase back, and I was happy to have money in my account. Ralph's was still undecided on whether or not to put me on the schedule, especially now with Dad's story naming me the only person of interest in Josh's case.

After my run, I planned on taking Cora to get ice cream. Before dinner. Because that's how this aunt rolled. All said and done, the folks and I were doing a good job keeping her spirits up and shielding her from the drama at her school. With Josh's death, the whole sexual harassment accusation seemed to be dead in the water. Funny, how if that accusation had never been made I wouldn't be in this mess. What a stupid thing to accuse a kindergartener of anyway.

After stretching out in front of my dad's office, I struck out with a slow gait, letting my muscles warm up as I ran through town. There were lots of hills in Wind River, and it wouldn't do to burn up all my energy right out of the gate.

I cut through the park and jogged past the fitness center and How Ya Bean. The Hunter Boot Moms were outside warming up, dressed in similar running attire and matching high-end running shoes.

"Hey." I jogged in place. To Annber I said, "It's Monday. I thought you had yoga today?" I realized my dates might be wrong. To Carlie I said, "Or was it you that has yoga? No, you're the swimmer, right?"

She said, "Not anymore, thanks to you."

Me? What did I do?

"Shut up, Carlie," Annber said, clearly the leader. "Let's run, ladies. These thighs won't slim themselves." She turned her attention to me. "What direction are you going so we can make sure to avoid that?"

They jogged off toward flatter land.

I jogged off in the opposite direction, through town

and toward a more challenging run. Though I run with earbuds in, I keep the music low. To do otherwise would be stupid.

A couple times, I checked over my shoulders just to make sure they weren't coming up behind me. As a collective, they struck me as organized and vindictive. I didn't want to bump into them at night or be caught unaware while running.

I crested the first hill, headed toward my parent's house. To the left of me was a new housing development and to the right the ridge that looked down into the wilderness preserve. Off in the distance, occasional tiny white peaks crested the Windy River's murky surface. The sun beat down and, without losing stride, I tugged off my long sleeve shirt and tied it around my waist, enjoying the cool breeze pushing against my tank-topped torso.

It was a beautiful day for a run and to soak in some vitamin D. The land flattened, offering a half-mile stretch of easy running. My stride evened out, my thighs happy to no longer be on an incline. It was when I caught my second wind that I caught air.

One moment I was keeping my pace even, and the next a car clipped me on the side, sending me ass over teakettle. I was upside down when I realized a car had hit me. Man, it had appeared from nowhere. I hadn't even heard it. Stupid electric car with no sound.

As I flew toward the windshield the weirdest thought came to mind. Why didn't electric cars wear bells? That way they couldn't sneak up on people.

The contact with the windshield sent me away from

the car and toward the ridge. I landed half on my shoulder, half on my back with a loud *oomph*. And followed that up with a grunt. Pain exploded through my entire body and I dry heaved from its intensity.

Disoriented and dizzy, I tried to stand, but slipped off the edge of the ridge where I'd landed.

Reaching for purchase but coming up short, I tumbled off the side at a quick clip, catching bits of dirt, grass, bush bits, and debris in my mouth and eyes. Each bumped elicited yikes, ows, and hisses.

The plummet seemed endless, but I finally came to a screeching stop in a raspberry bush. I screamed out in pain. The thistles were poking me in what felt like one thousand places. Truth be told, I would have rather kept rolling then stopped this way. I'd take my chances with a rock or something else any day over a prickly raspberry bush.

I laid there in my spandex shorts and my tank top, my T-shirt somewhere in my downward path I suppose, and wished I'd chosen something different to wear.

I was frozen, afraid to move. Stuck on my back with my legs splayed out and my left arm over my chest. Thankfully, my cell phone was strapped to my right arm in a plastic protective sleeve made for joggers. There wasn't a chance I was getting out of this without help. Unfortunately, digging into my right arm was the raspberry bush. I clamped my teeth together and whimpered as I moved my right arm into a position where my left hand could reach my phone. Thistles tore, snagged, and ripped at my skin.

I cried out again, but moved just enough of my arm that my hand could manipulate the plastic sleeve on my right bicep. Deftly moving my fingers, I unlatched the case and fumbled the phone out. I'd lost my wireless earbuds in the tumble so there was no asking Siri for help. The screen was cracked, perhaps damaged to the point of being unusable. I pressed the home button and said a silent prayer at the same time. When the screen lit up, tears of relief coasted down my temples. Or maybe those were tears of pain. Hard to say. Using my index finger and thumb, I called Leo.

"Samantha," he said in a rush. It seemed there was never a good time to call Leo. Chatter of several voices filled the background.

I swallowed. "Hey, you busy?"

"I'm at a tribal meeting. What's up?"

My words rushed out of me faster than Windy River's fast-paced current. "Oh well, I was just hit by a car and fell down the ridge toward the wildlife preserve, and I was wondering maybe if you could come help me because I'm being held captive by a raspberry shrub and all its thorns." I was impressed with how composed I sounded.

"You're kidding me, right?" A door slammed.

"Nope. No jokes. Really in a lot of pain here, Leo. So, think you can help? I hate to take you from your meeting but..."

"Did you call the police?" His words were coming out slightly breathless, like he was jogging.

Watch out for cars, I wanted to warn. "No, just called

you. I figured you'd get here faster than DB. I'm not his favorite person."

"I'm on my way," he said. A car engine turned over. "Tell me your location again."

"I'd just passed the houses by Eighth Street, and I was on that open stretch of land where the new development is going in. Before the dog park. About a hundred yards from the turnoff into the wildlife preserve."

"Before the turnoff?"

"Yep," I said. This time my voice wobbled. I needed to cry.

"Hang in there, Sam. I'm on my way."

"Okay, I'm going to hang up now," I said. "Because I need to cry, and I don't wanna do that with you on the phone, okay? Okay." I didn't give him a chance to respond. I hung up, let the phone drop on my chest, and unleashed my pain through what could be called body-wracking tears, but I was too afraid to move my body. My hip hurt. My head throbbed. My entire body burned from the needle-like thorns.

A cool breeze was coming in off the river. Leo was on his way. I just had to hold on to this tiny thread of calm until he got here. Panic and shock would not do me any favors.

An eternity passed before Leo showed up. He couldn't find me right away since the sun was going down and I was in the shadows of the raspberry bush.

"Samantha," he called. The beam of a flashlight swept over the ground.

"Over here," I cried, but my voice was thin and too airy.

"Samantha?" The sweeping beam paused, pointing forty-five degrees away from me.

I sucked in a deep breath and blew it out to say, "Marco."

"Polo," came his reply, his tone terse. The beam turned closer to me.

"Marco."

"Jeez." He was getting closer. "Polo."

"I'm over here, under the bramble." He might have heard the last part, but I'd run out of energy and had mumbled it.

Leo found me less than a minute later. He called to someone, and Ben Reynolds came to stand next to him.

Leo jerked his thumb in Ben's direction. "I brought a paramedic."

"Hey, Ben," I said. "I didn't hear the rig." The rig being a county ambulance.

Ben studied my predicament, hands on his hips. "You got yourself in quite a pickle here, Samantha."

Leo said, "Ben and I were at the tribal meeting when you called. That's why you didn't hear the ambulance."

Ben said. "I figured it wasn't worth the time to switch vehicles. You'd refuse an ambulance ride anyway."

He dropped to one knee and opened up a black duffle bag I'd just now noticed. He handed Leo a pair of gloves and donned a pair himself. From his back pocket, Leo took out a multi-tool. Ben took one out of the duffle then flipped it open to the knife function. He stuck it blade down into the ground.

As if the duffle bag was bottomless, he withdrew a blanket and shook it out. "As we cut away the cane, I'll drape the blanket over you to help protect you from more thistle."

"Sounds heavenly," I said.

As the guys worked, I tried to be patient. But biting back my cries of pain were increasingly difficult. Some thorns were deeply embedded. Leo tried to distract me by asking for details about the silent and deadly car.

I answered a few questions, then said, "I can't think about it, Leo. This hurts too much. I need to concentrate on not screaming."

They worked in silence while I focused on deep breathing and visualizing them getting done, how good I would feel being freed from the thorns.

It was full dark by the time Leo had wrapped me in the blanket. He held my head steady as he gently rolled me away from the bramble.

Ben said, "Let me take a look before we move her further. That was some fall you had, Samantha."

"You're telling me. You should see what I did to my phone," I said.

"You should see what the fall did to *you*," Leo said.

I glanced over Ben's shoulder and said to Leo, "Feels like we've been here before. Me getting bandaged up and you coming to the rescue. You have the same face now that you did then."

Ben glanced at Leo. "My mom would call that a dark scowl."

Leo wiped his hand down his face. "And I don't like this. I didn't like it then, and I don't like it now. Now can you tell me about this car that hit you?"

While Ben shined a light in my eyes and had me track his finger, I told Leo about everything I could remember. Ben felt all around my neck and shoulders, and cleaned the deeper punctures and scrapes. I followed my accounting of the incident with a rant about how electric cars should have bells or some type of wheezing sound so they can't sneak up on people.

"You're lucky you didn't break a hip or leg," Ben said.

I laughed with disbelief. "Yep, that's me, lucky."

Ben smiled. "From what I can tell. Truthfully, I'd like to get you to the hospital and do some x-rays. You're pretty banged up and scraped up, but nothing a tube of Bacitracin and a couple of pain relievers can't fix. You're gonna be sore for a while."

I nodded. "Bacitracin. I have some of that at home."

Leo snorted, "You should stockpile that, bandages, and meds. Keep a supply on you at all times. Carry them in a bag. You're going to need them all the time. I don't like this, Samantha. Not one bit."

I said to Ben, "He says that a lot to me. Like he thinks I enjoy being hit by a car." I rolled my eyes.

But my joke went flat.

Leo shook his head and said, "Come on, let me get you home." He pulled me up by wrapping his arms under my shoulders, easing me to my feet.

Ben said, "Can you bear weight?"

I tested my balance and my body's reaction to standing. I nodded.

Leo studied my face, looking for signs of discomfort. I masked as much as I could, but when I looked up at the hill I'd have to traverse, I couldn't mask the dread.

"Take a deep breath," Leo said.

Puzzled, I did as he requested.

He swept me up off my feet, one arm under my knees, the other around my back, and carried me up the hill with such ease I don't think he broke a sweat. Had I not been bleeding and aching, I might have felt something else. Something more akin to the romantic emotions brought on by chivalry. But there wasn't room for anything else as my embarrassment from needing to be rescued, once again, was taking up all the space.

16

THURSDAY

Josh didn't have family or next of kin, and word got out that, once the state released his body, the state would bury Josh in some random, large cemetery with no headstone. The VGS mom squad couldn't have that. They organized a fundraiser to cover the headstone cost for Principal Josh. And combined it with a celebration of life at How Ya Bean. Maybe the Hunter Boot Moms were afraid if they waited for whenever the state would release him, interest in supporting Josh would die down.

If they only knew.

Mom told me Alice shared with the school board and top city employees about hiring Gillian and Alice's suspicions regarding Josh. Gillian's findings showed embezzlement and money laundering well into six digits. Alice was on temporary paid leave while the school board did their own investigation.

Briefly, I considered the possibility that Josh might

have done this to himself, taken his own life because he knew he was busted, but that wasn't his MO.

My presence at the celebration wasn't welcome, so I planted myself on the rooftop of the fitness center with a listening device provided by Mrs. Wright, and my camera and hoped for a lucky break. This worked for me because I was bruised and achy from being struck by the car. Stretched out on a lawn chair on the roof was the threshold for my pain tolerance.

Two things I noticed. Lots of women attended the celebration, few men did. And none of these women were Laura Danner. I sat back in the lawn chair and eavesdropped with a six-pack of local IPA in a cooler and Mrs. Wright's headphones clamped over my ears. A giant disc that looked like one of those cones of shame that dogs wore was the receiver and I pointed it in the direction of the get-together.

The conversation below me was mind-numbing. Endless accolades about Josh and his character. He was great. So kind and helpful, always thinking of others. There were several remarks about me that were not as kind.

Leo startled me, coming from behind, and sat on the edge of my lawn chair.

I slid the headphones off. "Whatever happened to innocent until proven guilty? Some of those women down there are vicious. They're ready for me to be thrown in prison and the key tossed in the Pacific Ocean."

"Crime and fear bring out the ugliness in humanity." He wasn't in uniform. Black jeans and a light blue fleece pullover that hugged his body in all the right places. Of course, Leo didn't have any wrong places. With his sleeves pushed up, the eagle tattoo on his arm stared at me, as if trying to read my thoughts.

I looked away. "And what? Me running free makes them think I'm on some killing spree? That any of them could be next?" The comment gave me pause because the truth was the killer was still out there and not knowing why or how Josh was killed was unsettling. Essentially, anyone could be next.

"You're an easy target." He took a beer from the cooler and twisted off the top.

"Help yourself," I said sarcastically.

He gave an incredulous look. "You're not going to drink six beers. You're on pain medication and shouldn't be drinking one."

"I'm not taking the medication. It makes me loopy. Who can function that like?" I took a swig from my beer.

Leo nodded to the people below us. "Anything interesting?"

I shook my head.

"I've got something interesting." He rolled the beer bottle between his hands.

"And? Keep going."

He was toying with me. Butthead, but I refused to be baited.

"Consider this beer a thank you for what I'm about to tell you," he said with a smirk.

"If it's half as good as the buildup, I'll give you more of those beers."

Leo wagged his brows. "Oh, it is."

I clamped my teeth together to keep from yelling, "Just tell me already!"

Leo liked to push my buttons. He'd been doing it since we were in high school. If I didn't like his kid brother so much—and he wasn't half bad either—I'd kick Leo off my lawn chair and club him over the head with the cooler for being a brat.

"You're getting better at this patience thing," he said.

I raised my camera and snapped a close-up of him. "So many things I can do with that image." I snapped a few more. "If you don't start talking soon, I'm going to do something heinous with this picture."

"Like what?"

"Open a matchmaking account for you. Make a wanted poster. The possibilities are endless."

Leo chuckled. "There she is. That's the girl I know. Miss. Impatient." He tapped his beer against mine. "One of the houses on Eighth has a Ring camera and caught a picture of the Prius that hit you."

I sat up with a jolt but regretted it instantly, my hip aching something fierce. "Please tell me you got a plate."

"We got a plate."

I wasn't sure if he was serious or not. "For real?"

He nodded then pulled out two more beers from the cooler. "You're going to need this for the next part, though."

I discarded my empty in the cooler and twisted off the top to the new one. "Okay, I'm ready. Hit me."

"The Prius was a rental car."

"Aaaannd?"

"And it was rented by Josh Chapman."

I gasped. "How is that possible?"

"We looked at the video footage. The person who picked up the car is slight. Likely a woman but could be a slim male. The rental information says a woman, but I never want to assume. They wore a ball cap, never looked at the camera. We searched for the driver's license number and no match. It was bogus. They picked up the car in Seattle, and the attendant doesn't remember anyone unusual at all. Dropped it off in Portland, and nothing stands out to anyone. Both times the pickup and drop off were at busy times."

Josh Chapman?

"How could a woman pick up the car if it's in his name?" I was trying to sort through the pieces.

"Could have had a card with the same number in her name. ID was in Josh's name. It's not out of the ordinary to have a woman named Josh. As a woman who married a man who conned a town of people, this shouldn't surprise you." He gave me a pointed look.

"Because I still expect mankind to be upstanding, conning people will always surprise me, and when it ceases to, that's when I'll do something else." Not that I was a superstar PI or anything, but I dug this gig. Fighting for the underdog provided a power boost to my sense of self. Like I was making a difference.

"That's what I like about you, sweetness, an optimist at your core."

Leo's smile was dazzling. The kind that made girls do

crazy things like throw their undergarments at him. The strong angles of his face spoke to his strength and serious-ness with a potential for deadly.

But that smile. Holy cow. It hinted at a side of Leo that fantasies couldn't compete with. A sexy side that said he had skills in areas other than weapons and manhunts. Bedroom skills.

I pressed the cold beer bottle to my neck.

I shifted my focus onto his information. "Let's assume the killer is the one who rented that car and tried to run me down. Why? I'm the one on the hook for Josh's murder. Why hurt me and take suspicion off me?"

"Because the person isn't too bright? Anyone on your suspect list like that? Or maybe you're getting close to learning something?"

My suspect list was shockingly short. Jenna Miller was on it. I'd considered putting Laura Danner on it, but she didn't strike me as the type to off someone over water. Alice Andrews had motive but she came clean with the school board. What's the point of going through the trouble to off a man if one comes clean about one's motive?

He studied me. "Who's on your list?"

I pressed myself into the back of the lawn chair and bit out with annoyance. "Who's on your list?"

"*You're* the only name on the city's list," he said with the same amount of annoyance.

"Which is so stupid. What do they think about the computers and the padded invoices? The guy was embez-zling money from the school board, and he was laundering money. A practice he's done across the state before ending here. Why would I kill him?"

"Maybe you were in on it. With your mom being the mayor, one might assume you have inside access to city information. Plus, no one would suspect you. How the information is presented will make the pieces make sense. You're in a tough spot financially after what Carson did. You're also angry, and you took a trip to Hawaii over the summer. Where did that money come from?"

I went to answer, but he interrupted me with a wave of his hand. "Doesn't matter. We're spinning this to make you the bad guy. Josh propositions you with the money-making scheme, and you do it. Then he threatens to tell on you for whatever reason, so you kill him. Or maybe you were sleeping together, and he tried to break it off, so you killed him. Get what I'm saying? DB can find facts and situations and people to say they witnessed you and Josh fighting to give this story credibility and cast reasonable doubt on your innocence."

When Leo put it that way, my blood went cold. Logically, I knew spin convicted people. I'd even said this to myself when I went to the station. But deep down, I didn't believe people would think I was a murderer. I was *innocent*. That should be enough.

"Jenna Miller is the only person on my list. I thought about adding Laura but—"

"Do it," he said. "Don't rule anyone out because it makes you uncomfortable, Samantha."

He was right.

When trying to find out who killed Carson, my fake-husband, none of the suspects had been members of my community. Digging up their dirt didn't come with a sense of betrayal. Josh's death was too close to home.

Uncontrollable crying caught my attention, the sound of it coming from the headphones, and I put them back on while eyeing Leo. He moved to stand by the ledge, being careful to stay out of sight.

People were murmuring what sounded like consolation to the crying.

"He was such a bright light," the crier said between hitchy sobs.

I transcribed what I was hearing on my notepad and showed it to Leo. I couldn't tell who the crier was.

Leo read the sentence and gave me an eye roll. I pretended to gag myself.

"Oh, get control of yourself, Mindy. He was just a guy. Not a bright light," another woman said.

I wrote the response and showed Leo. He peeked over the ledge but drew back with a shake of his head. He couldn't see anything.

The crier, Mindy apparently, sucked in a heavy breath then said, "The man is dead, Danika. You could at least put your hate aside for the moment. We all know how you felt about Josh. I bet you're happy he's gone. We all know you wanted the principal job. I guess now you have it."

A curt laugh. "You're a group of fools."

Undeniably, Danika had oozed contempt for Josh at the open house. And based on the exchange between Josh and Danika the day he died, the two hadn't been on friendly, fun terms. I wrote Danika's name and the word suspect on the paper and showed Leo. He stepped near me and lifted the headphones.

"You're getting the hang of this." He let the headphones go so they slapped against my ears.

"Jeopardy," he mouthed, pointing to himself. "Wheel of Fortune," he said, pointing to me. I stuck out my tongue.

Then he did the most unexpected thing. He leaned forward and kissed my forehead, then brushed a wisp of hair off my face. He took another beer from the cooler, gave me a wave, and left.

I sat there for who knows how long listening to the women, thinking about Danika, the Hunter Boot moms, but mostly how the kiss had left me all tingly.

17

FRIDAY

I WAS SCHEDULED to be at AJ's later today.

But first I needed a quick chat with Danika Post, now VGS acting principal. Only I couldn't just breeze into the school lobby and request some time. I couldn't take the chance, afraid Mrs. Rivers would cause a scene. I continued to be the *numero uno* person of interest.

Instead, I waited in the school parking lot, hoping to waylay the counselor there.

My plan worked. I caught her as she arrived to start her day.

"Danika," I said, catching her between cars.

She squealed in terror and clutched at her chest.

I put my hands up in hopes of easing her fear. "Sorry, I didn't mean to scare you."

She stepped back, wide-eyed. "What happened to your face?"

"I fell into a bush."

She looked skeptical. "What do you want?"

"I want to know Josh better. I've been accused of killing a guy who I didn't even know."

She eyed me warily.

I pushed on. "I was taking pictures, that's all. You were there when he asked me to do it."

She nodded, hands still gripping her shirt and purse.

I leaned away to give her space. I learned this in one of the PI videos I watched. "And I'll be honest. I didn't think highly of him. His smile seemed fake, the way he shook my hand, clasping it between both of his, and," — I made the heart using my hands — "this whole spiel about a village to raise a kid and education is a three-hundred-and-sixty degree process, which doesn't make any sense."

She relaxed her arms. "Right, it's so stupid. If you do a three-sixty, you end up in the same place."

"Yes," I said emphatically. "But those Hunter Boot Moms didn't see it that way. They ate it up. And the way he touched all of them." I fake shivered. "He was skeevy, and I think you thought so, too."

"He's dead, so what does any of it matter?" Her stare was no-nonsense.

"Thanks for not accusing me of killing him."

"Oh, I'm thinking it. But more, I wonder what you want from me."

"I'm trying to figure out who actually killed him. And I was wondering if you might have any insight into that. Or you might have done it and need to get it off your chest." Saying it was worth a shot.

She laughed and slumped against a car. "I barely knew

Josh. Met him when I took the job here at the end of the last school year. I kept things at work strictly professional and made sure to keep him in his place."

"Why did I hear that you wanted the principal's job?"

Danika rolled her eyes. "PTC President Mindy. She spread that rumor. Yeah, I have my credentials in school administration, just finished them this summer, in fact. And yeah, I ultimately want to be a principal, and at a school like VGS, it would be amazing. But I also have little admin experience, and I know I have to put in the time. Mindy took all the info I just told you, omitted the part about needing more experience, and told the other ladies in the PTC I was gunning for Josh's job."

"How about your Aunt Alice? She wanted you to have the job, too, right?"

Danika nodded and pointed to herself. "I could do a better job of running that school without having any extra credentials. A chimp could do a better job than Josh was doing. He was so focused on making everything look good that he neglected the day-to-day stuff. Let me handle it."

"So you were doing his job, but without the pay or the title?"

She gave a half shrug. "I guess. When you put it like that..."

Our eyes met. I posed the question using an expression.

Her eyes widened, and she shook her head. "But I didn't kill him over it."

"I didn't kill him over touching me too much either, but here we are. Someone wanted to get even with him."

She continued to shake her head. "No. You want to know how I got even?"

I nodded.

"I applied for other jobs. I was offered a job with the Clark County School District in an admin role. I was about to get the experience I needed to move up when Josh died." She jabbed her finger in the air for emphasis. "And that job paid better, too. I resigned."

"When?" I hadn't heard anything about it.

"I emailed the morning he died."

"Was that what you were talking about outside the school the day he died?"

She pursed her lips for a second then said, "Yeah. He said I was smart not to list him as a reference because he wouldn't have given me a good one. He asked me to stay."

"Because you were doing all the work and he needed that to continue?"

She shrugged. "That's my guess, but who knows with Josh."

No other questions came to mind. "Thanks for chatting with me. Sorry to scare you in the parking lot. I'm kinda persona non grata in the building." I hitched my thumb toward the school.

"Oh, yeah, your name is mud." She smoothed down her shirt and skirt.

Back in LC, I texted Toby to see if he could find Danika's resignation letter. Doing so would help validate what she'd told me. Until then, I wasn't going to make any hasty decisions about her innocence or guilt.

The rest of my day was spent working for AJ. I swung

by *Click and Shop* for his groceries. Afterward, Simon and I spent hours at the dog park playing catch.

From the comfort of AJ's overstuffed plush leather chair and with my laptop on my legs, I pulled up the logged points from the tracker I'd put on Troy's car. Home, community center, grocery store, game store, home.

I stared at the screen, hoping something would jump out at me. Nothing did.

My phone rang, and the screen said it was AJ wanting to FaceTime. He knew I'd been tracking Troy.

"Hey," I said when his face came on the screen.

"Whoa," he said and pulled away from his phone, but only as far as his earbud cord would allow. "What happened to you?"

In the small corner of the screen was my image. My face was scored with small crisscross cuts. "I fell into a raspberry shrub, a ginormous, man-eating one." I'd worn a hat in hopes of hiding the marks. I pulled the brim down lower on my face. More red marks were slashed all over my hand and arm. I'd gotten used to them, but was seeing them all again through AJ's eyes.

"And it tried to eat you?" He sounded sincerely concerned.

"It would seem like it." Never mind my bruised hip from the car. But I kept that to myself.

"You're okay though?" His large brown eyes furrowed with worry.

"Yeah, I'm fine. Let this be a lesson to you. Never jog on a ridge with raspberry shrubs below."

"Noted," he said with a smile. "I'm glad you're okay."

"So... your brother. This is where he goes. Every day." I read him the list and the time spent at each location.

"Seems benign," AJ said, his face pulled tight in thought.

He'd called from the locker room. Behind him, a half-naked man walked by. Then another. All with towels around their waists.

I was insanely curious about the inside of a professional football locker room. The space was nice with rich, dark wood and light green walls. The team colors for the Pioneers were dark brown and kelly green. I wasn't sure how or why those were the colors, I couldn't imagine a frontiersman with a buggy all decked out in brown and green.

Another body walked by that I recognized. "Was that Keith McVay, superstar quarterback?" I nodded in the direction the body had gone. Keith was my age, single, and oh so very hot with his blond hair, blue eyes and a Wheaties-box smile. Last season, Keith had an average passer rating of one hundred and twenty, which meant he had consistent completions, lots of yards, several touchdowns, and had no interceptions.

AJ glanced in that direction then back at me. "Yeah." He sounded underwhelmed. "Back to my brother."

"Of course." Wait till I told my dad I'd seen Keith in a towel. Not that he would care about the towel part. That would be more interesting to Precious. "I'm heading to the community center soon. I want to be there a few minutes before he gets out. I want to talk to the staff. I figured tomorrow I'll follow him the entire day to see what goes down at those stops. They might look benign, but actually seeing it will tell us for sure."

AJ wiped a hand down his face. "I asked Tee-Roy to show me what some of these mysterious purchases were and he couldn't. Got all mad and accused me of not trusting him. Told me he was doing my stupid program, and this was the cost of it."

"What did he mean by that?"

AJ shrugged. "I suppose he means that if he has to do this community center program to stay out of jail, as a favor to me, mind you, then he's also entitled to a few of the things he wants. Troy has this huge entitlement attitude. I don't know how he got it because we came from the same house. We both watched our mom work three jobs."

"Except he moved here with you a few years ago and suddenly has a lot more," I pointed out.

"I work hard for this stuff," AJ said.

I laughed. "You sound like every parent in the same situation. You worked hard, but he didn't. Then your mom gets sick and even more changes." Thinking about Troy reminded me of Levi. "Hey, does Troy like football?"

AJ gave me a look that told me he thought I was stupid. "Does a bear crap in the woods?"

"Ha ha," I said. "I know you like football, but does your brother? Sincerely like it. Not just pretend because he thinks he's expected to."

That gave AJ pause. "He used to like it. Nowadays, I can't say for sure." He looked a little sad. "I barely know who he's becoming."

I told him about Leo and the weekend football program. "I'll text you his contact info."

"Yeah, do that. Thanks." AJ smiled. "That's a good idea, Samantha."

I glanced at my watch. Time to roll. "Okay, food is in the house. I picked up an awesome salad from the local restaurant in Wind River. There're some steaks in the fridge for you to grill tonight. Maybe ask your brother to have dinner with you and try to just talk to him about anything other than the touchy subjects."

AJ snorted. "That's everything."

"Maybe complain to him then. Make something up. Make him feel useful. I'll head down to the community center and see what's going on. I'll let you know if I find anything." I turned my phone to show Simon fast asleep in his dog bed. "This one's pooped. We played catch for over two hours."

AJ laughed. "You're the best, Samantha."

"Yeah, I know." I smiled. "Simon's easy to be with. I'm hanging up now," I said then pressed the button to disconnect. My hip was killing me from the softness of the chair, and I wasn't sure how I'd get myself out. I'd sunk deep into the cushions.

Setting my computer on the ottoman, I pushed it aside so I could slide out on my back. I landed on the ground with a thump, wincing from the pain. Simon lifted his head and wagged his tail.

"Go back to sleep, lazy," I said as I flipped over onto all fours. I pulled myself up using the chair's arm. This life of fighting crime was hard on my body.

After making sure Simon had access to water and food and LC was properly oiled up, I split for the Vancouver Community Center where Josh ran his Recode and Reshape class. Just because Troy's car was there didn't mean he was. I needed eyes on the scene for verification. Anything other than that was an assumption, and we all knew what they said about assuming.

Because Troy would recognize LC, I circled the building until I found Troy's car. It was parked behind the center. I parked in the front, tucked between two other large vehicles. I circled back to wait on a concrete bench with my backpack between my legs, Troy's car in direct sightline. I pulled my ball cap down to mask what I could of my face and pretended to read a magazine.

Five minutes after Troy's juvie class ended, he pushed through the doors, exiting the building. A scowl on his face, a backpack like mine flung over his shoulder. He didn't talk with anyone. Didn't look around or anything. Beelined it straight for his car. I reckoned juvie class wasn't all that fun, but I expected a smile or a look of relief to be done for the day.

A few minutes behind Troy was Levi. He strolled out of the building and stopped a few feet from the door after exiting, causing people to suddenly change directions. He pulled a vape pen from his pocket and began puffing his life away. I snapped a picture. Based on the aroma tutti-fruity again. Stupid kid. Dad's latest article said Washington State and a few states around us were banning flavored vaping juice.

I sent the picture to Leo. I ducked my head in hopes

Levi wouldn't recognize me. Once he had his vape pen going, he continued on his way.

I waited until Troy was out of the parking lot before I went into the building and followed the signs to the administration office. Such as it was. The center's office was a glass window in a wall in the main hallway. Through the window, there were several desks arranged in pods.

A pleasant-looking woman about my age was manning the front desk closest to the window. She had earbuds in and was focused on whatever she was typing. To her credit, she didn't look startled by my appearance and slid the glass open so we could talk.

"I was wondering if I could speak to the instructor of the Recode and Reshape Program," I said. I knew Josh was the instructor and was dead. But I wanted to see where this got me.

She grimaced. "The instructor who typically does the program is no longer with us."

I raised a brow and ignored the slight ache that came from the pull of skin across the cuts. "Something I should know about? I'm thinking of requesting this as an alternative for my son's probation, but maybe it's a bad idea." I touched a cut on my cheek, hoping she would infer the wrong meaning and think my son had done this to me. "But if the instructor can't stick around, that makes me wonder…"

She shook her head and leaned forward. "He died."

"Oh," I said. "Hopefully not by one of the students."

She shook her head again but wouldn't meet my eyes.

So, she knew Josh died of suspicious causes but wasn't going to elaborate further.

"Is the program not an option then?" I asked.

"Oh, it's still going. We have another faculty member facilitating the class until we know if the company that offers the program will send another instructor or not."

I smiled with false relief. "Can I speak with that person?"

She pointed down the hallway. "Room one-oh-seven. Kalan Johnson is the instructor."

I gave her a thumbs up. "Thanks." I shuffled off in the direction she pointed.

Room 107 was a large classroom with three rows of tables seating six to a row with computers in front of every seat.

Kalan Johnson was sitting at a computer clicking madly between pages on the screen. He was a slight man, like he didn't know what a carb was. The kind of guy weight seemed allergic to sticking to. His skin was the Pacific Northwest pale. His hair was blond and spiky.

I rapped on the doorjamb and said, "Knock, knock. You Kalan Johnson?"

He said, "Yeah," never once looking at me.

"Mr. Johnson. My name's Samantha True." I walked over to him and looked at the screen over his shoulder. "I wanted to ask you a few questions about Josh Chapman and the program here."

That got Johnson's attention. He spun in his chair to face me. "You a cop?"

"Private investigator," I said, reaching for my identification. Something on the screen caught my eye. Pay Forward For the Kids, Josh's company. "That's a dummy site." I tapped my finger on the screen.

Johnson turned back to the screen. "It's not actually. Because it's doing business. I thought it was a dummy at first, too." He pulled out the chair next to him and gestured for me to sit.

I did. I leaned into the screen.

He said, "What made you say it was a dummy site?"

I wasn't sure what I could share. "I've seen it before. I've been looking into Chapman, and this site came up."

He faced me. "I'm the IT guy here. I teach coding, website building, and all sorts of other stuff in adult ed courses. I know nothing about this Recode and Reshape Program, but they put me in here because they said Chapman was teaching the kids basic coding. How learning to code will keep a kid out of jail is beyond me, but here I am."

"I think it was more about them learning to work to a schedule and finding skills outside of whatever crimes they're committing," I offered with a shrug.

"Except many of these kids's parents are wealthy. The students have opportunity at their fingertips. It's the ones trying to get by that need the skill."

He had a valid point. "So you come in to teach coding, and you found this website?"

Johnson leaned back in his chair and let out a derisive laugh. "What I found was kids writing code to set up new products on the website."

"What kind of products?"

"Chromebooks, textbooks, and some were non-tangibles like service fees. Chapman gave each kid a list of code to write." He pointed to a stack of papers by him. "Then the kid uses mom's credit card to test the ability to purchase the products. Small amounts. Nothing major."

Warning bells were ringing in my head. "Small amounts that add up over time, I'd bet." To purchase products that were never delivered.

He gave me the trigger fingers to indicate I'd said the right thing "And you'd be right. What I can't find is the code that reverses those purchases or codes them as dummy purchases and not charge the card."

"So... all this is going into the coffers of," — I tap the business on the screen — "this company, which is really Chapman."

"Yup," Johnson said. Took me half the class to realize what was going on. These kids just come in, take their sheet, and get to work."

"Do they know what they're doing?" This could explain Troy's mood.

Johnson gave my question thought. "I think many of them do."

"Why didn't they stop when Chapman was killed?" I wondered out loud.

"Lots of different instructors came in. I'm guessing the kids didn't know where the con started and stopped. For all they knew, Chapman was the middleman. For all I know, that's true, too."

One thing I knew was there was at least one more person involved, and that person tried to run me down.

"Was there anyone else working with Chapman? Someone who said they were an employee of this company?"

"An IT person."

"I thought you were the IT person." I was pretty sure of his answer but needed to hear it out loud.

"I'm IT for the community center. This woman was IT for this company." Johnson tapped the screen.

Johnson had said this woman. This woman. Was Johnson on the up and up? Or had I walked in on something, and he was in on the con? He was of slight enough frame that he could have rented the car. This woman could be a lie.

I asked. "What did you have the kids do when you figured this out?"

"I had them watch Minecraft videos and talk about what types of coding were used in the making of that game. I couldn't think of anything better." He rubbed a hand down his face. "Jeez, now what do I do?"

I pulled my phone from my backpack. "I know who you should talk to." I dialed Leo.

18

WITH THE HELP OF JOHNSON, Leo and I were able to track the money trail to a specific bank. Getting the bank info would require a warrant signed by the courts.

For the average man, that was.

I had Toby, IT spy extraordinaire on my payroll.

I stepped into the hallway to make the call. We were after high time so I knew he'd get right on it. When I got back into the room, Leo was on the phone with Officer Gee, helping him write out a warrant.

I texted AJ and asked him to do a quick add up of all the charges on his card that came from Pay Forward For the Kids and to get that number to me ASAP. Wishing I could get it in minutes, I knew it might take hours. The life of a second-string quarterback was demanding, apparently. Whereas I had visions of him just tossing a ball on the field all day long, apparently that wasn't the case. There were films to watch and meetings to attend and runs to practice. I was surprised when he texted back five minutes later with a screenshot of the charges.

I showed the screen to Leo. "Based on this, my client has been scammed out of about three grand. His brother, Troy, has been in the program for three weeks. So averaging a grand a week. The program is twelve weeks." I turned to Johnson. "How many kids in the program?"

He shook his head in disbelief. "Twenty per quarter."

I asked, "And it runs every quarter?"

Johnson nodded. "Yeah, there are enough troubled teens to keep it going. In fact, Amy at the front said we have a waitlist."

Leo gave a low whistle. "That's almost a million dollars a year."

I said, "My client said he was told there would be some expenses throughout the program. What tipped him off was there was nothing to show for those expenses. When he asked his brother what he was getting for these charges, the brother couldn't give a direct answer."

Leo took my phone and studied the screen. "When you glance at this statement, it doesn't look to be a lot because all the charges are small enough. But when you add it up..." He shook his head. "Quite the scam."

"And your friend Levi is in this program, too. Your still-vaping friend Levi," I said with a pointed look.

Leo eyed me while he pulled out his phone. "I haven't had a chance to talk to him." He swiped his finger across the screen a few times then held the phone out so I could see it. He was calling Laura Danner on speakerphone.

"Danner Pest Control, Laura speaking."

"Hey, Laura. It's Leo Stillman."

"Officer, how can I help you?" She sounded wary.

"You're on speakerphone, Laura, because I have a quick question and in the room with me is the IT manager for Vancouver Community Center and a PI for a client that would like to remain anonymous. I'm calling about the Recode and Reshape Program. Is it okay if I keep you on speaker?"

A long enough pause that had each of us looking at each other.

She sighed. "Ask your question first, and I'll let you know."

"We were wondering if you had some charges on your credit card from a place called Pay Forward For the Kids Educational Services that are related to the program here?"

"I did. I asked Levi what they were. He couldn't explain it so I asked Josh. He explained they were startup costs for the program."

Leo asked, "Was it just the one week or every week."

"Just the one."

Leo looked at me, and I shrugged.

He said, "Okay, Laura. Thanks. Make sure Levi comes to football this weekend."

"Will do, Leo," she said and disconnected.

From Officer to Leo. She was definitely someone on the defense, but his simple and not threatening questioning had put her at ease. I made a note in my PI handbook to master that skill. Wheel of Fortune, my rear end.

Johnson was typing away on the computer and pulled up a screen with lots of numbers and letters on it.

He said, "I logged into what Levi Danner has been doing in class, and it's not what the others are doing. He sits in that corner." He pointed to the last row, farthest corner. The screen was turned at an angle that made it hard to see. "And it looks like all he did was surf the net."

"What sites?" I asked.

"Typical kid stuff. Bands and YouTube videos on gaming. But a few weird ones. The workout schedule at Wind River Fitness center and some newspaper articles."

Leo asked, "Articles?"

Johnson pulled them up. They were the articles on his dad's death.

My phone chirped. Toby.

"What did you find out?" I asked, stepping aside so not to talk over the guys.

"The account was cleaned out yesterday and transferred to another account in the name of J. M. Chapman."

Ugh, not again. "Any idea who this is? Don't tell me someone named Josh."

"Okay, I won't. Because it's not. That account was opened a few days before the transfer. I'll send you the picture of the ID they scanned into the system."

"Thanks, Toby. You're the bomb."

"Yeah, dudette. I know," he said before disconnecting. A second later, a picture of Jenna Miller popped up in my messages. J.M. Chapman was Jenna Miller.

I called Toby back. "Where does Jenna Miller's tracking device say she is?"

He tapped a few keys before he said, "Home."

"Okay, thanks." I disconnected and called Precious. "You free?" I asked.

"For what?"

"A road trip back to Seattle to visit our friend, Jenna."

Precious ohh'd. "What'd she do?"

"I'll fill you in on the way. I'm close to you so I'll come to your place."

"Give me fifteen," she said.

"Done." After hanging up, I shared with Leo everything I'd learned.

"How you obtained the information would not hold up in court. I can't do anything with it." He pressed his thumb against the spot between his brows, as if trying to ward off a headache.

"Not yet. You'll be able to when you get the warrant, but for now maybe we can be a few steps ahead. I'm headed to visit Jenna myself in a minute."

He took me by the elbow, worry furrowing his brow. "Samantha. Don't go. There's nothing you can do."

"I can ask her why she tried to run me down. I can ask her what she thinks she's doing. What game she thinks she's playing."

"And then what? When she pulls a gun on you and says she's playing the game of get-rich-quick, what are you gonna do?" he said in his haughty cop voice.

"I can't sit around here and do nothing. Am I supposed to watch TV or something while we wait for the warrant to come in? And how long will the bank take to get you the information? That will take what? Hours? Days?"

He stuck his hands on his hips but said nothing because he knew I was right.

"I just want to follow her. See what she's about."

"Do nothing else," he said sternly.

"I'll be careful. I promised I would when you told me I would have to clear myself, remember that? I'm on the hook here."

He pressed his lips together in frustration then said, "That was until you got hit by a car."

I patted his shoulder. "Cost of playing with bad guys. We were always dealing with a killer, Leo. Just one we underestimated." I winked and pulled away. I said to Johnson, "Thanks for all your help."

He looked between me and Leo. "Yeah, sure. I think. He looks worried." He nodded to Leo.

"He shouldn't be. I have a stun gun, and I'm not afraid to use it." I patted my bag. Following a flash of a smile, I split.

Precious was sitting in her SUV, engine idling when I pulled up. As we sped toward Seattle, I told her everything I'd learned at the community center. Including how the money trail ended with the money going into an account for J.M. Chapman, our Jenna Miller.

"Do you know she emailed me once the other day and thanked me for being so kind and for talking about silver linings. She even said she read one of the books I recommended and enjoyed it. I actually questioned my impression of her. Wondered if I was wrong." Precious's face screwed up in anger. "When we get there, I'm gonna—"

"Do nothing because this girl is a killer. She likely killed Josh, is probably the one who ran me down, and we now know stole a crap ton of money. We need a plan that involves more than you pushing her to the ground like you did last time." I tapped the console where the clock was. "And we've got only two hours to perfect it."

Precious sighed heavily and pushed back in her seat in frustration. "We should have stopped by Mrs. Wright's before we left."

In hindsight, that would have been a smart move.

"Let's talk through some options that go beyond us walking up to the door and pounding on it," I said.

"All I got is we stop and get a pizza and we knock on her door like we're delivering pizza but to the wrong address," Precious said.

"And then what? I zap her and hold her there until Leo gets a search warrant and can call the Seattle police to come get her? But I like the pizza idea. Let's eat one while we think it over."

We got two custom large pizzas from Mod Pizza located a handful of miles from Jenna's apartment. Then we sat in Precious's car and stared up at Jenna's apartment looking for signs of life while we ate.

Call me crazy, but the vibe I got from the place was that it was empty. She wasn't home. There didn't seem to be any movement in the place. Lights weren't going on or off. The curtains were open, and I hadn't seen shadows or someone moving around within like I did in the place below hers.

"She's not there," I said and smacked myself in the forehead with the cardboard pizza box twice. "Why would she take all that money and stay in that dump of a place? She split."

Precious was out of the car before me. We took the stairs two at a time.

She stopped to rap on the door, but instinct told me to go all the way. I turned the handle and found the front door unlocked. The door swung open to an empty apartment. Everything was gone. On the counter that overlooked the tiny kitchen was a donation slip from the Salvation Army with a list of itemized furniture they'd collected. Not the computer stuff, of course. She either took that or sold it elsewhere. But she hadn't left it behind for the cops to confiscate. The ankle bracelet, still blinking like it was attached, sat next to the donation slip.

I pointed it out to Precious. "That's disturbing."

"What do you make of this?" Precious said and jerked her thumb to a picture on the wall that hung in the exact spot Precious had suggested. It was a tropical scene, lapping waves with foamy tips breaking on a sandy beach, footsteps imprinted in the sand. Some were in stages of disappearing as the waves were washing them out.

Hanging from the corner of the frame was a small 3x5 Post-it note. Precious stepped closer. "See what visualizing and setting goals can do? You were right," she read, admiration in her voice.

"There's nothing to admire about a killer."

Precious harrumphed. "I'm admiring the determination. Because that gets results." She handed me the small yellow note.

It took a lot for me to not roll my eyes.

On the back Jenna had written, *Thanks for all the advice. I found my silver lining and plan to enjoy every dime.* She signed it with a J that she made look like a dragon.

Jenna Miller was drgnbait@techsavvy.com. Jenna Miller had sent Josh the email asking him to take the money and run away to Fiji. She'd always planned on ditching her tracking bracelet and going on the lam. Which means Jenna Miller lied about being done with Josh. She'd been in cahoots with him before and likely never stopped. Kalan Johnson had mentioned the Pay Forward for the Kids IT person, and I had hard money on it being Jenna.

I scrolled through all the information Toby had sent me on Jenna until I found her parole officer's name. I gave him a call, explained who I was, and that I was standing in Jenna's apartment, staring at her bracelet, which wasn't around her leg.

19

ON THE RIDE HOME, Precious and I binge ate through our frustration. Krispy Kreme donuts, a family-sized bag of M&Ms, fries from one drive-thru and burgers from another.

"We'd had her and let her go," I said for what was surely the hundredth time. I scanned the log sheet Jenna's parole officer gave me. The tracking bracelet showed one trip to Wind River, the day Jenna stole the briefcase. No other trips. Not that I thought this list was accurate.

"It's like I got so caught up with being a PI that I forgot all my life coach training. I *know how* to read people. *I knew* she was unstable, but I didn't do the math." Precious tossed a handful of M&Ms in her mouth. Some spilled from the side and went in between the seat cracks.

"Considering I'm the PI here, I feel doubly worse. Is doubly a word?" My stomach didn't feel so good. Like maybe I needed a salad.

"We really jacked this up," she said.

"Doubly," I added. I looked at the mug shot of Jenna her PO had provided me. It was more current than her driver's license photo. "I'm gonna see if the IT guy at the community center can provide other dates that place her in town besides when she went to meet Gillian. At a minimum, if DB thinks he can charge me, Lockett can use all this in my defense." Ugh, the thought alone made me want to barf. I crafted an email to Kalan Johnson and included Jenna's image, but sending it gave little relief.

I asked, "Do you think Jenna knew Josh had returned one of the two tickets to Fiji?"

Precious stared at me wide eyed. "And if she did, she would then know he planned to go without her, likely taking all the money with him."

I nodded solemnly, "Yep, leaving her once again high and dry and primed to take the fall. That, my fabulous friend is motive."

"We screwed the pooch here, Sam. Messed up."

I rubbed my temples, hoping to stave off a headache. "This case is too much."

When my phone rang, I glanced at the screen. Private caller, no number. Rachel. Calling from the ship phone.

"Hey," I said. Was I supposed to be with Cora? I wasn't able to take her to the beach because of the getting-run-down-by-a-car thing. The folks and I were trying to shelter her as much as possible from everything that was going on. In my opinion, we were doing a great job because she hadn't spilled any of this to Rachel so far.

"Are you kidding me?" Rachel screamed.

I held the phone away from my ear. I didn't need to put in on speaker because she was so loud, but I did because I had no intention of yelling back.

I said, "What—?"

"You're the prime suspect in Principal Josh's murder? Principal Josh was *murdered*? What is going on there? I swear to heaven, Sam, if Cora is in the middle of this, I will *never* forgive you." She said *never* with such venom a shiver of fear ran through me.

The best defense is a good offense. "Uh, did Cora tell you all this?"

A long pause. "Well, no."

What a relief. "That's because she has no clue. We've kept it all from her. Her life is all rainbows and unicorns right now." Saying unicorns conjured up visions of Unicorn Brew, and my stomach churned. I'd definitely overdone it on the sweets. Even the thought of them made me queasy.

"I'm trying to catch up on my news. We've been slammed here, and I was going through Dad's paper online when I saw the article." She was still irritated. "Someone could have told me."

"When? When you called Cora? Were we supposed to ask her to leave the room? That's not suspicious at all."

"You could have emailed me."

She had me there. Truth was, I'd been hoping Rachel never found out. Now, my next objective was to keep the full weight of the situation from her. "Except is this some-thing for an email? You said so yourself you've been slammed. Imagine getting that email and not being able to call home. We were trying to be considerate."

She huffed out a sigh. This was a clue I was winning. Time for the final drive down the field. "And soon Dad'll be posting an article saying I'm no longer the primary person of interest. Precious and I have discovered Josh had an accomplice. My guess is she'll become the primary. DB will keep me in there because he likes to torment me."

"An accomplice? What in the world was he doing? He seemed like such a nice man." She'd been bamboozled like the rest of the community.

In full disclosure, I felt smug that Josh hadn't wooed me. Like maybe I was getting better at reading people.

"Well, he was *not* a nice man, Rachel. He was a con man. He was skimming money from people, stealing from Laura Danner and the school board. He was bad, bad, bad." I shook my finger at the phone.

"When you say it like that it sounds like you didn't like him. I can see why DB thought maybe you did it. You're passionate about your dislike."

"That doesn't mean I killed him. Lots of people dislike lots of other people and don't kill them," I said.

"Who do you think killed him?" Her voice sounded tiny, scared. I supposed I would be, too, if my kid was attending the school where the principal was murdered.

"Cora's safe," I said. "We think the person who did this was the same one who helped him con other school districts. She's left the country." I add the last part for reassurance.

Rachel blew out a slow, steady breath. "I hate this

deployment. I hate that there is nothing I can do to protect Cora."

"Rach, Mom and Dad did a great job with us. They've got her covered. She's safe and happy. She misses you, but Dad keeps her distracted with football. She's gonna be a pro by the time you get home."

Rachel groaned then laughed. "I still kick butt in my fantasy league."

I laughed with her. Glad she sounded more relieved. "I can't get into a fantasy league around here because of Dad. I have to play anonymously online."

A loud pinging sounded in the background.

Rachel said, "Crap, I have to go. Some fake drill. Tell Cora I'll try to call on Sunday. Same time."

"Okay, take care of yourself. Love ya a bushel and a peck," I said. This was something that came from our grandfather on our mom's side. He used to say it to us all the time. Now we said it to each other and to Cora.

"And a hug around the neck," she said before disconnecting.

Precious gave me a look that said we dodged a bullet. "Glad she didn't know about the drive-by rundown."

I closed my eyes in relief. "No kidding. Can you imagine if she'd have wanted to FaceTime? I'll have to cake on the makeup for Sunday's call." My poor control freak sister could read trouble into anything.

Trouble with Josh's death was I had the who died and where they died, but I didn't have the why or how.

Jenna Miller's how: dunno

Jenna Miller's why: to take all the money

When we pulled up to my apartment, the day was close to ending. Streetlights were on, and the crescent moon was bright. Leo's cruiser was parked to the side of the building. We both saw it but said nothing. Precious followed me up the stairs where Leo sat in a lawn chair I'd set out on the landing. He looked beat. His five o'clock shadow looked to be two days worth of growth, scraggy and sexy.

His legs were out in front of him, crossed at the ankle, and his eyes were closed. Two bottles of local IP were by the chair.

I knew he wasn't sleeping. His hunting skills were too strong to sleep through two loud women clumping upstairs. "Are those the beers from my fridge?"

"Yup, you're all out," he said without opening his eyes. "I ate the cookies you had, too."

"There were cookies?" I plugged the six-digit entry number into the keypad that disengaged the lock to the front door. My place used to be my parents' vacation rental. I might have the luxury of living in a place my parents owned, but I was paying vacation rental prices for it.

I flung the door open, and from where I stood, I could see the small galley kitchen. A two-person bar was at the end of the kitchen counter. On it was a plate in my mother's dish pattern with the cellophane pulled back and crumbs. Nothing else.

"Were they good?" I asked him.

"Fabulous. Little heavy on the sprinkles." He sat up with a sigh and stretched his arms over his head.

Precious and I watched as his back muscles rippled under his shirt. Leo had always been a fine specimen of a man. Even in high school. His dark Native American skin would get richer from the time spent in the summer sun, and he'd come back to school looking like some folklore god.

"Good thing I ate my body weight in junk food on the way back or I'd be seriously ticked," I told him.

"Tell me about Jenna Miller," he said.

Between Precious and I, we filled him in on the events of our trip, the tracking bracelet, and the picture she left behind with the Post-it note.

"I'm guessing she offed him," I said. "I'm hoping this new information will help DB see the error of his ways and provide a new focus for this investigation."

Leo rubbed a hand down his face. He didn't look happy, and the sense that something bigger had happened while Precious and I were in Seattle settled over me.

"Just tell me," I said. "Like a Band-aid, rip it off."

Leo crossed his arms over his chest and ducked his head. "The toxicology report came back. The water bottles showed a slight trace of nicotine."

A picture flashed in my mind, the image of Josh holding a water bottle with pink water. I said, "Maybe it was those tablets he put in his drink. He had one that day he died."

Precious snapped her fingers. "Jenna knew about those tablets."

I watched Leo's face. His expression was impassive.

"Spill," I said. "What are you leading up to? Just say it already."

Leo sat up. "The nicotine levels in Josh's system were off the charts. Though the amount in the water bottle was small, it contributed to Josh's levels, but wasn't the primary source, after the vaping and patches."

"Nicotine?" I said. "Are we back to this mysterious vaping disease? Could the levels in his vial been too much?" Dad's article had said the CDC couldn't pinpoint a cause, flavored vape juice being the only common denominator.

Leo propped his foot against my railing and rested his forearm across his knee. "Yeah, it's possible. Doc is talking to the CDC to see if nicotine poisoning is a possibility for all those affected." Doc was the medical examiner.

Precious said, "I know nicotine is bad, but I never knew it could be used as a poison."

Leo nodded. "It can be. A few cases of someone being murdered by nicotine exist, but it takes a lot."

"So, we're back to Josh's death being a coincidence or possibly part of an epidemic?" I shook my head in disbelief. If either were true, Josh's karma caught up with him in a spectacular fashion.

"Maybe," Leo said. "But there was another vial in his drawer. Rolling around with items like fidget spinners, a few cell phones, a slingshot, and some rocks."

"Oooh," Precious said and raised her hand. "I know. I know. What are things a teacher confiscates?"

Leo tossed back his head and laughed. When he stopped, he pointed to her and said, "Jeopardy."

I grunted from frustration and snatched the beer from his hand then took a drink. "So what's that mean. That a kid might have something to do with this? That he confiscated bad juice off one of the kids? If that's true, I quit. I'll go full time at *Click and Shop*. No more of this PI gig. Because this is an elementary school we're talking about."

Leo stood. "The vial's being tested for toxins and fingerprints. As are the flavor water tablets Josh put in his drink. I'm making no assumptions until that information comes back. You'll know when I know."

FOLLOWING MY HIT-AND-RUN ADVENTURE, my parents gave me a gym membership to the local fitness center, a not-so-subtle message that they worried about me and didn't want me running on the roads. I'd gone to the gym before to do drop-in yoga classes. Now I looked forward to the luxury of going when I wanted instead of when I could afford it. My parents got no complaints from me.

The gym's downside was the Hunter Boot Moms. I expected to run into at least one of them at every class. They were exercise fiends, or so it seemed. I'd only seen Mindy and another one whose name I couldn't remember.

Today was the first day I braved doing something more than downward dog; I caught an early morning spin class. My hip felt better, though the bruise was an ugly brownish green the size of my head. No one had to see

that. The fast pace of the class was exactly what I needed
to take my mind off the bomb Leo dropped on Friday.

I had no idea what the outcome would be from the
fingerprints test, but whatever they were couldn't be good.
Either the police would have a new suspect or DB would
ransack my life looking for proof the vial belonged to me.
And with Toby in my life, the chances of an empty vape
juice vial being around were high.

Toni, the owner of the fitness center, was also the spin
instructor. Toni had graduated from Wind River five years
before me. She was solid muscles and intimidating. Obviously, she took fitness seriously, and there wasn't a muscle
on her body that wasn't chiseled. She sported a fake tan,
insanely white teeth, and long dark hair that looked brit-
tle. Like a good brushing would snap off strands.

We were twenty minutes into the class, Toni barking
orders for us to kick it up a notch, when we started doing
sprints, a sequence that comprised standing to peddle for
a count of four then on the saddle for a count of four, then
repeat. Toni's count was quick, and I was panting from the
exertion of trying to keep up. On the third cycle of sprint-
ing, I was on the up count when I noticed Leo peering into
the class.

The spin room was large and square with a series of
windows that looked out into the weight room. Someone, Toni I assumed, had taped motivational posters
over two-thirds of the windows. Only a small sliver of
exposed window at the top could be seen. I'd pop up
for the sprint, and there was Leo searching the faces of
the class participants. I'd drop back into the saddle,

and he'd disappear. We did three ups and downs before he spotted me and gave me the "urgent-eye," a pointed look that conveyed he had something big to say. On the fourth up, he signaled with a nod for me to come out.

I glanced at Toni. She was the sort who would passive-aggressively berate anyone for quitting halfway. I grunted with frustration and stayed in the saddle for the next pop up, bringing the peddles to a stop.

"No quitting, Samantha," she yelled without sounding breathless.

"I'll be right back." I pointed to the door. "Police are out there looking for me." Why I felt the need to explain, who knows.

She gave me a narrowed look then inspected the window on her next pop up.

Outside, Leo was waiting by the door. "Get your stuff. We have to go."

I pointed to the room behind me. "I'm in the middle of a class. I'm all sweaty."

Leo leaned in closer, and I resisted the urge to lean away. I had pit stains and no makeup on. My hair was in a ponytail that was listing to the side, and I couldn't remember if I had brushed my teeth after coffee this morning.

He said in a low voice, "The results from the vial in Josh's desk drawer came back."

"Did they find anything unusual in it? Too much nicotine?"

He dragged his hands down his face in exhaustion.

"No, standard bubble gum flavored vape juice, but they pulled fingerprints off the vial."

My heart stutter with anticipation. "And?"

"Josh's prints were on it. But so were Levi Danner's." He shook his head in disbelief. "DB has gone out to the Danner's to bring Levi in for questioning."

How would a vial from Levi's get to a school Levi didn't attend? Very clever of Josh to hide a vial in plain sight.

"What do you want from me?" I wasn't sure how I figured into this picture. Levi Danner was just a kid. A kid with a history of trouble and anger control issues. A kid who was part of Josh's scam program.

"I want you to talk to Laura. I can't imagine Levi doing something like this." At a closer look, Leo looked flustered. Maybe it rattled his cop senses to think he'd been coaching a kid who murdered a guy.

"You can't imagine. You have to stay unbiased," I said, using his words.

He pressed his lips together for a second then said, "I know. You don't have to remind me."

"Clearly, I do."

"Carl was my friend. He was Cowlitz. And we take care of people in our tribe. I need to help them."

"Being unbiased helps them—"

He interrupted and pointed to the door. "Are we going to do this all day, or can we go? I'll drive us to Laura's."

I didn't move. "Maybe I should go to Laura's. Without you." The Pilates class was letting out and soon my spin class would end, too. In moments we'd be surrounded by tons of ears.

He shook his head.

I snagged him by the elbow and led him toward the front of the gym. "Leo, if you show DB you have a vested interest in this, you'll be cut from the case. Frozen out. If you want me to help this kid, I need an inside man, and my inside man is you."

He studied me. As if my words made too much sense and he couldn't believe they came from me. Or maybe that was my interpretation when all he was doing was considering his options.

"If Levi did this, then he'll pay. But if he didn't, I don't want him railroaded by DB." He crossed his arms. "Don't go home, go directly to her. She needs to know this was important enough for you to drop everything."

I nodded.

He gave a small smile. "You're picking up this PI thing, Sam. Well done."

I laughed. "Now look who's Wheel of Fortune and who's Jeopardy."

Leo snort laughed. "Not in your wildest dreams."

I gave him a shove then headed for the ladies locker room. I scrubbed my face and patted down my hair before grabbing my gym bag and heading out to LC.

Leo was sitting in his cruiser in the parking lot on his phone. I gave him a wave as I pulled out of the lot and pointed my car toward the Danner's place.

By the time I arrived, DB and Cody Hinkle, the force's sergeant, were there. I pulled LC to the side of the yard and stepped out. I was witnessing a family's nightmare. DB was escorting Levi to the patrol car, his hands behind his back in cuffs. Laura was screaming at DB and crying. A younger girl was standing in the doorway sobbing. I figured her for the younger Danner kid, Lanie. Hinkle was escorting an evidence bag to the second patrol car.

"It's okay, Mom," Levi kept saying.

His face didn't look like it was okay. He looked seconds from crying. He was pale with blotches of red on his cheeks and neck. Like holding his tears back was burning him up from the inside out.

DB opened the patrol door and guided Levi in.

"No!" Laura screamed and bolted for DB, hands raised in attack mode. I was perpendicular to them and took off running. I caught Laura before she made contact with DB.

"Let go," she screamed as she flailed against me. "That's my baby."

"I know," I said in my calmest voice. "He's okay. Leo is waiting for him at the station."

"You can't take him," she wailed at a pitch so high I expected dogs to bark. She was fighting with everything she had, straining to break free from my grip.

"Laura," I said sternly. "You're scaring him. You're scaring your daughter."

Instantly, she crumbled in my arms, wrapping her arms around my neck, her body shaking from her sobs.

"It's okay, Mom," Levi said, his voice quivering.

She straightened, still leaning heavily against me. "I love you, Levi. I'll get you out of this as fast as I can."

He shook his head. DB slammed the door, cutting off anything Levi might have said in response.

DB approached us. "What are you doing here, Samantha? Come to gloat because you think you're off the hook?" When he crossed his arms, his biceps flexed.

I curled my lip at him before turning my attention to Laura. "Can you stand?"

"I think so," she said. She squared her shoulders and took in a deep breath.

I let go and took a step back. "Then go stand with your daughter." The girl looked barely out of elementary school. "Do you have family you can call? Maybe she should go to them."

Laura nodded. With shaky hands, she patted at her pants. "I think I left my phone at the shop. Lanie called frantic, and I just dashed over here." She glanced at the office building. "I'm not sure I even closed the door."

"I'll go check. I'll look on your desk for your phone. You can use mine if you want in the meantime." I held out my phone.

She shook her head, then moved toward her daughter, opening her arms to embrace her as she approached.

I turned to DB and tsked. "Shame on you."

"For what? I'm doing my job."

He was a pompous butthead. "Why didn't you bring Levi down for questioning?"

"Not that I owe you any explanation, but we were going to. But we served our handy search warrant first, and surprise! We found some questionable items and that, my dumb friend, means Levi Danner is under arrest."

I snorted in disgust. Then I went to the cruiser, I made sure to bump DB with my shoulder when I passed. I opened the passenger door and leaned in. "Listen to me,

Levi. Don't say anything. Not one word. You understand? Not to anyone. Even if they don't have on a uniform."

DB came to the door and started to close it. "Get out of there, Samantha, before I arrest you for obstructing justice."

I shoved it back open and kept my hand on it. There was no way I would win this one because DB was far stronger. But I was more determined.

"You understand, Levi?"

He nodded, looking like a deer in headlights.

I said, "A lawyer by the name of Tyson Lockett will come. He'll represent you. You can talk to him."

Levi nodded.

"Say this name, Levi. Tyson Lockett."

"Tyson Lockett," Levi said robotically.

DB was pressing at the door, and I knew he'd squish me. "Nobody but Tyson," I said as I backed away.

DB slammed the door and glared at me. "What do you think you're doing?"

"I'm balancing the scales of justice." I crossed my arms. "He's just a kid, DB."

"Who maybe murdered someone."

"I suppose it's encouraging you used the word 'maybe.' Though, just yesterday, you thought I did it. Keep that in mind." Score one for me.

"I don't think. I follow the clues. I follow the evidence."

I closed my eyes and took a deep breath to gather my wits before I slugged him. I opened my eyes and looked right at him when I said, "Trouble is DB, you couldn't follow a trail of anything unless it was littered with steroids, naked women, and protein shakes."

His expression said I bored him. "Your example doesn't work because that means I *could* follow a trail."

I huffed and stomped off to Laura. When I reached her, I said in a low voice, "I'm going to your office to make sure it's locked up. You make sure Hinkle sticks to the search warrant. Then I'll drive you to the station. I already told Levi not to speak with anyone, and I'll call a good lawyer for him. Call family. Bring help."

She stared at me, eyes round like an owl and glassy, probably from shock. A tear leaked out, another followed.

"Mom," Lanie said. "What's happening? Why are they taking Levi?"

Laura leaned the side of her head against the top of her daughter's. "They think Levi had something to do with Josh's death."

Levi's sister sighed heavily. "That's just great. Kids at school have been asking if we're preppers. If we think the apocalypse is coming. Now they're gonna give me a hard time because my brother is accused of murder."

21

MONDAY

LEO WAS WAITING outside the station when we got there.
I'd expected him to be inside with Levi. Laura's in-laws
took Lanie to their house, and I drove Laura to the station.
Lockett was on his way down from Seattle.

"He doesn't look happy," Laura said as she stared
at Leo.

That was an understatement. Leo was at Laura's
passenger door as soon as I parked.

"Don't get out," Leo said as he opened her door but
blocked her from exiting my car. "I have something to tell
you, and it's best you hear it while you're sitting down."

Laura gulped, the sound filling the quiet space. "Just
spill it."

"Levi confessed," he said.

In unison, Laura and I said, "What?"

I said, "I told him not say *anything*. Lockett is coming
down as we speak."

Laura said, "Confessed to what? Not for killing Josh. That's impossible."

Leo's gaze darted from me to her. "He said he killed Josh."

She shook her head wildly. "No, that's impossible."

I tried to shrink into my seat. Not only did I not want to be witness to this family's grief and troubles, I didn't want to compound the experience Laura and her family were having. Essentially, I was a stranger to them and seeing their most private problems.

Leo said, "I sent Samantha to help you, Laura. If you say it's impossible that Levi killed Josh, then you have to take action. Samantha is a private investigator. Let her help you prove Levi is innocent."

Laura glanced to me, then Leo. "It's convenient she was once the suspect and now my child is. How hard is she going to help?"

I looked to Leo for a sign that he thought I should speak up. He nodded.

"Laura, I didn't kill Josh, and even though I knew I was innocent, I wasn't about to leave my fate to the hands of DB Louney. He designated me as a person of interest only because I was in the room when Josh died. Are you willing to leave Levi's fate up to DB, his laziness, and the courts?"

Leo added, "Think about how easy it is to misconstrue information. You thought Samantha was guilty because of what? Her... err... husband's actions? You had no other facts. I can guarantee dissecting and misconstruing your life will happen if Levi goes to trial. Your past, your lifestyle, everything about your family, will be scrutinized and twisted."

"And how will hiring her stop that? It'll happen now that Levi's been brought in," Laura said.

"The best defense is a good offense," I said. "You have to go on the offense now. Don't wait. DB was determined to prove I was guilty, and I needed to prove I wasn't. That's how he's going to approach Levi's case. I've been working the case trying to prove my innocence. I can do that for Levi. I dug into the background of Josh Chapman. Josh wasn't a nice man. He may have looked upstanding, but behind the scenes, he was committing crimes."

Laura buried her head in her hands. "What have I done? All I wanted was to bring a positive influence into Levi's life. He misses his dad, and I thought Josh might fill that void, even a little bit would be a good thing." Her shoulders shook from her sobs.

Leo and I looked at each other over her bowed head, neither knowing what to do. I patted her shoulder in what I hoped was comfort.

"What happens now that Levi has confessed?" I asked.

Leo's expression was grim. "They're processing him now. He'll have to be arraigned, and the judge will decide if bail will be set. The prosecution is building a case as we speak."

Laura shot up in a snap. She trembled underneath my hand, and I pulled it back.

She pushed Leo aside and hopped out of LC. She spun to face us. "I can't believe this is happening. I can't believe all the damage Josh has done to my family." She pointed to me, her eyes large and wild. "There's nothing you can do to help me. You're bad luck or something. Just stay away."

Laura put her focus directly on Leo and stuck out her arms, crossing them at the wrist in a gesture that said she expected him to arrest her. "Levi didn't kill Josh. I did. He confessed to protect me." She shook her head wildly. "Though how he knew what I'd done is anyone's guess."

To Leo's credit, he didn't move. Not a flinch. I suppose this was where being a jeopardy smart cop came into play. "And how did you kill Josh?"

Laura heaved, her arms lifting then dropping as she kept them outstretched. "I poisoned him."

Leo waited. I waited.

She sighed again. "With pesticides. Duh." Her bravado was fake. After she said it, she'd immediately pressed her lips together, which did nothing to stop their trembling.

I'd put fifty bucks on Laura being a liar. She was too much of a mess. I suppose one could argue that she might be this way because she'd been cornered into confessing, but had she done it, she'd have never let her kid get taken away by the cops. One thing that wasn't fake was her love for her children.

Leo said, "And how did you use these pesticides?"

"Are you going to arrest me or not? I just confessed." She jiggled her arms in front of him, her voice wavering.

"Let's go inside, and we'll talk. Samantha will go get her mother so you can have a lawyer." Gently, Leo put a hand on her shoulder.

"Tyson Lockett is on his way. I'll get my mom until he gets here."

Leo gave me a nod. "Come on inside, Laura, and let's get this worked out."

I waited until they were inside before I hoofed it over to my mom's office. Her secretary waved me through.

I burst into her office, my hip aching slightly where I'd been hit by the car.

"Samantha," she said, coming to a stand. "I thought we bought you a gym membership so you wouldn't be running on the streets. I have one daughter on a ship in the middle of who knows what ocean and one daughter getting run down by hybrid cars but can't stay off the street. Is it too much to ask for just one of you to be boring and to stay home and do something like knit?"

I sucked in a large breath of air and blew it out slowly as I tried to catch my breath. "I just came from the police station."

She pressed her palms to her desk as if the hard surface was giving her strength. "I can't wait to hear this. Should I sit?"

I closed her office door behind me before saying, "Levi Danner was arrested for Josh's murder. Leo said they discovered nicotine in Josh's system. There was a vial of nicotine in Josh's desk with his prints and Levi's. DB went to Levi's house today with a warrant and found the same stuff there. He arrested Levi."

"Oh, dear," Mom said.

"That's not all. Laura then confessed to killing Josh. I think she's making it up. But you need to get to the station.

Lockett is on his way, but they need an attorney for now. Can you help?"

Mom sat and buried her head in her hands. "Poor Laura. That woman has the worst luck." She pressed the button on her desk phone to access her secretary. "Dana, cancel my appointments for the rest of the day, please."

Mom kept a mini fridge behind her desk and stocked it with goodies. Oddly, she liked her chocolate cold and her water at room temperature. From the fridge I helped myself to a Seattle chocolate San Juan bar and one of the few bottles of water she kept in there for those of us who liked it cold. I replaced it with the water from her stock by the fridge.

I leaned on the corner of her desk and ate half the chocolate bar in two bites. She took a chunk of my chocolate.

"Leo wants me to help prove Levi's innocence. I suppose Laura's now, too."

Mom reached for more chocolate. "Did she hire you?"

I held the remaining chocolate behind me, not willing to share. "No, I'm not sure what I'm supposed to do now. Can't butt into their business without their consent."

"I'll talk to her, but have Lockett talk to her as well. You need to get started on digging into possible other scenarios as soon as possible. If she doesn't hire you, she needs to hire someone."

Ever since DB had announced I was the person of interest without so much as looking into other suspects, I had this sour taste regarding the wheels of justice when left in the hands of law enforcement, and it wasn't a taste I wanted to have. On the whole, I believed those in law enforcement were good and well-intended, but wondered if the system wasn't severely jacked up.

"This is a stupid question coming from a PI, albeit a fairly new one, but aren't all people presumed innocent until proven guilty? DB was ready to throw me in jail and throw away the key." A frightening thought.

Mom leaned forward and crossed her arms on the desk in front of her. "I don't want you to think the justice system is broken. It's not. It's flawed, I won't argue that, but when done properly, the system works."

I played with the foil of the candy bar wrapper. "Is 'when done properly' the key?"

Mom gave her words thought then said, "Yes and no. If you were to poll police officers around the nation about how they go about solving a crime, the answers would vary. There's no right or wrong way. Some officers believe if they have a strong lead, they go with that until it falls apart, then they go to the next strongest lead. Others chase down every lead, big or small."

I scoffed. "Chasing down every lead seems like the right way."

"Sure, but in an investigative situation, time is of the essence. If the officer is chasing down every lead, does a trail go cold in the meantime?" Mom said.

She was right. There was no right or wrong. There were only people doing hard work, trying to find answers. Cops were people, and they weren't perfect and neither were their methods. Though I still didn't feel good about DB as he seemed too shortsighted for my taste. "So, DB is a chase-the-strongest-lead-until-it-fizzles kinda cop. Leo is a chase every lead kinda cop."

Mom nodded. "Neither will make you popular if something in the case goes wrong. And this is where working in the justice system gets hairy. People will always be ready to criticize the cop's methods, the lawyers, and even those who file the evidence. People's behaviors, lifestyles, and beliefs are called into question, not just the person on trial, but everyone connected with the case. Justice is rarely a cut and dry situation. Take Laura, for example. If she or her son get charged, you can bet their self-sufficient lifestyle will be used against them."

"But why? Who cares?" I still didn't get it.

Mom took another chocolate from the fridge. "Everyone, if it's the reason the crime was committed. We think serial killers and evil people look different, can be picked out of a crowd. But they aren't different. They look like everyone else. Focusing on the one aspect that made the evil person different from us is how people come to terms with people they know who commit crimes." She was matter-of-fact in her explanations. "No one lives a sanitized life that would withstand scrutiny."

"You and Dad are pretty vanilla," I countered.

Mom chuckled and said with a mischievous glint in her eye, "Well, we do like to play Mobster and Moll—"

I covered my ears and hummed. "I don't want to know this," I said on repeat to wash out the sound of her voice.

She laughed and pulled my hands from my ears. "In all seriousness, you need to think hard about being a PI. Cases like this will haunt you. Sometimes you'll wonder if you've helped a bad person go free. Sometimes you'll never know, and that's the really hard stuff to deal with. You'll also have to deal with people who associate you with the guilty party because you took a job."

"You're saying if I take this job, and if Laura or Levi are convicted and the self-sufficient thing looked to play a part, it'll create a negative connotation, and I'll be linked because of association." I shook my head.

"Exactly. You need to think of the endgame, the outcome, and consequences every time you take more cases like this," Mom cautioned.

Fear made rational people do stupid things. Fear over-rode common sense every time.

I'd experienced this and watched as it happened to others. This case could go sideways fast, and I'd be involved even more deeply than I already was. If either of the Danners weren't convicted, and no one was charged with Josh's death, my involvement would be scrutinized and the conspiracy theorists would have a heyday. Of course, the same would happen if one of the Danners was convicted.

I wasn't a stranger to being the odd man out. When you come from a family of overachievers and you're the underachiever, you get used to being overlooked and underestimated and talked about. That fact would work to my benefit with cases like this. If I took more. But there was no way I was walking away from this case now. Not after being the first person of interest and knowing no one was looking for the real murderer but me.

Mom brushed back a wisp of my hair that had freed

itself from my ponytail. "You could always open up your photography studio. Give your mom one less thing to worry about."

I met her gaze. "No, I can't. No more than you can just be the mayor of a small town."

The intercom buzzed, and Dana's voice came through. "Your schedule is clear, Madam Mayor."

Mom rolled her eyes. "Thanks, Dana."

Dana laughed then disconnected.

Mom opened a desk drawer and took out her purse. She slammed it closed with a push from her knee. "Time to go make sure Lady Justice has her chance."

I slid off the desk, crammed the last chocolate piece in my mouth, and ignored the slight shake in my hand. I might have been woefully unprepared as a PI, but I was determined to leave no stone unturned, regardless of the outcome. The truth of who killed Josh Chapman would come to light, and the right person would go to jail.

22

MOM STAYED LATE at the police station, working with Lockett and the Danners. Dad was at the paper putting stories to bed. I had kid duty. Hanging with Cora was a welcome relief after all the adulting I'd been doing. Truth be told, hanging with Cora or Simon the dog were the highlights of my day. Maybe that's why Precious looked for Bigfoot; it was a good escape from the real world.

Cora and I ordered pizza, splurged on the cinnamon sticks, and I let Cora drink her body weight in Sprite. A luxury Rachel doled out for good behavior.

Afterward, we did each other's makeup using bright blues and purples, gave each other wacky hairstyles, and let loose by playing Super Mario Cart. The Switch was a gift to Cora from my parents just because. They'd given it to her when we'd returned from seeing Rachel off. This kid of Rachel's was clever enough to rarely mention the gaming system when she talked to her mom. If Rachel thought the system was being overly used, she would limit it. I hated to tell Rachel that this adorable genius kid of hers was more like me than she'd like.

"You look like a clown," Cora said as she ate around the crust on her second piece of cheese pizza.

Cora had crafted large raccoon-like circles around my eyes.

"You don't think I should wear this blue under my eyes? I kinda like the effect." It made my face look sallower, and with the right shadows, kinda creepy. In the bright light of my childhood kitchen, I looked like I'd put my face on while sitting passenger in a monster truck as it jumped over vehicles. Like that commercial where the lady comes out of the airplane restroom with lipstick all around her mouth? She had nothing on me.

Cora shrugged. "Maybe. If you wanted to be a zombie."

"What do you know about zombies?" A scary topic for me in my thirties. What must a six-year-old think?

"The kids were talking about it at school." She nibbled her pizza an inch from the crust line before discarding it.

"In class?" Kindergartners knew about zombies? Man, times had changed.

"No, on the playground. Some older kids. They were saying Principal Josh was going to come back and eat our brains if we didn't give them our dessert at lunch." Her lower lip wobbled. "The dessert is really good. Like cake and Rice Krispies Treats like Mimi makes."

I pulled her onto my lap. "Cora, I'm gonna go to school and take care of these kids for you. Because no one should take another's dessert. That's just wrong on so many levels. But I want you to know there is no such thing as zombies. Never has been such a thing. It's all made up."

She pressed against me. "How do you know?"

"Well, I've been on this earth longer than you, and I've seen some things. None of them were zombies. Mimi and Grampi have been on this earth longer than me, and if there were zombies, Grampi would have put it in the paper. *Everything* goes in his paper. When you were born, you made the front-page news." I hugged her tight. "Those kids are being big meanies, and I'll fix that."

"Don't tell them it came from me." Her brow knitted in worry.

I shook my head. "Of course not. They aren't even going to know I'm there because of the dessert. You let me take care of this."

She didn't look reassured, but slightly... sad?

"What else is bothering you?" I rubbed her back, hoping she'd relax enough to tell me.

"I believe you when you say zombies are fake, but I thought if Principal Josh could come back as a zombie, then maybe my dad could, too, and I could meet him."

Man, this kid was crushing me tonight. Her dad, a Marine, died in combat before Cora was born. Rachel and Jeff planned to elope as soon as his deployment was over, only he never came home. Wrecked my sister and the rest of us.

"Oh, piglet," I said, using my sister's nickname for her daughter. "I wish you could have met your dad, too. But you know, just because we don't see him, doesn't mean he's not here." I explained that her dad was in the curls of her hair—Rachel's hair was straight. Or the brown of her eyes—Rachel's were blue like mine. I held her for a bit and told her stories about her father. Stories Rachel had told me. When we were both so maudlin I wanted to crawl into bed and hide under the covers, I changed things up.

"Listen, we can't go to bed sad. That won't do at all." Lately, the days had been filled with yucky people and bad acts. I needed some laughter or else my soul was going to shrivel and die.

"What should we do?" She slid off my lap and went for a cinnamon breadstick, a good sign. If she was up for eating, then she was up for more.

A movie would take too long, and I'd promised not to leave the house with Cora because I was a magnet for trouble so a walk was out of the question. My gaze fell on the Nintendo Switch.

Bingo.

I tightened the two ponytails on the top of my head, positioned to look like horns, and stood. "We need to dance more," I said.

I plugged in the dance game and set us up.

"Because we just ate, this might make you vomit. If you feel like the pizza is gonna revisit us, you run to the toilet and do it there," I said.

Cora wrinkled her nose. "That's gross."

"That's life, kid."

We started with an easy dance, but the third song had moves that were quicker and goofier. I made a few errors on purpose to make Cora laugh. My hip was throbbing and I'd broken out in a sweat, but we were having a blast.

Cora and I were busting a move. I performed a wild spin and in doing so caught sight of Leo and my Mom standing at the edge of the living room, watching us. The smile on my mom's face was pure joy. The one on Leo's was something else.

I was never going to live this down.

"Cora," I said. I'd stopped dancing. "Mimi's home."

Cora spun around and squealed. "Look, Mimi, we did each other's hair and makeup. Aunt Sam bought pizza and dessert sticks."

I eyed Leo, daring him to laugh. I refused to pull the ponytail horns out.

"How many pieces did you eat?" Mom asked Cora.

"Two, Aunt Sam ate four."

I gasped, insulted. "I did not. I ate six." I wasn't ashamed of my pizza consumption. I pointed to the box and said to Leo, "Help yourself. When's the last time you ate?"

He shrugged. "It's been a long day."

Mom said to Cora. "Let's get you to bed, piglet." She whisked her off to the back part of the house where the bedrooms were.

Leo held up a slice, but before he took a bite said, "I like this look on you. It's sexy in an other-worldly kinda way."

"You're a weirdo." I flopped onto the couch, exhausted, the day's events catching up with me.

He laughed then bit into his pizza. He brought the box from the table and sat next to me on the couch.

"How'd it pan out?" I moved my feet to give him room, but stayed laying down.

"Your friend Lockett is good. He got DB to not charge Laura with making a false claim and even made DB think it was his idea. She's gone home with nothing more than a slap on the wrist."

"But Levi's been charged." Essentially, the question was rhetorical, but I had hoped.

"He has. He's not helping his case either. Talking about how much he hated Josh. Talking about how Josh stole from his family." Leo finished his first piece and moved on to another.

"Do you believe him? Do you think he did it?" My mind couldn't comprehend a teen killing, even though I knew it happened every day. Case in point, school shootings.

"It's hard for me. I struggle to be objective. I've been taken off the case. I suppose my lack of objectivity is apparent to others." He looked pissed at himself.

"I think it's human nature to struggle with objectivity, especially when you've put effort into helping a person out." I nudged him with my toe. "These moments where you seem almost human are fascinating."

"What do I seem for those other moments? Superhuman? Godlike?" He winked.

"More like a freak of nature."

"Says the girl with makeup streaking down her face." He finished his pizza then grabbed my foot and held it tight with both hands, pressing his thumbs into the arch of my foot. "Looks like your injuries are getting better."

Human touch was good, usually. Human touch by a sexy man was amazing. I jerked my foot away.

I sat up and curled into the corner of the couch. "You want something. You're never this nice to me unless you want something."

He chuckled. "That's not true. I'm nice to you a lot... lately," he mumbled the last word.

I pointed a finger at him. "A-ha, you admit it. You've been awful to me in the past. You've been nice to me a lot lately because you've wanted something. I'm utilitarian. You need help and old, dumb Samantha will do."

He shook his head and frowned at me. "Not a bit of that is true. You're not old or dumb. You're tenacious. You're driven. Your sense of right and wrong is in line with mine. We're the good guys in a world that seems like it's gone crazy." He blew out a heavy sigh. "A teen kills a guy his mom is dating because the guy stole stuff from them? I don't believe it."

I was skeptical, too. Mostly because, if that was in Levi's personality, then all the previously perceived injustices toward him and his family would have had an overreaction from him of some sort.

"If I try to work this case on my time, behind DB's back, I might make things worse." Leo gave me a pointed look.

I straightened in surprise. "Are you saying you want *me* to work this case? Me, the PI you don't even believe took the PI test?" Which I hadn't. My not-legit husband had taken it in my name, without my knowledge, but Leo didn't need to know that. "Laura didn't seem wild about me getting involved."

"I need your help, Sam."

I blew out a slow breath. "I don't know where to start with this kid or his family."

"Keep digging into Josh. The clues are there somewhere." He pushed from the couch and retrieved a legal-size manila envelope half an inch thick. He tossed it to me. "I brought you something. Here is everything DB has. These are copies. You go through them and I'll go through them and let's see if we can come up with something."

I took the envelope. "What do I do when I've read them? Will this packet self-destruct? Should I eat the proof? Because we both know I shouldn't be seeing this."

He shrugged nonchalantly. "I trust you to not get caught with them."

Holy jeez, this was serious business. Leo asking me for help and telling me he trusted me. My PI star was rising.

I responded with the seriousness he needed to know I was capable of. "I'm on it."

He smiled and paused by the couch. "You staying here or headed back to your place?"

"Mine. Why?"

"I'll follow you home to make sure you don't come into trouble. Because as driven and tenacious as you are, you sure are unlucky." He chuckled while reaching for the empty pizza box.

We cleaned up, said good-byes, and Leo trailed me home. Before getting out of LC, I hesitated. Should I invite him in? Part of me wanted to, and that part was shocked. Because let's be honest, inviting him in for what? More conversation? As if. Truth was, I enjoyed having him around. Admitting that sent a burst of warmth to my girly parts that left them tingly.

I gave him a wave when I unlocked my front door, but he didn't immediately drive away. I watched from behind the blinds of my window. Did he think of me? Did his boy parts get tingly, too, when he did?

23

TODAY'S LIST of desired accomplishments was big. And the best way to go about getting it all done was to start small. I tackled the easiest tasks first.

My first stop was Ralph's to get back on the schedule as soon as possible. I needed the money. I might live simple, but LC's oil habit added up. Besides, I liked to occasionally buy fancy coffee like Unicorn Brew. It was the small luxuries, you know. Lason, my assistant manager, was happy to put me on the schedule starting next week.

From there, I drove to AJ's to give Simon attention and, hopefully, have a tête-à-tête with Troy. There were a million questions to ask. Did he know what he was *really* doing? That these "fake codes" they were plugging in were making charges. My guess was Troy knew. That would explain his mood changes.

Was it a leap to believe Levi knew what was going on as well? That's why he wasn't doing the coding. Only a *truthful* conversation with Levi would solve that riddle. And getting both, a conversation and the truth, was unlikely. At least for now. Because I wasn't hired by the family, but by Leo, I had to play my involvement with Levi and his family cool and casual.

At the Gunn residence, Troy wasn't around, and a quick text to AJ told me not to expect him. AJ was keeping tabs on him and had Troy working in the laundry room at the Pioneer's training facility. Poor communication on my part.

Simon and I played at the dog park for a while. I tossed the ball until his tongue hung from the side of his mouth. At home, I rewarded him with a big dog cookie I'd picked up for him from one of the local pet stores that made healthy dog treats. Easily, I was his favorite, and that made me happy. I liked the low demand relationship we had. Giving him cookies was no sweat off my back.

Leaving AJ's, I called Laura Danner and asked if we could meet. I'd let a day pass in hopes some normalcy would return to her life and she'd have a better presence of mind. This took some convincing, but she agreed to a short meeting after her visit with Levi. We planned to meet at How Ya Bean. I crossed my fingers that Unicorn Brew would be on the menu.

It wasn't. Apparently, June hadn't been feeling well so no special drinks were on the menu.

Knowing how June felt about others doing business at her coffee shop that weren't on the schedule, Laura and I snagged a table outside so we could talk.

Based on Laura's crossed arms and scowl and the

furtive glances from the other customers and locals walking by, I instantly realized my big mistake. Laura Danner wasn't going to have the informative chat I sought with the stares of speculation all around her.

"If you're more comfortable taking this elsewhere, we can go to my dad's newspaper," I offered.

"I have nothing to hide," she said loudly. Her gaze going from person to person, likely daring them to say something to her.

Precious said rumors about the Danners were circulating. Ranging from mild to extreme. The worst being the Danners were preppers, against government and societal systems, and building a cache of guns.

Those ideologies sounded more survivalist to me. And never mind that the Danners had a business and did contracts with *the man.* These facts alone negated half of the stupid rumors.

"What did you want to talk about, Samantha? Are you wanting to ask me if we're preppers? If we think the zombie apocalypse is coming?" Her jaw was set, angry. But her eyes were sad, filled with pain. "Let's see, I also heard I was caught up in a lover's triangle with Josh and some other unknown woman and asked Levi to take Josh out. And then—"

I waved a hand for her to stop. Then sat back in the chair and kicked my legs out, one ankle over the other. "When did being a prepper become a bad thing? I mean, we live within eyesight of four volcanoes. None of which are dormant. Maybe having a stockpile is smart. A prevention strategy."

After Laura studied me, her tightly crossed arms loosened slightly. "It's called homesteading. And it's about being prepared in case of an earthquake" — she gestured toward Mt. St. Helen's — "or an eruption."

"Makes sense to me. I'll be doing some stockpiling myself. I'd be stupid not to."

I tackled the other rumors head-on. "I don't know why people are saying the other stuff. It's ridiculous. Too much TV or social media."

A moment of acceptance passed between us. Laura notched back the tension a tad more and sat back in her chair. She gripped the armrest.

"You should rethink being seen with me, Samantha. People will start talking about you, too."

I snorted with amusement. "People have been talking about me since I was a kid. First, it was about my inability to learn to read, or about how I couldn't measure up to Rachel. Then there was the whole husband's a polygamist thing. And, of course, just a few days ago, I was the key person of interest in Josh's murder. Sometimes, I think it's my life destiny to give people something to talk about." I'd developed a thick skin over the years, but the secret was that no skin was thick enough.

Laura nodded slowly. "That's right, you *were* the key person in Josh's death." Her jaw trembled. "Now it's my teenage son."

I sat forward and leaned across the table as I set my paper coffee cup to the side. I wanted to take her hand or offer some comfort, but Laura Danner was holding life together with duct tape and bubble gum, and I didn't want to set her off. Not in public at least.

"I want your permission to investigate this case. I don't have faith in DB. When he focused on me, I'd started digging into Josh's background and I'll share all that with Tyson if you're keeping him as a lawyer. But I'd like to keep digging if you're okay with it."

"You're asking because you'll have to dig into our background, too, right?" She looked wary.

"For now, I'd like you to tell me what you can about Josh. About your relationship with Josh. I'm not going to dig just to dig. I'll use discretion."

Laura stared off over my shoulder, likely considering her options. "I can't afford to pay you. I don't think I can afford Mr. Lockett either."

"I can't speak for Tyson, but I won't cost you a dime."

Laura gasped in surprise. "Why would you do that for us?"

This was where the truth would pay off. "Leo believes in your son's innocence. And I believe him. I don't know you. I don't know Levi at all, but I do know DB and I do know what it's like to be falsely accused." I snagged my coffee cup and fiddled with the lid. "I was there when Josh died. It was awful. And though I wasn't in the Principal Josh fan club, he didn't deserve to die like that. And as long as DB is accusing the wrong people, Josh's killer is getting away with murder. That's why I'm doing this." I nodded as added emphasis to my words.

Laura studied me, maybe looking for a tell. A sign I wasn't as sincere as I seemed. She sighed heavily then said, "I was hesitant to date Josh, or anyone for that matter. Carl was the only one for me. I never imagined I'd be doing life without him." Grief marks were etched around her eyes and mouth, and as she spoke about Carl, holding back tears, those lines became more prominent.

"Josh asked you out?"

She nodded. "He was persistent. When he first moved here, I thought he'd dated June, but I could never confirm that. Had I been able to, I would have asked his ex for references." She gave a sardonic chuckle. "We should all ask each other for references."

"Some people hire a PI," I said, thinking of a previous case.

One of Laura's brows shot up. "I'll keep that in mind should I ever date again." She waved a dismissive hand. "Anyway, the more I hemmed and hawed, the more persistent he was. In hindsight, I think he liked the chase."

"Why do you say that?" Not that this would be out of character for most men, and Josh struck me as a player.

"Because in the beginning, he was great. Attentive. Made me feel as if there was no one else on earth like me, and he was the luckiest man alive. He was great with the kids. Levi wouldn't allow Josh in his life, but Josh was positive and continued to try to be Levi's friend. I appreciated that." She shook her head.

"And then?" I held up a small notebook as a silent way to request permission. Laura nodded.

"And then, as I started to believe maybe he was sincere and was as great as he seemed, he pulled back. Subtly at first, so much I didn't notice. Only in hindsight am I able to see it." She ducked her head in embarrassment, her cheeks pink. "It was so nice to have a companion again, someone to split a portion of the work with. I let that blind me to Josh's real nature."

"Which was?" I had my opinion, but I didn't want to be skewed by it.

"Josh thought he could charm his way into anything, or out of anything. You know the term 'sleight of hand'?"

I nodded.

"Sometimes Josh would..." She searched for words. "Come off as one thing. Attentive, dedicated, but I got the feeling it was to distract me from what he was really doing."

"Like helping himself to your water, gas, and stuff?"

Laura's lips thinned into an angry line. "The real issue wasn't that he helped himself, but how did he get the key to unlock the storage room to help himself? It was on my key chain. When I noticed the water gone, I immediately checked my key chain. The key was still there. And water wasn't the only item he stole. He also helped himself to toilet paper, various medicines." She waved her hand to stop me from asking the next question. "No illegal drugs or prescription drugs. Over-the-counter stuff. And gum. Josh had a way of twisting conversations so you doubted yourself. Maybe I had left out a spare key. Maybe he did ask me if he could take the water. I am overworked and stressed about Levi." She closed her eyes then covered them with her palm. "Josh was exhausting."

Something she said earlier struck me as odd. "Gum?

You stockpile gum? Is there something I should know about gum and start keeping it around the house, too?"

Laura looked at me through her fingers. "Only if you're a stress eater."

I smiled.

She continued, her hands dropping back to the table. "To not stress-eat an entire box of Oreos, I chew gum. I figure if we're having to tap into our stockpile for whatever reason, the situation will be stressful, so I horde gum."

"Why would Josh take your gum?" I couldn't recall having ever seen him chewing gum.

She tapped a finger on the table. "Get this. Josh was a smoker, or was trying not to be a smoker."

I clapped my hands with realization. "I knew that. I saw the patches under his shirt at the PTC meeting when school started." I pointed to my middle finger. "And he had some yellow staining on his finger."

Laura nodded. "Oh, he would have hated you knowing. He went to great measure to keep it a secret."

I curled up my lip in confusion. "Why? What's the big deal?"

"Because he felt like it didn't work with the persona of a high-standard, elite school principal. He was crazy about keeping the smoke from his clothes."

"I went to his house, and it didn't smell like a smoker lived there." No matter how a person tried to keep the smell of cigarettes out of their clothes, hair, and furniture, little bits always penetrated.

"He only smoked outside and usually in his underwear. He'd shower right after. In his defense, he was trying to quit." She pointed to me. "The patch was one tool he was using in nicotine replacement therapy."

I jotted that down in my notebook.

"He did all this so he could stop smoking cigarettes, right?"

Laura nodded.

"This nicotine therapy—"

"Nicotine replacement therapy."

"What was that all about? Was it working?"

She leaned across the table and in a lowered voice said, "Sorta. He'd ween himself to smoking only on special occasions."

Special occasions? "Like holidays?"

She barked out a short laugh. "He liked to smoke after sex." She quickly looked away but held up two fingers. "Two immediately afterward, and sometimes that gave him the stamina to come back for more. Then two more after that."

Now the smoking in his underwear made sense.

"That's the only time he lit up?"

She glanced at me, then away, still uncomfortable about her last comment. "As far as I know. If you want to know if the nicotine replacement therapy program was working, you'd have to speak to Boomer about that."

"Boomer Jacobson? Why do I know that name?"

Laura said, "His wife Carlie is on the PTC."

A-ha. Connection made. Carlie had been the one to bring up the sexual harassment with Cora, not Annber, the mom of the child whose shirt Cora had touched. Carlie's dislike for me had been crystal clear that day. In small towns, overlapping relationships was unavoidable. Boomer was Josh's doctor, Carlie worked with Josh on the PTC. Did they hang out socially? Did Boomer think Josh touched everyone as much as I did? Did he approve of his wife's adoration for the principal?

Laura continued, "All I know is that he couldn't resist after... well you know. This is how I figured out he was cheating on me."

"He was? With who?"

Laura shrugged. "I don't know that."

"I'm sorry, but I have to ask. How do you know?"

Laura glanced around before she said, "The cigarettes. By my estimations based on our... ahem... relationship Josh should go through a pack every five to ten days." Her look was pointed, her brows arched, asking me if I was picking up what she was putting down.

I nodded in understanding.

"Josh kept a trash can in his car. One of those *As Seen On TV* things with the soft sides and a lid and was supposed to be a natural odor eater. The Friday before he died, we went to dinner. On the drive home I finished a pack of gum and tossed it in the trash bag. I noticed two crumpled, empty packs. I confronted him on it. We had a huge fight and I ended it because I knew he was lying to me."

I hated to be the voice of doubt. "That doesn't mean anything. Those could have been there from a week ago or longer."

She shook her head. "Except Josh cleans his car out every Sunday. Like clockwork. Cleans out his car, washes it, and watches football. It's his day. Wouldn't even watch football at our house."

"And you're saying you weren't witness to all those cigarettes being smoked?"

Laura chuckled. "Not once that week. That's why it caught me off guard."

"Can't break a habit when you keep engaging in the trigger," I said matter of fact. Not that I faulted Josh for his habit or trigger. Only that he should have tried eating cookies or ice cream after getting nookie. He might have saved himself the stress and guilt that came with being unable to resist. What I faulted Josh for was having a relationship with someone and fooling around behind her back. If Laura's suspicions were correct.

"Talk to me about the Recode and Reshape Program." I tapped my pen against my notepad.

"What's to say? Levi was—is—running with a bad crowd." She sighed heavily. "He's been coming unraveled since his dad died." Laura pressed a palm to her temple. "Maybe we all have been. Anyway, Levi was caught shoplifting with these kids, and the owner pressed charges. Because it was Levi's first offense. I got him assigned to the Recode and Reshape Program." She snorted with derision. "Convincing Josh to take him in the program was another matter."

"I thought the kids were court-appointed, so why did Josh have the option?"

"Because this is a private program instead of the state-run one."

A program Josh owned and was using to run a scam. Having Levi enrolled could've blown the scam wide open.

I said, "I'm pretty sure I know why Josh didn't want Levi in the program."

The question was, did Levi know what Josh was up to and, if so, what did he do about it?

24

LAURA and I separated with my promise to loop her in on every development.

As if the universe was patting me on the back for such a fine client interview, it delivered to me Carlie Jacobson.

Not directly to me, but to How Ya Bean. She pulled up in a screech of tires, snagging a spot directly in front of the coffeeshop, her hybrid SUV extending over the parking space and into a crosswalk and blocking half of a bike rack.

Leaving her engine to idle, she jumped out and hotfooted it into the coffee shop. I followed her.

Two people were ahead of her in line. Dressed in a tennis skirt and sweater with pristine white tennis shoes, she tapped her foot impatiently.

"Hey Carlie. How ya holding up?" I asked as I moved into line behind her. "How's Boomer? Can't be easy when a patient dies."

She looked over her shoulder, curled her lip in disgust, then turned her back to me. "Get lost," she said.

"How are the PTC moms coping? Are you aimless little sheep without Principal Josh?" Antagonizing her hadn't been my goal, but her snootiness brought out the worst in me.

She spun to face me. "You're an awful person. I know they got the prepper kid in custody, but my money is still on you."

I shook my head. "Nah, I don't do men who smoke. I once dated a guy in college who smoked, and he was always chewing mints. I now associate the two, and it put me off mints, too." I leaned in close. "Because Josh only liked to smoke after sex the other party is probably past caring at that point."

Carlie turned a shade of pink that complimented the whiteness of her tennis attire. "I thought you and Josh were getting pretty familiar when we were here last." She reared back and scanned me up and down. "Wow, you do move fast. But I guess with your husband, or whatever he was, dead, you're probably lonely."

I chuckled then said, "Not that lonely. Never that lonely."

Carlie's face tightened with anger. "What do you want from me?"

"I'd like to ask you a few questions about Josh."

"Can I help you?" June said in a booming voice.

The line had moved quickly while Carlie and I had been trading insults.

Carlie rushed to the counter. "I called in a pick-up order."

June looked a hot mess. Her hair was sloppily pulled back into a bun that was slipping down her neck. Her T-shirt, what looked to be a man's undershirt, was decorated with coffee and tea splotches, her face devoid of makeup. June pointed to a to-go container with four drinks and fifth to-go cup next to it.

June glared at Carlie. "You need to settle up your account. No more running a tab. And you need to pick up Josh's bill, too. You can have the other mom's split it with you."

Whoa. Did I detect some anger? "Hey," I said to June. "How ya doing? I heard you might be under the weather."

June narrowed her eyes at me. "What are you talking about?"

The entire exchange was such a surprise and unexpected that, had Precious been telling me this story, I wouldn't have believed it. June was always happy and pleasant, and whenever she wasn't, she hid it well.

I put my hands up in defense. "Nothing. Ignore me."

Carlie mumbled, "I wish." From inside her shirt, from her bra I'm guessing, Carlie pulled out a credit card. When she tossed it at June, the plastic slid across the counter.

June glared at us both and mumbled something as she rang up the charges. After she handed Carlie back her card, Carlie turned to leave. She stared at me in disgust.

I went for broke. "When would be a good time for us

to talk? Are those drinks for the other PTC moms? I can come now."

Carlie clutched the cups close. "I never want to talk to you. Ever." She glanced over my shoulder and, as if possible, looked even more disgusted.

I turned to find DB circling her SUV. "Whoops," I said. She rushed past me.

From inside, I watched DB give her a hard time. Rightfully so. Agreeing with him was a weird feeling for me. He pointed to the half foot where her bumper was encroaching on the crosswalk. Carlie stomped her foot, which caused a drink to tumble from the to-go carrier.

Must have not been firmly placed in the slot. I glanced at the teens working the counter. They were watching the outside scene, too. The girl pointed to the boy behind her and rolled her eyes. Apparently, he loaded the to-go carrier.

I returned my attention to DB and Carlie. DB was taking out his citation book.

Carlie glanced back into the coffee shop. Her gaze met mine... and if looks could kill, I'd be pushing up daisies.

"You want a drink?" June asked. "Because if not, then get out of line."

I was staring at Carlie when inspiration struck. She wasn't going to talk to me. Ever. Unless something or someone changed her mind. And I knew just the something.

From my pocket, I pulled out a five and placed it on the counter. I snagged a bag of gluten-free, fat-free, no GMO hippie popcorn. "I'll take this," I said. Did I want to fall on my sword for a Hunter Boot mom? Nope. But I could see the bigger picture. I girded my loins, as they say, then went outside.

DB was telling Carlie all the citations he could stick her with.

With a loud *pop,* I opened my popcorn bag by clapping it hard on one side.

DB and Carlie looked at me. I tossed some popcorn in my mouth and said, "Keep going. I enjoy watching others get busted by DB. Usually he likes to give me a hard time. I'm surprised he hasn't already been in my face about being hired to work the Josh Chapman murder." I leaned against the large window of the coffee shop and ate more popcorn.

DB slapped his citation book against the palm of his hand. "Who hired you?"

I smirked. "You know I can't tell you that." Popcorn was flying in my mouth faster than words were coming out. "But it's no surprise people think you have the wrong person. I mean, just the other day you thought it was me. Funny, right Carlie?"

She looked at me, a scowl still creasing her features. But when our eyes made contact, I pointedly looked at her vehicle. Let's hope she was smart enough to read my intention.

Her eyes widened, but she didn't move.

"I have lots of questions, DB." I pointed to my back-pack. "I got a list of suspects in here that I'm sure you don't even know about. And when I break this case wide open, Carlie here can be my witness that I shared facts about the case, facts you ignored because you were busy handing out tickets for..." I gestured to Carlie's car.

DB faced her. "Why are you still here?"

She cast me a fleeting look of surprise then hustled around her SUV, climbed in, slammed the door and then sped off.

I had DB's full attention. I offered him my popcorn.

He put his citation book in his back pocket.

I tossed the bag into the nearby trashcan and dusted off my hands. "My work here is done. I'll be off. Have a good one." My apartment was in view of How Ya Bean. Spreading out all this information and having Toby do more digging was what I wanted to be doing. DB was an energy sucker, and I wanted to hold on to what energy I had left for the day. I took two steps toward home.

"Not so fast." He hooked me by the elbow and spun me toward him. "What gives you the right to butt into this investigation?"

"My private investigator's license." I put a hand up in protest. "And before you read me the riot act for that, know that I'm fully aware of my legal boundaries, and I have no intention of overstepping." I pointed two fingers to my eyes then back at him. "Because I know you'll be watching."

"I'm not worried about you or your PI skills," he said.

He was baiting me.

"Okay," I said with a casual shrug. I moved to lean against the empty bike rack, putting it between us. Trouble was, I was worried about his cop skills. Or lack thereof.

I kicked one foot up on the bike rack and leaned back on my hands.

"I have a confession from the kid. That's as good as gold." DB fidgeted with something in his back pocket.

"You also had a confession from his mom. If one was lying about their confession, why couldn't another?"

DB tsked. "You probably don't know this, mostly because you'd have to learn it in school, and we both know learning and school was hard for you—"

I rolled my eyes. "Says the guy who cheated off me in chemistry class."

"Or maybe it was just the reading of sentences."

"I'm dyslexic, DB, not dumb. What's your excuse?"

DB's expression went dark. "If you took the time to learn anything, Sam, you'd know that the odds of two innocent people confessing to the same crime are slim. In the world of crime, there is no such thing as coincidences."

He moved like lightning, which was surprising for such a bulky load of a guy. He slapped one end of handcuffs on my wrist. Before I could jerk my hand away, he clipped the other end around the bike rack.

DB laughed and put his hands on his hips. "I'd bet fast cash that you don't have a handcuff key."

I gave him my best annoyed face. "Ha ha, jokes on me. You win this one." I jingled the cuffs. "How about you undo these now?"

DB tucked his hands in his pockets. "This is why I don't worry about you as a PI. Or anything you think you might uncover in this case." He pointed to his chest. "I'm the big guns, and you're amateur hour."

"Those two don't work together. Maybe you're prime time and I'm local cable? Or maybe you're the big gun and I'm a marshmallow shooter. Or—"

"I get it, smarty pants. I'd love to know who you're gonna call to bail you out of this, but I've got work to do." He turned and strolled away, heading toward the station.

I yelled, "Just a minute ago you said I was a dummy. Now I'm a smarty pants? Which is it?"

When he kept on going, my temper elevated.

"I'm gonna call my lawyer. I believe you don't have just cause for this."

DB didn't care. He did everything like he was above the law because he was the law. And my mother, the mayor, didn't scare him.

"Sammy?" called a voice from across the street.

I turned toward it. My dad and Chuck, the guy who owned the local market and tech shop were at the front door of the newspaper.

"You need some help?" Dad asked, one hand on the door of his business.

I relaxed against the bike bars and used my free hand to wave him off, blocking my handcuffed hand with my body. "No, just waiting for someone."

Dad pause, glanced at Chuck, then back at me again. I smiled wide and kicked one foot over my ankle like I had all the time in the world.

If he'd seen the handcuffs, he'd already be over here. Worst case, he thought he might have seen them but was gauging how to react by my reaction. After what felt like the longest moment in time, Dad and Chuck went inside the newspaper building.

I breathed a sigh of relief. Last thing I wanted was for my mother to find out.

I fished out my phone and called Precious. She answered on the first ring.

"What up?" she said in the worst fake gangsta voice ever.

"Any chance you have a spare set of handcuff keys?"

Silence.

"Um, I don't know what you think I do in my free time, but no. I don't have any handcuff keys, much less spares. And before you ask, I don't have any whips or chains or masks or... wait, I do have a few masks from previous Halloween parties. Oh, and I might have a whip, but I certain—"

"Precious," I cried. "I'm cuffed to the bike rack outside June's."

"Oh, dare I ask?"

"DB's way of proving that I sucked as a PI. I suppose he's implying I'm unprepared for any or all circumstances." Begrudgingly, I admitted he was right.

"Okay, I'll see what I can do. I have a new client meeting in ten minutes so I'll need at least..."

"Ooh," I interrupted. "Never mind, I'll call Mrs. Wright and have her come." Not that I wanted to live that down either.

"Okay, but if she can't make it, text me."

"Done," I said, then disconnected.

I tried Mrs. Wright to no avail. Then I tried Mrs. Long, thinking maybe the two were entrenched in a mad game of MahJongg. No answer.

I called Toby, all the while purposefully ignoring the people passing behind me. Hoping if I didn't engage, they would keep on moving.

"Dudette," Toby said. "I'm driving a client somewhere. Can this wait?"

Toby freelanced as a private driver in between working for me, other odd jobs, and getting high. A loud squeal came across the line.

"How does Lady M like the car time?"

"She's not a fan," he said, "but I can't leave her at home." Another high-pitched squeal filled the space.

"How's your customer like that?" As a passenger, it would not be cool with me.

Toby cooed to Lady M, then said, "I'm not gonna ask and I'm driving over the speed limit. Before I forget, I sent those"—he cleared his throat to indicate I should pay attention— "you know, those one files you wanted. I sent them to your email."

I laughed. "Okay, thanks. Don't go so fast you get a ticket." *But if by chance you do, can you ask the cop for his handcuff keys?* "Listen, you don't have handcuff keys, do you?" My not-legal husband, Carson, had kept a supply space fit for an amateur spy hidden at the top attic space of his office. But the office burned down a few months ago.

"No, sorry. What's up?"

"No reason," I said then got off the phone as fast as I could. I wasn't up for repeating the story.

Someone cleared their throat behind me.

I dropped my head and closed my eyes, mortified to be caught. Darn it all.

I said, "How long you been standing back there?"

"Since you were talking to Precious," Leo said.

I groaned. The universe must get a kick out of sharing my embarrassing experiences, particularly with Leo.

He said, "Were you even thinking about calling me?"

I faced him and pointed to my shackled wrist. "Nope, because, for once, I thought maybe I could slink away with only a few people knowing this happened. Please tell me you stumbled upon me and gossip hasn't started making the rounds."

Wind River was small enough, the kind of town people pressed their noses to windows to watch scenes unfold before them while they speculated on the phone with the person next door.

"DB was telling anyone and everyone at the station."

I gestured to his street clothes. "You just get off duty?"

"Yeah, I have a tribal meeting in a few hours." He stuck his hand in his front pocket.

I sagged against the bike rack. "Please tell me you've got handcuff keys in there."

Leo whipped out a ring of keys. "As a matter of fact, I do. And I suggest you get one, too." He went to work on the handcuff.

"Consider it done. Any other sage advice you want to give me before I head down to the surplus store to stock up?"

"Yeah, try to imagine the worst scenario you can be in and get stuff to keep you from being in that scenario."

This was a vast improvement from him telling me to get out of the business. He freed me from the bar.

"I don't think my imagination is that good," I said, rubbing my wrist. "I never saw this coming."

Leo shook his head. "Maybe you should watch some thrillers."

Why not? The gist of my PI knowledge came from watching YouTube videos. It only made sense that my survival skills should come from a major motion picture.

I was doomed.

25

I'D SPENT the last few days going over Josh's calendar and other files Toby had sent over. I couldn't make heads or tails of it as Josh had used emojis instead of place, people, or event names for most everything. Some emojis were sports related, others hobby related. Occasionally, he would write in *PTC* or *Town Hall*. I'd gone through my phone last night and agreed with Josh; there were no good emojis for those two. Well, at least there were no *appropriate* emojis.

Having others look at the clues might provide some answers, so I'd set up a get-together of minds I liked and trusted. I prepared a simple brunch of fresh fruit, yogurt, muffins, and frozen quiche baked in my oven to make my house smell good and made me look like a pro. The team assembled at ten on the money Sunday, and I included Leo, who said his only task for his day off was to be one step closer to catching a killer.

Because I relied heavily on my visual skills, I taped three months of Josh's calendar to my wall in sequential order. On an adjacent wall, I taped the doctored invoices. From the office supply store, I'd bought a giant easel pad in case someone wanted to take notes. I documented in a weird shorthand that was like my own language. Well, Precious and Hue understood it, but they'd been in the trenches with me in school.

Leo was first to arrive. Dressed in dark jeans and a cream Henley, he looked relaxed but powerful. Always powerful. With broad shoulders and a posture that never slouched, he wore his heritage well. Proudly.

I, too, had dressed in jeans, only mine had holes in the knees and my V-neck T-shirt embroidered with flowers down one side had an eraser sized stain near my belly button where I'd almost dropped the blackberries and caught the bowl by pressing it to my stomach.

Let's be honest, I was too lazy to change.

He surveyed the walls, hands on hips. "Wow, I like looking at things this way. Gives you the whole picture."

"That's the point. You don't look at things as a whole?" This was as foreign a concept to me as my inability to break words down into bite-sized sounds had been to my teachers.

He nodded. "Sure, I print stuff out but not to this scale." He faced me and smiled.

"This is how I see the world," I said. "Hue, too." It was a defense mechanism, pointing out that his brother was like me.

Leo snapped his fingers. "Speaking of Hue, he sent me

this text with just emojis, and for the life of me, I cannot figure it out."

I held out my hand while he dug his phone from his front pocket. "Then you would hate the messages between Hue and me, minimal words."

He placed his phone in my hand, and I glanced at the screen then laughed.

Hue's response was a door, a man running, and a burst of wind.

"This means get the eff out." I typed back one-tear crying emoji followed by the snowflake and handed back his phone.

"Why didn't he just use GTFO?" Leo studied his phone. "And what did you say back?"

"Because GTFO requires too much work. Don't get me wrong. I use text slang all the time. LOL, LMAO, BTW, all those. But using pictures is easier for me. Sometimes I send my dad emoji sentences, too. I forget that they're more a riddle for him. You can always use an online search to figure them out." From my back pocket I pulled out my phone and showed Leo a recent text exchange between his brother and me. Over seventy-five percent of the screen was emoji sentences with one or two words sprinkled in between.

"Based on your exchange, you told Hue you were considering applying for detective. Which is awesome, by the way. Hue said GTFO. The crying face and snowflake say 'that's cold.' Because why not just say 'congrats' or party hat?"

"This is amazing. Like code." He spun and pointed to the calendar. "Like his code."

"Only his makes no sense." I stepped up to the calendar pages and studied them.

A knock at my door announced the arrival of Precious and Toby. Precious was dressed in a sweater dress with tights and knee-high boots.

Toby wore an ironic T-shirt with jeans that sagged. Around his neck was his empty vape pen swinging from a lanyard and Lady M's banana hammock.

When I peeked into the banana, Lady M peeked up at me from between the folds. She made a cackle sound.

I stepped back. "This sounds better than the sound she was making in the car the other day."

"Yeah, that was what's called crabbing. She wasn't happy to be in the car, but she's getting used to it now."

Precious got cozy on the couch. "Just an opinion here, but that trauma pet you got to help you with getting over being shot seems to be adding to your trauma. All this juggling for a squirrel that flies."

Toby pointed to the banana. "Since I've got her, I haven't thought about being shot once. It only comes up when I'm with you all. Like you're the trigger." He stroked the banana. "She's the best thing that's ever happened to me. And now that I can't vape, jeez, she's really helped calm my nerves." He looked at me. "But there might be times I'll need a babysitter."

"Why you looking at me?" I glanced around at the others.

"You have the most flexible schedule. And you owe me."

I reared back. "How you figure?"

"Do you want me to go into specifics? How about the time I was shot?"

I rolled my eyes and gave an exaggerated sigh. The time he was shot was Toby's favorite blackmail chip. "I need more than that."

Toby tapped a spot below the banana but above his waistline. "I feel it. Right here. That you and Lady M need to bond."

"Maybe that's hunger," Precious said.

"Can we focus on why we're here?" Leo asked the group. "It's a wonder you all get anything done."

I pointed to the walls with the calendars. "This was Josh's schedule for the last three months." I pointed to the other wall. "These are invoices he doctored and used to skim money from the school. Load up on food and let's dig in. He used some sort of code. What do you think of it?"

Leo said, "Why are there some dates missing?"

"Because we had to get this off Mrs. River's computer as the police already confiscated Josh's computer," I said. "And the computer I accessed from his didn't have anything on it."

Leo shook his head. "I'm gonna forget I even heard that."

Precious said, "If Mrs. Rivers was my secretary with access to my calendar, I'd use code, too."

I smacked myself in the forehead. "Of course, that's

why he did it." I stared at the calendar with a new awareness.

"Breakthrough." Toby pumped his fist in the air and then filled up his plate.

We all followed suit and sat in front of the papers tacked to my wall.

I recapped, "Josh, with the help of Jenna Miller, ran scams in Kitsap, but Josh started his life of crime in Jefferson County with stealing school property on a small scale."

Leo chimed in, "It wasn't until he was in Kitsap County that he moved into money laundering."

Money laundering, I explained to Precious and Toby, was done when a company appeared legit but its primary purpose was to funnel money through it. Like when Josh used school credit cards to purchase fake items from Pay Forward For the Kids, stolen money goes into his pocket. Padding the receipts was embezzlement.

Leo added, "And he stuck with his old favorite, taking items marked for disposal or reutilization and selling them. Even falsely marking good products for disposition services."

Toby took off his banana carrier and handed it to me. "Wear this for a while so I can spray this on me." He showed me a bottle labeled *Chill*, a face and mouth spritzer with a cannabidiol base. "All this talk of crime is making me jittery." He didn't wait for me to take Lady M, but slipped the cord over my head.

I said, "I thought she was supposed to help when you're jittery?"

"And she does, but she can't soothe me every time. And I don't want this spritzer to get on her. There aren't any studies on CBD and sugar gliders." He stroked the *Chill* bottle like he did his vape pen. Poor Toby jonesing for his vape pen. Going cold turkey must be hard on him.

Toby sprayed his face several times, misting the therapeutic water all over himself. Vanilla scent filled the space.

"You're like a walking aromatherapy ball. First your scented non-nicotine vaping and now this," Precious said.

I placed my empty plate on my coffee table then pressed my hands to my temples, frustrated. "I can't seem to get a handle on all this information. Here's what we know, let's start a list. Precious, write this down."

She moved to stand at the easel.

I said, "Put Jenna Miller. She's suspect numero uno. But there's also Danika Post. She said she resigned because she wanted an administration position. She wanted Josh's position but said she knew she didn't have enough experience. She and Josh had what looks like an unfriendly exchange just minutes before he died."

Toby stabbed a piece of pineapple. "And that email you asked me to look for, nope. Never happened. She never sent a resignation email."

I pointed to Precious who wrote Danika's name on the easel pad. "Then what were she and Josh arguing about that morning, and why lie to me?"

Precious wrote *LIAR* by Danika's name.

We left Levi's name off the list because I had a paper pinned to the wall that listed out Levi's claims and evidence.

Something Leo had said to me when I was the person of interest popped into my head. I gestured to the paper with the evidence we knew of. "If DB will look at the evidence and try to point it to Levi, why can't we look at the same evidence and try to link to someone else?" I pointed to the easel. "Like to Danika or someone. We also have nicotine poisoning the possible cause of death."

Leo tossed a pen into the air and caught it, his expression pulled tight as he thought. "It would have to be a heck of a lot of nicotine. It's so unlikely, I have a hard time giving this idea weight." He paused in his game of toss and met my gaze.

"Unless," I said and picked up my notebook, flipping through a few pages. "Unless someone knew about Josh's nicotine habit and used it against him." I tapped the pad. "Josh was in a nicotine replacement program. He wore a patch, well, likely two patches from the looks of it."

Leo sat up. "How do you know he wore two?"

"I saw their outline through his shirt when he stretched to shake Precious's hand at the open house." I sat on the arm of my couch next to Leo. I petted Lady M behind the ears. "And get this. He treated himself to two cigarettes after he gave his ladies *the business*. If you know what I mean." I waggled my brows for added emphasis. "Even when he was wearing the patch."

Toby asked, "You talking about sex?"

"Uh, yeah," Precious said and lightly slapped his shoulder.

"One question, though, did he smoke after he gave himself *the business*, too?" I asked. "Because it sounds to me like Josh liked *the business* a lot. And if he was getting it a lot and giving it to himself a lot, then that's a lot of cigarettes."

Leo said, "I'm guessing by how often you said 'a lot,' you think Josh was more than a few times a week guy."

"He struck me as the sort of guy who'd have women in every port. Sharing is caring, he'd say. And Josh really liked to show how much he cared." I made the heart shape with my fingers and put it over my boob like Josh had done. "My impression is that by showing us he cared, he wanted it reciprocated by sharing." I pointed to my lower lady parts.

Leo grimaced. "I don't want to know how you know that either."

"His ex-girlfriend told me."

Precious, twirling a lock of hair around her finger, paused. "His ex? Last I heard, he was dating Laura Danner, and they seemed serious. I don't know who he dated before her."

"According to Laura, she dumped him the Friday before he died." I shared her suspicions about Josh and other women based on the empty cigarette packs.

"That's flimsy," Toby said. "A million other things could explain that."

We all looked at him, surprised by his lack of paranoia. Typically, he would connect dots no one saw.

He spritzed himself with *Chill*, and vanilla mist floated toward me. "What? I watch crime shows on TV too, you know. I love Perry Mason."

Precious tapped the marker against the easel with

Danika's name. "Did Laura know who Josh might be giving *the business* to besides her?"

I shook my head. "But if I had to guess, and it would be a guess based on no fact, I'd start with Carlie Jacobson. Carlie had gotten ugly with me that Tuesday Josh died. She brought up the sexual harassment. Not Annber, the mom who complained."

In fact, I'd probably go through all the Hunter Boot Moms. Acolytes, every one of them.

Precious wrote the names Laura and Carlie on the paper with a question mark.

"When will the reports from the toxicology come back?" I asked.

Leo stretched. "I'm off the case. I have to wait until one of the other officers shares the info with me. I can try to login to see if a report's been filed and read, but DB gets a weekly list of who logins and looks at what."

I rolled my eyes.

Toby set his drink aside and reached for his messenger bag resting against the wall by the door. "You need a report. Consider it done."

Leo held up a hand. "Maybe not hack with me present."

Toby snort-laughed. "Is it hacking when you have the password?"

Once again, he had our full attention.

Leo said, "How do you have a password?"

Toby was clicking away on his computer. "I set up DB's computer system and tied it into his stereo and cheap-as-all-get-out cameras he bought online. He used the same password for each entry point even though I told him not to. I'm gonna go with his vanity overriding his common sense."

We waited a few beats.

Toby continued, "Yep, *DBstheMan* is his office password, too." Toby shook his head. "Civilians. So pedestrian."

Leo and I exchanged a smile. Precious patted him on the back.

Leo said, "But he'll see he logged in and know he didn't."

Toby gave Leo a look of disgust. "Dude, hackers use a creed similar to hikers. Take your trash with you. I'll leave no trace behind."

He made a few clicks, smiled, then looked at all us with a smug expression.

"Coming in hot," Toby said. The printer on my desk began to whirl as it warmed up. "Want anything else while I'm here?"

Leo shot Toby a look of disbelief. "Just get out."

Toby said, "For a cop, you sure are twitchy."

"You're breaking the law," Leo said.

Toby spritzed himself, then aimed it at Leo. "He gave me this password. How can that be breaking the law when he literally... Gave. It. To. Me."

"Semantics," Leo said.

I took the pages from the printer and scanned them but couldn't make heads nor tails of them. They were in cop code. I handed them to Leo.

He glanced at the sheets and gave a low whistle. To me

he said, "The medical examiner is ruling Josh's death homicide. Lethal dose of nicotine. You said Josh was in nicotine replacement therapy?"

I nodded.

Leo's mouth was a grim line. He flipped through a few pages then said, "This report states that the vape juice vial in Josh's desk had high nicotine levels. We knew that. But also the water tablets were laced with a nicotine powder, too."

"And the combination of those two plus his habit was enough to kill him?" I asked.

Leo continued to study the report.

Precious plopped onto the couch, her brow furrowed as she thought. "Who on our list was smart enough to know that a patch, some vaping, and a few cigarettes would be enough to do in a chronic smoker?"

I said, "Maybe the nicotine replacement therapy program puts a person on their max dose and everything he did after like smoking and an extra patch was too much?"

Leo shook his head, "Except the report says the vial in his desk, the one submitted into evidence and tested, had an unbroken seal. It had never been opened, so it hadn't been used."

Where had the additional nicotine come from?

I quickly scanned a nicotine replacement therapy site. "Precious, you asked who might be smart enough to know? We need to add this person to our list. Boomer Jacobson." I looked at my friends. "I think it's time to talk to Josh's doctor."

"OKAY," I said and tapped the clear two-way earpiece I'd just inserted. "Can everyone hear me?"

"Yep," Toby said. Lady Marmalade cooed in the background.

Precious shrugged. "I think I can, but you're also sitting right next to me."

"We'll test again when I get out of the car. Let's recap the plan—"

Toby groaned. "We've done this three times."

"Yeah, well, it's my butt going in there, humor me. I'll try to get Dr. Jacobson to open up about Josh. Maybe I can get him a little rattled and he'll slip up."

Precious sighed. "Are we sure we'll even know if he's slipped up? We're looking for a needle in a haystack here."

"Yeah, but we have Josh the magnet to help us." I was hoping Josh would be a trigger for Dr. Jacobson. If Josh was the player Laura thought, then maybe Carlie was who he was playing with? Was she the only one? The way Josh had used a simple conversation to touch me uncomfortably, coupled with how he'd touched others, my guess was no, he fooled around with several women.

I opened the door of Precious's SUV. "Hang here, be ready to rescue should I jack this up."

She touched her temple. "Visualize succeeding. Know what information you want and picture getting it. We outlined a strategy, stick to it."

"I picture a little birdie delivering all information. How nice and simple would that be?" I closed the door and headed for Dr. Boomer Jacobson's general medicine office which was housed in the end unit of the strip mall on the side of Wind River being commercialized. Dark tint covered the windows to allow for a client's privacy.

Toby had done as much digging, also called hacking, as he could but was unable to access Boomer's medical records. Scary the police were easier to hack than a small-town doc. What he found was Boomer graduated middle of his class, made a decent wage, and had a high mortgage. He and Carlie had two kids who attended VGS.

Inside, with one other person in the waiting room, I approached the receptionist.

"Hi, Samantha True, I have an appointment. New Patient." I handed her my identification and insurance card. This mining trip was gonna cost me in deductibles. I made a mental note to search the web if I could write it off as a work expense.

The receptionist, a young woman barely out of high school, with coffin-shaped nails painted purple and stick straight blond hair handed me a thin stack of papers and a clipboard with a pen on a chain. "Fill these out and bring them back when you're done."

"I had hoped these were online so I could get them done in advance," I said with a smile.

She didn't even feign interest. "Dr. Jacobson is old-school. Nothing is online."

This included social media accounts as well; I'd learned. Boomer didn't ask his clients to review him on *Yelp* or like on *Facebook*.

I filled out the forms. My pretense for being there was residual hip pain from being hit by the car. I reminded myself to add a slight limp.

I blew out a breath.

"Why are you panting?" Precious asked. "You know what I realized? We don't have a safe word. Like what if you need help, how will I know? So say something. Anything, and we'll call that the safe word."

Toby said, "Or yell 'I'm hit.' Or 'bad guy, bad guy' or—"

Dr. Jacobson opened the door to his back-office space and smiled at me. "Samantha, right? You can fill that out back here." He gestured for me to precede him into the back area.

Boomer Jacobson had wispy blond hair with a hairline slowly creeping back, and the ever-so-slightly emerging spare tire pressing against the golf shirt he wore under a white lab coat.

He led me down a short hallway. "On a scale of good or bad, which one brings you here?"

Did anyone answer good? And if so, why were they seeing their doctor?

"Bad, I think." My parents taught me not to lie. Uncertainty was how I circumvented that.

Toby said, "Bad? You need help?"

Dr. Jacobson said, "Bad, how?"

Precious said, "Sam, we need to know. Are you good or bad because I think we're all confused here?"

There were too many people talking to me, and I got frazzled. "Quiet," I said sharply.

Dr. Jacobson reared back. "I'm sorry."

I shook my head. "No, I'm sorry. I hit my head when I was hit by the car and sometimes putting my thoughts in sequence is hard. What I meant to say is when I let myself be quiet, that's when I notice how much my hip is hurting. This is where the car struck me." I touched my hip.

He held open the door to an exam room with the standard patient examination table, but also two chairs in front of a small desk. Dr. Jacobson gestured for me to take a seat on the exam bed. He stood in front of me. "How would you describe it? A throb, an ache, sharp pain?"

"A dull throb, but persistent enough to be annoying."

From there he did the standard muscle and strength testing. Afterward he stepped back and studied me. "It looks to me like this is just the natural process of healing. Make sure you get lots of protein and iron in your diet. If it continues, I can refer you to a specialist."

I gave him two thumbs up. "Sounds good. I've never been hit by a car before, and I didn't know what to expect for healing. It feels like it's taking forever, and I'm ready to get back out there and run."

"If you're patient now, you'll have fewer problems when you start running," he said.

"Your wife's a runner, right?"

In my ear, Precious said, "Now we're getting to the meat and potatoes."

"She's more a swimmer than a runner." Jacobson raised his brows. "You know my wife?"

"Carlie, right? My niece is going to VGS, and I was tasked with being the school photographer." I grimaced.

Jacobson snapped his fingers then pointed at me as recognition hit. "That's right. You were with Josh when he died. I thought I recognized your name."

I closed my eyes, wishing I could un-see that day. "It was awful." I shook my head sadly. "I wasn't crazy about the guy, but the way he passed did not look fun." I rubbed my hands up and down my arms to wipe away the heebie-jeebies.

Jacobson backed away to sit in a chair. "Creepy to think that someone we knew and my wife saw almost daily was murdered."

Once again, I stretched the truth. I figured if this became a rumor, it couldn't hurt Levi's case at all. Glancing toward the door to make sure it was closed, I lowered my voice. "Well, I heard... You know my dad owns the newspaper, right?"

He nodded.

"Well, I overheard that maybe Josh wasn't killed, but that he overdosed on nicotine. If that's such a thing.

They're only holding the kid until all the tests to
confirm the overdose are in."

Jacobson's eyes went wide. "He died from nicotine
poisoning?"

I nodded.

Jacobson's shoulders sagged in relief and, as if he'd
realized what he'd done, quickly said, "I supposed I imagined something gorier." He made like he was stabbing
the air.

As if, buddy.

Everyone with a lick of sense knew if Josh had been
eighty-sixed with a knife, that would have been in the
paper and I would be more than a person of interest.

I sat in the opposite chair. "Is it possible for someone
to OD on nicotine?"

Jacobson scratched his temple. "I suppose, if there
were other factors. Typically, too much nicotine makes
people sick, and when that happens, they cease engaging
in the nicotine activity making them ill."

I said, "If a person is trying to quit smoking, what
would they do?"

Jacobson leaned back in his chair and said, "Most
people try to stop by chewing nicotine gum and going
cold turkey, but then they fail. Nicotine replacement
therapy, though, has shown some success. Trouble is, the
triggers of smoking don't get addressed, just the
cravings."

I said, "Like Josh, rumor is he smoked two cigarettes
after," — I cleared my throat — "sex. Hypothetically, if a
person did that while wearing two patches, would that

cause an overdose?" I left out how Josh's water had traces of nicotine.

Jacobson shook his head. "Hypothetically, that person would need more. But not much more would be my guess. Two patches?" His look was questioning.

I nodded and held up two fingers. "What more can a person do besides gum and patches?"

Jacobson rubbed his face, "Nasal sprays, lozenges, and inhalers like Josh used."

Pictures flashed through my mind "Josh had an inhaler?"

Toby said, "I'm on it."

Jacobson's eyes went wide and he waved off my question. "Nicotine poisoning is rare. Nicotine as a murder weapon is even more rare. I think there are only a few cases, and the victim was poisoned over time. Plus, a few cigarettes here and there while wearing the patch isn't going to tip the scale."

I smiled. "What if, hypothetically of course, that person was giving *the business* to a host of women. Smoking, using the patch—"

"Yeah, that's a lot of nicotine, but again, I think they'd be getting sick and wouldn't be up to doing *the business,* as you put it. Maybe if that person were injected with a large dose at once, then I could see all the additional activity and patching would compound the effect."

Because Josh died from nicotine poisoning, that brought me back to square one. Where did the fatal dose come from? My who and where.

Boomer stood in front of me with a mini flashlight.

"I'm going to look into your mouth, ears, and at your eyes."

"But it's my hip," I said trying to keep my voice from reflecting my freaked-out state. An ear exam would produce my earpiece and I doubt I could pass that off as a large chunk of ear wax.

"Standard practice," Boomer said and lifted his brows expectantly as he pointed the flashlight beam toward my mouth.

Precious said, "Oh, crap, Sam. Get out. Get out now. DB is there." There was a scuffling sound and the chiming her car made when the door opened.

And here I thought DB was a crappy cop. Look at him following the clues. After yesterday's gathering at my house, Leo had left with the task to get some of this info to DB and the other cop on the case. Apparently, he'd done just that.

The universe had not only saved my butt but handed me an opportunity I wouldn't pass up.

"Is there something wrong with your mouth? Is that why you won't open it?" Boomer asked.

I was buying time. I smiled without showing teeth and shook my head.

A rap on the exam room door.

Jacobson gave me a sideways glance then moved to open the door. His secretary was there, and she whispered something to him. My guess was, "The cops are here."

Jacobson paled and looked at me. "Come back if you want that referral."

"Mind if I use the restroom before I leave?"

Jacobson shook his head, then exited, closing the door behind him.

I waited a beat then stuck my head out the door. No one was in the hallway. I jogged to the closed door across the hall that wasn't labeled with any sign.

Jacobson's office. Filing cabinets not included. I tried the next door. Another examination room. I surveyed the small hallway. Two doors on my right, three on my left. On my right was the exam room I had been in and the door to the restroom. To my left was Jacobson's office, where he and DB would likely come to talk any moment now, the second exam room and... I dashed for the last door. It was locked.

Voices came closer to the door that separated the front waiting room from me. I sprinted to the restroom and closed the door as DB and Jacobson came into the back. When the restroom light was on, a loud fan automatically engaged, making it hard to hear what the men were saying.

I said to Precious and Toby, "I'm gonna do some quick snooping. I'll be out in a flash." I took out my lock-picking kit and gave a silent thanks to Mrs. Wright.

Leo's voice came across the line. "I'd advise against that, Samantha."

"Crap." I eased open the door to the restroom and poked my head out. DB and Jacobson were not in the hallway. I had to be quick because, if DB wanted Josh's records, then we were both after the same thing. Before stepping out into the hall, I whispered. "Are you in your uniform?"

"Yes," Leo replied. "I'm on break."

"Then you should hand the earpiece to Precious." I dashed to the locked door and knelt before the knob. I let out a slow breath as I slid my tools into the keyhole like Mrs. Wright taught me. I felt the nooks and crannies of the lock and used my utensils like a key. The lock turned, and I grinned like a crazed monkey.

"I'm in," I said, incredulous.

"This is a bad idea," Leo said.

"Shut up," I said. My anxiety was shooting skyward. Getting caught by DB would not be a good thing. Inside, I scanned the cabinets looking for the C drawer. I whipped it open. This was where being a strong reader would have come in handy.

"Chapman," I said as I went through my mental system I'd learned in school on how to recall letters even though matching the sounds to the symbols didn't always make sense for me. "Ch," I made the initial sound.

"Ch?" Leo echoed.

"Letter C. Letter H," Precious said in the background.

I closed my eyes and pictured the shape those two letters made. "Got it," I said and pulled open a drawer.

Leo said, "What you're doing is breaking and entering."

I snorted. "Is not. I'm paying to be here, and the people here know of my presence." Spin, my dad always said everything came down to spin.

"Did you enter a space that was locked?" Leo again being all Johnny-law.

I flipped through the files but no Chapman. I took a

picture of the files with their names showing so Precious could double-check me later. Not that later would do me any good once I left. "If I did, would you really want to know?"

He groaned.

I eased the cabinet drawer closed. Now, how in the world was I gonna get out of here?

"Listen," I said, "I'm headed out. Everyone needs to be quiet so I can hear." I pressed my ear to the door. Nothing. But that didn't mean Jacobson and DB weren't standing in the hallway not talking while Jacobson looked for his keys or something.

This could play out two ways. They were either in the hallway or not. How I approached my exit would be the key. Ease open the door was a sneak-out. Flinging open the door was exiting without guilt.

I flung the door open, but not so much that it banged against the wall. I wanted to be quiet in case they weren't there.

And they weren't.

Luck was on my side.

Reengaging the lock, I eased the door closed then hoofed it down the hallway. I'd made it halfway, just past Jacobson's office door when it opened.

"Samantha?" Jacobson said.

I faced them and pressed my hands to my stomach. "Too many pain meds upset my stomach." I gave a chin nod to DB.

"What are you doing here, Sam?" DB stuck his hands on his hips.

"Not that it's any of your business, but I'm a patient here." I rubbed my hip. "Remember that hit and run that you all were supposed to be working on? Yeah, I'm the victim of that, in case you forgot."

"You always been a patient here, or is this something new?" DB asked.

I shook my head. "I'm afraid HIPPA doesn't allow the good doctor or me to tell you that information." I gave a finger wave. "I'm out. Have a good one."

"Wait a second," DB said.

Leo and I groaned in unison.

"You better not be here butting into you know what." He attempted to give me the old evil-eye stare that only worked when the receiver was afraid of the giver.

"What?" I said, feigning confusion.

"You know what," he said.

"What is this 'what' you're talking about? I have no idea what it is you're trying to say."

"Yeah you do," he said.

This was where growing up with the chief of police came in handy. You know how to push his buttons.

"No, I don't. Is this 'what' like an elusive yeti?"

He rolled his eyes. "Who said the 'what' was a yeti?"

"You did."

"No, you did," he argued.

"Actually—" Jacobson tried to interject.

"Whatever, this conversation is ridiculous. Talking with you DB gives me a headache," I said, then turned and rushed out of the office.

Precious's SUV was idling by the curb, and I jumped

into the passenger seat, ripping my earpiece out at the same time.

Leo, the be-in-control-freak that he was, was driving, and Precious was in the back.

Leo smirked. "That was some game you just played with him. Remind me to avoid that at all costs."

I pointed to myself. "Now who's Jeopardy and who's Wheel of Fortune?"

THE NEXT DAY, while Leo was looking into the inhaler Jacobson had mentioned, I took Cora to the park after school. I'd volunteered as a recess and lunchroom aide for the day and did my part as protective aunt, putting a stop to the dessert-stealing-zombie-trash-talking kids. Caught them red-handed. Following some cleverly emphasized words during my come-to-Jesus meeting, we all left understanding that their nonsense stopped today.

Wind River had done a fantastic job of meeting the needs of its residents, including those of the families with stay-at-home moms or dads. Our main park had a zip line that deposited people at the beginning of a mildly strenuous hiking trail that wound around by the river before circling back to the park. The playground was a kid's dream come true with a fort that looked like a covered wagon, swings, slides, and a merry-go-round.

We played for a while, me mostly doing the pushing

and spinning work while we talked about her mom, the small number of friends she had at school, and the bad dream she'd had last night. Amazing what a kid will say when they were distracted with play.

Poor Cora, her morale was low. Her self-esteem teetering.

"Wanna ride the zip line into the woods? I can show you a few tricks Grampi taught me when I was your age." Cora needed to do something that made her feel like a winner. And, frankly, so did I.

"What kind of things?"

I grabbed the chains of her swing as the arc brought her closer to me and said in a lowered voice, "Like how to start a fire?"

A fire pit with stone seats marked the halfway point on the trail.

She looked over her shoulder, her eyes wide. "I'm not allowed to play with matches."

I let go of the swing and gave her a push. "Who said anything about matches? I'll teach you old-school."

Cora jumped off the swing and landed on her feet like a cat. She spun to face me. "Okay, teach me."

This kid and her spirit! We made our way over to the zip line ladder. And by zip line, I was talking about thirty-five yards and no more than six feet off the ground with a large sandy pit underneath to catch the fallers. Zippers had two travel options. Hang onto the handlebars and away you go. Or sit on a set of handlebars with a center bar to lean into for support and a second pair of handlebars to grip. The zip line ended on a platform and made getting off the line easy. I fitted Cora with the bar between her legs and told her how to hop off when she got to the end.

"You set?" I asked.

She nodded.

I hesitated before making my offer. "We can walk to the trail, too. If you're nervous."

"I'm not nervous," she said. "I was looking at that guy over there. You said I should always pay attention to the people around me, and he's been watching us."

I scanned the space in front of us. "What man?"

"At your six," she said, likely repeating what she heard from TV.

From a kid who didn't know how to tell time I found this adorable. "My six is behind us."

"Over there," she said and pointed.

I followed her finger to my nine where I caught the flash of a man in a bright blue ball cap step behind the tree line. "When did you notice him?"

She shrugged. Another hard question for a kiddo with no time concept. I said, "Was it when we were on the merry-go-round or the slides?"

"Slides," she said. "Right before the swings."

Ten minutes ago.

"Was he with a kid?"

She shrugged again, so I let it go. "I'll keep my eyes peeled. Tell me if you see him again. Ready?"

She nodded.

Then, with her hands gripping the handlebars, I gave her a push.

Yes, we could have walked to the trail, but this was more fun.

At the end of the line, I led Cora through the trail and pointed out various flowers and how to identify poison ivy. I loved being in the woods. Rachel didn't care for it as much as I did, and that's why doing this with Cora felt like I was teaching her something. Giving her something maybe her dad would have had if he'd lived.

"When can we start a fire?" she asked.

I chuckled. "A fire is all about safety. You could burn the entire forest down if you don't set it up properly. Up ahead is a fire pit, and we can practice there."

Cora skipped ahead, notes from the theme song of her favorite TV show wafting back to me. This was what I'd tell my sister. That her child, though out of sorts to a degree, was still happy. Even though Cora's routine had changed, she worried about her mom, and was too young to process everything that came with her situation, she felt safe enough and loved enough to sing and skip.

Cora came to an abrupt stop and began to backpedal toward me. I jogged ahead, fearing a coyote or fox might be on the trail.

"What?" I asked as I tucked her into my side.

"I thought I saw that guy again." She pointed ahead but slightly to the left. "In the trees."

It was possible the guy she was referring to was ahead of us on the trail. He had slipped away before we did the zip line, and other side trails fed into the main one we were on.

"Don't worry, I got everything we need in here." I

bumped her with my backpack. Not that I thought we needed anything. Chances were high it was a day hiker like us, but I wouldn't discount my niece's feelings.

And having been handcuffed to a bike rack, I wouldn't discard being unprepared for the unknown either. I now pinned a small pouch with a spare handcuff key to the inside of my waistbands.

Having been a kid who had to go through life overcoming an obstacle at every turn, I'd found my niche in the outdoors and had learned to be prepared when outdoors thanks to my dad. Now, I was prepared for criminal incidents as well.

We came around a bend in the path that opened up to the fire pit and the stone seats that circled it. Cora ran ahead to look at the pit then turned back to me, excitement sparkling in her eyes.

I held up a hand, hoping to restrain her zeal. "Okay, we first have to make sure the area is clear." I kicked away a few branches. "We want to keep the fire contained."

Cora did a lap around the pit moving the odd branch or twig then gave me the thumbs-up as she plopped onto a rock next to me.

"One day, I want a backpack like that," she said in awe as I took out items from my pack. I handed her a bottle of water.

"Is this to put out the fire?"

I smiled. "It can be, yes, but I was thinking you probably needed a drink. We can use the sand and dirt around here to put out the fire." I laid out a ferro rod and a striker and explained the role of each. "When you're bigger, I'll teach you how to use the ferro rod with the back of the knife because having more than one way to make a fire is essential."

I explained the concept of tinder and kindling, and then together we built a small teepee of sticks using crushed dry leaves for tinder. "You can also use twine, dry moss, and crushed-up potato chips."

Cora was an engaged student with anxious hands ready to try her skills with the ferro rod and striker.

"It's not easy," I cautioned. "It can be frustrating." I showed her how to strike and explained how we wanted the spark to land as close to the tinder as possible. Then I handed my tools over.

Cora squealed. "This is so cool."

"I'm glad you think so. I thought the same when I was your age."

It took several strikes for Cora to make a spark. Then several more for her to strike and create a shower of sparks. Her small mouth was compressed tight as she worked hard.

"Patience," I reminded her. "It gets easier with experience."

When a spark landed, I placed my hand over hers to keep her from striking again, showed her the spark, then bent low to gently blow on the budding fire. Seconds later, it erupted into flames.

I wrapped her in a hug. "You did it!"

Cora shook her head. "My hand hurts. I don't think I'll be good at this." But the smile on her face belied her worries.

"Anything worth having takes work," I said. "Let me get a picture of you and the fire. Grampi is gonna be so proud." With my cell phone, I took a few images. It was then I caught sight of something in the trees. An unnatural color, bright blue, standing out among the autumn foliage. I sat next to Cora and distracted her with a granola bar and gummies then removed my stun gun from my backpack. I tucked it into my back pocket.

Logic told me this guy could be exactly what I told Cora he was—a day hiker. But my spidey-senses said otherwise. Maybe it was because we were only getting glimpses of him, like a fleeting butterfly. Whereas with day hikers and park goers, paths tended to cross, and this guy wasn't crossing. This made his actions suspicious.

Playing it cool became my game as I kept one eye searching the woods for him and the other on Cora. She'd be bummed to have to put out her fire moments after making it, so I let her enjoy her snack while marveling in her creation. When we were done, I proposed heading to the playground. Together we tossed dirt on the fire until it was extinguished. I dumped some water on it for an extra measure.

"How do you make a fire when it's wet?" she asked. Good question considering where we lived.

"I'll show you that, too, when it gets wet around here. It's the same way, the trick is finding the dry materials."

She took my hand. "Thanks, Aunt Sam. This was awesome."

"I think so, too." I gave her hand a squeeze.

She stopped short. "Look, in the trees. There's that

guy." She pointed like all children do with no concerns for subtlety.

Sure enough, ten feet from the trail was the blue hat. The man was distinguishable only by vague characteristics. He was taller than me, white, and not wearing a pack so not a day hiker.

I stepped in front of Cora, but kept us moving forward. "Hey," I called out to him. "Can we help you? You lost?" I had my phone in one hand, ready to press the essential keys.

When the hat turned toward me, I glimpsed half a face, a shadow over the top half.

I gasped, not believing my eyes.

"Hey," I yelled again. "You in the hat." I grabbed Cora's hand, and we jogged down the path toward him, me looking for a way to dart into the trees.

Blue Hat took off on a run.

I said to Cora, "It's okay. I think I know that person."

Her worried expression eased only slightly as we jogged down the path. If she hadn't been with me, I would have crashed between the trees after him.

"Hey," I yelled at him again. "I see you." And for good measure, I added, "Don't be a chickenshit. Come out here."

But he didn't, and we stayed in pursuit, albeit slow. And that's the thing. He wasn't speeding off either. We came around the bend that opened to the playground, and I crashed into Leo.

"I've been looking for you," he said. "Was just about to

call you." He gave Cora and I the once over. "You guys okay?"

Cora said, "Aunt Sam is chasing some guy in the woods. He's been following us."

Leo caught my eye, and I shrugged then resumed scanning the woods. Blue Hat had disappeared like the sun does behind clouds, only the trees were his cloak.

"Why were you looking for me?" I asked him.

"Break in the case and thought you'd like to hear." He gestured to the jungle gym ahead of us. "Feel like climbing Cora?"

"Can I?" she asked me. This wasn't seeking permission; this was her asking if we were safe.

"Totally, it's all good here," I said and smiled in a way I hope was reassuring. Inside, my mind was spinning as I tried to process what I'd just seen.

Cora trotted off.

Leo said, "You were right. The inhaler was with the evidence from his office. A mistake at the lab had it in the wrong evidence box. Thankfully, the bag was labeled correctly. Anyway, we tested the inhaler. Inside it was a toxin. Not nicotine."

He had my attention. "The inhaler was spiked?"

Leo nodded. "Ricin. It was one of those inhalers that marked the number of puffs a person takes. Only one was used. Boomer Jacobson was the one who gave Josh the inhaler, not the pharmacy. And get this, when they brought him in, the first thing he said was that Josh and Carlie were fooling around during her 'swim time'. You were right about Josh being a player. Any chance you recall Josh using the inhaler the day he died?"

My mind wouldn't conjure up the images of the day Josh died since it was too busy trying to piece together the last moments with the man in the blue hat.

I shook my head. "I'm sorry. I can't focus. I'll need some time. I'm... I saw..." I pointed to the trees.

"Did you see the one-with-nature flasher? We've had some complaints about a guy on the trail, flashing people. We haven't told the press yet, hoping we would catch him."

I scanned my memories one last time then shook my head again. "No, it wasn't a flasher. This is gonna sound crazy, but this guy, he was wearing a blue hat and it blocked part of his face but he,"—I gulped— "he looked just like Carson."

28

TUESDAY

THERE WAS no time to pursue the Carson look-alike, though I badly craved knowing if he was dead or not.

I mean, he'd been declared dead. And, yeah, I thought my brain was probably playing tricks on me. Add in my tendency to be a conspiracy theorist and doubter, and I was seeing Carson in weird places.

Okay, only two times so far—at the docks of the Windy River and today in the park.

After dropping Cora at my parents, I idled in LC and forced myself to get my head back in the game. Leo followed us to their house and stood outside my Jeep, his arm across the lowered window.

"If Boomer gets arrested, does that mean Levi will be let out?" Was my job done? Even though I'd resolved nothing and proved even less.

"Yeah, but ricin has to be found in Josh's system. And knowing DB, he'll wait until the last moment to arrest

Boomer and try to retain them both. Levi did confess after all."

"Why wasn't ricin found in the toxicology?"

"It's not something commonly tested."

I gave Leo a quizzical look. "Shouldn't a battery of tests be done to rule out everything?"

He smiled. "Not when all that costs money and when an easier, more obvious option is available."

I tapped a finger against my steering wheel as I thought about the recent turn of events. "Let me make sure I have this straight. The medical examiner said Josh died from nicotine poisoning based on the levels in his system, which were discovered because I saw Josh vaping and my dad mentioned the current epidemic with vaping lung. Eventually this points us to Levi because the police were looking for vaping juice and found a vial in Josh's desk with Levi's fingerprints on it."

Leo nodded.

"But no other substances or toxins were found in his system?"

"That we test for. The medical examiner always takes extra samples in case other tests need to be done later. Like we're experiencing in this homicide."

I squinted as I forced my brain to bring all the elements into one picture. "We have a vial of liquid nicotine in Josh's desk that had an exceedingly high nicotine content. We have flavored water tablets treated with nicotine that we think Jenna sent. And we have ricin in the inhaler that Boomer gave him." I raised a brow and looked at Leo in question. "Am I looking for one suspect or several?"

Leo shook his head in wonder. "The things I see on this job."

"Jenna wanted Josh dead because he'd burned her before, and she knew he'd do it again. He wasn't going to let her get her hands on any of the money." I snapped my fingers in realization. "That's why having the joint account with Alice Andrews's name on it helped Josh. The account did two jobs, blackmailed Alice and kept Jenna from accessing it. The only account she cleaned out was the Pay Forward For the Kids account."

Leo said, "Which, by no means, was chump change."

"Nope, but think of all the money left behind. I bet she saw his promise of Fiji as the ruse it was. Then Levi. He confessed to killing Josh because—"

"Josh was stealing from Levi's family and, according to Levi, playing his mom for a fool."

I sighed wearily and brought up something I'd been dreading that I'd discovered in my research. "I read online that nicotine is still used in pesticides in the US."

Leo nodded. "Yep."

"And I hate to even say this out loud, but it's possible that Levi could have been doctoring Josh's food when he ate at their house with pesticides that had nicotine in it. Untraceable in certain foods with bold flavors."

Leo was silent.

I continued. "I don't want to say this—"

"Don't." His lips pressed into a grim line.

"But that's a fair amount of circumstantial evidence

against Levi and not much against anyone else. Especially if ricin isn't found in Josh's system."

His jaw muscles ticked. "Levi didn't do it. I'm not wrong about this."

I held up my hands in defense. "Fair enough. I had to say it, though. I had to put it out there."

"Get to Carlie before DB does."

"You want me to confirm that she and Josh were playing naughty student and teacher?"

He nodded. "And anything else she can tell us about Josh. Did she know about the scams he was running? Take notes."

I screwed up my face in protest. "Hello, do you know who you are talking to? I don't 'take notes.' I put it all here." I tapped my temple. "And even if I did take notes, you simple humans with your ABC and 123 could never decipher my notes. You aren't fully evolved," I said haughtily.

Leo chuckled. "True. Call me when you're done with her."

I put LC in reverse. "Watch your six, officer. If DB finds out you're playing behind the scenes, you could get canned."

"You watch *your* six. No more phone calls after you've been attacked or hit by a car. I'm not a fan of those."

"I'm not a fan of making them." I looked over my shoulder in preparation to back out but then looked at him. "Do you really think that guy in the woods was your flasher?"

Leo bobbed his head as if he to say kinda, maybe.

"Does the flasher look like Carson?"

It was Leo's turn to let out a weary sigh. "The descriptions we have are a white guy, about Carson's height, and wears glasses."

"This guy didn't have glasses."

Leo stuck his hands on his hips. "Maybe the flasher got contacts."

Maybe. Or maybe Lockett wasn't joking when he said it would be just like Carson to fake his own death. I wasn't sold on the flasher theory. Though the alternative wasn't any better.

"Okay," I said with forced vigor. "I'm off to shake down Carlie Jacobson."

"I hope she talks," Leo called as I backed down the driveway.

Time to collect on when I distracted DB from giving her a ticket for her terrible parking job at How Ya Bean.

Using my phone's GPS, I drove toward the hills on the outskirts of Wind River, where the homes were new and large and the yard ridiculously small.

The driveway was devoid of cars, but I saw movement through the large front window.

Before I reached the walk to the front door, the garage door began to open. I paused and waited while it made its ascent.

Carlie Jacobson was tossing a tote and duffle bags into the car.

"Going somewhere?" I stepped into the garage.

She jumped and squealed, holding the tote over her

chest as if it were armor to protect her. She pointed a finger at me. "I have nothing to say to you."

I slapped my hands against my legs in false disappointment. "And here I thought a 'thank you' wouldn't be asking a lot. Guess the news is right, and we've become a society of all take and no give."

She narrowed her eyes. "A thank you for what?"

I pointed to her SUV. "For saving you from a ticket even though you rightfully deserved it. Got myself handcuffed to the bike rack for my efforts. You're welcome."

She grinned maliciously. "You deserved it."

I let her anger roll off me. "You're right. I deserve a thank you." I gestured like she should pay up.

"Never," she said.

I gently kicked a duffle bag that was on the ground between us. "Looks like you're in a hurry. Yet, I've got all day." I looked over my shoulder. LC was blocking her exit unless she went all-terrain and drove over her yard. The desperation in her eyes told me she was capable.

She tossed the tote she'd been clutching into the back. "If I'm here when they let Boomer go, he'll kill me."

I caught myself mid-eye roll. Typically remarks such as the one she just made were hyperbole, but in Carlie's case, her husband was downtown for homicide.

"Because you were sleeping with Josh?" I went for broke.

Carlie snorted. "Yeah, it's okay for Boomer to bone his dippy receptionist, but if I get my fix elsewhere, he has a conniption fit." She stabbed at the air with her finger for added emphasis.

"How do you know he was fooling around with his receptionist?"

She rolled her eyes. "I used to be his receptionist."

Fair point. "Boomer said you were seeing Josh during your swim time? When was that?"

She glared at me as she picked up the duffle by our feet. "You aren't going to pin Josh's death on me."

"I'm not trying to pin it on anyone except who actually did it. And I don't think it's a sixteen-year-old kid."

Carlie snorted. "Don't be so sure. Levi Danner caught me and Josh 'swimming'." She did air quotes and chuckled at her own joke.

Carlie's lack of empathy for others made me want to slash her tires.

She continued, "And he was pissed. Said some awful things to Josh. Threatened him, even."

"Threatened how."

"Said he would do whatever it took to get Josh out of his mom's life."

As threats went, that was benign. "Did Levi have a weapon?"

Carlie shook her head.

I sighed in frustration as I tried to make the big picture come into focus. Josh was dating Laura but sleeping with Carlie. Josh was also scamming companies and Recode and Reshape parents and.... Could he have been done in by a jealous husband? Perhaps all the extracurricular cons Josh had running were simply that and not the impetus for his death.

"You have to admit, a jealous husband is far more

likely to eighty-six someone than a teen protecting his mom's heart."

Carlie stuck her hands on her hips. "Sure, but which jealous husband was it?" She laughed bitterly. "Because Laura Danner and I weren't the only women to fill his calendar."

"Ah-ha, I knew he was a player. All that smoking had to mean something." I leaned against her SUV, trying to force the mental snapshots into one large picture.

Carlie snorted. "As if you didn't know. Puh-leez. He was priming you to make his move." She made a heart with her two hands and placed them over her chest.

"He was gross."

She let her hands drop to her side. "He was good. Like real good. He had moves like Jagger." She wiggled her hips. Then her eyes got glassy as she lost herself in a memory. She fanned herself. "He was like an addiction. I couldn't give him up. Even though I knew I should. He knew how to pay just the right amount of attention. Every time with him was like getting devoured and adored." She slumped against her SUV and wiped her brow. "Oh, lord, I miss him."

"Ew," I said.

"Clearly, you've never been devoured and adored."

"Hard pass," I said.

"You know, I think that's how Boomer busted me. Josh and his stupid pretense that he didn't smoke. Always asking me to get him more patches from Boomer's office. I had to stop when Boomer noticed they were missing. Then Josh went to Boomer to start nicotine replacement therapy. Had Josh not been so cocky Boomer would've never connected the dots between his missing patches, Josh, and me."

"Did you ever see Josh use an inhaler or anything like that?"

"Just the vape pen, but he said the flavors left a bad taste in his mouth." She laughed. "Like cigarettes leave a good taste?"

"It didn't appear to hold him back," I said.

"True." The wistful, longing expression returned to her face.

"Who else was he sleeping with?"

Carlie seemed in the mood to share now that she'd revisited Josh-time.

She pushed from the SUV, looking everywhere but at me. "I don't know for sure."

Lie. "Any guesses?"

"Every mom at the school?" she said with a laugh. "Josh didn't keep women long. He didn't like things to get complicated. He was going to replace me with you."

"What makes you think that?"

She gave me the once over, her lip curling up in disgust. "Because he was asking you to meet privately during the time we got together."

Ah, that explained the animosity. I shook my head and grimaced in revulsion. "Never."

She smirked. "You mean now we'll never know."

There was no point in arguing. She thought Josh was the-bomb-dot-com.

"I need to get out of here before Boomer gets

released." She looked worriedly toward the door into her house. "I don't want the kids to see us go nine rounds."

I inclined my head to outside the garage where a police car was parking on the street. "I bet they'll have a few questions for you first. Ask them when Boomer will get out. Tell them you need protection. If you're as scared of him as you seem, maybe you should have it recorded somewhere for future reference."

She looked past me and groaned. "You're a jinx, Samantha True, you know that? Wherever you show up, trouble follows."

"Yep," I said and pushed from her SUV. "Thanks for the conversation."

I passed Officer Gee as I was walking out and he was coming in. He side-eyed me, but I kept going.

I drove to the end of the street, my mind turning over everything Carlie had said. I texted Toby and asked him to dig around in Josh's email and look for possible girlfriends or lovers. He would also hack into Josh's text messages, too. Recalling Danika's behavior at the PTC meeting and at the Celebration of Life party, I asked Toby to spend extra time on her.

Using my phone, I accessed the images of Josh's calendar.

Thursday, swim icon. On his calendar for the Thursday we were supposed to meet about Cora's sexual harassment was the swim icon and a camera.

Was that supposed to be me? And, if so, was Josh's calendar nothing but him marking notches on the proverbial bedpost?

Frustrated, I banged my head gently on the steering wheel because chasing down all the women sleeping with Josh sounded awful, especially if they were going to go into detail like Carlie had.

Blech. I shivered in revulsion.

But I'd do it because if there was one jealous or enraged husband gunning for Josh, then potentially there was a second. And possibly a third.

How many people tried to kill Josh, and who was successful in their endeavors?

29

TUESDAY

IN THE MIDST of trying to get to the bottom of Josh's death, a dog across town required my attention.

Driving away from Wind River and the case gave me anxiety. Leaving the vicinity felt like I might miss something important, or worse, dropping the ball completely.

Truth was, I was stymied on how to uncover Josh's other lovers, emojis weren't enough. Precious suggested I ask in the weekly school email newsletter. I tucked that idea in my back pocket as a last resort.

In the meantime, it was me and Simon and a dog park where, hopefully, an epiphany would happen.

A girl could dream, couldn't she?

At AJ's, Simon greeted me at the door, tail wagging as he pranced in front of me.

"You ready for some fun, big guy?" I gave his head and ears some good rubs.

He barked in response.

"Well, come on then." I grabbed his leash and the bag of toys and treats that hung from coat hooks in the mudroom. "Let's do this."

What was great about a dog was they leave everything behind and enjoy the moment. This became my goal as well as Simon and I played hard at the dog park.

At AJ's house, I unleashed Simon and gave him a nuzzle of thanks. I said, "You love Sam, don't ya? You think she's awesome." He licked my face as affirmation.

"Yes." A voice from around the corner said. "We do think she's awesome."

I poked my head into the kitchen. AJ was making a smoothie that was the color of green baby poo.

"That looks gross." Pointing out the obvious was my superpower.

"If you put it in a travel mug that's not clear, you can't see it and you don't think about it. It's actually tasty." He held out the blender. "Taste?"

I shook my head. "Pass. How was practice today?"

AJ shrugged, but there was nothing nonchalant about the stiffness of his shoulders and the downturn of his mouth.

"That good, huh?" I poured cold water into Simon's water bowl, refilling it as fast as he was slopping it up.

"Being patient isn't a strength of mine." He stuck a straw in his green goo and began slurping it up.

I grimaced and pretended to vomit in my hand. AJ chuckled.

I said, "Don't you think patience needs to be a strength?" I held up my hands to the side like I was framing a TV. "It's a big game. The Pioneers need this win. But your competitors are known for kicking butt in the second half and you're down by two touchdowns. You have the ball. You're in the pocket, and the offensive line is doing their job. They're giving you time to find the play that will help you score. Patience would come in handy then, wouldn't it?"

AJ, still sucking down his drink, rolled his eyes. He then set his empty cup on the counter. "First, I have to get onto the field and be the guy in the pocket during a real game instead of practice."

I pointed to his cup. "You could make that drink for the QB. I bet his GI system will keep him out of the game for at least a week. No one can drink that and lead a normal life afterward."

AJ put his cup and blender in the sink. "I do."

I leaned against the counter. "So you say, but I won't be sticking around to find out if that's true. I want to talk to you about the Recode and Reshape Program."

"You want Troy here, too?" AJ gestured to the living room.

Slapping myself on the forehead in front of a client was probably not the smartest move to elicit confidence, but I did it anyway. Of course, I wanted to talk to Troy. Duh! Having not done so until now was a rookie move.

"I'll take that as a yes."

I nodded.

"Tee-Roy," AJ bellowed across the house.

His brother shuffled into the room wearing sweats and a baggy T-shirt. AirPods hung from his ears.

"Dude, you could have just texted instead of yelling," Troy said.

AJ crossed his arms. "I'm not going to text you when you're not even twenty feet away." He pointed to the couch. "Plant it."

Troy mumbled, "You're lucky I was between tunes." He dropped dejectedly onto the couch. "What did I do now?"

In an effort to build a bridge to Troy, I changed the narrative. "You didn't do anything. It's me. I need help. I'm hoping you're the guy who can help." I settled in the chair across from him and leaned forward, my chest down toward my legs. I wrapped my arms under my knees, presenting myself to him much like I do Cora, in a way I hoped wasn't threatening.

AJ took the seat next to Troy on the couch.

I said, "There were some things going on in your program that weren't on the up and up."

Troy crossed his arms and looked away. "I just did what I was told."

I held up my hand to stop him. "Let me start over. Someone killed your instructor at the Recode and Reshape Program, and I'm trying to determine if it had anything to do with what Josh was asking you all to do there."

Troy cut his eyes to me, his arms still snugly crossed.

I continued, "I'm guessing you knew something shady was going on."

Silence.

AJ's eyes narrowed, and I cast him a glare in hopes he'd get the hint and keep his mouth shut.

I pushed ahead. "Do you know that kid, Levi, in your class?"

Troy shrugged. "We weren't allowed to talk to people. Only Principal Josh."

I rolled my eyes. "He asked you guys to call him that?" I shook my head in disbelief. "I don't mean to speak ill of the dead, but what a douche. He asked the adults to call him that, too." I made my hands into little hearts. "He liked to make the heart with his hands and put it on women's chest." I made like I was barfing.

Troy laughed. "Yeah, that is skeevy."

AJ asked, "So you knew this Josh guy?"

I nodded. "He was the principal at my niece's school, and I was tasked with taking pictures for the yearbook." I paused, weighing if I should share the rest of the story. I went for broke. "And I was there when he died. Actually, I was the first person questioned about his death before the police moved on to Levi. I've since been hired to help prove Levi is innocent."

Troy's attention was all mine. As was AJ's.

"Just know when I ask you these questions, it's not to get you in trouble or anything, but to try to find out as much as I can to help Levi.

Troy sunk into the couch. "He hated PJ. That's what we called Josh. Everyone refused to call him Principal Josh. He wouldn't let us talk to each other. We even took breaks separately. But after class, some of us would hang and chat."

AJ asked me, "This Josh guy was doing what?"

I glanced at Troy, who instantly looked down at the floor. "Using the ruse of teaching kids coding, Josh was having kids buy fake products with their parent's credit cards."

AJ nodded as understanding dawned. "And we all just thought they were expenses for the program."

I said, "Yeah, sure. Except some people like you were expecting something tangible. I had my attorney look over that contract you both signed to get in the program. My guess is that Josh couldn't say the program had a monthly payment because of the upfront expense families pay. But it mentions possible additional expenses for technology or other digital media, whatever that is. Josh used that as his loophole to make extra charges on people's account." To get their kid into Recode and Reshape, each family paid three grand.

AJ pinched the bridge of his nose. "Only I started asking what the charges were for."

I gestured to Troy. "And he didn't have anything."

Troy ducked his head and mumbled. "That's when I knew something shady was going on. I went to PJ and asked him about the charges, and he said I must have made a few errors in coding, that there weren't supposed to be charges. He told me how to fix them. Your friend Levi confronted him, too. PJ used to make him sit in the corner and watch Bubble Guppies videos and write papers on the moral of the story. They didn't like each other much. That was clear."

Troy would not be a good character witness for Levi.

AJ said, "I remember those charges being refunded, but then a month later, they started showing up again."

"That's because he had me do it again. And this time I knew I wasn't making a mistake."

I said, "What did you do then?"

"I didn't know what to do. I knew what he was having us do was wrong, so I reported it to the IT lady in the office next to us and she told me she'd look into it. Nothing ever happened. Then I saw them making out in a car one day before class, and that's when I knew it was all a scam."

"You could have told me what was going on," AJ said, anger making his words sharp.

Troy went ramrod straight. "I tried. You kept telling me to straighten up and fly right. You never wanted to listen to what I had to say. You just thought I was trying to get out of the program."

It was AJ's turn to duck his head in shame. "You're right. And I've been consumed with my own issues that I projected onto you." He reached for his brother's shoulder and gave it a squeeze. "I'm sorry Tee-Roy."

"Nice," I said. "If more people communicated like that, we'd have less angry people in the world."

AJ gave me a million-dollar smile. "You can thank your friend Erika for that."

"Precious for the win," I said, and we both chuckled. I

held up one finger. "Quick question, Troy, do you know what day you saw Josh and the IT lady making out?"

Troy shrugged. "I didn't mark it on my calendar with a smiley or anything."

"No, but Josh might have," I said and pulled up the images on Josh's calendar on my phone. I showed the screen to AJ and Troy.

Troy's expression was one of disgust. "Well, considering we have class Monday, Wednesday, and Friday, it had to be one of those days." He pointed to the computer icon. "Maybe Wednesday?" He snickered.

I narrowed my gaze and stared at him. "What?"

"It's gross, really," Troy said.

"I love gross, tell me."

AJ chuckled.

Troy surveyed me with mild revulsion. "You're weird."

I smiled big and wide. "I've heard that before so it must be true." I wanted to know what had made this kid snicker. A memory of some sort, I'm sure.

Troy shook his head. "On the day I saw them making out, they were really into it. An elephant could have sat on the car, and they wouldn't have noticed. They were parked on the far end of the parking lot behind the school."

"You like to park there, too, I noticed."

Troy looked stunned. "How did you know that?"

"Educated guess." No need to tell him his brother hired me to spy on him. I gestured that he should continue with his story. "Go on."

"I just pretended like I didn't see anything, but once I got inside, checked in, and got to my 'station,' I realized I forgot my phone, and when I went back out, Josh was standing by his car in his skivvies, smoking a cigarette."

AJ said, "That's creepy and a little ballsy."

"Ballsy doesn't even begin to explain this guy." I faced Troy. "How many weeks ago was this?"

He shrugged. "Like the week before he died. Oh, and that Levi kid you were asking about? He was behind me and saw the whole thing, too."

QUITTING time for DB was five o'clock sharp. And, apparently, having two suspects for the same murder wasn't concerning enough to make DB stay late.

At five-fifteen, Leo opened the station's back door, for employees only, and let me in. Leo traded Gee for the night shift to provide me this opportunity. I'd done my part by sticking a tracker on DB's cruiser as a precautionary measure should he decide to return to the cop shop.

Tucked under my arm were printouts of Josh's calendar. "Is Laura here?"

He nodded. "Got here ten minutes ago. She's already in the interview room with Levi."

No room at the Juvie Inn was sheer luck for Levi and worked to our benefit, too.

"And Boomer?"

"DB had to cut him loose. Still waiting on the toxicology."

I followed Leo through the back hallway, around the break room, and to the last room in a row of rooms. I looked around confused.

"Exactly where is the jail?" I'd been here before. The police station itself was a large rectangle with the front portioned off for the receptionist and waiting room. Coming in from the rear, I faced a square of cubbies where Leo and others like him had their desks, a bullpen arrangement. To my right were a row of doors. The first being the ever-important restroom. Beyond that were two interview rooms and DB's office. To my immediate right was the break room.

Leo pointed to my left where a steel door with a window was the only decoration on the wall.

"Through that door are two cells. The jail."

The setup was like a scene out of a movie with a Podunk police station. Only this was real life, and we were Podunk. Something I often forgot because our coffee shop was first class and environs pleasing.

Leo led me to the interview room where I'd been held. He rapped his knuckles on the door then flung it open. He ushered me in.

Both Levi and Laura looked up at me in surprise. I returned the surprise when I discovered Lockett was in there, too.

"Dude," I said and held out a fist. We bumped knuckles. "Why didn't you tell me you were in town?"

He pulled out his phone and tapped it. "When's the last time you checked this handy dandy gadget?"

From my backpack, I pulled out my phone and glanced at the screen. The do-not-disturb-I'm-driving notification had automatically engaged, and I hadn't checked since I'd arrived, being too busy putting the tracker on DB and all.

A message from Lockett said he was in town and wanted to get together.

"Yes," I said and showed him the screen. "I'd love to get together after this."

Levi rolled his eyes. "Glad you all get to have a life while I'm stuck in this hellhole."

Laura slapped him upside the head.

Leo cuffed him on the shoulder.

I sat in the chair across from Levi and let the packet of the papers I'd brought flop on the table.

"Thanks for letting me crash this, Levi. I have some questions for you that I hope you'll be able to answer." I smiled, hoping it would break the tension in the room. Because he was right, when we were done here, I got to leave and do whatever the hell it was I wanted.

Levi glared. "I already told your lawyer friend everything I know."

I pressed my foot to Laura's toe, knowing she would likely come across the table at her kid for his bad manners. But his attitude didn't bother me. I probably would be just as belligerent.

"Yeah, but these are questions we just learned to ask.

And they're a bit sensitive." I inclined my head to his mom, hoping he'd read the clue.

His eyes darted between us.

I said, "I can ask people to step out."

Levi glanced at the one-way mirror in the wall that separated him from freedom.

"As if people won't be standing out there listening anyway," he snarled.

Leo jerked his thumb toward the glass. "No one is in there now."

Levi snorted. "How do you know? DB is probably out there, ready-to-use anything I say against me."

I turned my phone toward him and opened the app that was tracking DB. I leaned over the phone to get a look. I pointed to the map. "According to this, DB is down in Hazel Dell getting..." I leaned closer. "It's hard to tell. Donuts maybe? Nope, he's at the gym. Sorry, my bad."

Leo took the phone and inspected the information on the screen. He glanced at me. "You're tracking DB?"

"I defer to my lawyer." I pointed to Lockett.

Lockett chuckled. "Let's get on with this."

I winked at him while unfolding the printouts. "Okay, so here's what I know, and I need you, Levi, to correct me if I'm wrong."

He crossed his arms over the desk and leaned forward. "Ain't got nothing else going on," he mumbled.

Laura snapped, "You should be grateful all these people are here trying to help you."

"I don't deserve help. I hated Josh, and I threatened him," Levi mumbled.

"Was that when you caught him fooling around with Carlie Jacobson?"

Levi's attention was all mine. "Yeah."

"Did you threaten him when you saw him with the IT lady?"

Levi shook his head. "I wanted to, but this other kid was there, and I didn't want any witnesses."

Lockett shook his head in silent resignation.

"What day was it you saw him with the IT lady?

"He called her the computer dragon, and it was—" Levi looked up at the ceiling as if trying to backtrack time.

I placed a blank calendar in front of him. "This is today." I pointed to the square. "You were arrested this day." I subtracted seven days.

Levi hovered his finger over the page then pointed to Wednesday. "It was this day." He slid his finger to Thursday and said, "And this is when I saw him with that mom. They were doing it on his desk."

I placed a picture of Jenna Miller over the calendar. "Is this the computer lady?"

Levi nodded. I cut a glance to Leo.

Back to Levi. "Did you know what Josh was having the other students at the program do?"

Levi glanced at his mom then at me. "No, but it was something with coding. All I know is he wasn't making them watch stupid kid cartoons and asking them to write papers on the moral of the story. Like the guy even knew what morals were. He was shady, and I'm not sorry I threatened him. I'm not sorry he's dead."

Laura gasped.

Lockett said, "Maybe not say those sorts of things to anyone outside of this room. Or just never say them again."

I spread out two pages of Josh's calendar that spanned four weeks. "Does any of this mean anything to you?"

Levi scanned the pages up and down several times.

Laura said, "What teen did this? It's all emojis. This isn't Levi's. He hates emojis."

I put my attention on Laura. "You told me Josh was persistent in asking you out, but how did you two get together in the first place?"

Laura pushed away from the table and briefly chewed on her lower lip before saying, "We met when he asked us for a bid for the pesticide management for the school. But we got to know each other when Mindy Cunningham invited him to our book club. He asked me out every night after book club. I think I gave in around week three."

Pieces began to click together.

Carlie Jacobson was swim.

Jenna Miller was a computer.

Laura Danner was a book.

I said, "And book club was always Fridays?"

She nodded. "We always spent Friday and Saturdays together."

I flipped through my stack of paper and pulled out a Danner Pesticide invoice dated before school started this year. I passed it to Laura. "Does this look familiar?"

"This is the invoice for our service to the school. We maintain the facility monthly and bill them monthly." She scanned the page then gasped. She jabbed her finger at the bill amount. "That's not how much we charge, though. There's an additional one."

"Initially, you billed the school for eight hundred dollars." I needed clarification because I didn't want to make any assumptions and mistakes.

"Yes, and I was paid for eight hundred. But this one turned the amount into eighteen hundred."

I showed her the sheet Gillian had scanned and emailed me. "Yet the school paid eighteen hundred."

Laura looked shocked. "I didn't take this money."

I smiled kindly. "I know. Josh did. He was scamming the school and taking money from every pot he could get his hands in." I pointed to Levi. "He was having the students bill their parents' credit cards for items they weren't buying. The money was going into his account set up by this woman." I touched Jenna's picture.

I tapped my fingers on the calendar pages. "I couldn't crack this code. I couldn't see how it worked with the cons Josh was running. But I think the emojis are to indicate which women Josh was sleeping with. Computer is Jenna. Swim is Carlie, and Laura, you're the book. When I cross-referenced Josh's deposits from Pay it Forward For The Kids, they coordinate with the dollar signs Josh had on his calendar." I looked at Leo. "Do we know when he had appointments with Boomer?"

Leo stood and hustled out of the interview. We sat in silence, Levi looking at the calendars.

Less than a minute later, Leo returned, a sheet of paper in his hands. "I'll read the dates of his appointments and you check them against the calendar." He called out dates, but only a quarter lined up with Josh's calendar.

I shook my head. "They don't match. The appointments are spaced out and not in any pattern. I have a cigarette showing up every four days."

Laura sat up straighter in her chair. "Josh's nicotine replacement therapy was every four days. He was supposed to change his patch to keep from getting a rash, he still got them anyway. The journal was to reassess by looking through the previous four days of entries."

I asked, "He journaled?" I glanced at Leo. "Did we find a journal?"

Leo shook his head. "I went through the inventory list, and there were no notebooks or journals on the list." He held up a hand before I could say anything. Though my expression likely gave away what I'd been thinking.

He said, "I'll go through his office and home again. Not you."

I sighed in frustration and returned my attention to the calendars. "Who or what are tennis and unicorn? I don't want to assume football is that, football."

Levi pointed to the camera icon. "You forgot one. Camera."

I grimaced. "I think that's for me. Carlie said he had a habit of ditching women who were getting too attached or he no longer needed. Carlie said she would occasionally take extra nicotine patches from Boomer's office, but Boomer noticed they were missing so she stopped. That's when she said Josh started making moves on me. And he tried to fit me into his Thursday schedule." The thought alone made me want to throw up in my mouth.

Laura slapped an angry hand on the table. "What was I? His beard?"

Levi chuckled. "You're not using that word right, mom."

She glared at him.

I held up a hand to stop further spats. "I get what you're asking, Laura. And yes, I'm sorry to say that I do think you were a cloak of sorts for him. You continued to make him look upstanding."

She gave a wry smile. "I bet he got a kick out of dating the poor, lonely widow."

My next remark was cruel but had to be said, "Who he also used to scam more money out of."

Lockett leaned back and crossed one ankle over the other. "Crafty son of a gun, this Josh was. Money laundering, embezzlement, and having relations with several women who likely knew about each other but didn't care. A sociopath to be sure." He shook his head in wonder.

"I wasn't okay with the other woman. Women." Laura said with bite.

Lockett said, "You were the exception to the rule, and that's why he stayed with you. By being with you, should any rumors about his philandering circulate, people would come back to you and shake them off. 'Surely, Laura Danner wouldn't tolerate that nonsense'."

To soften the blow, Leo said, "It speaks to your good standing in this community and the fondness people have for you."

Laura wiped a tear from her eye.

Levi grunted and dropped his head onto the table. "I'm sorry I ruined that, Mom."

I said, "And tell me again how it was you killed Josh?"

Levi looked up at me over his arm. "I already told the cops this, and the lawyer." He jerked his head in Lockett's direction.

"But you haven't told me."

He groaned and crossed his eyes.

Seeing his response was the positive affirmation that Leo's gut was right. This kid didn't kill Josh. He thought about it. But who doesn't envision fantasize about life without the person who makes them insanely angry? Yeah, murder fantasies weren't good, but I was sure that's not what happened here. More like a poor decision with everlasting consequences by an impulsive teen. Either way, counseling was in order.

Levi hid his face, and a soft sob came from between his arms.

"Levi?" his mother said, stroking his hair.

He sat up with a jerk, tears streaming down his face. "I didn't want him to die. I wanted to make him really sick. I wanted to make him pay for using you and stealing from us. I went online and read about nicotine, and I knew with the way Josh smoked and wore those patches, he was one good nicotine exposure from vomiting his face off. That's what I was going for." He used his sleeve to wipe away his tears.

I encouraged him to continue. "So you...?"

"Added a dissolvable nicotine pesticide to some vape

juice and left the vials for him to steal. He was taking my vials all the time, saying he was doing it for my own good, but I know it was because he was using them."

"You're vaping?" Laura fairly screamed. "Have I taught you nothing? Have you seen the news?"

"How many vials did you add nicotine to?" I asked.

Levi shrugged. "One or two?"

Lockett said, "Which was it? One or two. Think hard."

Levi slipped his palm down his face and sucked in a ragged breath. He closed his eyes then said, "One. I had two set up to do, but I heard mom and Lanie come home, so I only got to one. I hid them in my shoe."

"Do you know which vials?" I asked.

Levi shook his head.

I said, "Close your eyes and try to picture it again. Even colors could help."

Levi did as I suggested. His eyes popped open. "I like only three flavors, tutti-fruity, marshmallow, and bubble gum. They have similar labels. But their safety seals are different colors. I dumped a lot of the juice out, added the extra nicotine, but made it look slightly used."

I said, "You mean the vial didn't look full."

Levi nodded.

I asked. "What color safety seal did the spiked vial have?"

Levi stared over my shoulder in thought. "It was multi-color. That's tutti-fruity."

I looked first at Locket, then Leo. "And the seal was broken on that vial?"

Back to Levi. He nodded.

I pressed. "And you hid them in your shoe? What about the bucket behind the shop?"

"I started hiding the vials under the bucket after Josh began confiscating them. I used to hide them in my shoe because no one ever looked in my shoes."

Laura mumbled, "He has the smelliest feet."

Levi rested his forehead on his palm. "But Josh saw me put them in my shoes. One day, I went to get one, and they were all gone. I even tried switching flavors, but he still took them. That's when I started hiding my vials behind the shop."

Lockett held up a finger. "Just to be clear, you're saying you poisoned only one vial and left that vial in your shoe. You're saying we'll find the correct vial because the seal is broken and the others are not because they are unused? And you're saying the vial you spiked was tutti-fruity flavored?"

Levi nodded. "And I didn't spike them."

Lockett continued, "And this is why you've been adamant about saying you killed Josh. Because you added a toxin to the vape vial?"

Levi nodded again.

Lockett shook his head. "Dude, any reason why you didn't tell me this in any of our several conversations?"

Levi shrugged. "You didn't ask in the same way she did." He pointed to me.

Leo jumped up and dashed out the door. He returned in seconds and handed Lockett a sheet of paper and kept one for himself. He said, "Item one hundred and thirty-six taken from Levi's bedroom is a vial of vape juice, seal broken. This item was found under your dresser in a tennis shoe."

Leo flipped the page. "Item fourteen. Bubble gum flavored vial taken from Josh's desk. Seal intact."

Lockett flicked the paper and smiled. "If this vial found in your shoe proves to be the laced one, then we have our win. We can prove you didn't kill Josh."

With his hands, Levi covered his face and began to sob. Through his tears, he said, "I'm so glad I'm not a killer."

31

TUESDAY

LEO ESCORTED ME HOME. The hour was late, and his pretense was my safety. Chivalry wasn't dead. But like me, Leo needed to review everything we'd learned today. This was how we processed. Lockett had canceled all plans since he went straight to work on proving Levi's case.

Using the keypad at my front door, I let us in and flung my backpack onto the floor by the foyer table, nearly knocking off the vase of fake flowers. A marble container used to sit there but...well, that's a story for another day.

From the fridge, I took out two IPAs and offered him one. He accepted the bottle and, while in the kitchen, picked up a Sharpie. While taking a long swig, he went to the calendar pages I had taped to the wall. On the side where the space was white, he began to write.

"Carlie is swim, Jenna is computer, you are camera, Laura is book, and cigarettes are when he was supposed to review his nicotine replacement therapy, journal and address where he was struggling."

"Something other than add another patch or have more smokes," I said. "What do you think the odds are that Josh's habit killed him? Could he have overdosed by his own actions?"

Leo shook his head. "I think someone shoved him over the edge. If Josh didn't ingest Levi's overdosed vial, then where did all the extra nicotine come from? Has to be more than those patches. Someone knew his vices and used it against him. Someone like the doctor or a lover."

"Someone being tennis, pencil, coffee, football, or unicorn."

"If any one of those is a person, then yeah." Leo stepped back and stared at the calendar. "Who else do we know Josh... dated?"

I rolled the beer bottle between my hands. "I'm guessing his other afternoon delights were married. That's why they're such a secret. But openly dated? Not even at the Celebration of Life ceremony was that talked about."

Accessing my laptop, I pulled up the information Dad and Toby had uncovered about Josh, and scrolled through it. I paused on a picture of Josh standing outside How Ya Bean with June, my mom, and Alice Andrews. The picture had been taken for Dad's paper, and the article caption that went with it was "Josh Chapman named new principal of Village Garden School." The photo was credited to one of Dad's staff photographers and listed everyone in the picture.

I showed it to Leo. "Why do you think June is in this picture? Am I reaching here, or is that odd?"

Leo studied the image. "Everything is reaching until it pans out. You should ask her." He paused. "Josh was there a lot, at How Ya Bean."

I nodded. "The PTC meetings were held there." I rolled my eyes. "How cliché is that? A bunch of hipster moms having their school meeting at a coffee shop."

"Carlie aside, are any of those other moms sleeping with him?" His tone was hopeful.

"Possibly, sure. I've already thought of that. Mindy Cunningham also runs the book club, so she ran with Josh in two circles. But those women can be catty, and maybe Josh knew better than to create a catfight. What do you know about Danika Post?"

Leo shook his head. "She didn't go to school with us. Moved here from the town over because she took the job at the school. She's had some trouble with her car being vandalized and has been to the station because of that."

"Recently vandalized?" Another reach? Maybe, but interesting. Do coincidences exist, or was this another clue?

He scratched his chin as he thought. "About a month or so. She kept sports gear in her car, and someone broke in and stole it."

"Is that it?"

"Happened three times. Same type of gear." He sat next to me.

"What was it?" My mind was pulsing with a variety of thoughts, trying to pull pieces together. I opened up my photo previewer on my laptop and scrolled through images I'd taken of Village Garden School and its patrons and staff.

"Rollerblades, yoga mat, and tennis racket and balls."

I stopped scrolling. "Tennis?"

The expression on Leo's face told me he knew where I was going with this. "Yeah, but also a yoga mat and rollerblades."

I pointed to the calendar. "What if Danika is tennis? Look, tennis is on the schedule back when he started dating Laura, but it's not on the schedule the week of his death." I handed him my laptop and beer, then got up and went to the wall. "In fact, tennis stopped showing up on his calendar six weeks ago."

Leo, who'd been clicking through my photos, stopped then slid everything onto the coffee table. He joined me at the calendar. "What was it replaced with?"

I ran my finger down the calendar, scanning Tuesdays when tennis had been scheduled. "Nothing specific. Two computers, one swim, coffee twice, and the unicorn twice."

Leo tapped the unicorn emoji. "This doesn't show up on a consistent pattern."

"Yeah, I noticed that. Maybe it's a boon or something. A cash windfall. Like the magical unicorn of goodness."

"Maybe," he said, staring at the wall. "I think you might be right about Danika and tennis."

I nodded in agreement. "I'll go talk to her tomorrow. Besides, she lied to me about resigning, and I'd like to call her out on it."

I plopped down on the couch, exhaustion hitting me hard. On my laptop screen was the picture I'd taken of June's schedule at How Ya Bean. She'd been a stickler for it. On the top, the Tuesday space was a coffee cup and the initials PTC.

"Look." I angled the screen toward him. "June put a coffee cup by the PTC meetings, and on Josh's calendar, he has a coffee cup on Tuesdays. You think that's the PTC meeting symbol?"

"Why not use a schoolhouse or a book or something?"

I laughed. "Because the brain associates how it wants to associate. Look at how Hue and I can have entire conversations using symbols. Maybe Josh put coffee to remind him to go to the coffee shop for the meeting. Maybe he got the idea from June and her coffee shop signs."

Leo slid down next to me and yawned. "I think you're on to something."

"I'll talk to June tomorrow, too."

He nudged me with his shoulder. "You're aware of what's happening here, right?"

I paused and tried to reread the situation. Up until a second ago, I wasn't aware of much other than fatigue weighing me down and stupid emojis that didn't make sense. Was Leo getting a different vibe? I'm not the best for reading social cues, as inference can sometimes be misinterpreted.

He nudged me again and chuckled. I sat there, like a bump on a log, clueless.

Little butterflies did a stutter-flutter in my stomach.

My entire past with Leo had been heavy with irritation, bordering on genuine dislike. Until the Carson thing. Something then changed the relationship between Leo and I, for the good. And I won't lie. I found him sexy as all get out. More so every day. But this friendship was new and blooming, and I didn't want to jack it up.

"Sam?"

Our first case was much like this one. Close to home.

Realization dawned. "Wait, are you talking about when I took pictures for Junior Greevy's accident, which really was—"

"Yep. This case is kinda like that. Our criminal here is likely someone we know. Just like it was back then."

I groaned. For two reasons. One, why would I ever think Leo was hitting on me? Thankfully, I didn't do something stupid like give him come-hither eyes. And two, I really hated it when bad guys were people I knew. Hated it so much I'd gotten out of the crime field and taken pics of babies dressed as bunnies for ten years.

He said, "You're handling this one much better than the last time."

I elbowed him, hard. "I had the flu. Who handles anything well when they have the flu? No one, that's who."

He tossed back his head and laughed.

"It's not funny," I said. "Someone we know and have spent time with likely killed Josh. And I was hoping it was Jenna because she's not one of us."

Leo instantly sobered, but his lips twitched slightly.

I narrowed my eyes in anticipation of what he was

going to say. I knew him well enough to guess a good teasing was about to come.

And it did. "You should be well versed in the get-close-to-the-criminal lifestyle. You married one."

I sprung to my feet and jerked my thumb to the door. "Get out."

Leo grabbed my hand and tugged me down to the couch. "Aw, c'mon Sam. I'm just giving you a hard time. You knew nothing about Carson and his intentions. Just like you know nothing about Josh's killer's intentions. We aren't superheroes. We can't read minds. And bad people hide among the good ones. If you stay in the business, you always keep that in mind. You aren't ever going to be free from the disappointment that evil is always so close."

I softened. "But I wish that weren't true. I hate to think I might have already talked to the killer and walked away none the wiser. I hate knowing they're out there playing us for fools and letting a sixteen-year-old kid take the rap."

Leo said, "I hate that this person will probably kill again to keep their secret."

I nodded in agreement. "I think that's the part that gets me the most. Anticipating another strike, hoping one doesn't come while trying to do everything to prevent it. It's like swinging at a ball, blind."

"You can always stop now. With the information Lockett has, the police should be reinvestigating the case. DB will have to put me on it. He's too short-staffed."

Appalled he would even suggest such a thing, I said, "I

made a promise to you and to Laura. As unnerved as I am —note, I didn't say scared—I'll see this through."

Even if the killer was someone I knew. Even if that made me more jaded and ate away at a bit of my happy parts leaving a fist-sized dark black void of cynicism that threatened to grow.

32

JUNE'S WAS my first stop. Coffee was needed if I had any intention of getting to the bottom of this case.

Last night I'd fired off an email requesting a meeting with Danika. Barging in and calling her a liar, then asking for information, wouldn't work. I didn't need how-to YouTube videos to tell me that.

The constant checking of my phone for a response made me look twitchy with an addiction to either coffee, my phone and the easy online access, or something more nefarious.

The line at How Ya Bean was six people deep. June was running the espresso machine. She looked rough, not fully over the flu. Her complexion was nearly translucent, and her hair was pulled into a messy bun that tomorrow would look greasy. She wasn't wearing any makeup nor dressed in her cute hipster fashion of leggings, short skirts, tight T-shirts, a cardigan, and Birkenstocks. Today she wore baggy sweats and a T-shirt that should reside in the rag bin.

I scrolled through my email. Nothing from Danika. Impatience getting the best of me, I called the school. Thankfully, the other office assistant answered and not Mrs. Rivers. She put me on hold as she transferred me to Danika. Three rings later, and the call went to her voice mail. I called the front office again and got the same woman.

Desperation to catch a killer made me lie. I told the assistant I wanted to make a donation to the school, but I needed Danika to tell me what to do. Danika was, after all, now in charge until a new principal could be hired.

The woman tsked, "I don't know why she didn't pick up. I can see her through the door, and she's just sitting there, messing with her purse. No one is in her office. Let me try again."

Three rings later, voice mail.

My right eye began to twitch.

"Can I help you?" the teen at the register said.

My turn. "Twenty-ounce white mocha latte, please." I shifted my focus to June. "Hey, June. How you feeling?"

She glanced over her shoulder at me, faked a smile, all while banging coffee out of the machine's portafilter. "I've been better."

I nodded in agreement. "I think we all have. Anything I can do to help?"

She shook her head while attaching the newly filled portafilter to the machine, then shifted to frothing milk.

This time she gave me a genuine smile. "That's a nice offer, Sam. Thanks." She poured dark brew into two cups and added milk. She then passed them to the kid working the station next to her. After, she stepped to the counter toward me.

In a low voice she asked, "I heard they arrested Boomer Jacobson. Is that true?"

I scratched my ear in hesitation, pondering what I should share.

She hurried to add, "I only ask because I want to know if the Danner kid will be let go. Shocked me to hear he'd been arrested. I thought maybe you might know more, considering your dad and the paper and all."

I shrugged, "You know as much as I do at this point. Boomer hasn't been officially charged, so that means Levi stays put until Boomer is."

Her reaction was unexpected. She broke out into a large smile. "I know this is mean, but I cannot wait to see Carlie's face when Boomer is charged. Serves her right. She has everything. A husband, kids, a nice house, and she messed it all up by having a fling with Josh."

I straightened. "You knew about Carlie and Josh?"

June snorted. "You only had to watch them for a couple weeks to figure it out."

"Josh was a piece of work," I said, letting my professionalism slip and my bias show.

June leaned against the counter. "He wasn't that bad. Broken inside. Needed lots of affirmation."

Did she forget that he forged some receipts of hers to collect more money and make her business look sketchy?

If so, then I expected people would begin their Principal Josh lament soon, and it would sound like those on the true crime shows. The old, "Oh, Josh. He was fun and nice. Not a mean bone in his body. Everyone liked him."

Only someone didn't like him because they killed him, and two other people attempted to harm him. So...

"Hey," I said intent on changing the subject. I pulled the paper out of my back pocket. "Do you remember this?" It was the picture of Josh being named principal but taken at How Ya Bean.

She nodded.

I grinned and shuffled awkwardly, playing up my discomfort. "This is a dumb question, but why was this taken here and not at the school?"

June looked at the picture and smiled wistfully as she likely recalled the day. "The school was being renovated and Josh didn't have an office. He worked out of here a lot." She pointed to the sign over the calendar. "Free WIFI and all that. Why is that a dumb question?"

I feigned embarrassment. "Because I knew the explanation had to be reasonable, but couldn't, for the life of me, figure it out." I lowered my voice. "Not much of a PI, am I?" I faked an awkward laugh.

June laughed with me. The front door chimed, and we both looked in that direction. Danika stepped inside. Our eyes met across the room, and a second later, she swiveled on her heel and rushed out of the shop.

"Hey." I chased after her.

I caught up with her half a block away. She was quick

for having a short stride, but my stride was bigger because of my long legs.

I grabbed her by the shoulder and spun her toward me. "I get the feeling you're avoiding me. Makes me want to know why."

She stepped back, but I anticipated her move and herded her against the building, boxing her in.

"I don't have anything to say," she protested.

"How do you know what I'm going to ask?" I placed my hands on my hips and stared her down.

"I'm sure it's about Josh, and I don't know anything." She wouldn't meet my eyes. She crossed her arms over her chest with each hand brushing away goosebumps on her upper arms.

I tsked. "Yeah, see. Your body language says that's not true. I watched several videos on this online, and I'm becoming quite the expert."

This got her attention. Her look was skepticism mixed with irritation. "Are you serious? You're learning to be a PI online?"

"Don't judge. Lots of programs are online now. I think even what you do can be achieved with online courses."

"Touché," she said.

I continued, "And how about you telling me why you lied? You didn't resign. What were you and Josh really discussing so animatedly that day he died? This time go with the truth."

She sighed wearily. "I told Josh I was going to quit."

"Because?"

She rolled her eyes. "Because he was a buffoon, and his mind was on getting laid twenty-four seven."

Click. Some pieces snapped together. "And this bugged you because..." I was confident I knew the answer.

"You're asking if I dated Josh, right? You want me to say it." She groaned and shook her head.

I nodded.

She leaned against the building, closed her eyes, and covered her cheeks with her hands to hide the pink stain of embarrassment. "I did. But not for long."

"Why not for long?"

She opened her eyes and gave me a pointed look. "Because I became privy to who he was under all that I'm-Mr. Do-right."

At this pace, we would be here forever. "Listen, I suck at picking up inferences. How about you just start at the beginning, lay it all out for me, and that way I won't make assumptions where you're leaving blanks. I could make some wrong ones, and that wouldn't be a lot of fun for either of us."

"You're as tenacious as your sister."

I smiled. "Thanks. We get it from our parents."

She laughed. "Josh hit on me two weeks after I took the job. I'll admit I was flattered because I thought he was handsome." She grimaced.

"Yeah, I get that. For most people his first impression is awesome. It's the second glance that shows his true colors."

Her eyes widened. "Exactly."

"But I get the feeling you didn't fall into his arms."

She shook her head. "I'd just ended a three-year relationship. I wasn't looking to date, or even to have a casual
fling. Josh offered that as an option, too."

I said, "What a pig."

Her smile was huge. "The more he pushed, the more I
resisted. He was like a dog with a bone. I'd say no, he'd
push harder. Then he started showing up at the tennis
club and asking me to play a few games. That's what wore
me down. You know what it's like when you meet a guy,
you learn all about what they like, but they don't take an
interest in what you like."

She waited for me to agree. I nodded, though Carson
had seemed interested in my hobbies.

"You guys started playing tennis together?"

"And a friendship formed, or so I thought." She
ducked her head, her long brown hair shading her face.
"Ugh, I'm so embarrassed."

"Why? I haven't heard anything that should make you
feel that way."

She looked up at me through her hair. "Because at this
same time, someone was breaking into my car, stealing my
racket and shoes, and once the coins from my cup
holder."

"How many times did this happen?"

"Three. It scared me. Particularly because the police
had no clue, and it felt personal. Know what I mean?"

Yep. "Because why continue to take your equipment?
To break into a car once and take everything, including
coins, is a crime of opportunity. To repeat it feels personal.

And who makes a killing pawning secondhand sports gear?"

Danika looked impressed. "Wow, those are some good videos you're watching."

I didn't bother to correct her that my assessment was common sense, not YouTube.

"This is the embarrassing part," she said. "I was nervous staying alone at night. I figured this burglar would escalate and break into my house. Josh offered to stay the night with me. He said he'd watch the car and see if he could catch the person."

"Did he?"

She shook her head and pressed her fingers to her cheeks. "He only offered as a way to try to get into my pants."

"You weren't sleeping with him?" It was a personal and invasive question, but I needed to know.

"Nope, drove him nuts. He would come over all the time. Just drop by and bring flowers or coffee or whatever. Little things. At work, there would be chocolates on my desk, and every time my racket was stolen, he'd buy me a new one. Part of me thought maybe he was breaking into my car just so he would have an excuse to stay the night."

I grinned. "Any chance you like true crime?"

She gave a one-shoulder shrug. "Yeah, and we had to learn about escalating behaviors and manipulation in school as part of our psych education."

"I'm sorry to pry, but why didn't you two, you know, bang uglies?" I hoped to keep our conversations light and not threatening. And to keep her talking.

She curled her lip. "Gross."

I waited for her to continue.

She sighed. "Because I don't do casual."

"I get that. I don't either. Or if I did, I wouldn't be good at it."

She pointed her index finger at me. "And I didn't know this at the time, but in hindsight, I think my instincts told me he wasn't who he pretended to be."

"How so?"

"He used to come over smelling like smoke. I asked him if he smoked, and he adamantly denied it. Said he was somewhere where people smoked. But he was coming around every day at this point. That meant between work ending and him showing up at the tennis club or my apartment, he went somewhere where there were smokers? Where's that? All the restaurants and bars are smoke-free."

I delivered my bomb. "Apparently he liked to smoke after sex."

Danika's smile grew. "I know. June told me that one day when I was getting coffee."

"June?"

"Yeah, Josh had been in there one morning and left when I came in. I made an off-the-cuff remark about how he probably had to rush out to get his smoking fix, and she told me he only smoked after sex."

My mouth gaped.

Danika continued, "I figured she knew what she was talking about seeing as how she'd dated him."

Laura had mentioned this but said she couldn't

confirm if it were true. Danika was about to do that for me. "June dated Josh?"

"Yeah, right when he moved to town. For a while, too. But he said it never was serious. Forgive me for being old-fashioned, but I think sleeping with someone makes the relationship serious."

33

INTENTIONAL OR NOT, Danika's revelation shifted my focus off her and onto June.

June?

Last night when Leo and I talked about the probability someone we knew had committed this murder, I'd secretly believed that to be Danika. Labeling her a murderess was easier to swallow than June. June, who never once made fun of me in school for not being a good reader, or for mixing up directions, and not knowing my left and right.

Nah, not sweet, smiling June. Her mother, maybe.

I left Danika by the wall and stumbled toward the coffee shop. Surely, June would have a reasonable explanation.

Though, if the murder wasn't committed by June, Danika, or Boomer, then I was back to square one.

Before I could reach the coffee shop, someone called

my name. I turned to find Toby rushing toward me. His yellow banana-shaped squirrel keeper swinging around his neck.

"Hey," he waved. "I've been looking for you." When he reached me, he bent over, placing his hands on his upper thighs and panted. Though Toby was a rail-thin man, it was clear he lacked sufficient stamina.

"You should work on that," I told him. "One day you might need to run for your life, and that won't be an option unless the person has even worse endurance than you."

He crossed his fingers. "I'm due some good luck, so I'll hold out hope that if I'm ever chased, it'll be by a sloth." He slid off the banana carrier from around his neck and looped it over mine. "I need you to watch Lady Marmalade."

"Wait, what?" The weight of the sugar glider was slight, like a little ball nestled between my breasts. When I looked into the pouch, her dark eyes blinked back at me.

Toby said, "She likes you and she hates being in the car for longer than twenty minutes. I have a lot of pickups to do today, so I'll be in the car most of the morning."

I jerked a thumb to point behind me at How Ya Bean. "I'm trying to get to the bottom of who murdered Josh. It might be June. Do you want Lady Marmalade exposed to that?"

He rolled his eyes. "June? Please." He snapped his fingers in sudden memory. "Oh, that reminds me. I found some of Josh's older calendars. They'd been deleted, but we all know nothing is ever really deleted." He snorted with IT derision, like the rest of us tech dumb-dumbs were stupidly unaware. Which was true to a degree.

He continued, "Anyway, for at least six months, Josh had a unicorn on his calendar every week. There are a few months missing, so I can't get a full picture of the time period."

"Was the first unicorn appearance the few months after he moved here and took the job at the school?"

Toby nodded. "Yeah, I also did a cross-search on unicorns in general to see if there might have been any correlation. They were trending. Have been for a while. Unicorn cake, shirts, and themed parties. Even your dad wrote a piece on how trends affect all towns and mentioned June's Unicorn Brew. I sent the article and pages to your email."

I swallowed past the knot of dread lodged in my throat and went to give Lady M back to Toby. "I can't—"

He covered his ears. "You owe me," he shouted as he backed away. "Remember when I was shot?" He turned and fast-walked to his eco-friendly eraser cap-shaped car.

I stared down at Lady M. "Looks like you and I need to talk to June. I should warn you, she could be a killer. If you have any of those magical, emotional support vibes in you, now would be a good time to share."

She cooed and stuck her head out of the pouch, looked around, then ducked back in.

Inside the coffee shop, June was nowhere. When I asked the teen working the register, she said June had gone to her office.

I hustled past the restrooms and to June's office. The

door was open; the lights were on, but when I stepped over the threshold, I saw plenty of bat-shit crazy stuff, but no June. Papers were everywhere, stapled in no discernible pattern to the walls and ceiling. Receipts, doodles of unicorns on scrap paper of various sizes, articles about the coffee shop, the VGS, Josh's appointment as the school's principal, his death and endless pages of engagement and wedding announcements.

It was like a tree exploded, or at the very worse, sprayed the room with paper-barf. Her computer was buried under piles of notes. I thumbed through them, skimming and scanning the pages for keywords, some papers looked to be drink combinations. Others were scribbles in various scripts and prints of June's name paired with Josh's surname. Mrs. June Chapman. Mrs. J. Chapman. Mr. and Mrs. Joshua and June Chapman.

The heat clicked on, and paper began to flutter under the forced air. The sound of crinkled paper was telling a story, only I didn't understand the words.

I would have sunk into the chair, stunned, but the chair had been pushed to the corner. A box full of paper reams in the seat. It appeared June had used the box of papers to stand on and staple—I stepped up to the paper on the wall—my dad's last article about Boomer being brought in for questioning. A large smiley face had been drawn in pink ink over the article. Next to it was a picture of the PTC committee. Carlie's face had been erased with such force, the paper was gone. The page overlaid another, and beneath it was the picture used in the article of Josh getting assigned the principal's job. June's image showed between the jagged edges of the torn paper.

Creepy.

Chills raced down my arms.

I whipped out my phone and started taking pictures, cursing my decision to leave my camera at home.

I paused long enough to dial Leo. My call immediately went to voice mail. Seconds later a text from him appeared.

It read: *In court. U ok?*

What did I say? That maybe June was the killer? Or at the very least had gone off the deep end?

I replied by sending a picture from the doorway of June's office. Then texted: *June's office.*

Moments passed that felt like hours.

His reply: *Whoa.*

Me: *You ain't kidding*

Leo: *I'm stuck here. Report it to DB. I'll let you know as soon as I'm out of here.*

Me: (Emoji eye roll) *Fine. Wanna wager he does nothing?* (Dollar sign emoji)

Leo: *Nope. Sucker's bet.*

I scratched Lady M's head as I backed out of the space. How had we missed this? Had the signs been right in front of us all along, yet we chose not to see them because it meant the unthinkable? A killer was among us.

My phone buzzed with an incoming text. Leo

It read: *Where is June right now?*

Good question. I searched the storage area and the ladies' room. No sign of her.

I replied: *In the wind?*

Leo: *Watch your back. Where are you headed now?*

Me: *The station.*

Leo: *Good, get out of there.* (Eyeball emoji and number six).

When this was over I would praise his attempts at emoji chat. Like telling me to keep an eye on my six. Instead, I took a shot of Lady M in her banana pocket and sent it. I replied: *babysitting. Cora pick up too.*

His reply was a thumbs-up.

I exited the coffee shop through the employee back-door, which emptied into an alley with parking spaces. June's car wasn't anywhere. I cut across the space and made my way to the police station.

Pamela waved at me when I entered. "Tell me you got something good in that banana get-up around your neck. The day has been stupid boring, and I need a little action."

I wanted to groan. Like her words were a jinx. My mood had shifted as I'd been in June's office. I couldn't shake the feeling that all those papers, fluttering in the blow of the heater, were harbingers of doom.

"It's Toby Wagenknecht's pet, Lady Marmalade. I'm pet sitting." I stood beside the front desk and let her peek inside.

"That's adorable. Can I touch her?"

I held open the pouch wider. "You can try. She's vocal about what she likes and doesn't like."

Pamela stuck her finger in and scratched Lady M's head.

Lady M cooed.

I said, "You're lucky. She doesn't do that to everyone." I nodded to the door that separated the waiting room from the actual police station. "Can you buzz me back? I need to see DB."

The annoying *zzz* of a buzzer filled the room, and I grabbed at the staff door, pulling it open. "Thanks."

The bullpen was only slightly more active than when I was here last night talking with Levi. The size of Wind River was reflected in our small police force. The staff was comprised of six patrol officers, one sergeant, one lieutenant, and two front desk managers.

DB was sitting in his office, a bagel hanging out of his mouth as he banged on his keyboard with his pointer fingers.

"Knock, knock," I said and did a finger wave.

He rolled his eyes.

"I see you were an apt student of keyboarding class," I said sarcastically. "Or is that the class you skipped because you were sacrificing goats and chugging steroids, trying to get the puberty gods to smile upon you."

He flexed one bicep, took out the bagel with the other hand, "You think the puberty gods smiled on me." He made his bicep pop up and down.

"The puberty gods giveth, the gray matter gods taketh away."

He glared but continued to flex.

I took a seat across from him and slid my phone onto his desk. "I'm coming by because I was just at How Ya Bean. Did you know June used to date Josh?"

DB stopped flexing and waved his bagel at me. "I don't bother with town gossip. And I don't care about other's social lives."

I pointed to my phone. "I had a few questions for her and went to her office to talk to her. She wasn't there. But all this was."

He picked up my phone and put his beefy steroid-strong fingers all over my screen.

"I took several, scroll through."

His brow furrowed. "What am I looking at? Are you telling me she's disorganized and a hoarder?"

"She had several articles about Josh. Lots of weird stuff, too, like engagement and wedding announcements." I wiggled my fingers to show I wanted my phone. "Look at this."

He handed over my phone.

I found the picture where Carlie had been erased, and I enlarged it. "Here she's literally erased Carlie from the picture, and you can see that's June under the paper." I handed him the phone.

He stared at it a while then set it on the desk. "I'll make note of this, and when I get a chance, I'll go out and talk to June."

"Why do I feel like it's more urgent for me than you?" Maybe because his tone sounded like he was just saying this to pacify me.

DB sat back in his chair and said with a mouth full of bagel, "Sam, I got a kid under arrest for poisoning his mom's boyfriend. I got a doctor who also tried to poison that same person because he was sleeping with the doc's wife. I got another person hiding in Fiji who fled with Josh's money because he was shafting her on her cut of the con they had running. And you want me to prioritize June because she's always wanted to be a bride not a bridesmaid."

I leaned forward. "Why do you say that?"

He snorted with a short chuckle. "Don't you remember in fifth grade when we all had to partner up and learn to do-si-do? Hue Stillman got partnered with June? Afterward, he couldn't shake her. She thought because they'd partnered they were dating. Started leaving him cookies and stuff in his locker." He pointed a finger at me and shook it. "*And* her senior yearbook statement said her life plan was to marry, have lots of babies, and be the best wife she could be." He blew out a cream cheese and chive breath. "I've always kept a wide radius away from June. She's the kind who'd deliberately trap a man. Thinks a smile is an invitation. She's trouble with a capital T." He pointed to my phone. "And she's a terrible housekeeper. Look at her office. Sloppy."

I curled up my lip. "Um, that's because her mind is coming unraveled."

"So now you're an FBI profiler?" He grinned wickedly.

"You're a dufus. This is a clear sign of something not good. It gives me chills to look at it. And it doesn't worry you at all?"

He shook his head. "Nope. Not enough to go out and talk to her right away. Yeah, I'll do it. But I got hotter fires right now. If you're so sure she's a nutter, why don't you go talk to her?"

My eyebrows shot up in surprise. Basically, I'd just been given permission by the cops to go out to June's. Leo couldn't argue with that.

Okay, he kinda could because we both know DB didn't always make the best decisions. I stood.

"You going out there?" He jerked his thumb in the direction June lived. "I'm certain she's harmless."

I shrugged. "Maybe, I'm gonna chat with Hue first."

Lady M stuck her head out of the pouch, took one look at DB, and hissed.

He said, "If you do and she's as crazy as you think, throw that thing at her." He pointed to Lady M.

"I'll email you these pictures," I said, then left.

Outside, I texted Hue.

Me: *June Rivers. Thoughts?*

Hue: (Bat emoji) (Poop emoji) *cray-cray* (man running away emoji)

34

HAVING WALKED to How Ya Bean, I used my walk back to my apartment to contemplate my actions. Too bad I lived really close to everything because Leo wasn't gonna be happy with the thoughts I kept having.

I dialed up Precious.

"Samantha True," she said in a harsh whisper. This was her fake angry voice. Because when Precious was for real angry, she stuttered. "I'd be mad at you if everything hadn't turned out well."

Having no idea what she was talking about, I went with it anyway. "Doubtful. When's the last time you've ever been *really* mad at me? Besides, I call to offer you the opportunity to ride sidekick and solve crime."

Her tone perked up. "Oh, do tell."

"First, why would you be mad at me?"

She sighed and lowered her voice again. "AJ and I had a meeting. He told me about the company trying to recruit him away. He said they're telling him a lot of what he wants to hear. Said you got to the bottom of the issue with his brother and how that Recode and Reshape program told AJ everything he wanted to hear, too, only it wasn't."

"Yeah, and we know why." I still wasn't making the connection to why she'd be angry.

She sighed. "*But...*"

Ahh, here it comes.

"AJ said the real clincher was when he thought about leaving, he just couldn't. Said he needed a person named Precious in his life."

Through my chuckles, I said. "Yeah, sorry about that. It slipped one day."

She laughed. "You should have seen my reaction. Or lack of one. There I was sitting across the table talking contracts and goals and he says, 'Sounds good, Precious,' and I didn't even notice. His brother was in the room, and he asked if we were dating."

At my apartment stairs, I sat on the second step. "That's funny. Troy thought AJ was calling you Precious as an endearment."

"Both Troy and AJ love you by the way. He said part of staying with me was keeping you as an assistant."

I was flattered.

"You'll still do it, right?"

I shrugged even though she couldn't see. "I always need money, so yeah."

She clapped, the sound echoing through the phone. "Excellent. Your turn. How can I solve this crime for you?"

I snorted. "As if. When you put it that way, I think I'll

go see June myself and try to find out why she's stapled paper over every inch of her work office. All about Josh, weddings, and engagements. I need to ask her about when she and Josh dated. But I don't need help to do that."

Precious gasped. "Shut the front door. You made all that up."

"I texted Hue because, apparently, when he and June got partnered in fifth grade square dancing, June thought that meant Hue was her soul mate. Hue said she was crazy, and he runs from her."

"Ooh, I remember that. She used to leave all kinds of treats and stuff in his locker. Remember how she used to just show up when we would be at the park or somewhere? She had that bike with the basket and rode it everywhere."

Of all the things I kept in my memory, that wasn't one of them. Yeah, I remembered June leaving Hue food. A crush wasn't unheard of in fifth grade, and Hue had always been easy to look at. Unlike Leo, he was quick to smile. I also remember her showing up at the park, but so did lots of other kids. What I couldn't see when I scrolled through my memory video was anything weird or out of sorts.

I said, "I'm having a hard time believing all this."

"That's why you're my favorite person, Sam. Because after years of having to prove to skeptical teachers and the like that you actually were dyslexic and not pretending, you still give everyone you know the benefit of the doubt."

"So do you," I reminded her.

"Because we're awesome. We can't surround ourselves with people who bring us down."

"Which is in direct conflict with my job, you realize that? And I'm asking you to go talk to June who might be a killer. That's getting surrounded by all shreds of darkness, if I'm not mistaken."

"You have to turn around the words you're using. Stop being negative. Be positive. Maybe by going we'll help June clear her name. Or to assist a person who might need intervention. We're doing a good service."

"I guess that means you're in, you're going with me."

"Duh," she said. Keys jingled in the background. "Where are you? I'll come to you."

"Sitting outside my apartment."

"How you want to do this? Bonnie and Clyde with guns blazing? Thelma and Louise with laughter and subtly covering each other's back?"

I scratched Lady M's head, and she cooed. "I'm babysitting Lady M so we have to include her, and no to the guns blazing."

"Ooh," Precious said. "The three of us can be a weird version of Charlie's Angels."

I laughed. "Sounds good. I suggest we pop over under the pretense that I was talking to her earlier and we didn't get to finish our conversation because I ran out to catch Danika. And we want to know if she's okay. I don't want to get into an altercation if we can help it. Go over, check things out, be snoopy without being suspicious, and bail without getting hurt."

The engine to Precious's car turned over. "Sounds solid. I'll be there in fifteen."

We disconnected, and I continued to stroke Lady M.

Having her present was a stroke of good luck. Interpreting our intentions would be harder for June with a sugar glider in a banana pocket hanging around my neck. Totally not threatening.

I checked my pack for my stun gun and then patted my waistline for the pinned pocket with the spare handcuff keys. I texted my dad and told him where I was headed and that I expected to be on time to pick up Cora. This action had two benefits. Someone other than DB and Precious knew where I was going, and if I didn't show up at the school and they called someone to come get Cora, Dad would know what to do.

He texted a thumbs-up.

Now all I had left to do was wait for Precious.

35

WEDNESDAY

JUNE LIVED with her mom out toward the northern part of town, where the houses were on acres.

Lady M cooed as we drove.

"I don't know why she doesn't like being in the car with Toby. She's perfectly fine with us."

Precious said, "Because he likes to listen to that techno music. Must drive her nuts, a girl of her quiet temperament."

Precious slowed as we approached, and I pointed to the driveway. "June's car's here."

The houses out this way were older and offered more square footage, and the lots were grand.

"Okay, we're just popping by to check on her and I'll ask another question about Danika. Make it seem like I'm sniffing up the wrong tree." I nervously rubbed my palms down my leggings.

"Got it," Precious said and parked behind June's car. She winked. "In case she tries to make a run for it."

"Does she strike you as the run for it type?"

Precious arched a brow. "If she's the killer and is letting a kid take the fall, yeah, she does."

I felt itchy with apprehension. "You're right. I've got to stop thinking of this as June but instead a murderer." I sucked in a deep breath, blew it out slowly, and then said, "Let's do this."

At the front door, I rang the bell. Twice. Finally, June opened it a crack and peered out. "What are you doing here?" Only the left side of her face and shoulder were exposed.

I said, "We were talking earlier, I got distracted by Danika, and when I went back, you'd disappeared. I wanted to make sure you're okay. I know you've been out a lot, and well…" I wasn't sure how to finish. Because she had been out a lot, and I never even brought by so much as a can of soup.

June cut her eyes to Precious. "What about you?"

Precious hitched her thumb toward me. "I'm the driver. Lady Marmalade doesn't like to be behind the wheel."

June's eyes narrowed. "Lady Marmalade?"

I pointed to the squirrel carrier. "Toby's emotional support animal. I'm babysitting."

June studied the pouch, then me. "Does it work?"

I said, "Does what work?"

"The emotional support animal."

Precious and I exchanged a glance, silently asking

each other if we thought it worked. I shrugged as I hemmed and hawed. "Maybe it works?"

Precious nodded. "Maybe. Lady M is so tiny, so maybe she can only dole out so much emotional support."

I said, "And Toby's trauma was big so maybe he needs something like a horse."

"Or elephant," Precious said.

June said, "Well, I can't imagine being shot was easy."

We murmured our agreements.

June asked, "Can I hold her?"

"No" was on the tip of my tongue when Precious said, "Sure, but we have to come in because we don't want her to run away. She loves the pouch, but when we take her out, she gets scared and might take off."

June swung open the door.

Based on how she'd used the door as a cloak, I half expected her to be wearing something not appropriate, but she was dressed in the sweats and T-shirt she'd been wearing at the coffee shop. Though she looked paler than normal. But in the PNW, we all lost color as winter approached.

I mentally slapped myself on the head. Making excuses for June wasn't how I was going to get to the bottom of Josh's murder. Developing the skill of being unbiased, of training myself to see what was in front of me and not what I wanted to see was what would make or break me as a PI.

I mentally clicked on my photographer lens and tried to see June that way.

She let us into a cream and light blue living room

immaculate to the point of being unfriendly. One wrong move, and the room looked mussed.

June gestured for me to hand over Lady M.

"I'll start with the pouch. Don't take her out yet. She feels safe there, and she needs to get to know you." I slid the pouch from around my neck and over June's.

Upon closer inspection, June looked fried. She had bags under her eyes that were heavily disguised by concealer. Her sweats and T-shirt had coffee splatters, and her nails were chewed to the quick.

"You look tired," I said with a soft, hopefully non-threatening voice.

June sighed wearily and scratched Lady M's head with her index finger. "It's the coffee shop. Wearing me out. I don't know how much longer I can keep the hours."

Precious, not one to be intimidated by anything or anyone, sat on the couch. "I hear ya. Being a business owner is hard. Even though my office closes at five, I often talk to clients after I close for the day."

June said, "Yeah, but at least you have a life. I can't get good help to stay, and the teens I hire don't understand what quality work means." She rolled her eyes. "If one more tells me that working at a coffee shop's fine but they hope to get a real job one day, I will lose my mind."

Afraid of the couch, I leaned against the wall. This also gave me a better full view of June. "At least you both have steady jobs. I currently hold three different jobs, and one of my employers is my best friend."

"You seem happy, though," June said.

"Happier than when I was working for Toomey.

Taking picture after picture of families and kids with parents that had unrealistic expectations wore on me."

June stopped stroking Lady M and pointed that same finger at me. "Exactly. I started the coffee shop because I didn't want to work for anyone. But I'm a slave to that shop. No nightlife. No time off. All while my childbearing years go flying by."

Precious fidgeted with her ponytail. "I would think the coffee shop would be a great place to meet men."

June barked out a bitter laugh. Lady M hissed.

"You know who I met at the coffee shop? Principal Josh."

Before me was a golden opportunity, but I had to tread lightly. "You and Josh dated for a while, right? Was that before or after he went after Danika?"

June straightened, and her features tightened. "That little twit in her cute tennis skirt and stupid laugh." A mask of rage distorted June's face.

In a squeaky voice I could only assume was a poor imitation of Danika, June said, "Caramel Latte with skim milk please. You make the best drinks, June. If you could figure out how to skim the fat out of them, I'd be in here more often."

Looking uncomfortable, Precious shifted on the couch. I kicked one leg out over the other and crossed it, hoping to convey the opposite of Precious. I was trying to tell June she was safe with me if she wanted to share her heart out.

I said, "Annoying, I'm sure, especially as she was making moves on your man."

June's eyes went large. "Right! I had Josh right where I wanted him. Then she came along."

"And where was that?" I asked. "Where did you have Josh?"

She rolled her eyes at me. "You know. Thinking about marriage. Looking at making things between us permanent. I even had an offer to take on a partner. That way I could focus on being Mrs. Chapman, having babies, and being at all his job functions." She held up her index finger. "Just once I want to sit with the PTC moms. Sit on the other side and have someone serve me, cater to me. Those bimbos take what they have for granted."

Telling June that her pushing Josh toward marriage was likely the precise action that drove him to Danika wouldn't go far. Logic had no seat on this crazy train.

Time to crank up the cray-cray. "And after Danika was another woman and then another. That must've pissed you off."

Precious caught on; she was quick like. "And dating Laura, a woman with kids, would make me have all sorts of bad feelings."

I added, "And a whole lot of ticked off when the man I was hoping to marry starts dating a woman with kids because it's a safe bet that she's not going to settle for casual. I mean, I have a lot of rage for Carson, and he was already dead when I found out the truth." Or at least I thought he was.

Precious let out a long, loud hoot. "You can bet your sweet patootie I'd have it out for any man who did that to me." She crossed her leg and let her foot swing, as if this were a conversation in all fun and not one with a potential killer.

June nodded. "Revenge is a dish that's best served cold."

Goosebumps rose on my arms. Yeah, if she eighty-sixed Josh, she waited until he least suspected it.

June stared at Precious. "Why haven't you married? Aren't you and Connor still dating?"

Connor was Precious's on-again/off-again boyfriend. They'd been like that since ninth grade. Their relation-ship could be summed up by saying, they were a couple when it suited them.

Precious waved a dismissive hand. "Connor's busy in Canada building a reputation in the front office of a hockey club. I'm here. I don't want to be there. He doesn't want to be here. Until that issue gets resolved, which it won't, we'll keep doing what we're doing."

June's tone was laced with disgust. "Which is cheat on each other with anyone and everyone you can."

Precious uncrossed her legs and straightened, a sign her patience was waning. She pointed a finger at June. "Hey, Connor and I have been nothing but honest with each other from day one. Unlike you and Josh. He never told you he was a user, and you forgot to mention you were marriage obsessed." Precious was frustrated. Her voice rose and she stood, jamming both hands on her hips. "I mean, come on June. You want to be married? Join one of those dating sites. The purpose of those is to marry people off. Why spin your wheels on a loser? Because playing the victim here doesn't work for me. You have plenty of options. Not taking those is all on you."

Precious the life coach was in full action. She continued, "What I think the truth here is this. Josh was the first guy to pay you a lot of attention. Probably because when you dated other guys, they picked up on how needy you are. Josh didn't care because he had a primary objective. To use you. And you let him."

June went from pale to pink. Either embarrassment or fury or a little of both. By the bulge of her eyes, I was going with fury. Like a steam engine primed to explode, June lost it.

"Get out," she screeched. She pointed a shaking finger at the door. "Get out of my house. Now, you bitch. What do you know about dating? Men fall at your feet. But for girls like Sam and I, we have to work harder. Bring more to the table."

Now wasn't the time to be offended, yet I was.

Speaking of tables... On the coffee table was a foot-tall statue of an angel reading a book. The diameter small enough to wrap a hand around. June swooped it up and rushed at Precious.

Lady M began to hiss loudly, her head popping out of the pocket.

As she skirted away, Precious pointed a finger at June, keeping the coffee table between them. "Hey, relax, I'm just trying to help you get to the root of your issues so you can move forward and find true love."

June was frothing at the mouth. "Josh was my true

love. He was everything." She swung the statue wide, missing Precious by a foot.

I jumped between them, palming my stun gun. "Give me Lady M, and we'll get out of here."

"You think I imagined a future with Josh? That he never led me to believe it was possible? Well, I'll show you." She pivoted and then dashed from the room, climbing the stairs two at a time, taking Lady M with her.

I faced Precious. "Way to go."

She looked chagrined. "I can't stand people who are determined to play the victim. I couldn't help myself."

"Did you forget she might've killed someone? Wonder if she'll say the same thing? That she couldn't help herself. He'd made her so mad she poisoned him with a scone or slipped something in his drink."

The memory of the day Josh died hit me hard, like a punch to the solar plexus. I watched him finish his Unicorn Brew coffee then toss it in the trash outside the school. Moments later, he was collapsing in his office.

I bent over and slowly blew out a breath. "June killed Josh and I know how she did it."

36

"ARE YOU GOING TO THROW UP?" Precious asked.

For a moment, I thought I was. I straightened, covered my mouth, gulped several times, then shook my head.

We were in a killer's house. "We should leave," I said, but looked up the stairs. Lady M was up there. Yeah, she was just a sugar glider, but she was Toby's sugar glider, and I'd been charged with protecting her. Like Rachel had charged me with Cora. What kind of person would leave Lady M behind?

A dead one?

"Oh, God." I pressed the heels of my hands to my temples. "I'm going to do something stupid." But not without confessing my sins and hopefully triggering timely assistance.

I sent Leo a voice text: "At June's. Came over to check on her and things went south fast. Precious with me. I think June put vape juice in Josh's Unicorn Brew drink. She used a vape vial left behind by Levi. Send help."

Then I tucked my phone away because I knew what he would say, and I wouldn't leave.

Precious grabbed my shoulders. "We need to visualize getting Lady M and getting out of here and make a plan. Quick."

I tried to do as she said, but all I could see on a loop was Josh chugging back the remnants of his drink and tossing it. June herself told me Levi had two vials of marshmallow vape juice at How Ya Bean. She put it in the lost and found. She'd taken those vials and spiked Josh's drink. Being a non-smoker, June wasn't so crazy or careless that she'd actually go buy vape juice. And her hours at the coffee house made traveling out of town to buy vape juice more difficult.

And the hit and run on me? Mrs. Josh Chambers. Who wanted to be his missus more than June? Not Jenna.

I said, "Let me go up first. Wait about five minutes and come up after. We want to corner her without her knowing she's cornered. Or if it gets hairy fast, I need you to bail."

Precious nodded. "Visualize success."

I moved to the stairs and called out, "June, we're leaving. I need Lady M, and we'll get out of your hair. Can I come up?"

Silence.

I climbed halfway up the stairs. The top opened up to a wide hallway with rooms on both sides. "June? We're sorry we upset you."

The landing was empty. I went up a few more stairs. "June?"

Nothing but my voice. I glanced back at Precious. She shrugged then shooed me forward.

Easy for her to say. She was downstairs.

I stepped onto the landing, stun gun in hand, and eased up to the first doorway with caution. The one on my right looked to be Mrs. River's room.

How dysfunctional was it that June continued to live at home? I couldn't help but wonder if that played a part in her obsession to be married. Or maybe Mrs. River's knew June was a few coffee beans short of a cappuccino which could explain why she was quick to point the finger at me.

A few feet forward, I glanced into the door on my left. A large bathroom. No June.

I crept ahead. My phone buzzed in my pocket, but I ignored it.

Second door on my left was another bedroom. But it was a hot mess of crazy. Like June's office. One entire wall was covered with pictures of June and Josh. I surveyed the room, no June, but two other doors. Both closed. Likely a closet and... I wasn't sure.

A large double-pane bay window with a built-in seat brought in lots of light. Had the room not been plastered with pictures, it would have been a pleasant space. A large bed was in the center, covers disheveled. On the dresser were several containers with what looked to be home-made creams. Two flowering plants, with closed buds, sat on each end of the dresser. Being the outdoorsy type, I knew a few things about plants. It helped to avoid poodle dog bush, poison ivy, and the like. The closed buds were the tip-off. A plant from the nightshade family. I leaned forward and smelled. Nicotine plant, or *nioctiana.*

From behind me June said, "He used to get wicked bad rashes from the nicotine patch. I made him homeopathic salves to help."

I turned and found June dressed in full-on wedding attire, white gown, veil, and the angel statue clutched between her hands like a bouquet.

Lady M and her pouch hung from June's neck.

"Um." I was at a loss for words.

In a rustle of taffeta and crinoline, she swooshed up to the dresser and picked up a jar filled with white cream.

"How's your nose?" She undid the lid and shoved the jar inches from my nose. "What do you smell?"

Afraid to sniff the stuff, I pretended to by breathing in through my mouth.

June huffed in frustration. "I said smell it." The jar lost inches and was now centimeters from my nose.

Afraid, I took a tepid whiff. "Eucalyptus?" I clutched my stun gun, glad I had brought the mini and hoped June wouldn't see it.

June tossed back her head and let out the creepiest maniacal laugh I'd ever heard. In real life.

Lady M hissed, her pitch higher, a sign she was getting even more agitated.

She tossed the jar on her bed. "That's what Josh thought, too. Eucalyptus is great for masking other scents."

"Like nicotine?"

She snapped her fingers then pointed at me. "Bingo. The nicotine patches gave him a terrible rash. Poor, sweet, too-stupid-to-live June made a special salve just for him."

The June I grew up with and the person dressed in head to toe white were not the same. Referring to herself in the third person had made that abundantly clear. Madness had taken over. Something in her eyes was wild and dark and vacant.

"And in that salve you added nicotine?" An educated guess on my part.

"Yep, Josh was such an addict. But desperate to pretend he wasn't. Just like all the people with their smart-phones glued to their fingers. Pretending they need it for work. Josh pretended he could get his fix from an alternative like gum or a patch." She snort-laughed. "But he loved cigarettes because he loved blowing smoke rings. He would blow them and try to stick his—"

I clapped my hands over my ears. "Shut up! I do not want to know anything about Josh and his smoking proclivities."

June's laugh was bitter, her mouth twisting at an ugly angle.

I nodded over her shoulder to the wall of photos. "Is this what you were talking about downstairs. Your future with Josh?"

She spun and swept her arm the length of the wall. "Tell me I imagined that he wanted a future with me. I gave him everything he wanted." She gestured to her body.

And he gave her nothing, I noted. Instead, he tapped

into her desires and played upon them to get what he wanted. Not that his actions justified hers, by any means.

She pointed to the wall. "Go, look at them."

I stepped closer and scanned the various images. Josh and June at the beach, Josh and June hiking. Josh and June dressed in traditional wedding garb, in swimsuits, and ski attire. From a quick glance, in nearly all the photos, Josh had been photoshopped in. On many of the others, someone, I'm guessing June, had put her head over the woman's body and Josh's over the man's. A modern yet twisted way of playing paper dolls.

"Did Josh ever see this?" Because if he had and it didn't have him running scared, then I wasn't sure what to make of that side of humanity.

When June didn't answer, I turned and caught the last bit of her train slipping out the door.

A second later Precious cried out, "H-h-holy crap, S-S-Sam!"

From down the hall, June screamed. "You think you can have whatever man you want, you greedy cow."

I rushed from the room in time to see June take a swing at Precious, knocking her square upside the head with the angel statue.

Precious, who'd been coming up the stairs, fell sideways and crashed against the wall. Precious's eyes were wide, blood streaming down the side of her face. Dazed from the blow, she lost her balance trying to right herself, arms wind-milling as she fell back into the empty space of the stairwell.

"No!" I screamed, my hand going out in a hopeless

attempt to catch Precious as she fell. Fear and disbelief had me rooted.

June spun toward me, rage etched in the dark grooves on her face as she hurled accusations. None of them made sense.

Lady M popped up out of her pocket, emitted a loud screeching hiss that paired well with June's crazy-ass rants. When this was over, Lady M would need her own emotional support animal.

I gave two sharp short whistles, the way Toby taught me, and Lady M scrambled up June's chest, causing the madwoman to swat at her like a camper does a pesky mosquito and bop herself in the mouth with the statue. The scene would have been funny if I weren't so scared.

Lady M launched herself off June's chest toward me. I caught her with both hands, apologizing for the stun gun in my palm that was probably digging into her. She trembled in my hands. Poor thing was as frightened as I was.

Hanging from the wall was a basket of fake flowers next to a picture of hand-painted blooms. I stroked Lady M as I cooed my apologies, then stuck her in the hanging basket, nestling her in the heads of the fake hydrangeas. She burrowed lower.

June was two arm lengths away, her pitch escalating. I needed to take her out and get to Precious sooner than later.

"Hey," I said in a deep booming voice, much like my father had done when Rachel and I were children to get our attention.

June narrowed her gaze at me, but at least she had shut her mouth.

I continued, "If Precious is hurt, I'm gonna lock you up myself. You're a crazy person."

June began to walk toward me, raising the angel statue, primed to strike.

For no understandable reason, a picture filled my brain of the Seahawks hiking the ball then scrambling for action.

When it came to self-defense, clearly my system short-circuited because this image made zero sense and would probably get me killed. But then the image played out, and inspiration struck. I pulled a running quarterback move. I rushed to June, got within swinging distance of the statue, and dropped into my version of a baseball slide that football players use.

I slid right into June's legs, her voluminous skirt covering my middle body, and knocked her down.

Right onto me.

The statue bounced across the floor. The angel's head popped off, my stun gun sliding behind it. Out of reach from both of us.

"You've ruined everything," June yelled in my face, then went for my eyes with her fingers.

Her veil was draped over one shoulder, and I used it like a rope to bring it across her face and neck, tugging it tight. Her head turned to the side as the massive amounts of clips and pins she'd used to secure the veil tugged at her scalp.

She clawed at the veil. I held it tight with one hand while searching the floor for my stun gun with the other.

"This veil looks stupid on you," I said and gave a tug. Some pins gave, and the headdress slid to the side and forward. One more tug, and the entire thing would come off. Time for a new plan.

I was trapped under her weight and the excessive fabric of her tacky-ass dress.

She grabbed at her veil's headdress and ripped it off, then flung it to the side, the netting raking across my face.

"You've ruined everything," she repeated.

Maybe she was stuck in a goofy loop? Goofy loop was no joke and no fun. It was when the brain got stuck on one thing and couldn't break out of the cycle to see a way out. Only this time, her goofy loop was telling her to hurt me. And she was stuck with her intention to do just that.

She clocked me on the side of the head with a resounding slap.

I returned the favor but used a closed fist and aimed for her face, hitting her square on the nose.

She reared back, sat upright, blood spurting everywhere.

June's face contorted in fury as she stared at the blood spattered on her white gown. "Look what you did. You ruined my dress! You've ruined everything!"

"That dress made you look fat, anyway." Whatever it took to knock sense into her was the plan. And to keep her attention on me and not what I was trying to do. Though, this could easily work against me.

June's eyes went wide. "You're a hateful, bitch, Samantha," she spat.

I stretched my arm out as far as I could, patting my fingers across the floor hoping to connect with my stun gun. "Says the woman who killed her lover."

She lunged at me, dropping her entire body weight on my chest as she cupped her hands around my neck and squeezed.

37

WEDNESDAY

WITH ONE HAND SEARCHING, I wasn't able to effectively block her and was left to use my fist to pound at whatever part of her I could reach.

Stars burst before my eyes, my body was desperate for oxygen. Though, I didn't need any stars to tell me that. The burning in my lungs had been the first tip-off.

I bucked and fought, but each exertion of energy cost me precious oxygen.

"You ruined everything," she screamed in my face, spittle dropping onto me.

I suspected at any minute now I'd pee my pants. Fear was creeping in fast, increasing my panic.

Ugh, how awful would it be for Leo or DB to find my body with my purple face and urine-soaked pants?

I didn't want to go out that way.

With what was probably my last stretch—darkness was cloaking my vision and blinking wasn't holding it back—I patted the floor to my side, slightly above my shoulder line.

My middle finger brushed against the rough edge of something fabric. I prayed it was my stun gun which was encased in a thick, protective case. Though one I could zap through.

I strained toward the object, while choking and gurgling, desperate for air, and pulled the petite weapon what had to be millimeters toward me.

June let go of my neck and grabbed both sides of my head, grasping my hair.

I gasped, taking in only small bits of air as my throat worked to acclimate to the sudden loss of pressure and increase in air.

"You ruined everything," she repeated. June was definitely stuck in the goofy loop.

Scary for me, because the goofy loop was fueled by primitive actions. There would be no reasoning with June.

She whipped my head up then banged it once against the floor.

A burst of pain erupted through my skull. But the little oxygen I was gifted was enough to give me the strength to stretch just a tad further. I cupped the stun gun in my palm, fumbling for the trigger button.

June slapped me again, and the stun gun slipped from my hand as zingers of pain shot through my arms and neck.

I coughed and wheezed as I gasped for air and struggled to process the pain.

June's hands returned to my neck and commenced their squeezing.

My bladder hinted that I could only take one more big hit, and it would let everything go.

Anger surged through me. I was not going to die. I was not going to let Precious die. And I certainly wasn't going to wet my pants.

Patting the floor again, I found the stun gun easily, this time the trigger button was aligned with my thumb, and I flipped it to turn the stun gun on.

I swung my arm, and the little power pack of lightning volts arced toward June, catching her right under her left armpit. I pressed and held the trigger down.

Electric currents shot through her. She arced upward while her body was wracked in small repeated convulsions. Instantly, her hands tightened then loosened as she convulsed then fell on top of me, unconscious, her head resting on my shoulder.

I pulled back, but for good measure, or maybe out of anger and fear, I went at her one more time, sending another nine million volts through her.

I wasn't proud of the moment, though I wouldn't apologize. Call it a goofy loop if you wanted. All I could think of was making her stop, making the pain go away, and not dying.

Not dying was important to me.

I considered shocking her one more time. Instead, I attempted to roll to the side, but the recent lack of oxygen left me weak. Sleep called to me. But fear told me to stay awake, that I needed to run. Unfortunately, what my brain said to do and what my body could do didn't align.

A loud bang came from down the stairs, and in the distance, someone called my name.

When I tried to call out, nothing but garbled junky sounds came from me.

June twitched, and I turned my head toward hers. Her eyes were open and her mouth was working as if she were trying to say something.

I gave her another short zap.

Footsteps thundered up the stairs. "Samantha?"

Leo rushed to my side and took the stun gun from me. I clawed to get it back.

"I'm here. I've got you covered. You're okay," he murmured.

DB appeared over his shoulder. "Jeez. I said go talk to her, not get into a fight with her." He pointed to June. "Told you she was man-trap crazy."

I shot him the bird.

Leo lifted June off me and rolled her onto her back.

DB bent down and gently sat me up. "Can you stand?"

I shrugged. "Presh," I whispered, my throat burned as I tried to make sound.

DB gestured down the stairs. "EMTs are with her now. Probably has a bad concussion, but she's okay."

He helped me to rest sitting against the wall then moved away to June.

Leo came over and inspected my neck and head. "We need a medic up here."

When his thumbs gently probed the bruises around my neck, I winced.

"You're gonna have a hard time talking for a while and a fair amount of pain. But you're alive."

Little bit. I held up my thumb and forefinger with only a sliver a light shining between them. I smiled.

"It's not a joke, Samantha. You're lucky." He searched my face, fear written across his own.

I smoothed the crease over his brow. "Sorry," I mouthed.

He nodded, then lowered his forehead to mine and sighed deeply. I held onto his shoulders, finding strength through him.

DB cleared his throat. Leo pulled away.

DB said, "This is beautiful and all, but I'm gonna need some insight as to what happened here. You think you can write it all out?" As he said the last part, he rolled his eyes. "Who am I kidding? You write in abbreviations and symbols."

I shot him another bird. Then I gestured for Leo to help me up.

"I'm not sure that's a good idea, you likely have a head injury," Leo said.

I gestured for DB to help me up. When he did, I indicated he and Leo should follow me. DB had handcuffed June, who was also propped up against the wall. Her lips were clamped tight and she glared hard at me as I walked by.

Sergeant Hinkle was assigned to watch June as I led DB and Leo into her room.

Tapping into my bad-ass gesturing skills, I told the story of June and her obsession with Josh. Of course, the pictures on the wall told a lot, too. Leo filled in a lot of gaps, as well.

I showed them the salve, the nicotiana plant, and mimed how she applied it to his rashes. Adding more nicotine to his system.

After walking them through that, Leo called my dad and told him what happened, then he escorted me to the ambulance outside. But not before I collected Lady M from the fake hydrangeas. Her banana pocket was covered with June's blood so the paramedic made me a temporary carrying case from a sling and ace wrap.

Precious and I rode to the hospital together.

"We did it," she said as she held an ice pack to side of her head. "By the hair on our chinny-chin-chin."

I nodded in agreement. Then we fist bumped.

Glad to be alive.

38

ANOTHER BEAUTIFUL DAY where the sun was highlighting the blue sky. I was going to enjoy every day like this before the winter rains started, no matter what condition I was in. The slight chill in the air was refreshing as the bandages around my neck were hot and stifling. But the doctor insisted, saying they worked to remind me to tread slowly with food. As if the shooting pain I was awarded with each swallow wasn't reminder enough.

Leo and I sat on my balcony, our feet on the railing, a cooler of hard cider between us. I was on a soft food and liquid diet until my throat healed. We were both dressed in jeans, me in my favorite Seahawks sweatshirt. Sadly, I noticed a tiny hole at the cuff. I would wear this thing until it was threadbare.

Leo had worked until the next day processing the scene. He was enjoying a rare day off with me. I suspected he was hovering to make sure I was okay and not moments from going into delayed shock.

I was grateful to be alive and didn't have time for shock.

Precious had stayed a night in the hospital because of her concussion and was recuperating at her parents.

My parents and I were trying to keep what we could from Rachel. Dad, torn between being a newsman and a father, had written his article with a keen eye on limiting my role. This made the police happy as well.

Leo flipped through a packet of papers then handed them to me.

He said, "Based on the latest toxicology report, no ricin was found in Josh's system. The official ruling in Josh's death is homicide was the manner of death and cause of death was nicotine poisoning."

I wrote Boomer's name and a question mark on a piece of paper.

"He's been charged with attempted murder. He's out on bail and will probably lose his medical license." Leo held up one finger. "But not his wife. She's sticking by his side. I suppose she finds the fact that his jealousy made him try to kill someone attractive."

I grimaced.

"According to the rumor mill, their house is going up for sale." He reached into the cooler and took out a second beer, putting his empty bottle in the recycling container I'd dragged out. "You know about Danika, right?"

I nodded. My mom had told me the school board

promoted Danika to assistant principal, and she was to take part in the hiring of the new principal.

From his pocket, Leo withdrew a folded piece of paper and handed it to me. It was a check for my services drawn off his account.

"I don't know your going rate. If this isn't enough, let me know and I'll write a second check."

I stared at the check in longing. I liked money, paying my bills on time, and little extra luxuries like coffee and ice cream and a new shirt or something. Any extra coming into my account was a good thing.

I ripped up his check and dumped the little pieces into the recycling bin.

Leo set down his beer and stared into the bin. "What did you do that for?" He looked between me and the bin, shocked.

From my back pocket, I took out an envelope and showed him the small bundle of hundreds. "Laura," I mouthed and tapped the envelope. After I'd been released from the hospital last night, Laura had been at my apartment when I got home, this envelope in her hand. Leo had given her the heads-up about June.

She'd caught me tired and unable to argue, pressing the envelope into my hand and thanking me profusely. I couldn't take her money *and* Leo's.

I scratched out the gist of this info on my notepad.

Leo nodded in understanding. "The vial Levi added the nicotine pesticide to was the one under his dresser in the shoe. He's not off scot-free, though. The DA is looking at whether they should charge him for attempted murder.

Lockett pointed out that doing so would give any defense lawyer June hired ammunition should they go to trial. Having another person, Boomer, charged with attempted murder was bad enough. Adding two would help her. But Lockett's confident that Levi will get more community service time, and that's it. He'll be spending more time with me working at the food bank, on the reservation, and at a soup kitchen every week."

"Ooh," I whispered and pulled out my phone. I tapped the screen to show I wanted him to look.

The email was from AJ. In it, he told me the Recode and Reshape Program was canceled, and families were in limbo while they waited for the courts to determine what would be an appropriate way for the kids to serve out their sentence. I gestured that Leo should merge his program with this one.

He shook his head. "I'm spread too thin as it is. With the department being limited in staff and helping out with the tribal council and reservation..." He rubbed a hand down his face ending with a scratch to his chin. "Actually, you might be on to something. Text me the contact information."

I smiled and elbowed him.

"I didn't know you knew AJ Gunn. I bet you like that, football fan that you are." He cut his eyes to me.

I rolled mine. Then rubbed my fingers together in the money sign.

Leo's brows arched. "He was a client?"

I nodded. Nondisclosure contracts prevented me from telling him AJ was a client of Precious's first.

Leo said, "June's singing like a canary. Telling anyone who'll listen that she'd been slowly poisoning Josh over the long term. Confirmed what you said about how Levi had left some vials behind and she'd put them in the lost and found, but he never came back for them. She said that Tuesday you all were at the coffee shop was when she put it in his drink?"

I gestured like I was taking pictures.

He nodded. "Yeah, she said that, too. Said Josh had stayed the night with her. Praised her for being so good to him. Told her she'd be the perfect wife as she was tending to his rashes with her homemade salve."

I shook my head in disgust at both of them, June and Josh. Him telling her what she wanted to hear the most, all the while she was poisoning him. And all this happening in the same house with Mrs. Rivers. Who, according to June, liked to take a nightly Ambien and shut out the world.

Leo agreed. "June said Josh loved Unicorn Brew. It was his favorite drink. Apparently, she held it over him. She would only make it on the days after they hooked up. Which is why she sporadically served it."

Yep, that's what the calendar showed.

Josh had to know June was crazy. I guessed that was why his visits were not as consistent, but his compulsive nature and narcissism filled him with hubris, which ultimately led to his death.

I never want to blame any victim. Regardless of his skeeviness, Josh didn't deserve to be murdered. Dirty rotten that he was. But I had trouble being remorseful for those who played with fire and got burned. Either way, the end of this case didn't come with warm feelings of satisfaction. Instead, I was saddened by the behavior of adults. By people who should have known better, people in influential positions.

Leo sighed and tilted his chair back. "June said she was feeling guilty about the nicotine in the salve, but he didn't seem to have any adverse signs of too much nicotine, so she let it go. But then he hit on you."

I jerked upright, my beer sloshing from the bottle.

"What?" I whispered and forced as much indignation into that one word as my swollen vocal cords would allow.

"Yeah, apparently, she'd grown wise to his moves, and when she saw him do the heart thing,"—he tucked his beer between his legs and made a heart with his two hands and held them to my chest — "she knew you were next in line and was sick of sharing him. Sick of all his unkept promises. She said she just snapped. So she spiked his Unicorn Brew."

I made like I was dry heaving. Then croaked, "I would never ever with him." I went back to fake vomiting.

Leo laughed. "Yeah, well, June thought everyone wanted a piece of him and you were no different."

I circled my finger near my temple to show I thought she was crazy.

Leo's expression changed, saddened. "I think she probably has a mental illness. Or maybe I'm just saying that because I can't wrap my mind around June being a killer."

Or letting a kid take the fall for it.

I tapped his shoulder to get his attention as he seemed lost in thought. I mouthed, "Jail or hospital?" Meaning, where would June end up?

Leo shrugged. "All depends on how they charge her, the deal she takes, if she takes a deal, or what the jury decides if she doesn't."

We sat in comfortable silence. When another unanswered question came to me, I wagged my finger. One more. Just one more question.

He arched one brow.

I pointed in the park's direction and made like I was running, then opening a trench coat to flash people.

Leo's brow furrowed. "You want to go to the park and run?"

I gave him my are-you-serious face. Until now, he'd been right on with all my gestures. Now he was misunderstanding me? I wasn't buying it.

"Stripper," I whispered.

He grimaced. "I can't see you doing it for a living. Privately, sure. One client only, though." He winked.

I punched him in the shoulder.

"Flasher," I croaked and made like I was whipping open and closed a pretend trench coat.

Leo looked puzzled. "I'm not speaking from experience here, but typically aren't bedroom games naughty nurse and sexy UPS man? Or naughty teacher and student?"

I fake gagged at the last one.

Leo laughed. "If you're asking me to play naughty flasher and cop,"—he looked at his watch— "I've got some time before I have to hit the sack. I have an early shift. This would make things kinda awkward between us afterward, but we'd sure have fun in the meantime." He wagged his brows and awarded me a cocky grin.

Wow, I was flattered, I think. More confused. Was he coming on to me? Only now I forgot what I wanted to know because a vision of Leo in my bedroom was blocking out everything else.

Heat flooded my body, and I resisted the urge to wave my hand or rapidly pull my sweatshirt in and out in an effort to fan myself.

I wasn't deft enough to come back with something witty. Tomorrow, I'd come up with the most awesome response or zinger. But today, right now, I had nothing but naughty images of Leo filling my brain.

Focus!

I swiped the beer from his hand. "Carson," I whispered. "Have you caught the flasher, forest stripper?" For added guilt, I clutched my throat and pretended that him forcing me to say all that came at a great and painful cost.

He snatched his beer back. "You can't seriously think it was Carson that day. And no, we haven't caught him, but another person was flashed the other day and they described Bart Pettiford."

I crossed my arms and shook my head. The guy I'd seen hadn't been Bart Pettiford. Yeah, Bart was a tall, thin, and had brown hair like Carson but...

Maybe the idea of Carson being alive was playing tricks on me. Not having full closure could do that to a person, I supposed.

Leo said, "You think you could have seen Bart that day?"

I shrugged and mouthed maybe, then let the idea go.

Leo pointed to a car that had pulled up to the curb. It was Toby.

"I ordered Thai food."

I clapped my hands in excitement.

Leo said, "I got me the good stuff. I got you soup."

I frowned, even though he'd ordered wisely.

Toby climbed my stairs, swinging a brown bag. A new felt banana hammock hung from his neck. Lady M's new pouch.

I pointed to the pouch and asked Toby if she was okay by giving him the thumbs-up then thumbs-down.

He smiled. "She's good. Took a while to calm her down, but we've been listening to Mozart and she's been cooing."

He set the bag at Leo's feet and took the pouch off so I could see inside. Lady M blinked up at me. Thankfully, she didn't hiss. I gave her a scratch, happy we all came away relatively unscathed.

My phone chimed. A message. I swiped to pull it up. A video from Rachel, and based on the expression on her face, she wasn't happy. Word must have gotten out. I grimaced and pressed play.

"Samantha," she screeched like one of those Howlers in the Harry Potter films, the ones where the parents sent a scathing dressing-down in front of all your peers.

But this message wouldn't shred itself and disappear when it was done.

Rachel vaulted into her rant. "How hard is it for you to stay out of trouble just for four to six months? One small deployment. That's all I asked."

Leo and Toby laughed.

"Unreasonable expectations," Leo said to Toby. "Trouble dogs her every step."

They bumped fists. I rolled my eyes and bit back a smile. If trouble dogged my steps, then I was glad to have these guys by my side.

———

Ready to read more Samantha True? Sign up for notifications for when the next book is coming out. Click here to be the first to know.

MEET KRISTI ROSE

Hey! I'm Kristi. I write romances that will tug your heart-strings and laugh out loud mysteries. In all my stories you'll fall in love with the cast of characters, they'll become old, fun friends. **My one hope** is that I create stories that *satisfy any of your book cravings* and take you away from the rut of everyday life (sometimes it's a good rut).

When I'm not writing I'm spinning (riding a stationary bike- I'm obsessed repurposing Happy Planners or drinking a London Fog (hot tea with frothy milk).

I'm the mom of 2 and a milspouse (retired). We live in the Pacific Northwest and are under-prepared if one of the volcanoes erupts.

Here are 3 things about me:

- I lived on the outskirts of an active volcano (Mt.Etna)
- A spider bit me and it laid eggs in my arm (my kids don't know that story yet)
- I grew up in Central Florida and have skied in lakes with gators.

I'd love to get to know you better. Join my Read & Relax community and then fire off an email and tell me 3 things about you!

Not ready to join? Email me below or follow me at one of the links below. Thanks for popping by!

You can connect with Kristi at any of the following:
www.kristirose.net
kristi@kristirose.net

JOIN KRISTI'S READ AND RELAX SOCIETY

I hope you enjoy this book. I'd love to connect and share more with you. Be a part of my Read & Relax Society and let's get to know each other. There, I'll share all sorts of book information. You're guaranteed to find an escape. You'll also be the first to know about my sales and new releases. You'll have access to giveaways, freebies, and bonus content. Think you might be interested? Give me a try. You can always leave at any time.

If you enjoyed this book I would appreciate if you'd share that with others. I love when my friends pass along a good read. Here's some ways you can help.

Lend it , Recommend it , Review it

XO, Kristi

CPSIA information can be obtained
at www.ICGtesting.com
Printed in the USA
BVHW071022200521
607794BV00001B/76

9 781944 513344